WARHAMMER®
40,000

D1387509

CHAOS CHILD

BY

IAN WATSON

BOXTREE

Published in the UK 1995 by
BOXTREE LIMITED
Broadwall House
21 Broadwall
London SE1 9PL

First published in the UK 1995 in hardback by
BOXTREE LIMITED

10 9 8 7 6 5 4 3 2 1

Typeset by SX Composing Ltd, Rayleigh, Essex.
Printed in Great Britain by Cox & Wyman Ltd, Reading, Berkshire.

ISBN: 0 7522 0772 5

Illustration on cover by Mark Craven

Jacket design by Head Design

Illustrations by Dave Gallagher

A Timeline for the Warhammer 40,000 Universe

Millennium	Event

15th   Humanity begins to colonize nearby solar systems using conventional sub-light spacecraft. At first, progress is painfully slow. Separated from Terra by up to ten generations in travel time, the new colonies have to survive mainly on local resources.

The Dark Age of Technology

20th   Discovery of *warp drive* accelerates the colonization process and the early independent or corporate colonies become federated to Terra. The first alien races (including the ubiquitous Orks) are encountered.

The development of the *Navigator gene* allows human pilots to make longer and faster 'jumps' through warp space than was previously thought possible. The great Navigator families, initially controlled by industrial and trading cartels, become a power base in their own right.

Humanity continues to explore and colonize the galaxy. Contacts are established with the Eldar and other alien races. A golden age of scientific achievement begins. Perfection of the *Standard Template Construct* (STC) system now permits an almost explosive expansion to the stars.

The Age of Strife

25th   Humanity reaches the far edges of the galaxy, completing the push to the stars begun over ten thousand years before. Human civilization is now widely dispersed and divergent—with countless small colonies as well as many large, overpopulated planets. Localized wars and disputes with various alien races (especially the Orks!) continue, but pose no threat to the overall stability of human-colonized space. Then, two things happen almost simultaneously. First, humans with psychic powers begin to appear on almost every colonized world. Second, civilization starts to disintegrate under the stress of widespread insanity, daemonic possesson, and internecine strife between these new "psykers" and the rest of humanity. Countless fanatical cults and organizations spring up to persecute the psykers as witches and/or degenerate mutants. At this time, the existence of the creatures of the warp (later known and feared as daemons), and the dangers they pose to the human mind with newly awakened psychic powers, is far from understood.

Terrible wars tear human civilization apart. Localized empires and factions fight amongst themselves as well as against fleets of Orks, Tyranids, and other aliens whose forces are quick to seize the opportunity to sack human space. Many worlds fall prey to the dominance of Warp Creatures whilst others revert to barbarism. Humans survive only on those worlds where psykers are suppressed or controlled. During this time, Terra is cut off from the rest of humanity by terrible warp storms, which isolate the home world for several thousand years, further accelerating the ruin of humanity.

The Horus Heresy

30th   Humanity itself teeters on the brink of the abyss of extinction. Civil war erupts throughout the galaxy as the Emperor of human space is betrayed by his most trusted lieutenant, the Warmaster Horus. Possessed by a daemon from the warp, Horus seduces whole chapters of humanity's greatest warriors—the Space Marines—into joining his cause. When the final battle seems lost, the Emperor defeats Horus in single combat, but only at the cost of his own humanity.

His physical life maintained by artificial means, and his psyche by human sacrifice, the Emperor begins the long task of reconquering human space. With the creation by the Emperor of the psychic navigational beacon known as the Astronomican, the foundations are laid for the building of the Imperium, as it is to be known in the 41st millennium. Fuelled by the dying spirits of those psykers who would otherwise fall prey to the daemons of the warp, and directed by the Emperor's indomitable will, the Astronomican soon becomes an invaluable aid to Navigators throughout the galaxy. Interstellar travel becomes even easier and quicker, while the repression and control of psykers and creatures from the warp releases much of humanity from its hellish bondage.

The Age of the Imperium

41st   Throughout the portion of the galaxy known as the Imperium, humanity is bound within the organizations and strictures of the Administratum. The Emperor grows ever more detached from the day to day concerns of his mortal subjects, while the Inquisition works ceaselessly to protect humanity from the ever-present dangers posed by renegade psykers and the terrible creatures inhabiting warp space. The armies of the Imperium—the Guard and the almost superhuman Space Marines—maintain a constant vigil against the threat of invading Orks, Tyranids and other aliens. But still the numbers of psykers increases steadily, and other more sinister groups associated with Warp Creature domination continue to gain ground . . .

YEAR 40,273 *Accompanied by Assassin-courtesan Meh'lindi, Secret Inquisitor Jaq Draco is sent by his superior, Baal Firenze, to planet Stalinvast to witness the extermination of Genestealers on that world. Although the purging succeeds, the mysterious "Harlequin Man" Zephro Carnelian lures Draco to discover a plot whereby a group of secret Inquisitors and other cryptic conspirators hope to infect the human race with a mind-controlling psychic parasite known as the hydra. While pursuing the trail laid by Carnelian, Draco inadvertently causes the extermination of all life on Stalinvast. In a space-hulk in the warp, Draco discovers that Firenze is one of the principal plotters. In search of the evasive facts about the hydra, Draco travels to a chaos world in the Eye of Terror with Meh'lindi and Navigator Vitali Googol and the Squat engineer Grimm. From there, they escape to Earth. Forced to behave as renegades, they penetrate the imperial palace to confront the Emperor with their mystifying discoveries. Draco's audience with the Emperor is awesome yet deeply ambiguous. Draco flees and hides himself in suspended animation in the hope that subsequent events will provide enlightenment regarding the hydra conspiracy and the conflict of intrigues within the Inquisition and the Secret Inquisition.*

YEAR 40,373 *Inquisitors are being murdered as Draco awakes from a century spent in stasis. He needs to find an Astropath to eavesdrop psychically on what is now happening. Despite signs of impending insanity on the part of Navigator Googol, Draco's ship reaches the world of Luxus Prime where Slaaneshi cultists are in rebellion. Googol succumbs to daemonic possession, but Jaq and Meh'lindi are reunited with Grimm. Together they find a new Navigator, Petrov, and abduct the Governor's Astropath, Fennix.*

It transpires that the alien Eldar Harlequins are about to stage a dire ceremony in orbit around Stalinvast, and that a rejuvenated Baal Firenze is intent on attacking the Eldar habitat with the aid of Space Marines, ostensibly to seize secrets of the Webway by which the Eldar travel through the warp.

Jaq and his companions can only infiltrate the alien habitat if Meh'lindi can be surgically freed of her Genestealer body-implants so that she can use Polymorphine to adopt the appearance of an Eldar. Discovering that her former superior, Tarik Ziz—now a renegade—has fled to planet Darvash along with a surgical team, Meh'lindi succeeds horrifyingly in having the implants dissected out of her.

The companions enter the habitat while a space battle rages and Marines are invading—led by a psychotic Firenze. In pursuit of Zephro Carnelian, Jaq and his comrades give chase through the Webway—accompanied by Captain Lexandro d'Arquebus of the Imperial Fists (whose previous exploits are recounted in Warhammer 40,000: Space Marine*); though Astropath Fennix loses his life.*

Arriving on the ravaged Craftworld of Ulthwé, they are captured and learn of the alien plan that Jaq should become possessed by a daemon, and purged, and illuminated—so as to serve the Eldar in their manipulation of the mysterious Emperor's Sons (or Sensei Knights), and help bring about the mutual annihilation of the cosmos and Chaos as foretold in the Eldar's prophetic Book of Rhana Dandra, *which is kept in the legendary alien Black Library hidden in the Webway.*

A squad of Marines rescue Jaq's party. They flee into the Webway, though Navigator Petrov loses an arm to clingfire. In an agony-vision sent by dead Fennix, Petrov perceives through his warp-eye the route to the library. Emerging on a warped world, Lex engraves the route permanently upon Petrov's third eye while Chaos Marines are attacking.

By the time Jaq's party reach the Black Library, all of their Marine escort are dead except for Lexandro. A Phoenix Warrior kills Meh'lindi, devastating Jaq. Petrov attempts treachery, and is killed.

Bearing the Book of Rhana Dandra, which is encrusted with a fortune in jewels, and also carrying Petrov's lethal warp-eye which Lex cut out, the armourless Captain and Grimm and heart-sick Jaq set out to find a world where they can hide while they try to decode the alien book of fate. Jaq broods obsessively about a rumoured crossroads in the Webway where time and reality can alter, and where he might somehow bring Meh'lindi back from the dead—if he becomes illuminated by conjuring a daemon into himself and then exorcising it . . .

CONTENTS

Chapter One

Runes

"You failed," the Harlequin hissed at Zephro. "You weak human fool."

The expression upon the Harlequin's chameleon mask was one of contempt and ridicule. Even the alien's kaleidoscopic costume—so buckled and belted and beribboned—seemed to mock Zephro Carnelian in his own mischievous motley garb of green and red triangles, which had seemed so harlequinesque to him.

In his tricorn hat with its ostentatious crimson plume, was Zephro merely a clown? Merely a human monkey who aped the scintillating quicksilver Eldar?

"So you're illuminated, are you?" jeered the Harlequin.

Zephro winced inwardly. Should he appeal to Farseer Ro-fhessi, his patron, his friend? (Hopefully still his friend, if indeed Ro-fhessi had ever fully been that!)

If his friend had overheard, no attitude was evident. The horse-like visor of Ro-fhessi's crystal-studded helm hid the Farseer's expression. This was no time to intrude on Ro-fhessi—not when Ro-fhessi's mentor Eldrad Ulthran was about to cast the runes. All thoughts should be upon the impending divination. Zephro should rejoice that he was privileged to watch—whatever the outcome might be. Hostility from one of the group of Harlequins was understandable, acceptable.

Maybe Zephro's presence wasn't so much a privilege as a woeful necessity—due to his role in the fiasco which required this divination.

Fiasco? No . . . catastrophe.

Seen from space, Ulthwé Craftworld resembled an ornate coral-like cathedral with the dimensions of a major moon, though horizontal, not globular. Embellishing its surface, like gems studding a serrated golden shield, were domes. Nowadays many of those domes were dark. Others glowed with only ghostly light. Given several hundred years of peace, the psycho-plastic wraithbone of Ulthwé would repair itself entire and empower itself anew until the shield gleamed and the gems shone.

Peace was tragically lacking.

Immediately astern of the Craftworld there floated a swirl of brightness and murk. Held in stasis like some baby spiral galaxy, that swirl was Ulthwé's major gateway to the Webway. Through there, Wraithcraft could reach far stars. That swirl was no propulsion system for the Craftworld itself. Soaring ether-sails propelled Ulthwé into its flight away from a vaster and more terrible eddy several scores of light years further astern. These days the Eye of Terror seemed to be expanding more quickly than Ulthwé could outrun it.

Here in this interstellar gulf the harvest of energy was tiny. The Craftworld could only sail slowly.

How soon would extreme jeopardy compel the digging up of spirit stones to be implanted in the metal combat-bodies of Wraithguards? If those artificial bodies were destroyed, the spirits temporarily enshrined in them would be lost irrevocably.

How soon must the Avatar of the War God be awakened? The Avatar's berserker fury would wreak havoc upon foes—yet equally upon the whole terrain where a battle was fought; even if that terrain was precious Ulthwé itself, already so often ravaged.

Eldrad Ulthran laid down his staff and his long sword. He removed his helm to bare his head. Silver streaked his hair. Each of his movements was so stately—in keeping with a sacred moment, to be sure, yet nowadays Eldrad was always slow. It was as if Eldrad Ulthran was wading through an invisible syrup of time before coming to a final halt.

From a pouch at his belt Eldrad took the rune stones. He threw one of these upon naked wraithbone. Then he formally announced the subject of the divination, which was simply the latest in a grievous series upon the same theme.

"Inquisitor Jaq Draco!" Eldrad declared. "Draco who penetrated the Black Library!"

Aye, such a fiasco; such a catastrophe . . .

Eldrad—and Ro-fhessi and Zephro Carnelian and the Warlock Ketshamine and half a score of Harlequins—were in the Dome of Crystal Seers.

Due to raids by the forces of Chaos all too many zones of Ulthwé were devastated wastelands, hideous blotches of ruin. Such gloomy wildernesses were of use only to the Black Guardians and Aspect Warriors as combat training grounds.

Other regions still retained their sublime elegance—slender pyramids and fluted towers rising from amidst groves of trees which seemed sculpted of jade.

This Dome of Crystal Seers was a place of especially sacred beauty and daunting power. It was here that the wraithbone core of Ulthwé was exposed nakedly underfoot, that gold-flecked creamy wraithbone. Elsewhere in the Craftworld the psychopotent, quasi-living core was cloaked by loam and turf, or by marble or mosaic floors . . . or else by rubble and ruin.

Here, from the naked essence of Ulthwé, rose millions of trees of wraithbone. Each towering tree had grown from the spirit stone of a dead citizen, to unite their souls with Ulthwé's very being. In glades throughout the Dome numerous crystallized bodies also stood rooted. Those were Farseers who had become totally attuned to this place—as Eldar Ulthran would soon become. It was several years since Eldrad had left the Dome itself. It was several decades since Eldrad had last travelled out of Ulthwé on any such expedition as had rescued Zephro from the clutch of Chaos, well over a century earlier.

The most ancient and tallest of the wraithbone trees actually grew through the dome into space. That pellucid air-retaining dome was a hybrid of substance and of energy. It easily tolerated piercing by the trees. Topmost limbs of trees were tendrils questing outward from a transparent and softly luminous shell—into the black lake of the void.

Within that dark lake above, stars were tiny lamps. Many had been swallowed aeons since by the lurid gangrene and bile and jaundice of the Eye of Terror, which was all too visible through the dome. Nightmarish irreality was engulfing ever more suns and mutating ever more worlds into habitations for monsters and daemons.

If invaders from the Eye finally overwhelmed Ulthwé, not only would its defenders die but the wraithbone forest would be shattered. Ten thousand years of heritage and afterlife would disintegrate—yet not into pure oblivion, oh no. All the spirits of the dead would be sucked into the psychotic torments of Chaos . . .

"Draco found and entered the Black Library!" declared Eldrad.

Indeed, indeed. Hidden in the Webway itself, guarded by terrible forces, its location known only to Great Harlequins, that repository of knowledge about daemons should have been forever secure unless a guide led the way. Draco simply could not, should never, have been able to find the Library unaided, let alone enter it.

Yet he had done so.

Even worse, Draco had robbed the Library.

Warlock Ketshamine leaned his lofty frame upon the hilt of his Witch Blade so that its point pierced the naked wraithbone. Ketshamine's mask was a bleached skull, awful and inscrutable. The Warlock's swirl of hair was dark as coal. His flaring black sleeves and tent-like skirt displayed huge prints of runes such as were writ on the stones. Ketshamine too had once been a Farseer who scryed the shifting flux of probabilities. Ketshamine had eschewed the study of prophecy in favour of the more lethal uses of psychic power.

"Draco stole the *Book of Rhana Dandra!*" called out Eldrad.

Aye, the mutable book of fate itself: *it was missing*. It was gone from the Black Library in the Webway—because of damnable Jaq Draco.

It was Zephro who had involved Draco in the affairs of the Eldar.

Not without good reason! Not without approval and guidance. Not without Draco's name being present in the book of fate.

"Did Draco steal the *Book of Rhana Dandra* to rehabilitate himself with the Imperium? Where did he take it to? What will occur?"

So saying, Eldrad threw all the other stones. He stared at their pattern on the wraithbone, and at the shapes of the runes themselves. The Farseer was entering a trance. Already the runes were beginning to glow as they became channels for energy—not only the energy of the psychic ocean which enfolded material reality, but also the spirit-energy of bygone seers, by virtue of this direct contact with the wraithbone.

The runes were warming. As they warmed, so their shapes shifted subtly.

Heat began to radiate from those stones.

Orange heat. Red heat.

In a high eerie voice Eldrad cried out: "In robbing the Black Library Draco suffered a tragedy—a tragedy so terrible that he may likely become insane!"

A tragedy? This was new knowledge, sieved from the psychic ocean.

"What kind of tragedy?" The question burst impulsively from Zephro.

Ro-fhessi waved an impatient hand at his human protégé to silence him. Eldrad was peering into the web of future probabilities. Draco's 'tragedy' was responsible for the likelihood of him becoming insane. Thus his tragedy figured in the flux of cause and effect. Of the tragedy itself, which had already occurred, only the fact that it had happened could be gleaned, not its precise nature.

Dread clutched Zephro. It had been the Eldars' dire plan that Draco should be ensnared by daemonic possession—and then led to salvation. Draco would become illuminated, like Zephro himself, and immune to Chaos.

Draco would become an Illuminatus. As such, he would help seek out and gather together the human Emperor's undisclosed Sons. The Emperor had sired those Sons before He was crippled and encased in His golden throne ten thousand years previously. He did not know of their immortal existence. Those Sons were psychic blanks to Him. Nor did the Sons understand their own nature until Illuminati enlightened them.

The Sons would become Sensei Knights, forming the Long Watch. When the Emperor finally failed and when Chaos surged to devour the cosmos, those Sensei Knights—all of whom were aspects of the Emperor—would fight the last fight. Or so they believed . . .

The Eldars' name for the last battle between reality and Chaos was *Rhana Dandra*. In the Eldar book of fate it was written that the outcome of this final battle would be cosmic cataclysm, the mutual annihilation of Chaos and reality. This at least would be preferable to the triumph of Chaos.

Chaos! Four major Gods of Chaos already existed, like malign rival monarchs amidst the countless potent entities of the warp. When the proud star-spanning Eldar civilization collapsed in psychotic spasm ten millennia previously, the foul deity Slaanesh had coagulated into existence.

If the feebler human race collapsed, a fifth senior Power of Chaos would emerge, finally to unhinge reality and sanity.

But there was an alternative . . .

In the psychic ocean of the warp, fed by whatever was noble in mankind, a force of goodness could coalesce: the Numen, the luminous path, the light for New Men, to renew mankind.

Such a frail hope! Eldar Farseers had glimpsed that the Numen could emerge when the Emperor finally failed—if his Sons were fused in mind-fire, if they were consumed to give birth to a phoenix of salvation and renewal. Thus the apocalypse could be averted. Farseers would steer a luminous numinous renewed cosmos. The Eldar would regain a measure of glory.

Supposedly Jaq Draco was to play some small yet crucial role in this process. Alas, the exact nature of that role was shrouded in mystery.

Now Draco had stolen the book of fate.

Maybe he did so out of sheer revenge! Draco had discovered the plan to engineer his possession by a daemon, and his subsequent purification. He had reacted very negatively.

If Draco were now to become insane—why, madness was only a membrane away from daemonic possession. Madness was an open doorway for a daemon. Draco was unsupervised. He had with him the precious potent *Book of Rhana Dandra*! Such a catastrophe, such a disaster.

Terrible doubt assailed Zephro. What if the Eldar did not *really* control the majority of the Illuminati—and thus the Emperor's Sons? Zephro owed his very salvation to the Eldar—as did other Illuminati. Yet it was a fact that renegade Illuminati were trying to create a psychic doomsday weapon with which to lash out at loathsome Chaos and at aliens alike.

Those renegades were busily infesting worlds of the imperium with an insidious psychic parasite. The Hydra parasite would lie dormant for centuries. At some moment in the future it would suddenly fuse the human race into mind-slavery. The slaved minds of trillions of hosts would lash out in a lethal paroxysm— the most likely result of which (so Farseers feared) would not be a purifying purge but the unleashing of the fifth Chaos power.

To sabotage this dangerous plan, Zephro had infiltrated the Hydra conspiracy.

What if he was only a catspaw? What if other secret Illuminati existed unknown to him—who had purged themselves of Chaos, and who were also trying to gather in the Emperor's Sons to create a true Long Watch? What if the activities of the Eldar, and his own activities, were merely a travesty of that genuine search by illuminated individuals, a genuine search which was indeed nudging the Numen closer?

What if the intoxicatingly persuasive Eldar were so sure of the inevitability of the Rhana Dandra apocalypse that their aim was merely to consume the Emperor's Sons in the hour of cataclysm—so that the mutual destruction of Chaos and cosmos should be absolutely guaranteed, and nothing whatever survive?

Zephro must not give a place in his mind to such doubts! He was feeling alienated because of the Draco disaster. Because some Harlequins now despised and blamed him.

Ro-fhessi did not blame him. Surely not.

Runes fluxed and shimmered. Stones glowed white hot. Energy was surging through those stones, from warp into wraithbone, from wraithcore into warp. Even the trees of wraithbone shivered. Away in the groves the crystalline statues of Seers would be vibrating.

"Where might Draco succumb to insanity?" shrilled Eldrad. "Where in all the worlds?"

A thunderclap came—an ear-piercing *crack*.

For a moment Zephro imagined that one of the rune stones had exploded.

No! The sound had come from above—from the dome itself.

Up there, where one particularly titanic tree pierced through into space, a vessel had impacted. The ship's contours were shifting weirdly. One moment it resembled a scarab. The next, it seemed like a crab. Coruscating with malign energies, its frontal claws were ripping at the substance of the dome.

Beyond it drifted another incoming ship.

Moments earlier those vessels hadn't been there. Oh, but they had been. They had been cloaked in invisibility. They had been veiled from Eldar lookouts by sorcerous shielding.

As the first ship burst through the dome, plasma gushed from its snout. Gobbets of compact superheated gas incandesced against one massive tree—and then another. Shattered trunks toppled upon shorter trees, snapping them. The scream of escaping atmosphere might have been the agonized voice of the ravaged trees.

Already the shriek was dying to a whistle as the dome resealed itself—only to be ripped open a second time, by the following ship.

Slowly the first intruder was descending. Rotating upon its axis, it jetted plasma in every direction other than where the divination had been taking place . . .

. . . and where it was still taking place! Never before had Chaos mounted a raid upon this place of power. Yet for a while the urgency of the divination outweighed the demands of the violent intrusion. Pray that enough Guardians and Aspect Warriors responded to the intrusion. Eldrad shrieked at the stones, *"Where in all the worlds? Show me! Show me!"*

Where indeed? As soon seek a needle in a haystack, or a bug in the coat of a cudbear. Draco's possession of the book of fate seemed to block perception, blinding the Farseer to the infernal Inquisitor's whereabouts . . .

From the Black Library Draco would have fled through the Webway, that maze of energy-tunnels through the warp. Many exits and entrances existed on human worlds, unknown to their inhabitants.

"Show me!"

What was shown was something else entirely.

Nausea assailed Zephro—and with this came a fleeting vision. He saw a nightmare landscape of volcanoes and plains of lava and jagged crags. In a sombre sullen sky lightning of many colours flickered: incessant discharges of unnatural energy. From a precipitous peak there rose a skyscraping black tower. On top of that tower glowed a great crystalline eyeball.

Oh, but this brand of nausea was all too familiar to Zephro. It was the sickness of daemonic influence. With a surge of will Zephro dispelled it.

Had the others seen the same vision? No longer could they delay reacting to the attack. Warlock Ketshamine discharged bolts of energy from his Witch Blade at the descending ship. Those eye-searing pulses reached the vessel. Immediately they were deflected into the forest, as if from a sling, harming the wraith-bone.

The ship was going to land upon the great scar it was creating for itself.

Harlequins plucked shuriken pistols and laspistols from holsters hanging amidst all the belts and scarves and buckles of their tight bright cling-suits. Those suits were gyrating with rainbow hues. Each Harlequin was becoming a will o' the wisp.

Black Guardians had emerged in the distance, cradling long-barrelled lasguns. Their golden helmets were the heads of bees attached to the bodies of upright ebon warrior-ants. On their back-banners was the rune of the eye shedding a tear of passionate vitriolic grief for the sufferings of Ulthwé.

Spiders were swarming from out of the naked wraithbone. Those tiny white spiders materialized out of the very substance of the bone itself. Thousands of spiders, tens of thousands, in psychic defence of the Craftworld! A carpet of these spiders rippled—towards the white-hot rune stones.

Of course! The stones were acting as a psychic beacon. The rune stones were in such an intense state of activation that they had guided raiders to the Dome of Crystal Seers.

Spiders surged over the stones, sizzling into steam. More spiders followed. More again, to quench the runes. The divination was certainly at an end. How appalling that it had attracted not the hoped-for truth but disciples of Chaos instead!

An urgent sending assaulted Zephro's sensitized consciousness—and an image:

Of a domed abandoned wasteland elsewhere in Ulthwé. Of intrusion through a Webway portal—by armoured Chaos Marines! Chaos warriors were spilling forth, attended by deadly Daemonettes, the creatures of Slaanesh. Emergency, dire emergency . . .

A second attack was under way—conducted by vile perversions of human warriors who had once been so proud and noble,

but whom Chaos had subverted ten millennia previously, and
who were now the timeless standard-bearers of vicious depravity.

*The battle-standards rising from the backs of those erstwhile Marines
were so grotesquely obscene as to sicken witnesses of the intrusion; and
Zephro shared their nausea . . .*

The profile of the foremost vessel had stabilized. That ship had
become rectangular—with razor fins, with pincers at the bows.
The following ship was still fluctuating as it descended, wreaking
more havoc upon the sacred forest.

High above the dome, a third raider swam into view. But out
there in space a Wraithship of Ulthwé was sailing to the attack.

The Wraithship's high sails tacked in the thin ether. Ether, ha!
To a large degree it was radiant pressure from the Eye of Terror
itself which the Wraithship used to propel itself and manoeuvre.
Upon its deck a fusion cannon opened fire dazzlingly.

A moment later the third raider ballooned with a light so intense that sudden shadows of trees were like physical blows from
great cudgels impacting all across the beloved terrain. After-
images wrought bars of darkness and blinding streaks upon
Zephro's vision.

So much psychic surge! In stroboscopic flashes he was glimpsing that wasteland, elsewhere in Ulthwé.

*Aspect Warriors were responding to the invasion. Howling Banshees,
in their white and red armour, were advancing. Imbued with the spirit of
their shrine, those females would be uttering stunning mind-shrieks.
Their masks were screaming feral faces. Energy pulsed from their laser
pistols. Their power swords would be humming in anticipation.*

*Daemonettes rushed at the Banshees. Oh those daemonettes so desir-
able as regards the swell of thigh and bosom and curve of loins, so lethal
in other respects! How jealous of the Banshees they were. How eager to
rip the Eldar females apart with the pincers of their hands. How keen to
impale a Banshee upon the barbed prongs of their tails.*

*Behind came the Chaos Warriors. Crustacean codpieces jutted from
their armour. They toted such obscenely shaped bolt guns. And those
banners! Displaying such gross bizarre erotic icons!*

*Scorpion warriors of Ulthwé were attacking on the flank. Striking
Scorpions! How nimbly they darted. Agility was their defence against the
explosive bolts which ejaculated from the bolt guns of the Chaos renegades. Agility, and strong green armour banded with funereal black.*

Scorpions fired shuriken stars from their pistols. Stars glanced off Chaos armour. Those Striking Scorpions were so alert for a chance to rush in and deliver their sting. Once they were at close quarters the pods in their helmets would discharge stunning psycho-conductive needles. The final coup would be by chainsword . . .

From the grounded vessel, yet other Chaos Marines were emerging accompanied by a mob of beastmen.

These Marines were burdened with heavy bolters and lascannons. How angular their power armour was. Shoulder pauldrons were rounded, yet as for the rest—such cruel angles! Above their helmets jutted vanes like axe-blades. Their very stance was angular. They sported blasphemous totems which would have wrenched at the mind of any devout imperial Marine—mockeries of honour, mementoes of foul victories over former battle brothers.

"Renegades of Tzeentch!" cried out Ro-fhessi.

The beastmen were swifter than the Chaos Marines. Shaggy-legged, they only wore light armour. From their brows twisty horns jutted forward. Clawed paws clutched bolt guns. From scabbards at their waists they pulled cutlasses. Their hooves were stamping marks of Chaos upon the bare wraithbone. Oh yes, these were creatures of Tzeentch—of the Power of Mutability, of Change the Destroyer.

"I glimpsed the *Watchtower*," Zephro called out by way of extra confirmation.

Aye, Zephro's psychic vision had been of the Tower of the Cyclops. Zephro had recognized it from horrific sketches which Ro-fhessi once allowed him to see. That tower stood upon the Planet of the Sorcerers in the Eye of Terror. That planet was the stronghold of magicians dedicated to the Lord of Change. Those had once been true Marines. Nowadays their king peered through the warp by means of that cyclops eye. He spied upon the realm of reality—greedy to find arcane trophies . . . such as sacred rune stones.

Those other Chaos Marines who had invaded the wilderness were blatantly servants of Slaanesh, the Power of Perverse Lust. Was it by coincidence or by malign collusion that both groups had chosen the same occasion to attack?

Black Guardians fired their lasguns at the beastmen and their

masters. Marines of Tzeentch responded by discharging lascannons and heavy bolters. Many bolts hit trees. Penetrating deep,
the bolts exploded. Mighty trunks quivered from bole to crown. A
Guardian was blasted apart by a bolt. Another was burnt open by
a lightning spear of laser energy . . .

The defenders of the wilderness—those Banshees and Scorpions—were all
close-range fighters. Where were the airborne Swooping Hawks who
could drop grenades from above?

In the wraithbone forest Harlequins shimmered from place to
place. Once in motion, they were virtually invisible. Pausing
briefly, they fired las-bursts and streams of tiny razor-stars. So
few Harlequins!

Where were the Aspect Warriors? Where, where? Were they
diverted by that other assault far away?

Where were the anti-grav platforms for scatter-lasers? Terrible
though the use of such weapons would be amidst the sacred
trees!

Where were the shuriken shrieker cannons? Where were the
wraithcannons?

Harlequins darted. Harlequins vanished and reappeared.

Tzeentch yearned to unleash destructive tidal waves of change
throughout the cosmos—to unhinge continuity itself.

The king of the Planet of Sorcerors must have sensed the loss of
the book of fate. He must have detected earlier divinations carried
out by Eldrad Ulthran. His Chaos raiders had certainly been
guided in their final approach to Ulthwé by Eldrad's latest and
fiercest effort to locate the *Book of Rhana Dandra* and its thief. Oh
fate was cruel.

Those shapeshifting ships had arrived here through the warp.
They had emerged into ordinary space very close to Ulthwé indeed, so as to take its defenders by surprise. Wraithships were
forever on patrol around Ulthwé. There was no star nearby to
bend space so that incoming vessels must emerge billions of kilometres short of their goal. A raider might materialize suddenly
above the Craftworld itself—especially if guided by such a
psychic beacon as Eldrad had been obliged to light.

Those other Slaaneshi Marines had come by breaking into the

Webway and following some psychic scent. Upon their world there would be a gateway from long ago. That gateway would have been sealed. What could have weakened the seals? What could have laid the trail of scent?

An earlier intrusion which had produced that wilderness had come from a Chaos world which tilted crazily to and fro like a rocking plate. Aspect Warriors had driven the surviving Chaos Marines back to their roost there. They had witnessed a landscape of lunacy. In the sky of that world they had spied a daemon of malign delight sitting upon a low sickle moon.

Surely the present Slaaneshi invaders came from that selfsame world. An Eldar adept had sealed the rupture. What could have re-opened the Webway to Chaos but an intrusion into their world from *this* side of the seals?

The trail led back to Ulthwé. The meddlesome intruder must have been Jaq Draco himself when he had fled away from the Craftworld to find the Black Library. Through malice or through stupidity Draco had breached the seals.

Damn Draco and damn him again. *He* wouldn't have lingered long on that world with its daemon-in-the-moon. Just a fleeting visit. Oh the damage he had caused!

Preceded by beastmen, the Marines of Tzeentch were making headway through the glades. They were aiming for where the rune stones lay extinguished under a mat of spiders, the divination aborted. If lascannons had been able to recharge more rapidly, progress might have been even speedier.

Picked off by Harlequins, beastmen were dying. Spiders were trying to dissolve into those beastly bodies through the fur and hide, distracting the beastmen's attention. Chaos Marines seemed almost indomitable in their advance. Shuriken stars and laser fire veered off those enchanted angular suits. The Marines' loudspeakers brayed a hideous skirl of *Tzeentch, Tzeentch*. And then a roar of *Magnus, Magnus, Sons of Magnus*.

Oh yes, Magnus had been their founder and their primarch. Nowadays he was their sorcerer-king in the Tower of the Cyclops. These were some of his self-styled Thousand Sons.

The Eldar plan involved the dying Emperor's biological sons, who were unknown to Him-on-Earth. Here came savage Sons of another stripe. Oh the bleak loathsome irony of it!

Eldrad Ulthran pointed the Staff of Ulthmar, summoning and focussing its energies. Ketshamine discharged his Witch Blade once more. Psychically, Ketshamine was messaging for support. Where were the Aspect Warriors? Where were the anti-grav floaters with heavy weaponry?

Damn Draco forever. May he go mad and become the plaything of a daemon.

No, but he mustn't. He must be found.

Yet how, when Ulthwé itself was so assailed?

Other Craftworlds would join in the search. The loss of the *Book of Rhana Dandra* was a calamity for the whole Eldar race. Spies would search. Harlequin players would rove through the Webway to human world after human world, risking their lives and staging spectacles as a pretext for their presence.

Zephro sighted his laspistol at a lumbering beastman who waved a cutlass. Zephro was preparing to kill and to be killed himself.

Into view, at last, came an anti-grav platform. The platform jinked its way amidst the soaring trunks. Behind it flew Swooping Hawks. Their wings shrieked through the air, a blur of hues.

There was hope! Forlorn hope.

Chapter Two

Pilgrimage

A wild region of a southerly continent of the planet Karesh consisted of boulder-strewn goat pastures. Beneath those rugged pastures were limestone caverns. In a certain cavern was an exit from the Webway.

Below ground, phosphorescent lichens flourished. From the other side of the cavern the misty blue glow of the Webway might have seemed to the casual eye to be merely a more intense patch of natural luminosity. Thus was the terminus camouflaged.

In any case, why should anyone have come down from the surface to search? Such caverns were huge and spooky and dark. Idle curiosity was rarely wise.

Evidently some goatherd had intruded at one time or other. Maybe he had been searching for one of his animals which fell down a shaft or strayed too far into a cave. Facing the opening to the Webway was a cairn consisting of three billygoat skulls. The horns poked defensively at the blue tunnel, as though to impale whatever might emerge.

The skull-cairn implied that the locals were primitive folk. Lex suggested re-entering the Webway to find a more advanced world. Jaq was still deep in shock at Meh'lindi's death, and felt unable to make a decision. Lex and Grimm debated the issue.

To re-enter the Webway would be to take such a random risk. They needed food and drink and rest. They had to hide. They had to think. In their hands was an alien book of fate—written in inscrutable script in a language which none of them knew, not now that *she* was dead.

The book was a key to so many secrets. This business of the Emperor's Sons, for instance! Since the book supposedly contained prophesies about the final apocalypse, there must be details about those Sons in this book—if the Sons genuinely existed. One only had a Harlequin's word for this, and Zephro Carnelian's too. Both parties could have been lying. This book was the proof. The proof couldn't be read.

Nor could they risk contacting any imperial authorities. The Inquisition numbered in its ranks profound experts upon the Eldar race. Those would have sacrificed an arm to be able to scan this book. Alas, the Inquisition was infiltrated by conspirators and at war with itself. Jaq had been branded a heretic and renegade.

What of the place in the Webway where time supposedly could turn backwards? Back to a time when Meh'lindi was still alive? Better not think of that! Not even Great Harlequins knew where that place was—if it existed at all. Only someone supremely illuminated might be able to find such a place. An extraordinary magician . . .

Such as . . . a master of this book of fate? Such as . . . someone who had undergone daemonic possession, and redeemed himself?

"You're still in trauma," Lex told Jaq sternly at the mere mention of such matters.

"I shall pray for clarity," said Jaq numbly. He didn't pray.

"Listen," said Grimm, "I once visited a farming moon so superstitious that wheels were even banned. 'Cos wheels represented godless science. Perils of witchcraft, hmm? Even on *that* moon there were anti-grav floaters and a swanky capital equipped with a spaceport."

Karesh proved to be a similar planet. Not that wheels were prohibited—but the rural peasantry were whelmed in ignorance and dread.

Finding one's way out of the cavern took a while. Half an hour after surfacing, they had spotted a goatherd. The fellow fled at sight of the trio. An hour's trek brought them to a hamlet of drystone hovels.

Stunted peasants were in awe of Lex's superhuman stature. Was that mighty chest of his—with the ribs beneath his muscles all fused into solid bone—a *human* chest? What were those sockets in his spine? (Aye, through which his lost armour had once interfaced with him!) The peasants were leery of Abhuman Grimm. They were dismayed by stern Jaq, and by his scaly mesh armour. However, their dialect was comprehensible—so this world could not be too detached from the Imperium.

Dimly the peasants remembered tales of a team of powerful strangers roving a neighbouring province once upon a time, equipped with dreadful weapons, rooting out deviants.

Psykers were feared hereabouts. The sign of the horns was used to ward off evil, which must not otherwise be spoken about too much. Offerings must be made to a nameless menace, which was at once terrible—yet also benign, in so far as it kept its distance. Was this menace the Emperor himself, dimly understood? These peasants eased the trio on their way in the direction of 'the city' with offerings, including a new beige robe for Jaq, and a great loose homespun vest for Lex, which had been the property of a local prodigy, a farmer of grotesque obesity.

The 'city' proved to be a tatty town, although furnished with a landing field. Peasants would drive surplus goats there for slaughter. Far away across a sea, goats' brains were much in demand by gourmets. It was in this town that the trio finally discovered the name of the world they were on—a detail which had been beyond the goatherds' ken.

Planet Karesh.

Its capital was Karesh City. Once a fortnight, chilled brains were flown to Karesh City from this province. Otherwise, the region might have been even more isolated. The next such flight was due only a couple of days later. In exchange for bed and board at a hostelry near the landing strip, Grimm reluctantly surrendered a finely-tooled silver amulet depicting one of his ancestors.

With one of the smallest gems prised from the cover of the *Book of Rhana Dandra*, Lex bribed the pilot of the cargo plane.

Another tiny gem bought them lodgings in Karesh City. There it fell to Lex and Grimm to scrutinize the register of interstellar shipping due to call at this world. Jaq continued to be riven by grief for

his dead Assassin-courtesan. Was he obsessed by the quest for
the luminous path and for truth—or for the supposed occult place
where he might snap the spine of time itself and bring Meh'lindi
back into existence? Sometimes it seemed to Grimm and Lex that
the latter might be the case. Surely this was just the consequence
of bereavement. Having encountered an Inquisitor of the stripe of
Baal Firenze, Lex respected Jaq's tormented loyalty to truth. Since
Meh'lindi had died serving Jaq, some of that loyalty had become
symbolised by Meh'lindi for the time being.

Lex understood all too well how deeply the death of close comrades could affect a person. Inscribed repetitively upon the bones
of his left hand, from which he had once dissolved the flesh in
acid, were the names of two fellow Marines who had died
decades ago.

Yeremi Valance and Biff Tundrish, from Trazior Hive, Necromunda.

The chirurgeons of his fortress-monastery had grafted new ner-
vewires and synthmusclefibre and pseudoflesh in the aftermath
of Lex's self-imposed penitential ordeal. Decades later, Lex's
hand still itched inwardly with the memory of those names.

The interstellar merchant and passenger ship *Free Enterprise of
Vega* seemed suitable as a route out of Karesh. According to the
register its captain held an ancient hereditary free charter. This
captain ought to be a man of honour, unlikely to murder passengers if he suspected that their baggage was valuable. The
captain wouldn't wish to lose his imperial charter to trade freely
where he chose without too much obligation to the merchant fleet
administration. An enterprising spirit such as he would surely
want a huge ruby such as could buy half a dozen interstellar trips.
He would be discreet.

What clinched the matter, for Jaq, was the destination of the
ship.

Sabulorb!

Meh'lindi had once walked upon Sabulorb. Three years prior to
meeting Jaq, that very planet was the scene of her bravest and
most harrowing feat. In the gruesome guise of a Genestealer
hybrid Meh'lindi had infiltrated a Genestealer nest. She had
killed the Patriarch. She had escaped alive.

To walk where she had walked, albeit with horror in her heart.
To see what she had seen. To be where she had been!

*

In their hotel suite, its windows plasteel-shuttered for privacy, Grimm raised a possible objection.

"Look Boss, I agree it's over a century since she was there, 'cos of all the time you spent in stasis. Sabulorb might still be infested."

Genestealers were furtive. They tried to establish their control by guile. To penetrate society from behind the scenes by using normal-seeming hybrids as a facade was their goal. To prey on society until it could be monstrously transformed.

The plasteel shutters were embossed with floral motifs. Fragrances seeped from tiny grilles in the hearts of the metal flowers. Walls were richly brocaded, and topped with a frieze of blossoms. A painting framed in filigree depicted a gauze-clad nymph dancing provocatively and inviolably upon a Venus Mantrap in a steamy jungle.

"Do you reckon," asked Grimm, "that her killing the Patriarch resulted in any kind of public exposure of the menace? She went there in secret, remember."

Oh indeed. Her visit had been a cruel experiment on the part of the Director Secundus of the Officio Assassinorum. Meh'lindi had wrought some havoc, but clandestinely. She had reported back only to the Director Secundus of her shrine.

"That Genestealer coven could still be patiently beavering away under another Patriarch and another Magus," Grimm pointed out. "They could have covered up the harm she did them. Huh, there might have been other covens in any case. What's the chain of authority for anyone intervening?"

Lex pondered. Untold hours of study in the scriptories of the fortress-monastery had been devoted to the traditions of the Imperial Fists, his Chapter. He had also familiarized himself to some degree with the intricacies of imperial organization. Very few people could possibly grasp all of those in any great detail.

"As I recall," said Lex, "the shrine ought to have notified the Adeptus Terra. It should have informed the Administratum. The Administratum ought to have mobilized a chapter of Marines . . ."

In a galaxy so vast, with so many urgent demands upon less than a million Space Marines—and with billions of officials involved in the imperial bureaucracy alone—decisions might be delayed for years, dire though Genestealers were. The outcome could take decades.

Grimm scratched his hairy rubicund cheek. "That Director—
Tarik Ziz, damn his soul—could have suppressed her report—not
wanting his nasty experiment to be known. Nothing might have
happened yet. Taking up residence on Sabulorb could be risky."

Jaq grimaced.

To walk where she had walked!

Grimm and Lex visited the captain of the *Free Enterprise*, on board
his vessel at the spaceport, to enquire about commercial prospects
on Sabulorb and its political stability, with a view to booking passage there. Alternatively, they might wish passage to a different
world aboard his ship. The magnificent ruby which Lex showed
to the captain spoke volumes.

Lex himself did not speak much at all, leaving this to Grimm.

Already, back in the tatty town an ocean away, with Grimm's
assistance Lex had torn the long-service studs from his brow with
pincers. Lex retained the studs in a pouch. He must become incognito. Surrender of the studs had been painful to Lex's soul, if
not physically daunting. Was not an Imperial Fist able to endure
most pain? Did not a Fist privately relish pain?

Lex's sheer musculature might nevertheless proclaim Space
Marine to anyone who had ever encountered the legendary warriors or who had watched devotional vids. That tattoo on one
cheek, of a skeleton fist squeezing blood from a moon, might
identify his actual chapter to an aficionado. This hypothetical person, observing the eight livid puckers disfiguring Lex's brow,
might conclude that he had been discharged in disgrace. If even
better informed, this person might wonder why Lex had been released from his vows at all instead of being sentenced to
experimental surgery, and his organs harvested for pious use.

Lex was most unlikely to meet such a totally knowledgeable
person. With his coarse vest and groin-cloth and great bare leathery legs, Lex seemed to be a barbarian slave owned by Jaq, whose
trusted factotum Grimm was.

Should anyone ever spy the patchwork of old scars on Lex's
trunk, where potent extra organs had been implanted by Marine
chirurgeons, those marks would imply that Lex must have been
savagely whipped to make an obedient servant of him—after his
capture from some feral world, probably. If anyone caught a
glimpse of those spinal sockets, why then, at some stage the slave
had been used as a servitor cyborged to some bulldozer or crane.

As to the injuries in his brow, Lex must have been impaled in the head with a multi-toothed cudgel, and his thick skull had survived the impact.

To further the barbaric image, in public Lex suppressed his fluent and gracious command of Imperial Gothic. He parodied the scum lingo of the lower levels of his erstwhile home-hive on Necromunda. He was a Fist, a thinker. He could pretend cleverly.

Grimm and Lex learned from the spry elderly captain that Sabulorb was most certainly politically stable . . . nowadays. There had been (whisper it) Genestealers on that world. Blessedly, Space Marines had cleansed the planet around seventy-five standard years earlier. Space Marines, no less! Ultramarines, by name! The captain plainly made no mental connection between those Marines and the barbaric giant who stood in his cabin.

"Uh, did any of those Ultramarines stay on?" asked Grimm. "To set up a recruiting base?"

They had not done so. The cities of Sabulorb had required a good deal of repair before the economy got back on track. Much devastation had occurred, and many deaths. Be assured: that was all in the past. Sabulorb had passed through its phase of reconstruction into relative prosperity once more. Moreover, this was Holy Year on Sabulorb. Pilgrims were flocking there with fat purses.

How perfect for the trio that Sabulorb expected many visitors from other worlds . . .

How predictable that there should have been so much damage and death three-quarters of a century earlier. That action by Ultramarines had occurred twenty-five years after Meh'lindi visited Sabulorb. Hardly a rapid response by the Imperium—though speedier than some responses. Had a clerk mis-routed a report? Had Tarik Ziz suppressed the information? Had intelligence about the infestation come from some other source?

Whatever the reason, twenty-five years had allowed the covens to become much stronger, and their response to a challenge correspondingly more violent. Yet even so, Sabulorb was clean.

The journey from Karesh to Sabulorb consisted of an initial plasma-boost outward to the jump-zone on the periphery of the Karesh system. This took over three days. Then came a jump through the warp, of only twenty minutes, yet bridging light years. *Free Enterprise* emerged on the outskirts of the Lekkerbek system, a prosperous port of call.

Inward, once again for several days. Outward, once again for a few days more. A second similar jump took *Free Enterprise* to the edge of the Sabulorb system. Since Sabulorb's sun was a massive red giant, the journey inward required almost a week.

In all, including stopover on Lekkerbek: a journey of almost three weeks.

During the whole of this time Jaq remained secluded in the suite of three connecting cabins. Lex preferred not to show himself. But Grimm roamed the ship, as a mechanically-minded Squat would.

Amongst the passengers already on board were scores of pilgrims, and scores more boarded at Lekkerbek. All were agog to be present at the unveiling of the True Face of the Emperor—a ceremony which occurred only once every fifty standard years, in Shandabar City on Sabulorb.

So as not to disabuse pious fellow passengers, Grimm refrained from enquiring too specifically into the nature of the ceremony. Plainly many pilgrims had saved for half a lifetime to afford the trip. To behold their God's true face would bless them utterly, guaranteeing peace everlasting for their souls, and bliss. These fervent folk presumed that Grimm and his reclusive master and his seldom-glimpsed slave were on the same pilgrimage.

In private, Grimm was sarcastic enough about pilgrimages in general to merit a warning snarl from Jaq.

"Would you appreciate your own Squattish ancestors being mocked, little man? Those are *your* object of reverence. We cannot gainsay these people's devotion!"

Lex nodded agreement to this reprimand. In his own area of the suite Lex was often praying to Rogal Dorn, Primarch and progenitor of the Imperial Fists—those Fists whom he had, some might say, deserted. Through Dorn, by proxy, he prayed to the Emperor on Earth.

Lex also spent time studying a scanty *General Guide to Sabulorb*. The captain sold copies to the pilgrims, but he had handed one gratis to Grimm since the ruby was so spectacular.

The *General Guide* contained hardly any information about the Holy Year ceremony itself. Pilgrims would already know all about it. Mainly the guide discoursed about the planet; and this was of compelling interest to Lex, who was accustomed to assessing the vital statistics of a world thoughtfully prior to combat.

To circle its giant sun took Sabulorb ten of Earth's years. Each season lasted for three whole years. The inhabitants counted in standard imperial years.

"That's sensible of them," remarked Grimm. "Otherwise, imagine asking anyone's age! Gosh, I'm almost two years old; I'm getting married. Oh dear, I'm eight years old; I'm dying."

Due to the small tilt of its axis all the seasons of Sabulorb were similar: cool. Its sun was huge but diffuse. It did not radiate a great deal of heat.

Much of the three great flat continents of Sabulorb was covered by cool deserts (and permanent ice-caps shrouded the poles). Deserts of grit abutted on deserts of pebbles or of sand; and one must beware of the pernicious powder deserts. A circulatory system of rivers stretched long irrigating limbs throughout those continents, from freshwater sea to freshwater sea.

One might imagine that those rivers had been dug as giant canals at some time in the distant past—and that the basins of the seas may have been blasted out by unimaginable explosions. Debris had formed the deserts. The basins had been filled with water pumped from within the planet's crust.

Here and there on land were what might be ancient ruins, eroded to stumps. Or were those natural formations? In the seas, according to the guide, algae and vast weed-mats yielded oxygen. The waters teamed with fish and froggy batrachian creatures which lived on the weed-mats. On land, herds of camelopards and pygmy camelopards grazed belts of vegetation along the rivers. Those quadrupeds sported humps and snaky necks. Scaly-hided sand-wolves preyed on them.

"Huh," said Grimm, "life's too simple on Sab—"

Where was the biological link between the amphibians of the seas and the grazers on land? What's more, the balance of camelopards and sand-wolves—of prey and predator, which must constantly seesaw up and down—was too simplistic in a cosmos which generally indulged itself in a fester of pullulating life-forms preying upon one another in a chain of ravenous consumption.

"Somebody or something kitted the planet out—"

No such life-forms could have arisen on Sabulorb of their own accord. A red giant became a giant by expanding. Once, that sun would have been much smaller and hotter—and Sabulorb would have been a frozen world far from its luminary. While expanding, that sun would have swallowed any warmer inner worlds. Faced by impending destruction, intelligent creatures on one of those doomed inner worlds may have prepared Sabulorb for habitation.

Or perhaps, with its rumour of ruins, Sabulorb was akin to Darvash, the desert world where Tarik Ziz was in hiding. (Oh, to boil Ziz alive in his dreadnought suit! That would be incense to Meh-'lindi's soul.) Aeons ago, Darvash had undergone some preliminary planetary modification at the hand of some elder race. The ancient edifices on Darvash had been huge and intact—not weathered away to stubs, as on Sabulorb.

"I think the Slann visited Sabulorb vastly long ago," suggested Lex. "Hence the batrachian creatures in its seas . . ."

Decades earlier, in a colossal hangar of the fortress-monastery, as a cadet Lex had witnessed a mottled frog-like Slann war-mage being marched away in chains to the domain of the surgeon inter-rogators. So little was known of the Slann. That race was supposed to be even more ancient than the Eldar. Slann may even have uplifted the Eldar to civilization long ago. They may have seeded life on Earth. Now they mainly stayed in their redoubts north of the galactic pole. Because the Slann were reputed to be dangerously powerful, the Imperium generally left them alone.

"Yes, *Slann*, I'd say—"

Jaq cared nothing at all about the Slann or about the origin of Sabulorb, although Grimm had listened with interest to Lex's speculations.

"Quite a bright bit brute you are," Grimm had commented. Lex had merely chuckled ominously, and relapsed into his mockery of scum lingo:

"Runt grunt. Bigman hear 'im. Bigman hunt 'im."

"Oh I shiver in me boots," said Grimm, though not quite so cockily.

They also absorbed the dialect of Sabulorb through a hypno-cas-que provided as another bonus by the captain. Other passengers were obliged to pay.

The Sabulorbish language was full of -*ings*. "Be giving me alms." "Be riding this camelopard." Everything was larded with present participles as if partaking of sacred time—or of eternal timelessness.

*

Forever Meh'lindi was in Jaq's thoughts, unshakably, agonizingly. Whenever he lit incense in his sub-cabin, the smoke writhed, hinting spectre-like at the silhouette of his Lady of Death.

Surely his devotion had undergone a bias for which he would once have scourged himself on grounds of heresy.

Had he lost his clarity?

Or was it the case that by allowing the memory of Meh'lindi to haunt and torment him, and by letting this obsess him, he might crank up obsession to a perfervid state of mind—aye, of psychic mind!—which would transcend all ordinary bounds? Dared he invite possession by a daemon of deadly lust so as to conquer the daemon within him, and thus become illuminated—immune to Chaos, able to scry and use the secrets of the *Book of Rhana Dandra* in the service of righteous duty? And maybe to bring Meh'lindi back as well . . . He must not think of this possibility! He must not let Captain Lexandro d'Arquebus of the Imperial Fists, his barbaric slave, suspect that his former wild words still haunted his thoughts.

He must purge such thoughts. He must lock them up in a private oubliette. Truly the notion of retrieving Meh'lindi from beyond death was an impossible and demented fantasy!

Jaq recalled the two occasions on which Meh'lindi had wrapped her lethal tattooed limbs around him, ecstatically—though for a higher purpose.

Meh'lindi had served him well, and thus the Imperium, so excellently. Let her image in his mind (and in his very nerves!) continue to serve *obsessively* as a means of whetting his consciousness—as a personal icon, a fetish, feeding him energy in a manner akin to Lex's bond with Rogal Dorn! Aye, inspiring Jaq tormentingly to strive to the very bounds of sanity, and perhaps beyond—and beyond again, into purity sublime.

This would not be heresy, but true fidelity and consecration, in the service of Him-on-Earth.

Alone, Jaq toyed with the speckled pebble on a thong which he wore around his neck—Meh'lindi's bogus spirit-stone. It hadn't fooled the Eldar for long. Eldar souls might indeed suffuse into stones, but human souls didn't. The stone was only a pretty pebble.

Might it serve, nonetheless, as an amulet for Jaq? As a focus for his own psychic consciousness, to imbue that faculty with agonized passion?

If there was any actual resonance with Meh'lindi, this resided in the Assassin card in Jaq's Tarot pack. That card from the suit of Adeptio had once come to resemble Meh'lindi closely. Did it still do so? In the wake of her death, had the resemblance faded?

From his robe Jaq removed his Tarot in its insulated wrapping of flayed mutant skin. Closing his eyes—by feel and by concentration—he stripped open the cards, and cut them.

There she was: Assassin of Adeptio. The cropped raven hair, the golden eyes. The flat ivory planes of her face. She was bare to the waist. Tattooed beetles walked across her dainty breasts, decorating old scars. She was so lithe, such a wonderful weapon. Jaq's eyes could have bled. Her image in the psycho-active liquid-crystal wafer was so waxen and stiff. Her eyes were so empty. She was death itself now. She was oblivion.

The cards! Oh stupidity! Zephro Carnelian's mocking image must still haunt the pack, an infiltrator in their midst in the guise of a Harlequin! Carnelian might be able to snoop on Jaq through the card.

If the trio were to hide successfully, that Harlequin card would have to be destroyed, not merely insulated. Why hadn't Jaq thought of this until now? Ach, his capacity for analysis was askew because of the tragedy.

If a single card was destroyed, the integrity of the pack would be impaired.

Before wrapping the cards again, Jaq slipped Meh'lindi's image into an inner pocket. He had no need of protection and insulation against *her*. The Assassin card was the perfect icon, and fetish, and memento mori.

Free Enterprise was due to make its second jump through the warp.

Jaq, Lex and Grimm were waiting for the warning klaxon in the little lounge connecting their cabin-cubicles. Let passengers and crew only think the purest thoughts while the ship was in transit through the sea of lost souls—where predators lurked!

Jaq removed the thong, and pebble, from around his neck. He held the speckled stone over the mouth of the disposal chute for Lex and Grimm to see.

"I must cleanse myself of distractions," he said.

"Aw, don't, Boss," protested Grimm.

However, Lex nodded solemnly.

"Aye," said the giant. "Just as I removed my service studs."

Jaq let the stone fall—to be incinerated, and the ashes voided into space.

"More distressingly," Jaq went on, "I must also destroy my Tarot pack in case Carnelian can trace us through it."

Just then the klaxon wailed. *Free Enterprise* was entering the grey realm of the immaterial, awash with psychic currents. May they not be assaulted by gibbering entities, scratching at the hull. May they not be trapped in a maelstrom, to become a lost space hulk in which drifted mummified corpses.

Where more appropriate for Jaq to dispose of the cards? Probably the ashes would not pass directly into the warp, due to the ship's energy shields; but rather would disperse into vacuum once the *Free Enterprise* emerged into reality again.

Down the chute Jaq rid himself of his own significator card—of the high priest enthroned and gripping a hammer. Ice-blue eyes. Scarred, rutted face. Slim, grizzled moustaches and beard. Might he become as blank to scrutiny as any of the Emperor's fabled Sons were to their paralysed sire.

The Emperor's spirit imbued these cards, which He had once allegedly designed. If the fervent pilgrims could only have seen Jaq consign to ashes the Emperor card itself, that grim blind face encased in the prosthetic Golden Throne!

Jaq rid himself of the Space Marine card. Let Captain Lexandro d'Arquebus be anonymous. The card had begun to duplicate Lex. An olive complexion, notched by duelling scars. Ruby ring through his right nostril. Dark lustrous eyes and pearly teeth.

Jaq dropped the Squat card down the hole.

"Oops," said the little man, as if a queasy flutter had upset his stomach for a moment. Whether the card had resembled Grimm or not was a moot point. All Squats looked much alike with their bulbous noses and chubby red cheeks, their bushy red beards and prodigious handlebar moustaches. Grimm's ruddy head of hair had grown back by now with typical Squattish vigour.

Most Squats who travelled outside their home systems— usually to serve the Imperium—dressed similarly, in those beloved green overalls of theirs, and quilted red flak jackets, and forage caps and big clumpy boots.

Jaq barely blinked at the contaminated Harlequin card. Into fire, into ash, into void. Away, away, quickly.

Many more cards flew down the chute.

The Daemon card from the suit of Discordia presented itself. Jaq hesitated because it was flickering.

"What you seen, Boss?" Grimm also saw, and groaned.

In the past, this card had adopted the semblance of the hydra: a writhing knot of jelly tentacles, due to cross-contamination from the Harlequin card. Now it was a daemon pure and simple—if such a thing were ever simple. Snarling fangs, cruel claws reaching out. It flickered.

Of a sudden it was altering. The hideous face was puckering. The neck was shrinking. The head sank low into the chest. Curved horns shifted.

Instinctively Jaq cast an aura of protection. But he still held the card.

"Dump it!" squawked Grimm.

The daemon's body fluctuated so! Mocking faces were appearing all over its skin, only to vanish again. Lips were opening as if to speak. Cruel thin lips. Fat slobbery lips. Twisted lips. Opening and closing. Opening again elsewhere.

Lex gasped at the sight—in a way which suggested *recognition*. "In Dorn's name destroy it!"

Jaq knew the image well enough from restricted codexes he had once scrutinized in a shielded daemonological laboratory of the Ordo Malleus.

This was Tzeentch, the Changer of the Ways, the would-be Architect of Fate. Recollection of studying that image once upon a time on Earth, in the bosom of the inner Inquisition, brought to this malign mirage almost a twinge of nostalgia as well as of horror.

Tzeentch embodied the path of anarchy and mutability and turmoil, whereby to unpluck the threads of events. Was it Change itself with which Jaq must risk meddling perilously, rather than rampant Slaaneshi desire?

To seek a route to the place in the Webway where time and history might twist! Where Meh'lindi might still be un-dead! From which she might be summoned back!

Anguish gripped Jaq. Lex seemed paralysed by the image he

witnessed, as if his strength was enchained. Grimm almost gibbered but the little man's babblings were as froth; babblings about the danger of summoning a Daemon whilst in the warp itself . . .

That froth was bothersome.

"I already cast an aura of protection," snarled Jaq. "I have my force rod ready!" He stared at the card.

Might Tzeentch preside over the first stage of his transfiguration en route to illumination? One of Tzeentch's Greater Daemons, some cunning playful uncaring Lord of Change? Was this the meaning? Nevertheless, Jaq would keep a hidden kernel of his own spirit intact . . .

Oh *temptation*.

Smoke formed uncanny patterns around the Daemon's head, pregnant with revelations, with visions.

The card could be a litmus of the perils besetting Jaq. A gauge of his progress. A warning signal.

Sanity reasserted itself. Grimm was right. If this situation continued, instead of pure thoughts horrors might coagulate around *Free Enterprise*. Were those horrors already suckering to the hull, scritty-scratching at the welded plates, cackling, seeking entry? Pink, long-armed blurs would rush through the ship. So it was written in the *Codex Daemonicus*.

But to incinerate this card . . .!

To whom might he pray for guidance now that he had burnt the Emperor card, director of the pack? To His Lady of Death, perhaps?

Lex uttered a strangulated grunt. He lurched slowly towards Jaq as if tearing chains of adamantium loose from rock.

"Hear me!" Jaq cried. "As I am your Lord Inquisitor!" Lex paused, perhaps glad not to approach closer. "If I'm ever to use the *Book of Rhana Dandra* I must meddle with *some* occult forces. I'm fully trained to cope. This card can warn me—like a radiation monitor," he sang out at Grimm.

Jaq wrapped the Daemon card securely in the mutant skin which had formerly protected and insulated the whole pack.

"There, it's safe—"

All of the remaining cards he consigned to oblivion.

A regular Captain of Space Marines such as Lex might rightly be appalled by a glimpse of Chaos. He wasn't a Terminator Librarian, a psychic specialist. Yet he had staunchly endured a brief sojourn on a Chaos world. The glimpse of Tzeentch had seemed to ravage Lex inwardly, as if kindling anew some ancient nightmare. With horny fingernails Lex scratched at his huge left hand as if he might tear away the flesh and lay bone bare. Or else to inflict some pain upon himself?

Lex was detaching himself spiritually from this brief episode. Jaq could hear the giant praying softly, "Light of my life, Dorn of my being."

Lex eyed Jaq with composure. Some trauma inside of Lex had been contained. Not to be voiced.

"I'm guided by your knowledge," he told Jaq.

"I shall be very careful in all we do," vowed Jaq.

Aye, careful that he did not alienate his companions.

As to prudence . . . why, a man could stand on a clifftop eyeing a maelstrom down in the sea for hours, calculating every twist of its swirling currents. As soon as he leapt from the cliff he would bid farewell to all solidity and stability.

After a further interval the klaxon sounded again. *Free Enterprise* was safe in the far outskirts of the Sabulorb system.

In a dream the spectre of Chaos haunted Jaq . . .

The Harem of Lord Egremont of Askandar had occupied a hundred square kilometres at the heart of the vaster metropolis of Askandargrad. Until two days before, the immense Harem had been a walled Forbidden City within the greater city. Half of this Forbidden City was now in ruins. Fires blazed. Smoke billowed into the sullied sky where two suns shone, the larger one orange, the smaller one white and bright.

From north and from west, twin swathes of destruction cleaved through Askandargrad to converge upon the ravaged prize of the Harem.

Astride the massive, much-breached wall between Harem and metropolis—formerly the only point of entry—Lord Egremont's sprawling palace was an inferno. If he were lucky, the Lord-Governor of Askandar was dead.

As were so many hundreds of the élite Eunuch Guard. As were thousands of soldiers of the defence force. As were many of the Maidens of the Harem. If they were lucky.

In the ruin of what had been a splendid bath-house, Jaq crouched with three of the Eunuch Guards. Burly men, the

Eunuchs were bare-chested save for scarlet-braided leather waist-coats. Golden bangles adorned their muscular arms. The belts of their baggy candy-striped trousers were home, on one side of the waist, to a holster for a bulky web pistol, and on the other side, to a scabbard for a power sword.

Sufficient unto the policing of the usually peaceful Harem, these weapons! The web pistol, to entangle any intruder or rebellious resident. The power sword, to decapitate if need be.

Sufficient, until now . . .

The Eunuchs' uniforms were soiled and torn. One had lost the topknot of hair from his shaved skull to a near miss by a flamer. His scalp was seared pink. Another nursed an obscenely decorated and contoured bolt gun lost by an injured invader.

The ivorywood roof of the bath-house had fallen in upon the perfumed waters of the long white marble pool. Timbers and tiles had crashed upon naked bodies. Some bathers had died instantly. Some had drowned. Once-lovely bodies were broken and submerged. Some victims still whimpered, injured and trapped by wreckage yet able to gasp air.

A stretch of side wall had partially collapsed. Through the resulting gap, from behind a barrier of marble debris, Jaq and the Eunuchs were witnesses to vile revelry in the once-delightful plaza outside where terracotta urns of floral shrubs lay shattered.

Were the screaming tethered female prisoners hallucinating while abominations were perpetrated slowly and perversely upon their flesh? The Slaaneshi Chaos Marines had certainly used hallucinogenic grenades—as well as bolt guns and meltaguns and terrible chainswords, and heavier weaponry too. Were hallucinogens intensifying the already appalling sight, and the implacable cruel touch, of pastel-hued armour exquisitely damascened with debauchery upon the breast plates and the shoulders? Was that which was already monstrous being multiplied far beyond the brink of sanity?

A few tormentors had shed items of armour, exposing grotesquely mutated rampant groins, their organs of pleasure bifurcated and trifurcated, with squinting eyes sprouting from them, and with drooling lips.

Others had no need to shed armour. Chaos Spawn had materialized: lamb-sized creatures with legs of spiders and bodies of imps, and with questing tentacles and phallic tubes. Jaq himself almost believed that he was hallucinating. A snake-like umbilical cord connected these spawn to the swollen groin-guards of their master—who stood back, roaring and whinnying with delight, as they guided the spawn in the ravishing of their captives, soaking up the sensations of these roving external members.

Corralling other hysterical captives were beastmen slaves armed with serrated axes. A Chaos Techmarine monitored these slaves. His armour was studded with spikes. Each shoulder pauldron was in the shape of giant clutching fingers. He wore a nightmare helmet shaped like a horse's head, eyes glowing red.

One of the shaggy beastmen drooled and dropped his axe. The beastman reached out a paw to caress a particularly voluptuous captive.

Immediately the Techmarine adjusted a control-box strapped to his forearm.

The disobedient beastman's metal collar exploded, severing his head. The head fell. It bounced and rolled amidst the captives even as the beastman's body was tottering.

Two Eunuch Guards lay maimed. A Chaos Medic in fancy armour opened up one of them with a long knife and pulled out the writhing wretch's entrails to sort through. The Medic snipped a gland loose and deposited it in an iron flask bolted to his thigh. From that gland some drug would be extracted, to induce deranged ecstasy.

This sight was too much for one of Jaq's Eunuch companions. "Hasim!" he moaned. "My friend!"

Before the man could be stopped, he was scaling the barricade of broken marble, web pistol in one hand, power sword in the other.

The energy field of the sword blade shimmered, a blur of blue. The pistol was cumbersome with its cone of a nozzle and its underslung canister of glue. Blundering forward, the Eunuch fired the pistol. His aim wavered. A murky mass of tangled threads flew from the nozzle. The mass expanded in the air. Even so, the cloud of stick threads missed the Medic—and wrapped around the Techmarine instead, clinging and tightening.

The Medic had seized his chainsword from the ground. The sword whirred. It buzzed like furious killer bees. The sharp teeth throbbed into invisibility as they spun around. With seeming delight, and with one hand behind his back, the Medic met the Eunuch.

How shrilly the teeth of the chainsword screeched as they met the energy field of the sword. An electric-blue explosion of power ripped teeth loose, spitting them aside. The Medic's metal-sheathed arm was vibrating violently as if it might shake apart. No doubt such sensations only pleasured the Medic. The guard of the chainsword had locked against the power blade.

From behind his back the Medic swung his long surgical knife. He drove the blade into the belly of the Eunuch. The sword fell from the Eunuch's hand, suddenly inert. The web pistol tumbled too. That former guardian of the Harem staggered backward, clutching at the hilt of the knife.

He tripped. He fell. He squirmed to and fro. The Medic roared with satisfaction. Such an injury wouldn't bring quick death—but plentiful opportunity to operate upon the man while life endured.

Of course, other mutated Marines were heeding the place from which the Eunuch had come. Abandoning their pleasures, they were bringing bolt guns to bear.

Meanwhile the contracting web had tightened upon the Tech-marine's armour. Threads cramped one of his gauntlets upon that control box.

Maybe the Techmarine sought to activate the frenzy circuit, to goad the beastmen into a killing rage directed at the wrecked bath-house.

A collar exploded. A shaggy head was blown from its neck.

A second collar exploded.

A third. A fourth . . .

Jaq woke from the memory-dream, sweating coldly.

Chapter Three

Riot

At Shandabar spaceport, after much queuing, Grimm was able to exchange a minor gem for a bag of local shekels. Pilgrims thronged the port, which served long-distance aircraft as well as spacecraft. These pilgrims were merely the latest arrivals, many from other continents of Sabulorb.

Since many of the pious preferred to conserve their funds for lodgings and the purchase of relics, it proved possible to hire a limousine with fatly inflated tyres and dark windows for transport into the city. Destination: any bureau specializing in the long-term leasing of property. Jaq had no wish to stay in one of the crowded caravanserais such as Meh'lindi had once used, pretending to be a governor's daughter from another solar system.

Shandabar was a dusty, chilly metropolis of considerable size. Even so, it was packed. According to the driver of the limousine the regular population was two million. Right now the number had swollen to at least six million.

Along the northern fringe of the city flowed the two-kilometre wide river Bihishti, the water-bearer. To the south was the Grey Desert. Dust and grit frequently blew across Shandabar, though it was rare for a storm to deposit more than a few centimetres' depth of granules. Still, by custom, tyres were balloon-like—both on cars and on the multitude of carts pulled by morose camelo-pards with long snaky necks and splayed feet.

From armoured vehicles, police kept an eye on the surge of

humanity—of robed pilgrims and touts and pickpockets and beggars and jugglers, of slaves and artisans and missionaries, of
zealots who preached to the passing crowds, of porters and huck-
sters and couples foolishly in love. The sky was of copper colour;
the red sun was vast. Many buildings were domed and arcaded.

After viewing holographs of several suburban mansions, Jaq
chose that which seemed the most secluded and well-fortified. A
great diamond was perfectly acceptable as a deposit upon a ten
year lease. Doubtless the property agent rejoiced in the inflated
commission which he would finesse.

By the time the driver had taken them to a quiet southerly
quarter, the great red sun was beginning to set, protractedly. A
curved maroon lake of sun still bulged up into the sky. Several
stars already showed.

The boundary wall of the property was topped with lethal wire.
The limousine halted outside wrought plasteel gates. Half a
dozen cloaked fellows armed with autoguns were passing by.
These paused to eye the limousine.

The driver seemed unperturbed. "Being vigilante patrol," he
explained.

Grimm demanded the keys to the vehicle before he and Lex
and Jaq stepped out, to be challenged by the vigilantes.

The little man introduced himself as the new major-domo of
this mansion. He gave his own name, which was common
amongst Squats. The name of the grim new master of the house
he gave as Tod Zapasnik, which was how Jaq had decided to be
known in Shandabar. The hulking barbarian slave merited no in-
troduction.

The leader of the vigilantes condescended to inform the new
residents that during the time the mansion had been empty the
lethal wire on top of the wall had apparently lost its power. A few
days earlier, a party of fanatical pilgrims had climbed into the
grounds to roost in tents overnight, when the temperature would
become bitter.

"Not breaking into mansion itself, Great Sir," the man said to
Jaq. "Cutting precious bushes for kindling, and felling trees for
logs. Previous owner neglecting payment to our virtuous patrol."

Jaq snarled at Grimm. The little man distributed shekels to the vigilantes. In bygone days Jaq might well have cursed their leader for his blackmail and his blasphemy. What did such a person know of virtue? Virtue was dedication, virtue was consecration. Virtue was an Assassin-courtesan who had only ever embraced him twice, and on each occasion for an excellent reason.

As new residents of this district, the trio should not provoke needless antipathy—but rather, respect.

"Being well able to protect ourselves and our property, however!" Jaq advised. From within his own cloak emerged *Emperor's Mercy*.

Eyes widened at sight of that precious ancient bolt gun plated with iridescent titanium inlaid with silver runes. Only two explosive bolts actually remained in the clip, but Jaq had his laspistol too, fully charged.

Grimm toted *Emperor's Peace*, with a single bolt remaining in it. He loosened the holster of his laspistol.

From the webbing on his back underneath his vest, Lex pulled the bolter which still had a full clip. He transferred a laspistol to the multi-purpose holster which by now was strapped to his thigh. Hitherto the holster had remained mostly empty. With several compartments, it was such as a slave might carry tools in.

During the couple of weeks they had spent on Karesh, Grimm had failed to obtain any extra ammunition for the bolt guns. Their bolters could still speak once or twice before falling silent. Quite a few times, in Lex's case. The laspistols would serve well.

Gloom was deepening. Shadows stalked the streets. The driver of the limousine coughed impatiently.

Tucking *Emperor's Peace* away after this demonstration, Grimm unlocked the gates. He thrust them open to admit the vehicle, and returned the keys to the driver. After glimpsing such guns, *he* wouldn't dream of revving and absconding with luggage.

"Be waiting just inside," the little man ordered gruffly.

As the chauffeur complied the chief vigilante was eyeing Lex's bare legs and scant attire. He pulled up the collar of his cloak. He shivered.

"Getting cold already," he observed.

Lex snorted contemptuously. He was trained to endure extremes of cold, or of heat. His anatomy was modified accordingly. Under his skin was the quasi-organic carapace in symbiosis with his nervous system, enabling him to interface with power armour via the spinal sockets. The carapace also served as insulation. What did these mundane fellows know about cold?

The slave flexed muscles such as few could have seen before. "Soft bods," he sneered in scum lingo.

The vigilantes were all shrinking well out of the way. Was this in awe?

No! Brown shadows flitted mansionward along the street. A dozen shadows. A score and more. Of a sudden a chant arose, of *"His face, True Face, His face, True Face."*

"Who blocking the path of His true pilgrims?" cried a frenetic voice. "Pilgrims returnin₃ to their tents with holy relics! Moving aside, moving aside—in His name!"

Grimm's eyesight was acute. Squats had evolved in gloomy caves and tunnels where lighting had once been scanty and power was strictly rationed. "They only got stub guns, Boss," he said.

Handguns which fired ordinary bullets were the hardware of a commonplace low-life gang. Notwithstanding, Jaq called out: "Warning you! Circumstances changing. Throwing down guns. Removing tents peacefully from this property!"

Needless slaughter was not the imperial custom. All too often, circumstances might compel bloodshed to sustain civilization and stability and sanity and faith, but it was always a matter for regret. Sheer carnage was the style of lawless heresy and of Chaos.

The reply to his warning was a *crack-crack* like the snapping of twigs underfoot. Slugs whined past. A slug pinged against the open gates. Others ricocheted off the boundary wall.

Intoxicated with expectations of the coming religious spectacle, the devotees were besotted with a sense of personal righteousness.

Then even more righteous bolt guns spoke.

RAARKpopSWOOSHthudCRUMP

  RAARKpopSWOOSHthudCRUMP . . .

A bolt ejected. It promptly ignited. Propellant powered the bolt on its way. The bolt impacted. It tunnelled and exploded. Flesh and bone or a vital organ erupted. It was ever this rowdy way.

By contrast, laspistols were silent in operation. If the aim was inaccurate, the scalpel-blade of energy soon dispersed. Whenever a laser-pulse met its target: such a lacerating flare-up, such a scream of agony, if the victim still had the breath and lungs and heart to scream.

Perhaps ten of the pilgrims had fled. A score more lay dead or dying, almost all thanks to the laspistols.

Quite a minor massacre.

The vigilante leader returned. In the dying light he eyed those bolt guns with a sort of devotion.

"Being Space Marines weapons, Great Sir, not so? Grandfather telling me of when Space Marines were coming, him just a kid. Purging the aliens in our midst. Pilgrims collecting *relics*, right enough!"

From around his neck the man pulled a thong. Momentarily Jaq twitched. Yet what dangled from the thong was a burnished bolt—which the vigilante proceeded to kiss.

"Where getting that?" demanded Grimm.

"Being sold here in Shandabar as relics."

The Marines must have left unused clips of bolts behind, items compelling adoration.

"Gimme that," demanded Lex. "Belonging here." He slapped his gun.

Surely the vigilante would refuse to surrender his talisman. By what authority other than muscle did Lex presume to make such a demand?

Yet no . . . A mesmeric sense of seemliness appeared to overwhelm the vigilante.

"To be seeing such guns fired . . .," he murmured. Reverently he handed over the bolt. He gazed at the litter of corpses. "Sending a sanitation squad in the morning, Great Sir."

"Being grateful," said Jaq. "My slave will be using the pilgrims' tents as body-bags, and dumping them here in the street."

Most of the sun had sunk by now. Stars were brighter. Sabulorb possessed no moon. If it had, seas might have spilled far inland every day, so low was much of the land. The power propelling the slow flow of the rivers must have been centrifugal Coriolis force due to the planet's rotation. Good citizens would not wish to corrupt their minds with such arcane matters, the province of tech wizards.

According to the *General Guide*, the holy city boasted three major temples in addition to countless lesser shrines to the God-

Emperor. Each temple was sited near where an ancient city gate
had once been, during the early millennia of the colonization of
Sabulorb.

It was towards the easterly Oriens Temple that the trio set out
on foot early on the following day. Later they might buy a balloon-wheeled vehicle. Jewels from the *Book of Rhana Dandra* would
easily make them shekel millionaires many times over, should
they sell those all at once, which only a fool would do. Walking
was the best way to understand a city, even if hours of tramping
were necessary.

Oriens was the temple where Meh'lindi had been. Oriens was
where she had found the Genestealer coven. They must walk in
her footsteps. They must seek for more relics identical to that
which the vigilante had worn.

On their way to the Oriens temple they spied, far along a great
boulevard, a massive edifice quite out of keeping with the local
architecture. In place of domes and arcades: soaring buttressed
battlemented walls and a central spire.

"Looks rather like a Courthouse," said Grimm with a qualm.

No such institution was marked on the meagre city-map of
Shandabar in the *General Guide*.

Nor had they noticed any mirror-masked Arbitrators patrolling
the crowded streets hitherto.

"Better take a look later on," suggested the little man.

As the trio approached the place where the Oriens Temple ought
to be, buildings became flattened ruins. A whole neighbourhood
had been devastated, and nothing done by way of reconstruction.
Even so, pilgrims were converging through the dusty rubble.
Soon, what a swarm of touts there were! Not to mention beggars
and fortune tellers, souvenir sellers, and vendors of savoury tit-
bits such as stuffed mice or mulled wine. Booths and stalls and
kiosks mushroomed all over, as if a fair was being held upon a
former battleground.

Amidst the devastation, trade was thriving. Customers were
legion. Touts buzzed like wasps around juicy fruit. Would-be
guides accosted visitors.

To prevent pestering, they hired a guide—a skinny middle-
aged fellow whose very appearance seemed something of a deterrent. Due to some overactive gland the guide's eyes bulged. At

some time a knife slash had cleft his upper lip. Perhaps he had
been operated upon ineptly because of a deformity. As though as
a consequence of his cleft lip, words spilled out of him volubly.

Samjani was his name.

"Thanking for hiring, three Sirs, coming here to Shandabar to
be beholding the divine visage!"

"Yours not being too divine, eh Sam?" commented Grimm.
"Business being slow for you compared with the other guides?"

Samjani grinned hideously. "Normally no one bothering about
facial beauty, not here at Oriens." He leered hideously. "Not here
where deformed hybrids were once lurking!" To what fine dramatic effect Samjani used his split lip and bulging eyes, to suggest
the half-human spawn of Genestealers. During normal times he
would be a fine, frisson-inducing guide.

"Conceding, short-Sir, that my looks are jinxing my luck a little
when pilgrims being mainly intent upon the Holy Face."

Indeed, the face of Him-on-Earth would be unveiled two days
hence at the Occidens Temple.

Clarification about the nature of that ceremony could await a
visit to the Occidens. Meanwhile, here they were at Oriens where
Meh'lindi had once been.

Yet where *was* Oriens amidst all this ruination?

Samjani led them up a mound of rubble.

"Being before you!"

Amidst the detritus, across a wide area, vents gaped. Those
vents evidently gave access to a subterranean maze of tunnels,
catacombs, chambers and crypts. Debris had been cleared from
below ground. Ladders led down into those tunnels which had
once been infested by the deformed coven—their heartland,
which had finally been cleansed by armoured space-knights, a
legend come to life. Of course this was a rightful place of pilgrimage. Though why had the Oriens Temple never been rebuilt?

"Priests of Occidens not wishing rebuilding of Oriens, Sirs—"

It transpired that there had always been rivalry between Occidens and Oriens. Although lesser in status, Oriens had grown
rich because it hosted a giant jar containing clippings from the
Emperor's fingernails. He-on-Earth was immortal. His spirit
reached throughout the galaxy. As if still joined to His person,
those nail clippings continued to grow slowly. Priests of Oriens
would shave off parings from the divine fingernails, set those in
silver reliquaries, and sell them to devotees.

Whereas the Occidens Temple could only display the True Face once in a holy year, every fifty standard years.

The coven had subverted the entire temple administration of Oriens. Their Magus had become High Priest. When all the coven were slaughtered by the Marines, and the temple razed in the process—along with much of the neighbourhood, which the temple had owned—no administration existed any longer.

The local Pontifex Urba et Mundi should have appointed a new High Priest for Oriens. However, during the uprising of Genestealer hybrids this dignitary of the Ecclesiarchy had been assassinated in his palace. By virtue of seniority, *his* rightful successor should have been the High Priest of the imperial cult of the Occidens temple.

"Comprehending me, three Sirs?—"

The elderly High Priest of Occidens had refused to appoint a new High Priest to Oriens. However beholden an appointee might be to begin with, new power would soon banish old allegiances. Piously the High Priest of Occidens had insisted that first of all his own elevation must be properly ratified by higher authority. His argument was that if ungodly monsters had polluted one of the major temples of the holy city, how could the high priest of any other temple be worthy to elevate himself?

"Years being spent compiling a heresy report—"

Finally this report was dispatched thirty light years to the office of the Cardinal Astral, who was responsible for a diocese many hundreds of cubic light years in volume. Since the report had not been properly submitted by the office of the Pontifex of Sabulorb (he being dead and unable to sign), a clerk returned the report, according to Samjani's gossip.

In the meantime the scrupulous High Priest had died of old age. His acting successor resubmitted the report along with a request for his own formal ordination as senior cleric—which was rightly the business of the vacant office of Pontifex on Sabulorb.

Thus the decades passed by.

The ruins of Oriens proved as worthy of pilgrimage as the erstwhile Hall of the Holy Fingernail. Beneficiaries were the guides and vendors—who all paid a hefty tithe of their takings to the supervising Occidens Temple.

"Ultramarines woz here," said Lex.

"Indeed, big-Sir."

"Aaah . . .' '

Lex could not quite sustain the role of uncouth barbarian in such a context. He must examine certain relics on vendors' trays.

The majority of these relics proved to be forgeries: mere solid models of bolts—with no armour-piercing tip, nor propellant, nor mass reactive detonator, nor explosive.

After careful scrutiny, Lex advised Grimm to purchase two genuine explosive bolts. The proposed price was ridiculously inflated, steep as the sky. Lex was lofty too, and massive. The vendor dared not refuse Grimm's offer after Lex flexed himself and growled about counterfeits and blasphemy.

Finally they came to the exposed crypts.

As Jaq gazed down from above into one such crypt, his lips formed the name *Meh'lindi*.

In the guise of a monster she had crept through that very chamber which was now vulgarized by gawping sightseers, none of whom knew a scrap about her anguished bravery, no more than any of these guides did, nor anyone else on Sabulorb apart from Jaq himself and Grimm and Lex.

Such vulgarity! Jaq could have leapt down into the crypt with a scourge. He could have flailed about him to cleanse these ruins of infatuated tourists. How dared they obliterate her dusty footprints of long ago with their own trivial tread?

"Descending now to be viewing the monsters' lair?" prompted Samjani.

Deep in his throat Jaq growled at their guide, who was one of the instruments of vulgarity. Why should he not growl like a beast? Might he not need to wind his desolate passion up to a pitch of frenzy and temporary surrender of his own rational will?

Hastily Grimm intervened. "So what happened, Sam—I'm meaning what was happening to that jar of fingernails, eh?"

"Smashing and scattering during fighting, Abhuman Sir. His holy nails still turning up amidst rubble, often difficult to be identifying."

"I bet they are," agreed Grimm.

"Keeping a nail for oneself being punishable by flogging. All surviving nails being in safe keeping of Occidens. Half-shekel fee for finding one here!"

"Nails still growing, eh?"

"Nails under lock and key at Occidens, never being on display."

"You amazing me."

"During time of my great-grandad many bloody brawls were occurring between the disciples of the nails and followers of the True Face . . .' '

Jaq wandered from vent to vent, pausing to gaze down in lengthy bitter reverie. Lex attended him silently.

For Lex, too, this was a place of potential purity despoiled by peeping Toms and Tabithas. Here was a place where Marines had fought valiantly and victoriously; and where some had no doubt died, their progenoid glands to be harvested respectfully by medics.

The blue-hued Ultramarines had come; they had cleansed; they had gone—leaving behind seeds of legend and by no means as many unused explosive bolts as the trade in relics suggested.

How it would have heartened Lex to obtain a whole satchel of ammunition clips. Yet might he not then have felt himself to be all the more an impostor? Someone aping a Marine on account of his brawn—when he truly was a Marine in reality! Aye, a renegade knight who had torn the service studs from his brow . . .

Let Rogal Dorn, the dawn of his being, remain with him through this time of self-imposed exile, for a greater good.

Despite Grimm's best efforts, at this meditative moment Samjani suddenly scurried to accost Lex. Goggling and leering enthusiastically, he exclaimed, "*You* could almost be pretending yourself an Ultramarine, big-Sir!"

Pretend? How so? By leaping down into a crypt, wearing no armour at all? By dashing through crowded tunnels, *fighting* his way through all those Toms and Tabithas!

Pretend to be an Ultramarine—when he was rightfully a *Fist*!

Lex's hand swept back reflexively, the broad bat of his palm about to swat Samjani.

Grimm interposed. "Sam! There's a Courthouse in this city, ain't there? Being a Courthouse, being a Courthouse!" he babbled.

Lex withheld himself. The Courthouse, yes indeed. Oh, if he broke their guide's neck—if he knocked his head off—this wouldn't matter one whit to a Courthouse. Yet that a Courthouse should be here, where none had been mentioned by Meh'lindi: ah, that could be a nuisance.

Mundane crimes were of no concern to an imperial Court-house. Murders and robberies: let the local police take care of those. Crimes against the Imperium were the business of a Court-house. What were the trio seemingly involved in, but terrible covert treason?

Did Samjani realize the narrowness of his escape? Impassioned pilgrims who hired him might often be volatile in their behaviour.

"Being a Courthouse, certainly," chirped the guide obligingly. "Construction commencing just a few years after the Ultrama-rines were visiting . . .' '

It figured. The subversion of an important temple of the im-perial cult by sly inhuman hybrids—and the corruption of this world's administration—was proof of laxity. Laxity was a crime.

According to Samjani the hereditary Governor of the time—Hakim Badshah—had been absolved of heresy along with his family. The Badshah dynasty could continue. Massive fines upon the Badshahs paid for the precinct Courthouse which took ten years to complete, and for its maintenance.

Samjani mentioned that the gates of the Courthouse were generally closed. Those judges within seemed mainly involved in their own affairs and intrigues.

Jaq was paying attention by now.

"Are the Marshalls of the Court leading no regular patrols through Shandabar?"

Not to Samjani's knowledge.

"Are the Judges sending no execution teams in search of offen-ders?"

Samjani seemed not to know what an execution team might be.

"People killing themselves readily enough," Samjani said. He refused to elaborate. Perhaps he was merely alluding to the re-ligious rivalries and brawls.

Presently they left the crowded wasteland, and their informant, to walk across the city in the direction of the Occidens Temple, by way of that Courthouse, so as to study it. The trek could take two to three hours, if one paused to admire lesser shrines or the great fish market or the camelopard stockyard, with its vista of the Governor's palace not far beyond.

*

When they came close to the immense Courthouse they watched
for a while from the far side of a broad thronged thoroughfare.

The looming sprawl of the Courthouse occupied a whole city
block. Evidently several hectares of buildings had been demolished to make way for such an edifice—unless those buildings
had already been casualties of the Genestealer uprising.

Stout walls soared upward, inset with hundreds of lancet windows which were too slim for any human body to squirm through
yet which would serve excellently as firing slits. Bastions jutted.
Buttresses were fortified. Grimacing gargoyles poked from
beneath crenellated parapets and pinnacled turrets. Surmounting
the central spire was an orb in the shape of a grinning skull. All
along the upper reaches of the Courthouse, an imposing frieze
ten metres high bore the repeated motif of a jawless skull interspersed with the motto *PAX IMPERIALIS LEX IMPERIALIS*.

The Emperor's Peace, the Emperor's Law . . .

For Lex to see his own name coincidentally writ high and huge
seemed such an indictment of his own desertion of duty—as
though that frieze were displaying the names of notorious
criminals!

"Huh, well me own name ain't up there," joked Grimm. "They
ain't looking for me yet."

Were the Judges looking for anyone in particular? True to Samjani's account, the great ornamented plasteel main gates were
firmly closed.

This could be due to the sheer crush of pilgrims during the
holiest time of a holy year. Judges in residence mightn't wish a
paste of people to be squeezed through their portals willy-nilly
into whatever great courtyard lay behind those gates.

The reason could also be, as Samjani implied, that this Courthouse had become preoccupied by its own internal politics, since
Sabulorb seemed genuinely pacified.

Jaq recalled a Courthouse he had once visited, on a warmer
world. Its gates had always been wide open. Vigilant Arbitrators
had scanned the crowds within its courtyard. That courtyard had
supported a whole community of arguing petitioners who might
have been camping there for weeks or months on end, and of
caterers who served herbal teas and spiced cakes to the petitioners, and of cooks who brewed and baked, and of clerks who took

depositions, and of legal counsels who coached petitioners in the
phrasing of their depositions, all of which concerned niceties of
imperial decrees which had been delivered hundreds or even
thousands of years earlier. Some petitioners might spend half
their lives in that great guarded yard, which was only the outermost region of the Courthouse. The most devout suppliants
might even become recruits to the ranks of the warrior-Arbitra-
tors, their original legal case no longer of any significance to
them.

Here on Sabulorb it was otherwise. The Court was closed.

Jaq said to his companions, "There's a lot to be said for acting
under the very eye of the law." Pious hubbub almost drowned his
words. No one else nearby could have overheard. "The law's
gaze ranges far. It may not notice what is beneath its very feet."

Grimm nodded at a towering viewscreen mounted on a gantry
at the next intersection. Beneath, offerings were raining into a
great bronze bowl, their tinkling quite inaudible. At present the
viewscreen was blank. Many other viewscreens were mounted at
regular intervals.

The little man accosted a pilgrim for information. Lo, those
viewscreens had no connexion whatever with the Courthouse nor
even with ordinary police surveillance.

Six million people could not reasonably hope to witness the unveiling of the True Face directly. To behold the unveiling on
screen anywhere in this holy city was deemed equivalent to being
a direct eye-witness. Spectators would even gain a clearer view on
a screen.

"I don't accuse the Judges of laxity," said Jaq. "But perhaps
they're more interested in their own splendid power than in rigo-
rous investigations. This is sometimes the temptation. A
Courthouse can seem a world unto itself."

Behind those gates, beyond whatever courtyard, would be an
immense labyrinth of halls and dungeons, armouries and bar-
racks, firing ranges, scriptories and archives, warehouses and
kitchens and gymnasia and garages. A Courthouse wasn't unlike
a fortress-monastery, a sovereign domain where the robed Judges
presided over the Marshalls of the Court, and those Marshalls
over the well-armed dedicated Arbitrators who would enforce the
law of the Imperium, were it to be violated.

"I presume," said Jaq, "that the present Lord Badshah hatches

no plots—no more than that Hakim Badshah did. Why should
he? He can pay for the upkeep of this Courthouse through taxa-
tion. The local administration was purged of hybrids years ago.
Judges must consider their mere presence a sufficient curb upon
treachery. This is wrong, *wrong*—yet it suits our purpose. We
might be more conspicuous in a smaller city. Anyway, we ought
to remain near the spaceport—unless we can detect an unknown
opening to the Webway buried under desert sands!"

To detect such an opening, by using Azul Petrov's amputated
rune-eye . . .

The dead Navigator's warp-eye had been imprinted with a
route to the Black Library which was in the Webway. Might the
eye somehow signal the presence of a Webway portal?

Yet how might the lethal eye be used, except to deliver a killing
gaze? And why should any hidden opening exist on Sabulorb?

They had only proceeded a hundred metres more—bringing
them near to that great bronze bowl beneath the viewscreen—
when a hectic babble arose from ahead, far louder than the
regular hubbub. Like a storm-wind an outcry rushed through the
host of people, in a medley of divergent dialects:

"*Displaying the True Face early—!*"
   "*Dey dizblay dze Drue Face—!*"
      "*Prieshts shtarting dishplay Hish fashe—!*"
         "*Ostentus vultus sancti—!*"

It could only be a wild rumour. Those viewscreens remained
blank. The priests of Occidens couldn't possibly be unveiling the
True Visage in public two days prematurely.

Such a rumour was readily believed by pilgrims who had
travelled from the far side of the planet and from other planets of
other stars. To miss the crucial moment would be intolerable, ex-
cruciating. To miss out, after fifty years! Rumour spread like a
firestorm.

Here came a variation on the rumour, which seemed to lend it a
crazy logic:

"*Being private viewing for those who are bribing—!*"
   "*So many bribing, private viewing being public—!*"
      "*Being classed as public viewing—!*"

Those viewscreens remained ominously blank.

The consequence was panic. The crowd was surging. From side

avenues, pilgrims stampeded into the surge. A tide of bodies
heaved and thrust and clawed and screamed. Jaq and Grimm and
Lex fought for refuge in the lee of the bronze bowl. Even when
empty, the bowl must weigh a tonne.

Part of the mob alongside the Courthouse began to appeal
dementedly. Fists battered on the Courthouse gates. A thousand
voices demanded justice.

"We paid—!"

   "We were paying—!"

      "Pious pilgrims petitioning—!"

Was this supposed injustice within the jurisdiction of the
Courthouse? Not at all. Of course it wasn't.

A violent affray at its very gates was of vital concern to a Courthouse. Fists thumping on the plasteel gates were engaged in
criminal assault. From high lancet windows lasguns soon were
pointing downward. Clamped to the long slim barrels were
tubes.

From loudspeaker-gargoyles a voice boomed forth:

*"CEASING AND DESISTING FROM THIS ASSAULT ON THE
GATE OF A COURTHOUSE, GOOD CITIZENS AND PILGRIMS!
REMOVING YOURSELVES PEACEFULLY IN THE EMPEROR'S
NAME!"*

Yet the assault continued.

Again the gargoyles blared:

*"DESISTING AT ONCE! NOT DASHING YOURSELVES
AGAINST THE ROCK OF A COURTHOUSE, PILGRIMS! DIS-
PERSING! BE NOT COMPELLING LETHAL RESPONSE!"*

The appeal was in vain. The battering at the gate persisted.

Moments later it seemed as though the unseen Arbitrators
above were scattering large silver coins upon the crowd. Coins by
way of a token refund of the costs which pilgrims believed they
had incurred in vain. Coins by way of additional offerings to the
Emperor, which pilgrims might pluck up and toss into a bronze
bowl.

The coins began to explode amidst the crowd.

"Frag grenades!" exclaimed Grimm, ducking low.

Fragmentation grenades, no less. Those tubes coupled to the
lasgun barrels were grenade launchers.

Each grenade was shattering into scores of zipping razor-sharp
slices. These tore through clothing. They lacerated flesh. They

severed arteries and windpipes. They maimed and blinded. They slashed runes of blood upon upraised hands and cheeks.

Such a slipping and a screaming there was. Such tormented frenzy, as of goaded beasts. Quite a few pilgrims carried about them some weapon other than a simple knife or studded brass knuckles. Only a fool walked any world without some protection. Stub guns appeared. Handbows. Even some laspistols. What were people who hadn't yet been injured or blinded to *do*? Should they wait for more grenades to rain down? Wait for pulses of laser fire? Running away was almost impossible. Too many other bodies were in the way. Upright bodies. Staggering bodies. Collapsed bodies.

Armed pilgrims fired back at those lancet windows. They fired bullets and mini-arrows and laser pulses. Small chance of scoring a hit, or even of aiming straight. Yet now the very Courthouse, and justice itself, were demonstrably under attack.

Smoothly the main plasteel gates rumbled open—and the crowd heaved.

Inside of the gateway, further access was blocked. Three armoured vehicles stood alongside one another, wreathed in engine fumes.

On two of these vehicles heavy stub guns were mounted. On the middle one, an autocannon. The roofs of all three vehicles were platforms for a team of Arbitrators. Eerie reflective visors rendered the Arbitrators featureless. How dark their uniforms were. They were so many ebony robots with mirror-screens instead of faces.

From grenade launchers popped such a cocktail of frag and choke-gas and flash-flares. Then the serpent-mouth muzzle of the autocannon blazed solid shells. From the big stubbers clattered a storm of heavy bullets.

Shells and bullets reaped a swathe through the dazzled, gasping, bleeding mob. Another swathe, and another. Heavy bullets ricocheted off the bronze bowl behind which Jaq and Lex and Grimm were sheltering.

This Courthouse was like a cudbear pestered while hibernating in its den. Or a nest of death-wasps.

Chapter Four

Mayhem

With each impact of a stray bullet the bowl rang like a bell. The note did not linger. Nor did the trio wish to linger. Yet except in the ever-widening killing zone around the Courthouse gateway hardly any open space existed. Everywhere else there was an undulating herd of hysterical humanity.

Those guardians of justice need not have opened the gates. Their gates were of plasteel. Their walls were massive.

Any assault upon a Courthouse, however misconceived or provoked, was such a snub to imperial authority. How could the Arbitrators have stayed ensconced in their stronghold in the face of defiance? Perhaps the conduct of the pilgrims wasn't really tantamount to rebellion. Yet if there was no overwhelming response the incident might lead on to worse defiance. Moderation on the part of the Courthouse could so easily be misinterpreted.

Had some Judge been poring over books of precedent for months in anticipation of some such incident? The holiest of days was at hand. This city was packed to the seams with fervent visitors. Shandabar was no hive-world city, but right now its population seemed similar in density. Judges rejoiced in a proud tradition of launching shock troops against rioters. Order could so easily tumble into disorder beyond the capacity of the local police to contain.

The autocannon and the heavy stub guns fell silent. Arbitrators leapt down from the vehicles. Firing energy packets from their lasguns, they fanned out. At first they hardly bothered to aim into a seemingly limitless host of pilgrims. Due to the lumpy carpet of corpses, the Arbitrators' footing was unsteady, and their progress leisurely. Their helmets filtered the lingering choke-gas, which had not drifted in the direction of the crouching trio.

In hope of escaping death, many pilgrims began to throw themselves face-down. This exposed the armed resisters in their midst as targets for more precise surgery. Energy packets flew further, causing more distant pilgrims to dive.

So it happened that for their own safety more and more pilgrims further and further away prostrated themselves. Prostration quickly gained a momentum of its own. A tidal wave of kowtowing spread outward. Bodies forced other bodies down willy-nilly.

Where the trio sheltered, all bodies bowed low in the general direction of the Occidens Temple—as though in abject adoration of Him-on-Earth. Such limitless homage filled the whole locality. Pictures of this scene could have been included in devotional vids, were it not for all the blood and untold hundreds of trampled corpses in the background. A picture in sepia might have disguised the bloodshed.

The Arbitrators had ceased fire. They were stepping across a field of limp or grovelling flesh—like some invigilators of prayer whose duty it was to punish any worshipper who raised his face.

Thus was the human cosmos righteously controlled for the salvation of souls. Thus was disorder curbed. Thus was the superfluity of humanity pruned. In defence of law and stability the harshest measures were often, tragically, mandatory.

At this spectacle of governance exercised to such potent effect Jaq felt a spasm of heartfelt reverence. He experienced such a poignant nostalgia for simplicities—not that his career as an Inquisitor had ever been simple, but long ago it seemed to have been so lucid in its purity by contrast with the tormenting dilemmas which now beset him.

Yet a moment later a frisson of horror at the carnage shook him. How much death could be justified by the demands of discipline and stability? But he knew the answer. The alternative—of cosmic anarchy—was infinitely worse. If the Imperium failed—or *when* it failed—the cruellest Chaos would reign, and reality itself would fall apart.

"Now we get going!" declared Grimm.

Across the stepping stones of ten thousand sprawling pilgrims.

"No!—" Lex called out, too late. His hand missed clutching Grimm to drag him back behind the bowl. The little man was bustling on his way, shoulders ducked, big boots bounding across living bodies. Away, away, before the dark faceless Arbitrators came close in their tour of inspection. Probably Grimm was right, and Lex was wrong in this instance. Without another thought, Lex hauled Jaq into motion.

"Run, Jaq, run!"

The impact of Lex—even of Jaq—upon prostrate bodies was more momentous than Grimm's had been. Bodies squealed and writhed or reared in injury or protest. Injured or offended parties were too slow to delay Lex's dash, or Jaq's.

"Halting, in His name!"

"HALTING NOW!"

Arbitrators had noticed the decamping trio, which was what Lex had hoped to avoid.

An Abhuman—and a giant, and another man: what made *them* act so guiltily? That absconding Squat might have been overlooked. He wasn't a big fellow. Squats weren't worshippers of the Emperor. Their tech skills were merely useful to the Imperium. The Squat must have been caught up in the confusion by chance.

A decamping giant as well? And another robust individual too? A trio was more than coincidence. Could this be a case of *ringleaders*?

Arbitrators were giving chase. Three of them. One for each fugitive, should the three split up. Merely to shoot the fugitives in the back would be to lose a source of intelligence under interrogation in the dungeons of the Courthouse. Thus it was as a snatch squad rather than an execution team that the three Arbitrators pursued.

How it went against the grain for Jaq or Lex to run away as though they were criminals! Those mirror-masks were keeping up a nimble pace across backs and buttocks and heads. The fugitives had a good start and were even gaining distance.

A side alley hove into view—a gullet crowded with hectic pilgrims. These ecstatics seemed to imagine that a viewscreen, which they couldn't see frontally, had lit up with the Unveiling. This must be why the mass of worshippers were cringing in adoration. Ignorant of the truth, the pilgrims elbowed and clawed.

Grimm hurled himself amidst them upon hands and knees. He was a grotesque child scuttling and scrabbling his way through adult legs.

Lex barrelled into the jam of bodies. All of his weight of muscle and ceramically reinforced bone carved a path. Jaq was immediately behind him.

"STOPPING THOSE MEN!"

Now there was more elbow room—and even open space, merely confined by alley walls. Some pilgrims were still plunging in the direction of the boulevard. Lex cannoned into several deliberately to knock them over. Grimm, up on his feet again, tripped a couple with his big boots. Fallen bodies writhed on cobbles.

The trio turned a corner and raced.

They had entered a cul-de-sac. They skidded on animal bones and offal. A dead dog lay butchered and trussed. Over a fire of coals, a second dog was charring on an improvised spit, left deserted. The proprietors of the barbeque had dashed off towards the boulevard. Had they supposed that the distant detonation of grenades was the popping of celebratory firecrackers?

At first glance, there seemed little choice but to turn tail and collide with the Arbitrators.

For generations gangs of kids had sprayed graffiti in this appendix of an alleyway. Names and obscenities in rotund script rolled across the stone walls—and also across an iron door, which they almost camouflaged.

A second glance sent Lex rushing shoulder-first towards the door. Any external handle had long since been broken off. Lex crashed against the iron. Rust cascaded. The door groaned.

A second time he hurled himself. The door yielded with a screech of snapping hinges. He forced it open.

Within was a dingy warehouse. Protected by gratings, some small dirty skylights provided meagre illumination.

What lay piled along all those ranks of plasteel racks? Oh, those were saddles—and bridles, and reins, intended for camelopards.

Glance back: lasguns at the ready, the mirror-faced Arbitrators leapt around the corner, into the cul-de-sac. Jaq and Grimm were hardly through the doorway before Lex was heaving a rack of saddles over as a blockage. The Arbitrators responded by opening fire. Packets of energy exploded against plasteel shelves and tumbled saddles—and winged inside the warehouse too. Outbursts of energy lit the interior stroboscopically as the trio hastened, ducking behind racks, towards a more massive door with a wicket set in it.

This wicket was sure to be locked. Manual bolts secured the greater door. Who would expect anyone to want to break *out* of the warehouse? Lex heaved a floor-bolt upward, hauled a roof-bolt downward. From behind came the sound of Arbitrators clambering over or through the obstruction.

Give them some pause for thought! Tugging the bolt gun from its hiding place behind his back, Lex fired a single shot along an aisle, *RAARKpopSWOOSH*.

CRUMP.

Arbitrators were highly trained, zealous men. They ought to recognize the characteristic noise of a bolter. Surely this merited a few moments' reflection. Was that gun a relic of the Ultramarines' visit decades ago? Was it contraband from off-world? Had some local gunsmith succeeded in jerry-tooling such a weapon?

Perhaps Lex's action only increased the zeal of the Arbitrators. The trio fled into a road seething with pilgrims who seemed enraged. As Lex fought a way through a torrent of persons, the furious buzz was of *murdering mirror-heads*—or of *mirror-heads murdering*. The babble was so confused.

Jaq reeled, and clutched at Lex.

"Somewhere in this mob there's a telepath. I can sense him! A psyker. He's terrified. He's sending out chaotic images—"

Aye, muddled images of the massacre, which had assaulted that psyker's senses with so much pain and so many death agonies. Pilgrims who possessed any trace of psychic sense were picking these images up. Everyone was already so highly strung. In this road there was none of the desperate mass prostration, as there was on the main boulevard. Voices cried dementedly:

"Murder—"

"Mirror-heads!"

Those who shouted could have no clear idea whether 'mirror-heads' were engaged in murder, or whether it was essential for themselves to kill anyone who fitted such a description. Hysteria was becoming ever more rampant by the moment, infecting almost everyone, whether remotely psychic or not.

Lex craned his neck. He glimpsed the masked Arbitrators emerge from the warehouse. Jaq and Grimm only heard the howl of the mob. For several seconds the trio were borne backwards by a homicidal tidal surge towards the Arbitrators. Then they were free.

They escaped along a less crowded lane which forked and forked again.

They ran and then jog-trotted until they came to Shandabar's fish market, where all seemed normal.

A host of stalls occupied several dusty hectares, arcaded on three sides. Under the vast red sun trade was brisk. Fishmongers were bawling the virtues of the harvest from the broad Bihisti and from the nearest freshwater sea—fresh or dried, salted or pickled. A glutinous tangy reek pervaded the chilly air. Of the panic and deaths near the Courthouse there was no realization here, no more than there was awareness in any of the glazed bulging fishy eyes peering blindly from slabs and boards.

Grimm panted.

"Oh me legs!' Reckon . . . that mob . . . minced the mirror-heads?"

"Probably," said Lex. He scratched at his fist in frustration. "It wouldn't have been right for us to kill representatives of imperial justice. They were just carrying out their duties. I oughtn't to have fired that bolt. I apologize."

"Why?" asked Grimm.

"Those Arbitrators could have reported the use of a bolter. Could have started an investigation."

"With detectives visiting every rental agency on the offchance of tracing us?"

"I don't suppose we really drew much attention to ourselves, considering the mayhem. I've noticed big guys on the streets as well as little squirts."

"Squats," Grimm corrected him tetchily. "I've spotted a few of us as well. Engineers off starships, probably. Us Squats like to travel and see the sights. If I do run into one of my kin I shan't be doing any hobnobbing, let me assure you. Us three don't really stand out—not with all these pious lunatics around."

"Devout souls," Jaq corrected him.

For a brief while the little man hyperventilated. "In my book," he resumed, "there's generally summat weird 'bout most pilgrims. Grossly fat, or got a squint, or a goitre size of an apple on the neck. Or a skin disease, or webbed toes kept well hidden. Bunch of freaks, if you ask me."

"Our book," said Jaq, "is the *Book of Rhana Dandra*."

"Which we can't read, 'cos it's written in Eldar, and the script's impossible."

Jaq shrugged. "I wonder how much local animosity there is towards the Courthouse, aside from sheer dread of the Judges . . .? What happened back there was a mere reflex action of goaded animals. I'd guess that the Marshalls of the Court will feel the need to show more presence now. As Grimm says, there's a whole haystack of people, even at normal times—and only a few needles to probe it with. I rejoice bleakly in the religious rivalries here. Those will sow confusion."

He mused. "We may need to make contact with criminals—to integrate ourselves, and protect ourselves from the attentions of the Courthouse. Crime, after all, is everywhere. We ourselves are similar to criminals."

Grimm grinned. "Cosmic jewel-thieves, eh?"

Jaq was eyeing Lex, who nodded soberly.

"Transgressors against the Imperium, my Lord Inquisitor. Seemingly so. Temporarily. Until we understand. Until we can report back to trustworthy authority."

"If the Inquisition is at war with itself, Lex, what authority can we trust?"

"I realize that! My own chapter is beyond reproach. Yet our Librarians could merely report to the Administratum."

"Which would notify the Adeptus Terra. The Inquisition would intervene. Which faction of the Inquisition?"

Lex bowed his head briefly, as if praying privately to his Primarch.

So at last they reached the vast sandy area outside the complex of domes which was the Occidens Temple. A few thousand expectant pilgrims were already camping. Thousands more milled. There was a heady aroma of incense and of grilling fish kebabs—no sooner cooked over braziers than sold—and of spiced wine, and of bodies. Acrobats performed atop tall poles for all to see. Fortune tellers fanned versions of the imperial Tarot. Cripples begged for alms.

It was possible to wend one's way to the fore, in a slow journey of well over a kilometre. This the trio did.

*

Around the temple stretched a strong plasteel crush-barrier manned by armed deacons. An elevated walkway draped with rich brocades ran from the top of the temple steps out to a splendid platform overlooking the barricade.

At a gate in the crush-barrier, a deacon was soliciting sumptuous offerings for the opportunity to enter the temple—which was otherwise closed to worshippers now that the unveiling was so imminent. An armed sexton would guide those who paid lavishly. These privileged persons would behold the actual sacred aumbry cupboard where the True Face was kept.

Tomorrow—on the eve of the unveiling—offerings must be twice as sumptuous as today.

Here was the origin of the rumour which had caused hundreds of deaths and injuries. Someone had misunderstood; and the misunderstanding had been compounded.

A fat bald man, accompanying his squint-eyed daughter, had handed over a fat purse of shekels, which were being counted. For most pilgrims the cost of admission was too steep, whatever special virtue might accrue.

Jaq was consumed with curiosity—with the Inquisitor's desire to know, and know. From a pocket he produced a small emerald of the finest water.

Rather than spiriting Jaq's offering away out of sight, the deacon held it up to the light. Did he suppose such a jewel was false? Even in the dull light of the red sun, the sparkle said otherwise.

Grimm dragged on Jaq's sleeve. Amongst the crowd a tall woman—grey-gowned and hooded—was peering intently.

"Meh'lindi—" gasped Jaq. It was her. Her ghost. Within that shading hood the face was . . .

No, that wasn't Meh'lindi's face. He mustn't delude himself. The features merely bore a resemblance. And the height, the lithe stance. Already the woman had turned away so smoothly that she might never have been watching at all. She was distancing herself amongst the throng, losing herself. Already she was gone from view.

"That lady was eyeing our sparkler," said Grimm.

"Forget her," Jaq said distractedly. The woman hadn't been Meh'lindi at all. Of course she hadn't been. Meh'lindi was dead, gutted by the power-lance of a female Phoenix warrior. As to the resemblance, why, there were only so many possible permutations of physical appearance amongst human beings. Billions of variations certainly existed on the human theme—yet in a galaxy of a million populated worlds trillions and trillions of people seethed. Somewhere in the galaxy there must be several people who appeared to be identical *twins* of Meh'lindi. Dozens more people must bear a striking resemblance to her.

No one could match Meh'lindi. No one!

The sexton who guided the trio was a wiry weasel-faced elderly man. A laspistol was tucked in the girdle of his camelopard-hair cassock.

"On entering our temple, first of all you are encountering—"

—a portico crowded with the carved and crumbling tombs of previous High Priests, hundreds of those . . .

In a huge colonnaded atrium beyond, a forest of incense sticks burned soporifically. Sweet smoke ascended through vents in the domed roof. This chamber resembled a colossal thurible . . .

Further beyond was the basilica, patrolled by armed deacons.

"Fifty side chapels being dedicated to fifty attributes of Him-on-Earth—"

Innumerable candles were burning. Millennia of smoke had deposited a coating of soot and wax on most surfaces. The great hall was a place of light, yet because of the soot the dominant impression was of darkness crowding in upon effulgent lumination to quench it.

"Paying attention, travellers, to the great wall-mosaic depicting our blessed Emperor's defeat of Horus the rebel—"

This mosaic was actually kept clean of wax and smoke. It had been cleaned so many times that its details had almost been erased. That fat man and his squinty daughter were gaping at the mosaic, while their escort waited impatiently.

Next was an oratory for private prayers. Jaq and Lex only bowed their knees briefly. At the rear of the oratory hung an ancient curtain interwoven with titanium threads. That curtain was so frayed, save for the tough titanium, that one could see through it mistily into the sacristy beyond.

Through the curtain, and through a resplendent grille-gate.

"—being of arabesque tungsten, the grille."

In the sacristy, by the light of many candles, an aumbry cupboard was foggily visible. The cupboard was so gorgeously decorated in silver and gold as to dazzle any spectator who did not view it thus through a veil. Armed sacristans stood guard alongside the aumbry, softly chanting a canticle.

"That holy aumbry itself being triple-locked. Within is reposing a rich reliquary. Inside that reliquary is resting the True Face of Him-on-Earth—"

That precious treasure was only ever exposed to injurious sunlight in holy years. In the interval between such rare public exhibitions the Face was occasionally shown briefly by candle light in the sacristy to munificent donors, for half a minute or so.

"No such private viewing being permitted during Holy Year—"

But lo: high above the veiled entrance to the sacristy there hung in shadows a gold-framed picture executed in ink upon camelo-pard vellum. A picture of a lean and rueful though glorious face.

"Travellers: that being a copy of a copy of the True Face of Him!"

Inside the sacristy, two indentured artists were labouring painstakingly to produce similar copies.

"Being expensive to buy?" asked Grimm nonchalantly.

Why, two priests known as the Fraternity of the Face were always selling such copies in one of the chapels of the basilica. The sexton would guide the trio by way of that chapel on their return.

More than ten thousand years in the past—enthused the sexton—when the Emperor had roamed the galaxy in the flesh one day He had wiped His face upon a cloth. His psychic energy had imprinted that cloth with His visage. After so many millennia the original cloth was frail. That was why the artists copied from a copy.

"A copy being shown to the crowds?" enquired Grimm.

The sexton's expression darkened. His hand brushed the butt of his laspistol.

"The True Cloth being shown!"

Jaq stared up at the dim face on the vellum.

When he had seen Him-on-Earth in the huge throne room ath-rob with power and acrackle with ozone—amidst hallowed battle-banners and cherished icons—the face which had been framed in the soaring prosthetic throne was that of a wizened mummy. Such potent soul-stripping thoughts had issued from the mind within that mummy that Jaq had almost been annihilated. How could a mite comprehend a mammoth?

Would Jaq ever return to that throne room, illuminated within himself?

How dared he contemplate allowing any daemonic power access to his soul, in the hope of exorcising and illuminating himself?

The trio declined the offer to purchase a copy of the Face.

"Already giving our only real valuable for a squint at the sacristy," lied Grimm.

When they were heading away from the barricade through the host of pilgrims and tents, a scrawny liver-spotted hand clutched at Jaq's hem.

"Charity for a registered cripple," croaked an elderly voice.

Smouldering thuribles of incense dangled on chains from a gibbet-like frame. Backed up against the base of this frame was a rickety cart with small iron wheels. Upon the cart crouched a rag-clad crone. Her face was wizened with age. Her stringy long hair was white. Yet her rheumy blue eyes were keen with a light of tense intelligence. In those eyes was a quality of anticipation for which expectancy of coins alone could hardly account.

Grimm scrutinized her circumstances. The thurible-gibbet protected this cripple from being trampled accidentally. A handle jutted from the rear of her cart. It might be pulled or pushed. Here she crouched under the cool red sun, begging.

"No respect for the elderly on most worlds!" grumped the little man. He fished in one of his pouches for a half-shekel. "Oh, your legs being all withered away, Mother." This was plain to see: two brown sticks were folded unnaturally. Was Grimm about to shed a sympathetic tear? The crone's cart smelled of urine.

Grimm withheld the coin temporarily. "Who's wheeling you away at nightfall, Mother?"

Aha. Had her legs perhaps been broken by her own greedy family so that she could serve as a source of income?

"Temple servant pushing me into a shed," she replied. "Servant assisting me, kind sir."

"Was the temple breaking your legs, Mother?" Surely the Occidens temple did not need to create and exploit cripples, pitifully to swell its coffers . . .

The crone rocked forward, as if in sudden anguish from a cramp of the bowels.

"Oh yes, it was breaking my legs!" was her reply. "Yet not in the way you're meaning."

Grimm hunkered down by the cart. Soon so did Lex, and Jaq . . .

The crone's named was Herzady. One thing she had never been was a mother. Defiantly she declared her age to be eleven years.

Who else upon Sabulorb would dream of counting their age in local years? She had lived long enough to arrive at double figures. She had endured more than a hundred and ten imperial years — the vast majority of them spent in this cart. Grimm was impressed by Herzady's longevity, even though to a long-living Squat a century was rather small beer.

"Pretty impressive for an ordinary human being, particularly in such reduced circumstances!"

A century earlier, as a young girl, Herzady had attended that holy year's unveiling in company with her pious parents. During the bedlam which ensued, her mother and father both lost their lives. Herzady's legs were permanently crippled. A compassionate priest had taken pity and provided this cart. For decades Herzady had awaited the next holy year. When the unveiling came again she was watching from a safer place than on the previous occasion.

Bedlam?

Oh yes. At the unveiling fifty years later there had been homicidal bedlam again, due to the hysteria of pilgrims intent on seeing . . . what could not be seen.

Could not be seen? What did she mean by this?

Why, Herzady had been all ears and eyes for decades. She knew that the Visage had faded, aeons since, into invisibility. On the climactic day of holy year when the High Priest of Occidens in splendid procession carried the reliquary out along the walkway, briefly to open the sacred container, what he would expose to the gaze of hundreds of thousands of pilgrims was a cloth which was *blank*, apart from a couple of stains vaguely located where eyes might have been.

"Pilgrims are glimpsing almost nothing, Sirs! How they are straining and struggling to see!"

Consequently a vehement riot would cut short the ceremony. What about those copies . . .?

Ah, the earliest copy had been made by laying sensitive material upon the precious faded cloth until a psychic imprint was transferred. This imprint was then piously embellished.

"Huh," said Grimm. "In other words, invented!"

This account of the invisible True Face filled Jaq with an eerie sense of awe at the sheer devotion of so many of the Emperor's subjects. What did it matter if pilgrims were besotted? What did it matter if they would die or be injured just to catch a fleeting glimpse of the cloth which had once wiped His Face? Their agonies were as nothing compared to the eternal agony of Him-on-Earth. The veneration of pilgrims would pass into the psychic sea of the warp, flavouring it with benediction.

Kneeling beside Herzady's cart, Jaq found that he was able to pray.

For a while.

Gently he said to Herzady, "Being crippled—crippled because of adoring him—you are partaking in His vaster malady."

"I am waiting," she replied bleakly, "for many more persons being crippled and killed the day after tomorrow—as surely must be happening. Then I am dying contentedly."

It was to witness this calamity that Herzady had endured indomitably throughout the five decades since the previous holy year! The crone's persistence was pathological. Her lucidity was madness.

Futility flayed Jaq's briefly-boosted faith, as surely as the gulf of time had erased the True Face. He rocked from side to side.

"That Courthouse, hmm?" Grimm said to Herzady. "You been overhearing talk 'bout the Courthouse? Involving itself much in the life of this holy city?"

Did Grimm suppose that they might wheel the crone away in her cart to their mansion in the suburbs, to become their informant about matters Sabulorbish?

The little man prompted her: "Hundreds of people dying outside that Courthouse earlier on today. All imagining the True Face being unveiled early—and panicking."

Galvanized by shock, the crone sat bolt upright upon her twisted shrivelled legs. She gasped tragically. "Herzady missing so many deaths . . ."

Her wizened face spasmed in pain. A thin spotted hand fluttered to her chest. She slumped over.

Lex checked her pulse. In his hefty hand her wrist looked no wider than a pencil. Herzady was dead. Of a heart attack, of a broken heart.

It was Grimm who reached to close the crone's gaping empty eyes.

"Huh," he said, "saved meself half a shekel, anyway."

Two days later, of an afternoon, they had struggled to a position at the very rear of the great square.

Although Grimm had been reluctant to come to the unveiling, Jaq was intent on studying the pious madness of a multitude possessed by rapture to the point of derangement where injuries and deaths would be as nothing. There were lessons to be learned about passion, obsession, possession. About derangement of the senses and the soul.

How untypically warm and foetid it was in the square this afternoon due to the exhalation of so much breath and the closeness of bodies rubbing together.

How many people in this press had already fainted or asphyxiated during the hours of waiting? What a roar arose as—presumably—the True Face was borne forth at long last. How the spectators convulsed. It was as though that sea of people was a vast pan of water which had reached boiling point. Or perhaps a pan of hot oil.

"Oh me blessed ancestors!" yelped Grimm. The little man was crushed between Jaq and Lex. Exerting his enhanced musculature, Lex forced wailing pilgrims aside, perhaps cracking ribs in so doing. The long high sandstone wall of a nearby house was indented with shallow niches—as if a line of statues had once kept vigil along there, or as though that ancient wall had been squeezed and rubbed into that crinkle-crankle shape by sheer pressure of people during so many similar unveilings in the past.

Lex tore pilgrims loose from a niche. He was a massive bulwark against the heaving tide of frenzied humanity. He offered partial shelter to Jaq and Grimm in his lee.

Grimm huff-puffed to replenish his lungs. How many chests were being crushed in the crowd? The little man squawked disgustedly. Grimm could, of course, see nothing whatever other than the nearest bodies.

Jaq was inhaling odours of hysteria. Lex alone could see clearly over heads and hoods and hats bearing True Face badges— although the focus of his vision was a full kilometre away.

"Priest's opening the reliquary," he bellowed. A greater roar came, briefly drowning his voice.

"Crowd's surging against the barrier—"

Inevitably that barrier would have given way soon, and the walkway would have come crashing down—were it not for the guardian deacons in their white surplices.

At first, the deacons used humane stun-guns to subdue the excesses of enthusiasm. Pilgrims who had camped to the fore had merely guaranteed themselves a stunning into unconsciousness upon their flattened tents. A rampart of stunned bodies arose all along the barricade.

The rampart rose higher as frustrated pilgrims climbed up over bodies, and were stunned in turn. Soon that rampart of bodies was imperilling the security of the barrier. By now the gorgeous High Priest had shut the reliquary and retreated. Pilgrims still pressed forward.

Deacons discarded their stun-guns. Probably those guns had run out of charge. The deacons must resort to autoguns and shotguns. Now they fired high-velocity caseless shot and low-velocity fragmentation shot. The giant red sun which filled a quarter of the sky grew even ruddier as though soaking up the blood which was being shed. Dust stirred up by thousands of milling, stamping feet might be to blame for the deepening of the sun's hue.

It was only with difficulty, and with bruises, that the trio eventually extricated themselves from the edge of that square. In spite of all the deaths in the vicinity of the temple many pilgrims' eyes sparkled brightly. Their eyes might have been doped with belladonna. Many were weeping with joy. Some warbled to themselves, "Oh the True Face!"—even though they had seen next to nothing.

That night Jaq dreamt his dream of Askandargrad again . . .

One by one, all the collars of the beastmen had exploded—and their heads had been shorn from their shoulders.

Some of the squealing maidens were tethered to one another.

Some, to shrubs jutting from shattered urns. Some tethers hung loose upon the ground. If only some of the maidens might escape their fate while they were temporarily unsupervised. If only *one* of them might escape—and not fall foul of other marauders, and hide herself somewhere in the ruins.

Help was on the way. Just days prior to the invasion by the renegades of Chaos, Space Marines of the Raven Guard had re-fuelled on Askandar and their ship had departed for the jump-zone. Messaged by Astropath before the Governor's palace was destroyed, the Ravens had now turned back. They would reach Askandar in another two days. Potently armed, black-armoured Raven Guards would hurl themselves against the raiders. Pray that the daemonic sights they saw did not require battle brothers to be mindwiped subsequently, to save their sanity.

It was almost as if Chaos had deliberately planned to taunt the Ravens . . .

If only some captives might escape! But the din of exploding collars had swung attention toward the maidens.

"In the Emperor's name fire that weapon!" Jaq ordered the Eunuch beside him. Suiting deed to word, Jaq peered over the barricade and discharged his own bolt gun at one of those terrible parodies of a righteous knight.

RAAARK—

The male and female rune of Slaanesh was emblazoned provo-catively on that Chaos warrior's knee protectors. Unlike his accomplices, his obscenely moulded armour was enamelled in purple and gold—a sardonic flaunting of the ancient colours of his Chapter before evil perverted it.

The bolt hit the left side of his breastplate. It penetrated at least some way. *CRUMP*. It exploded. The warrior swung around, arms flailing.

RAAARK—.

The Eunuch also fired. The vambrace shielding the target's forearm intercepted the bolt. *CRUMP*. An arm was crippled. Pray that sufficient damage had been done to the invader's reinforced chest to collapse a lung! The renegade was still swinging around—almost as if dancing a solo waltz. Pray that this was a dance of death.

RAAARK. RAAARK. Both men fired again, then ducked a

moment before a torrid hiss gushed across the marble barricade. Air was being superheated by a beam from a meltagun. Moments later: a terrible roar! The beam had caught the upper ends of some fallen roof-timbers jutting from the bathing pool. The moisture in the wood had vapourised. The timbers exploded. Daggers of wood and splinters flew like quills discharged by an enraged Hystrix beast. The other Eunuch shrieked. Several jagged darts had struck him in the shoulders. He reared, clutching at those goads. *Shwooosh* . . . The beam from the meltagun caught his exposed head. In a trice his eyes vapourised, and his chubby cheeks, and all of his face. It was as if his head had been sprayed with an instantly-acting acid which stripped his head to a skull—a skull within which the brain liquified and boiled, grey steam surging from his ear-holes and bursting upward from his rupturing fontanelle. The dead Eunuch sprawled upon broken marble.

Resin in the stumps of timbers had ignited. Flame capered above the pool clogged by debris and by bodies, some of which were still alive. From outside came such callous laughter. Jaq clawed at the surviving Eunuch.

"We must get away!"

The Eunuch stared at Jaq, madly.

"You shouldn't be here in a maidens' bath-house!" he bellowed. Sanity had deserted him.

Oh, what the Eunuch said had *once* been true. Just two days earlier the Harem had been forbidden to all full men, except for Lord Egremont.

And except for a young imperial Inquisitor—here to investigate rumours of a perverse Slaaneshi cult in this guarded inner city of women. Lord Egremont's grand experiment in benign population control had bred certain mischievous frustrations. Egremont was an idealist, and his reign had been genial, if eccentric. Askandar had thrived.

Oh fools, to espouse such a cult! For now the consequences were all too painfully apparent. Agonizingly so! Corrupted Chaos Marines had come to reap the harvest of idle folly, laying waste to Askandargrad and sadistically ravishing the Harem.

The Eunuch glared at the obscene bolt gun in his hands. He began to turn it around. He moved the muzzle towards his mouth.

"Help will be here in two days," hissed Jaq.

Laughter! So close, outside! To risk a look would be to lose his life. To stay any longer would be suicide. Swiftly Jaq withdrew, scrambling past timbers and spreading flames, keeping low.

Behind him: *RAAARK—CRUMP*. The Eunuch had shot himself. By doing so perhaps he had saved himself from a death more abominable and prolonged.

Once more, Jaq woke shivering.

Chapter Five

Thief

The mansion which they had rented consisted of three storeys. A dozen rooms on each. Extensive cellars below. Furnishings were ebon. Floors were of black slate. In some respects how like the funereal interior of Jaq's lost starship was this mansion! Lamps stood everywhere, reminiscent—at least in the way that their light reflected glossily—of the electrocandles in icon niches aboard *Tormentum Malorum*.

Jaq wished all curtains to remain permanently closed, blanking off the view of surrounding leathery shrubbery, tracts of silvery gravel, the great red sun, the high perimeter wall, and a neighbouring rooftop.

From room to room there now scampered a little bearded monkey. It was like an imp, bright-eyed and brindle-coated. Grimm had bought this miniature parody of a human from a street vendor. That was because Lex had remarked, on noticing the creature perched on the vendor's shoulder, "As a Marine is to a Squat, so a Squat is to that monkey."

"Huh, well I'm sick of being the short-arse," Grimm had said. Jaq made no objection to the purchase.

The busy solitude of the animal struck a chord with Jaq. The monkey had no mate of its own kind. Yet it constantly quested, as though around the next corner or in the next room it might surely discover a partner. How exasperatedly the creature sometimes chattered at its vague reflection in shiny surfaces.

The monkey would try to groom Grimm's bushy red beard, hunting for lice or fleas. He didn't bother to give it a name.

A week after the day of the unveiling it was this monkey whose squeaking and scuttling to and fro upon his bed woke Grimm in the dark chilly early hours.

The little man still recalled dreaming about a fire-fight inside some caves. He and a few bold Squat comrades were taking on a horde of Orks. Those raucous messy green-skinned aliens were armed with thunderous crude blunderbusses. The gaping mouths of the barrels spewed nuts and bolts and showers of sparks and plumes of fumes. With decent bolt guns Grimm and his cronies were busily accounting for those alien thugs. *RAARK, SWOOSH, CRUMP. RAARK, SWOOSH, CRUMP.* This was a battle of systematic versus disorderly noise.

Grimm wished to resume such an entertaining dream. He was about to swat the pesky pet aside—when a dark figure loomed. *Lex.* Just had to be Lex. Using only two fingers, Lex picked up the monkey by the neck, squeezing slightly to silence it. Leaning low over Grimm, Lex murmured, "Carry on snoring just as you were. Do so, and listen to me."

Snoring? Snoring? Had that been the source of the dream!

"RAARK," said Grimm, sounding like a carrion bird with a sore throat. "SWOOSH," he breathed out slowly. "CRUMP," he uttered.

As Grimm strove to imitate what must have been the sound of his snores, and as Lex held the monkey dangling, still alive, a chagrined Squat listened.

"There's an intruder somewhere. Gone down to the cellars, I think—"

Lex had detected the intrusion with his Lyman's Ears, which replaced the ordinary internal arrangement of tympanic membranes and auditory ossicles and spiralling cochlea. Thus to protect a Marine against motion-sickness. Hearing was also enhanced. Irrelevant sounds could be filtered out.

Lex had been asleep. Yet a Marine only ever slept with half a brain. The other hemisphere remained on alert stand-by. Lex was roused. He had been monitoring the progress of the prowler. In spite of Grimm's rumblings the monkey must have heard faint noises too.

"RAARK," repeated Grimm. Dressed only in his calico drawers, he slid out of bed. He took his laspistol from beside an empty

pot of beer on a side table, and emitted a final strangulated
SWOOSH—of someone whose snores had either stopped
naturally or who had succumbed to asphyxiation.

Nude apart from his webbing, Lex held a laspistol in the hand
which was not busy with the monkey. He could hardly release
the animal: it would resume a frantic squeaking. Should he
simply snap its neck? Perhaps it had been trying to serve a pathetic kind of purpose. Still holding it, the giant padded softly with
the little man in search of circumstances down in the cellars.

A solitary night-lamp burned half-way along a stone passage. The
door to one of the cellars stood open. That door was the stoutest
of any down here. That cellar was the one in which the jewel-
encrusted *Book of Rhana Dandra* was kept, in a locked iron chest
chained to a wall. The faint light of an electrolumen glowed from
within, dimming and brightening—in motion, evidently in somebody's hand.

A lock was grumbling softly, slowly. A lid was creaking open.

Grimm was first through the doorway. Ducking low, he fired
his laspistol at the roof of the chamber—so as to startle and distract. The packet of energy blossomed against the fan-vaulting.
Like a flower of phosphorus briefly it illuminated stone tracery,
intercurving ribs. It lit up the ebon lectern which Jaq had bought
so that the enigmatic volume could be examined conveniently, if
not understood.

And in that brief flash: an inky silhouette was stooping over the
opened iron chest. A figure dressed in such darkness that reality
might virtually be absent there—excised and cut out. That
absence was already straightening, turning lithely. The face was
inky. Only eyes to be seen. Yellowy, feline eyes. How tall the
dark silhouette became.

*Could it be an Eldar, come to recover the book of fate? Could the black
figure somehow be an imperial Assassin?*

Having dazzled, light died. Nor did the electrolumen any
longer shine. Darkness was doubled. A rushing passed by
Grimm, wafting at his hirsute skin.

Of a sudden the doorway was blocked by something as sturdy
as any reinforced door. At the same time a frantic squeaking was
scuttling past Grimm's horny bare feet. Lex had discarded the
monkey so as to seize the interloper tight. Fighting, writhing,

kneeing were all in vain. Who could break free from such a muscle-enhanced, ceramically-reinforced embrace? Not the black shadow-person.

"I got him! Light lamps, Squat!"

Yet it wasn't a *him*. It was a *her*. The blackened face was a woman's. A human woman's, not an Eldar's. So very like Meh-'lindi's after she had sprayed synthetic protective camouflage skin over her features! No filter-plugs in the nostrils, though . . . Her garb closely resembled an Assassin's costume. No red sash was around her waist to conceal a garotte or toxins . . .

Recognition dawned upon Grimm. "It's *you*!" he accused. "You were in the crowd outside Occidens. You were goggling at our emerald."

Of course it was her. That tall lithe woman had exchanged her grey gown for a black body-stocking—which was almost identical to the clingtight garb which Meh'lindi had formerly worn. How appropriate for a thief—who hoped to steal through the night un-seen so as to steal . . . *treasure*.

Jaq's torn old robe had wrapped the book of fate. The wrapping had been opened up by the thief, exposing all the glory of jewels which crusted the binding. Resting upon the book was a little black bundle. The thief had just begun to open this bundle when she was interrupted. The bandanna was loose, but still hid its contents.

The woman remained passive in Lex's grip, which he did not make the mistake of slackening.

"Quite an uncommon thief," said Lex to Grimm, "to have cir-cumvented the alarms, and to have found her way down here, and to have picked so many locks."

"For a moment," the little man exclaimed, "I thought she was an Eldar or an Assassin!"

The woman's eyes widened. Lex growled at Grimm for his in-discretion.

The woman asked, "Why should there be an alien or an Assas-sin in your cellar?" She spoke the same standard Imperial Gothic as theirs.

"You ain't from Sabulorb, lady. Who sent you?"

Lex shook her.

Lips pursed, the woman considered Grimm's question.

"How close are you to death?" growled Lex. "That's what

you're thinking. If you say that no one sent you, then no one knows what happened to you."

Yearningly her gaze strayed towards the jewelled book.

At that moment the monkey leapt upon the lip of the chest. It stared at all the gems, sparkling in the lamplight. It reached—yet those jewels were all firmly fixed. Took a knife to prise one out, not tiny monkey fingernails! With quick motions the animal's little hands completed the unwrapping of the black bandanna. Chattering to itself, it burrowed. It lifted a bauble inky as night.

"*Don't look there!*" Averting his own gaze, Lex shifted a hand to cover the woman's face.

The bauble rattled into the bottom of the chest. It had struck iron, and so was out of sight. Lex restored his hand as a fetter upon the woman's arm.

The monkey shrieked piercingly. It clutched at its head. A moment later fur and fragments of scalp and skull and brain sprayed the fan-vault and the stone walls. The animal's head had only been the size of a large grape, yet flecks hit Grimm and Lex and the woman.

Grimm rubbed his soiled brow. "Just as well I didn't bother giving the damn thing a name! Now at least we know that Azul's eye works. I thought the whole point was to let would-be thieves find out for themselves, by the way, big fellow?"

"We can't interrogate her if she's dead," snapped Lex. He hauled the woman deeper inside the cellar as if proximity to what had killed the monkey might be as a useful means of persuasion.

The woman said hesitantly, "If I had opened the black wrapping would *my* head have exploded?"

"Not necessarily," Grimm said darkly. "You might have choked. You might have swallowed your tongue. Your eyes might merely have popped out of your head."

"Toxin?" she asked. "Assassin's toxin?"

"Naw," sneered Grimm, "a dead Navigator's warp-eye. Now the eye's somewhere in the chest and I'll have to feel around with me own eyes shut tight."

"*What are you people?*"

"Who are *you*, knowing about Assassin's toxins, eh?"

"I'm a thief," the woman said. "I came to Sabulorb for rich pickings because of the Unveiling and all the pilgrims. I was watching at the temple to see who seemed wealthy. I followed you. I observed this mansion, avoiding the local vigilantes. That's all—"

Grimm licked some monkey tissue from his moustache. He spat upon the floor.

"What's happening?"

Jaq had come wrapped in his beige robe, laspistol in hand. As soon as he saw the black-clad woman he lurched and moaned. The exclamation *"My Assassin!"* escaped his lips.

"No she ain't, Boss," said Grimm. "She's a thief. She was trying to rob us. Me poor monkey took the brunt of the booby trap 'stead of her. Azul's eye worked a treat. Mistress of thieves she has to be, to get in here! She knows about Assassins—somehow!"

Jaq glanced at the headless animal, its stump of neck gory.

He said, "I must find a lapidary who can pare a monocle from the warp-eye carefully—for me to wear with a protective patch . . ."

The captive stared at this newcomer in dread—which she did her best to mask. What were these people indeed?

Jaq demanded of her, "How did you come by Assassins' clothing? Why are you wearing it?"

"For camouflage in darkness," the woman protested. "To blend in. Why else, why else?"

"You really are quite like her," he mused. "And yet, not close enough . . . A caricature of her!" Jaq was pointing his laspistol at her now. He would not fire while Lex still held her. "You would have stolen the book just for its jewels. Now you know that it's here."

She burrowed within the encompassing custody of Lex. "I don't know what it is!" she cried. "Yes, I do know about Assassins!"

So the thief talked, to save her skin for a while longer.

Her name was Rakel binth-Kazintzkis. *Binth* signified that she was the daughter of a father named Kazintsk. Rakel's wild home world was where black-clad Assassins obtained the raw material for the drug which enabled trained Assassins to alter their appearance by will-power. On Rakel's world postulant Assassins and initiates would practise shape-shifting and predatory stalking and slaying amongst its primitive population. On Rakel's world people knew Assassins well. Though not as acquaintances or friends.

That drug came from a lichen. Psychic shamans of her world would boil the lichen and drink the juice. Then their own appearance would change. They would take on the guise of spirits of the dead.

Grimm grunted approval at this honouring of ancestors.

Those spirits were wise and harmonious guides—yet Rakel had begun to doubt their effectiveness after her brother had been killed and impersonated by a black-clad practitioner.

To Jaq it sounded as though those local shamans risked attracting daemons rather than benevolent forces. Maybe not! Otherwise, would the Assassins—who were clearly of the Callidus shrine, Meh'lindi's very own!—have used this world as their secret bailiwick, source of Polymorphine, and practice turf?

The inhabitants of Rakel's world couldn't help but breathe in spores of the lichen at fruiting time. A weak form of the drug pervaded their bodies, and the bodies of local animals too. All could alter their appearance temporarily to a certain extent. Yet not to the extent that Assassins achieved!

What the Assassins did was harsh and terrible. They refined the lichen, distilling it time and again in their laboratories into a pure product of enormous potency.

A female Assassin could become a male, and vice versa. Much training was involved—deep concentration—and pain as well, though Assassins seemed almost immune to pain.

Assassins would sometimes capture native inhabitants for fatal and agonizing experiments.

This was normal practice. Devout Marines surgeons must experiment upon mind-slaved prisoners and failed cadets in their unending programme of research into the capacities and shortcomings of those organ implants which rendered such a man as Lex superhuman . . .

Assassin scientists studied the stability of metamorphoses. A captured inhabitant of Rakel's world would be injected with the pure drug and forced to alter—and sometimes even released, attended by a swarm of spy-flies which would watch his doomed struggles to retain his new shape. Being untrained to Assassin standards, unable to focus and control sufficiently—and because the drug was pure—sooner or later the experimental subject would go into agonizing flux, his body distorting, organs and limbs softening and reforming terribly till finally he dissolved into protoplasmic jelly.

This much Rakel knew about Assassins.

One day a rogue trading ship had set down upon her world. It landed near to her nomadic home. Rakel had ingratiated herself with the captain so that when his ship departed in haste, warned off by her tales of the black-clad users of this planet, he had taken her with him in gratitude.

After learning many useful tricks while travelling from star system to star system, and becoming a skilful thief, Rakel had deserted her captain. She had been in Shandabar now for several months, consorting with criminals and preparing to rob pilgrims. She had never dreamed that she would set eyes on such a treasure as lay in the chest.

How had she located it in this large mansion?

Thief's instinct. People often thought that cellars were the safest place. Head for the stoutest door with the toughest lock.

"Just as well you didn't *open* the book looking for pretty picture," said Grimm, "or you might have become one of the pictures, for us to stick pins in."

He was improvising. The *Book of Rhana Dandra* contained no such pictures. If Rakel were by any chance spared, she would avoid the book unless she was prone to Pandora Syndrome.

Jaq nodded. He kept his laspistol pointed at their captive.

"Useful informant on criminals, her?" muttered Grimm tersely. "Useful contacts?"

"Are you magicians?" she murmured to Lex, limp in his grip.

"Far from it!" he growled.

Was Jaq so far from pursuing such a course? With his free hand Jaq pulled from an inner pocket of his robe a folded red sash. Meh'lindi's sash. Did Rakel see the sash as a tether for her hands? As a gag? No, she *recognized* what it was.

"Assassin's sash," she hissed.

"Yes," said Jaq, "and tucked inside this sash is an ampoule of Polymorphine . . .' '

"Poly—"

"That's the technical name the Callidus shrine of Assassins call the pure drug by. The drug you've been talking about."

Rakel squirmed ineffectively. "I told you the whole truth! I swear it! I don't have any confederates, only some business acquaintances. Receivers of stolen goods. Shoot me dead with your pistol," she begged, "but don't inject me with *that*."

Jaq nodded to Lex and Grimm. "We need to consult together privately. For the moment we shall lock her in the adjoining cellar. Fetch some plasticated wire, Grimm. Scurry! Lex, kindly bring her next door."

Grimm soon returned to the neighbouring cellar with flexible black-coated wire.

"Frisk her for lock-picks first. No, what's the use of that? You probably wouldn't find them all. Nor any hidden digital weapons, nor poison. Even a body has its hiding place. Remove all her clothing first before you tie her hands and feet."

Did Rakel misunderstand their purpose? Did she imagine she was to be violated by this near-nude giant and this hairy dwarf and the bearded, rut-faced man—before her body was injected and thrown into agonizing flux?

While Grimm stripped off her body-stocking, Lex shifted his grip from limb to limb. How attentively Jaq studied their captive's anatomy, analyzing the cusp of the breast, the flexure of flank, the crease of buttock.

"Clean her face and hands," he ordered. Because of the camouflage paint her features now contrasted bizarrely with the creamy whiteness elsewhere.

In a corner of this cellar stood a basin and ewer and rags, deposited by Grimm after the washing of the lectern on its arrival. The water was stale and dirty, but it served.

At last Rakel was left in darkness; and Jaq led his companions away from the door.

"I regret our rough discourtesy," he told them. (Would Meh-'lindi have even flinched at such treatment?) "There'll be worse if *she's* to survive. I must not care about her too much."

"You want to inject her with Polymorphine," said Grimm. "You want to make her into an exact Meh'lindi. But how?"

From his gown Jaq produced the Assassin card, which was the perfect representation of Meh'lindi.

"With this as psychic focus, little fellow."

"I thought you burnt 'em all apart from just the Daemon card! So you kept hers after all . . .'"

"We can employ this to save a life, at least for a while. We can make use of an expert thief. If I'm ever to understand the book we need to lay hands on an Eldar language programme for a hypno-casque. If there's such a thing on this world, I would say it'll be in the Courthouse."

Judges were mainly concerned with internal security, yet it was a fact that the Eldar sometimes meddled in human affairs. Somewhere in its data store the Courthouse should have the means to interpret alien language messages. It would indeed require an expert thief to sneak into that battlemented citadel, evading the mirror-masked Arbitrators . . .

"That lady deserts people," Grimm reminded Jaq.

"That's why she must be *bound* to us—so that she will never dare desert me. That's why we shall force her into the exact mould of Meh'lindi." Such torment was in Jaq's voice. "She must believe that only by regular psychic reinforcement of her new appearance, using the card in my keeping, does she escape going into agonizing flux."

Grimm asked softly, "Is it true she would go into flux?"

Jaq lowered his voice. "I insist that it is true."

"I see . . .' '

"Bear in mind," added Jaq, "that some criminals may well have sources of information within the Courthouse, however pure the Judges and Arbitrators are themselves. I must pray for guidance. I must meditate. Then we shall act."

Jaq took himself off along a dark side-passage towards a little crypt.

"What you reckon, big fellow?" whispered Grimm. "Will having a living replica of Meh'lindi around here be good for the Boss's mind?"

Lex considered.

"I think," he said finally, "this may divert Jaq from futile obsession. No matter how exact the duplication, the mind in the body will never be Meh'lindi's."

"Yeah, wean him away. That's what I was thinking to meself . . ."

In the stygian crypt, Jaq knelt, eyes closed.

If he were ever to lose the image of Meh'lindi from his mind, he would be discarding an epitome of duty and dedication, of bravery and perfection.

And what about *desire*? Desire which could bring frenzy, especially when frustrated!

Surely he must court frenzy if he were to pass beyond delirium into illuminated purity. Would not that woman, Rakel, in her transformed body, frenzy him by her sheer physical presence — and at the same time frustrate him profoundly by her essential difference from Meh'lindi?

Desire! Cousin to *lust*, to the Slaaneshi passion! An Inquisitor should rightly avoid the experience of desire. Had he truly *desired* Meh'lindi? Her beauty had been bizarre. Though not in the dark. Her tattoos hadn't phosphoresced. Her tattoos weren't luminous like an electrotattoo, when one willed one of those to shine. In the dark there had simply been the twisting alphabet of limbs, to be read as a blind person reads.

What words had Meh'lindi's limbs spelled in the darkness? Desire was something beyond language and beyond reason. Was this merely another way of saying that desire was a state of madness? Desire operated without analysis or explanation. It functioned in a space devoid of explanation — in a veritable void of logic. In that void the most powerful superstition could arise, overthrowing the familiar parameters of duty and sanity. To lose guidelines was to become chaotic. It was to court a kind of Chaos — out of which what new sort of order might arise?

Beauty, pah! What was mere beauty worth?

Could Jaq be said to have *loved* Meh'lindi? Hardly! How could he respond to her with love — were she even *alive*! In his thwarted desire, foreshortened by death, lurked deep mystery and paradox . . . and thus a route to illumination.

Probably it was sheer fantasy to imagine that, even if illuminated, he could ever find the legendary place in the Webway where time could reverse — thus to call Meh'lindi back into existence in her own living body from before the time she was slaughtered. Hadn't Great Harlequins searched in vain for that rumoured place for thousands of years?

Yet could he accept that Meh'lindi's fierce spirit had simply dissolved into the sea of souls when she died? Hardly! If he became illuminated, and led Rakel into the Webway — so close to the warp! — yes, led her, transformed by Polymorphine into the absolute twin of Meh'lindi in body, might not Meh'lindi's spirit be attracted irresistibly to that duplicate body? Might not Meh'lindi regain flesh and blood?

Mind and body would melt together. The consciousness which

had been Rakel binth-Kazintzkis would be displaced—like some lesser daemon, exorcised! Meh'lindi would be Meh'lindi again, entirely.

It's a curious phenomenon that people generally look exactly the way their personality suggests that they *ought* to look. Or to put it another way: that a person's personality is utterly appropriate to their appearance. To explain this phenomenon some ancient poet wrote that "soul is form, and doth the body make". So therefore if a body became perfectly Meh'lindi's, Meh'lindi's soul must surely heed the call—the compulsion of identity.

Should Jaq have scourged himself for harbouring personal concerns and personal passions?

Not when he must energize himself to frenzy in the service of truth!

Thus Jaq meditated.

Lamps were lit, and Rakel was untied.

Hunched naked upon a flagstone, she listened with wide-eyed horror to Jaq's explanation of what must happen to her—as an alternative to her demise by laspistol. Death was no longer an option for her, unless the transformation failed.

"The transformation will not fail!" vowed Jaq. He entrusted the Assassin card to Grimm to hold constantly before Rakel's eyes throughout the agonizing process of metamorphosis. "Rakel: you must focus on this image the whole time. I shall guide you as regards tattoos upon the body. Those are blazoned eidetically upon my mind—"

Likewise upon his heart . . .

Meh'lindi had been richly tattooed in black, to disguise and embellish scars. A fanged serpent had writhed up her right leg. A hairy spider had embraced her waist. Beetles had walked across her bosom. Her surface was tattooed—and hair-trigger lethal. Rakel must imitate that surface perfectly. What of the depths? Why, Jaq had twice been admitted to those depths, to purify and consecrate Meh'lindi; with Meh'lindi's full consent, and with more than consent.

Assassins were trained to tolerate pain, to banish pain. Rakel wasn't trained. If her concentration failed she might go into flux.

"Be staunch, female!" Lex advised her. "Pain is the teacher and saviour. *Dolor est lux.*"

Rakel gritted her teeth then managed to say: "Women *do* give birth, you know—"

"Have you given birth?" enquired the giant.

A shake of the head.

"Well then," said Grimm, "you're about to give birth to yourself, to your brand-new self."

Now and then a scream tore its way out of Rakel's throat as her body remoulded itself.

"Concentrate! The serpent's neck bends leftward—"

Often Rakel whimpered, like a beast caught in a bone-crushing trap.

"The voice: a little less husky—
    "Now the right breast smaller—
        "Golden eyes: think golden—!
        "Flatter, the face—!
"More muscle in the calf—
    "Just a fraction longer, the legs—!"

What a litany of invocations. Rakel's whimpers were the responses. Somehow she managed to keep her gaze fixed upon that Tarot icon which Grimm held out before her, while her own flesh and bone racked her, there upon the flagstones.

At last a counterfeit Meh'lindi stood unsteadily in the cellar, supported by Lex. In Jaq's eyes was a harrowed awe and a kind of appalled adoration. Almost, idolatry. What else was Rakel but an animated idol of his Assassin-courtesan?

Jaq retrieved the Assassin card from Grimm. The card was hotter than the warmth of Grimm's palm could have caused.

"Rakel—" Jaq addressed her harshly. He resisted the self-beguilement of calling her Meh'lindi. "Rakel, this card is one thing you may never steal. Without my psychic boost you can never use it on your own."

As he was restoring the card to an inner pocket of his robe, the card met resistance. An obstacle sprang free. Liberated from its wrapping of flayed mutant skin, another card fluttered to the floor. A tiny flat Daemon of Change leered at Rakel's metamorphosis.

Lex shuddered. He gulped. He lurched, letting go of Rakel. She staggered against a wall, but supported herself. In reflex Lex stamped forward to tread upon that terrible image—with his huge *bare* foot.

"Dorn, light of my being," he chanted.

"Get yourself off it!" Jaq threw himself against Lex. "You could brand yourself!"

Grimm was on his hands and knees, battering at Lex's tough toes. Lex yielded. Gingerly the little man seized the Daemon card. As if it were a burning coal, he restored it instantly to Jaq. Jaq wrapped the card tightly, and hid it.

"You're sorcerers, aren't you . . .? That jewelled book . . .! I'm so hungry I feel I'm con-con-consuming myself!" Rakel's teeth chattered. The idol was shivering violently as if she might wobble apart.

"Feed her!" snarled Jaq. "Feed her with the best in the kitchen, Grimm! Open a stasis chest. Heat foetal lamb and tongues and kidneys. Find a blanket for her, anything to cover her."

Lex cast around. "Where's her black costume?"

"I need to examine it."

"I'll bring a blanket from a bed—" Did Lex wish to be alone for a while?

"Grimm can see to blankets as well as food. You stay here with me, Lex."

Jaq averted his eyes as Grimm led Rakel away. Lex eyed that transformed anatomy with what seemed more than mere curiosity.

"Will she stay stable?" he asked, anxiety in his tone.

"I'm sure she will. The Assassin card stabilizes her. Yet your re-action to that Daemon card, both now and aboard the *Free Enterprise*, compels me to put an inquisitorial question to you, Captain d'Arquebus."

Briefly Jaq willed the electro-tattoo on his palm to display its daemon face. "I speak now as a Malleus man, of the inner In-quisition, whose primary concern is daemonic activity," he said solemnly. "In your past career as a Marine, have you ever had acquaintance with the Power known as," and Jaq lowered his voice, "*Tzeentch*? Have you ever had contact with, or knowledge of, this Power? Confess to me, Lex, if you have. Confess to me. In the Emperor's name tell me. *In nomine Imperatoris!*"

That mighty man blanched. He knelt.

"Yes," he murmured.
Haltingly the story came out . . .

It was many decades earlier, long before Lexandro d'Arquebus became an officer. It was in a cavern of a mining world inhabited by Squats loyal to a rebel lord named Fulgor Sagramoso. Lord Sagramoso's followers had captured Lex and his companions. The captive Marines had been chained down. They were to be sacrificed to the Changer of History. The corrupted Lord Sagramoso himself underwent vile bodily changes. Such disorienting nausea had plucked at the very foundations of Lex's being. He had witnessed daemonic possession. He had known the sickness unto death.

Blessedly, Terminator Librarians of the Imperial Fists in lustrous armour had come blasting their way into the cavern, storm bolters blazing with salvation.

Because of their bravery and endurance Lex and his two surviving comrades had been judged worthy to remember their experience rather than being mind-wiped to ensure their sanity. Lex and Yeremi and Biff had sworn never to tell any of their other battle brothers about the phenomenon of *Tzeentch*.

Lex hadn't sworn not to tell this to an Inquisitor. That memory from the past still disconcerted him hideously.

"You endured a close encounter with Chaos," Jaq said respectfully—absolvingly. "You understand how tortuous our cosmos is, and thus how ingenious—even devious—the champions of truth must sometimes necessarily be."

As devious as Jaq himself?

Was this confession of Lex's another indicator to Jaq that the route to illumination might well be through Tzeentch rather than through Slaanesh? Through mutability, rather than through lust?

Was it possible to balance the two Powers so that a person became simultaneously possessed by both, and therefore fully by neither? Could there be jealous conflict between rival daemons? A war in one's very soul! Thus daemons would mutually disable one another, allowing their intended victim to squirm free to salvation and immunity! Could it be?

From inside his robe Jaq drew his force rod. He kissed its tip sacramentally.

"With this instrument are daemons dispelled . . ." He offered the rod to kneeling Lex, also to kiss.

"If I was ever . . . possessed," mumbled Lex, "could your rod save me?"

"Or slay you. Or both."

"And I, you, likewise?"

Jaq frowned. "Only a powerful psyker may use this rod."

A psyker, untrained, was a potential magnet to daemons. If a trained psyker such as Jaq were to abuse his training and subvert his own sanity, what might he conjure?

"What became of your two comrades?" asked Jaq.

Lex scratched fiercely at his left hand.

"Biff died fighting Tyranids," he said simply. "Then Yeri died too. Everyone's destiny is death."

Jaq frowned. "Except for those supposed immortal Sons of the Emperor! If they truly exist. Supposedly their destiny is death too, in the bonfire of souls which kindles the Numen!"

If those Sons existed. Wherever they might be.

Chapter Six

Robbery

Away from the mansion it wasn't too difficult to remember to call Jaq *Tod* or *Mr Zapasnik*. Inside the mansion itself, the moment inevitably came when Grimm referred to the Boss as "Jaq" in Rakel's hearing.

"Jaq," Rakel said tentatively as the foursome sat at table later, "the food in your house always seems to be so wonderful."

They were eating purple Sabulorb caviar and medallions of yellow *mahgir* fish poached in spiced camelopard milk.

Rakel's voice was really quite like Meh'lindi's. Meh'lindi would never have made any such remark. To Meh'lindi it had always been a matter of pure indifference whether she ate a raw rat or a ragoût to fuel herself. Jaq's knuckles whitened as he clutched his plasteel fork.

"Huh!" blustered Grimm. "Never call the Boss that in public! And it's *me* who's the chef. Anyway, you shouldn't seem to enjoy your grub so much."

"No, I sympathize," Jaq said to Rakel with an effort. "You've had your body altered by the thing you most fear—so that I can safely trust you rather than kill you. How much trust do I bestow?" He glowered briefly at Grimm. "Rakel: my name is indeed Jaq, and I'm acting under cover. Deeply under cover. I am an Inquisitor. Do you know what an Inquisitor is?"

She did know. She paled. She had visited numerous worlds. On one of those planets an inquisitorial purge of heresy had been underway.

*

They had allowed Rakel to return to her former lodgings, with
Lex as escort, to retrieve her stolen valuables and to bring those
back to the mansion to keep in her new room on the second floor.
Rakel's accumulated treasure was trivial compared with the
jewels still encrusting the forbidden book in the cellar.

Jaq insisted that Rakel must exercise gymnastically. For this
purpose Grimm had obtained a range of equipment, now housed
in a chamber adjacent to hers. Bars, pulleys, beams.

As a nimble thief, Rakel had never neglected her body. Now
she must hone herself supremely. She would become a fitting
shrine for Meh'lindi's spirit! Yet Jaq did not tell her this. The
nominal aim was to keep the false Meh'lindi occupied and exercised and expend her surplus energy.

Rakel had fretted that such strenuous activity might disrupt her
new body. But no, reinforcement was the goal, so Grimm assured
her. In the curtained house Rakel was adjusting to her new companions, bizarre though their own mysterious goals might be.
The atrocity which had been inflicted on her was . . . surmoun-
table. What other choice did she have than to align herself with
this trio?

As major-domo of the household Grimm could always find
ways to busy himself, especially in the kitchen. Lex also exercised
solo, observing the proper Marine rites. Nevertheless, Lex craved
more than exercise and prayer. To Grimm—who had been preparing spare ribs of camelopard in a spiced sauce at the time—Lex
had confided his mounting urge to scrimshander. He yearned to
inscribe a fine image upon a bone.

The little man suggested using a camelopard rib after Lex had
sucked it clean. This provoked Lex to fury. Did the Abhuman not
understand that Lex could only engrave scrimshaws upon the
bones of fallen comrades? Maybe he might honourably decorate a
bone of someone who had belonged to another devout chapter.
Alas, no corpses of Ultramarines had been buried on Sabulorb.
All who fell would have been returned to their fortress-monastery.

Did Grimm, with his supposed reverence for ancestors, not
understand this?

Lex was frustrated.

Grimm had mentioned this matter to Jaq.

*

"This world was once infested by Genestealers," Jaq told Rakel at the dinner table. "Do you know what those are?"

Yes, her criminal contacts had told her about the infestation by Old Four-Arms.

"Not all hybrids may have been destroyed," said Jaq. "The Courthouse does not seem to be exercising enough diligence these days. I do not suggest that the Courthouse is contaminated. However, an Inquisitor must always harbour many suspicions — and often act secretly. You may have seen an Inquisitor storming about on that other world you visited. The best work of the Inquisition is often pursued unseen, until the crucial moment. That book downstairs contains secrets about Genestealers and their origin."

Did it? Did it not?

They're bred by Tyranids, Lex almost said; but he kept silent.

In the Tyranid hive-ship, in that evil leviathan shaped like a snail, Biff and Yeremi had died . . .

"To read the book I shall need something which is probably stored in the Courthouse. I must not reveal myself prematurely to the Judges. So your arrival is timely. However, you must be tested. *We* intercepted you, after all."

Thanks to Lyman's ears. Other victims of crime would not have Lyman's ears, but even so!

"I'm told," said Jaq, "that the Oriens Temple was once home to the ancient thigh bone of a Marine, housed in a reliquary." The real Meh'lindi had told him this. "I wonder whether that thigh bone survived the destruction of the temple? I wonder whether the Occidens Temple sequestered that bone, just as they have done with the Emperor's fingernails. Find out, Rakel, find out from your criminal contacts! If that femur is hidden away in Occidens I want you to steal the bone and bring it here for Lex to ornament with his graving tool."

"Oh yes indeed," said Lex. "Oh *yes*!" His fists opened and closed as though already grasping the revered bone.

Why Lex should wish to engage in such an activity was not to be confided. Rakel knew Lex's name — but not his identity.

"Ask about illegal *cults* as well," continued Jaq. "Is there any cult devoted to metamorphosis — or to revolutionary change? Is there any cult devoted to lust and wanton pleasures of the flesh?"

Rakel ventured to ask: "Is that why I should not praise the food we eat, no matter how fine it is?"

"Not at all! We eat well because austerity narrows one's perspectives."

Grimm tilted his pot of ale. "You usedn't to allow any alcohol aboard the good ship *Tormentum*, Jaq." These days, Grimm had been allowed to provision the larder with beer and wine and even some of the strong local *Djinn* spirit. Jaq himself still drank no alcohol. For Lex, with his supplementary preomnor stomach and his purifying oolitic kidney, indulgence would be futile.

"Alcohol disorders the senses," Jaq explained. "I may need to exploit disorder. *You*, Rakel, in your new Assassin shape should not express sensual preferences regarding food. It isn't fitting."

Jaq placed the Assassin's sash upon the table. From the sash he removed three small hooded rings, baroque thimbles.

"Wear these on your fingers, Rakel."

With a professional, if puzzled, eye Rakel was assessing the possible value of these supposed items of bijouterie.

"You crook your finger suddenly just so." Jaq mimed. "These are rare digital weapons of Jokaero manufacture. One fires a toxic needle, the next a laser beam, and the third is a tiny flamer. Each will fire once. We have no means to replenish these. They are only for use in case you are cornered, with no other means of escape."

Rakel eyed the three digital devices, and the three other persons seated at table.

"See how we trust you!" sneered Grimm.

"You wouldn't take *me* out," Lex growled at her, "not with toxin nor flame nor laser burst. Even blind, I'd break your back."

"And your body would soon go into flux," said Jaq.

Nodding, Rakel slid the three digital weapons on to different fingers.

"You're perfect," Jaq said bleakly.

The little man dabbed a finger in the spiced milk and sucked as if on a teat. "Huh, this sauce is getting cold!"

Rakel was no longer a free agent. No longer was she even herself, physically. But then, what did freedom signify? What value was there in the freedom to tote a valise of stolen gems and drugs and imperial credit tokens and such from star system to star system, paying bribes and sweeteners in the process? What value was there even in a *self*, in this cosmos of untold trillions of selves? If anything defined her 'self', it was thievery, the purloining of material aspects of other people with which to embellish in private her own identity.

In this mansion she had attained, inadvertently, a whole new counterfeit identity, forged upon her very flesh. Wasn't this a perverse kind of triumph? Now she had a mission and a mandate to steal, bestowed by a clandestine Inquisitor. Wasn't this a perverse kind of recognition?

She proved to be a useful intermediary. Her main contacts were the Shuturban brothers, two dark moustached men whose father, now elderly, had been a camelopard driver and smuggler. Chor Shuturban was sly, she explained. Mardal Shuturban was rash and quick-tempered.

The Shuturbans had been most intrigued by the alteration in Rakel's appearance since last they had seen her. Indeed, at first they had been quite sceptical that Rakel *was* Rakel—until she reminded them of previous illegal dealings known only to herself and the brothers.

So had she undergone major surgery at the Hakim Hospital—and recovered already? She was obliged to tell Chor and Mardal—exaggeratedly—about the lichen juice of her home-world, and how this made her people masters and mistresses of disguise. She had actually been in disguise prior to this—so she claimed, with a twisted smile—and now they beheld her true self. She spoke of shape-shifting chemicals in her blood. Chor had muttered about wizardry.

Chor Shuturban did indeed know the present whereabouts of that thigh bone. It had been retrieved from the ruin of Oriens in its severely damaged golden reliquary when a tunnel was cleared of debris during his father's time. Occidens deacons had been supervising the excavation. Shuturban Senior had made it his business to learn where so much crushed wrought gold was taken. The reliquary had been locked inside an altar in one of the side-chapels in the basilica of Occidens.

While the elder Shuturban was musing about the future of that gold, a tetchy camelopard had kicked him in the gut. His pain wouldn't subside. Some organ must have been ruptured. It was only when he went to Occidens to pray in that particular chapel, and when he vowed never to desecrate it, that he was healed miraculously.

The reliquary must still be there to this day. Due to religious rivalry, how long might the relic remain out of sight, unexamined—and maybe in time become forgotten? No pledge prevented his sons from disposing of the gold if someone else should choose to loot the altar.

Fifty side chapels were in that basilica. Some of the altars were of adamantium. One was of ivory, dedicated to the Emperor's teeth. The majority were of plasteel. In exchange for a half-share of the precious metal Chor Shuturban would tell Rakel which was the chapel. Rakel had promised to consider this offer.

"Logically," said Jaq, "it should be the chapel of His Thighs . . ."

Rakel had already arrived at the same conclusion. Occidens was open again to the public, after the paroxysm of the unveiling. On the way back from the Shuturbans' premises she had visited Occidens to pray her way around the so-called Stations of Him-on-Earth, as hastily as was compatible with decorum.

Many body-bags of camelopard hide cluttered the basilica, unclaimed, the odour of decay almost masked by the prevalent sweet incense drifting from the atrium. Because pilgrims had died in adoration of the True Face, they merited a time of display in the basilica. Body-bags were all tied at the necks, exposing to scrutiny the head or remains of a head. This was for identification—yet also so that a miracle could be recognized. A corpse might remain uncorrupted, demonstrably blessed by Him-on-Earth. Invariably there were one or two such miracles. These miracles vindicated all the deaths which might otherwise have seemed, to a heretic, to mar the climactic ceremony of Holy Year.

In the basilica, unfortunately, there was one chapel dedicated to His Left Thigh, and another chapel to His Right Thigh.

"Do we flip a shekel?" asked Grimm after Rakel had delivered her report.

Jaq scowled at this irreverence. "It will be the *chapel sinister* where they hid the bone. The left-hand one. Leftward is the side of formulae, occult science, guile, and secrets."

Lex agreed. It was on the bones of his left hand that he had inscribed the names of dead Biff and Yeremi.

"The priests wouldn't disregard the customary symbolism," Jaq stated.

Rakel's best route into Occidens would be through one of the

apertures in the dome of the atrium, through which the smoke of
incense vented. Clad in black, she would descend on a thin
strong rope like a spider on its silk, then drop cat-like to the floor.
At night, when the temple was closed, no armed deacons might
be on patrol in the atrium of the basilica. She had noted that residents of the temple—as opposed to visitors—rarely glanced
upwards. Upwards was wreathed in smoke.

From the atrium she would proceed silently into the basilica.
Apply lock-picks to the plasteel altar. Heave out the reliquary,
heavy with gold.

"Heavy on account of the femur too," insisted Lex. "Marine
bones are big, and reinforced."

Rakel glanced at him curiously, but did not question.

Next: open a body-bag.

"Hide the corpse away inside the altar?" queried Grimm.

"*No*," said Jaq. "That would be sacrilege."

Put the reliquary inside the bag along with the body. Tie the
bag up again. Return to the atrium. An accomplice would let
down the rope for Rakel's retrieval.

"Am I to be on the rooftop?" demanded Grimm. "What sort of
solo test is this?"

Rakel smiled wanly. "There'll be other ways into the temple.
Sewers, for instance. I'm sure Chor Shuturban will tell me if we
promise enough gold. Wouldn't we prefer to amaze him?"

She wasn't Meh'lindi. Meh'lindi would have found a way in
through the sewers, contorting herself and dislocating her limbs if
need be. Yet Rakel was cleverly analytical.

The morning after robbing the altar she would present herself
at the temple accompanied by a burly slave. She would identify a
head poking from the bag. She would weep with mingled grief
and joy. The slave would help her carry the burden away.

And if the reliquary proved too large, even in its crushed state,
why, the night before she would cut off the head of the corpse,
hide the headless body, then fasten the head to the top of the reliquary. The reliquary would substitute for the body.

"Hide, *where*?" demanded Jaq.

"I'd hoped to make use of the altar," Rakel said humbly.

"Sacrilege. Blasphemy."

"Indeed," said Lex.

"I suppose," grumped Grimm, "this means I might have to

haul up this rotting headless corpse on the end of the rope after you've climbed it?''

"A thief uses every means she can," said Rakel.

Jaq said sternly, "You're attempting to manipulate us to compensate for what has happened to you."

Rakel shrugged. "I serve you," she said, "in whatever way I best may."

Jaq's eyes widened at this echo of his dead Assassin-courtesan.

"It's a plausible plan," he acknowledged.

"Just so long," jeered Grimm, "as you don't fasten *yourself* inside the body-bag as a way of getting out of the temple! Even with verdigris and cosmetic slime on your face the priests might decide you were uncorrupted, and a miracle. Ach, that prompts a thought. Don't you reckon a corpse that's getting a bit high might fall to pieces en route to the roof?"

"I shall take a net with me," explained Rakel. "A net with a narrow mesh. Plenty of suitable fishing nets are on sale in Shandabar."

"A net with a corpse in it," muttered Grimm. "What a haul."

"I feel *corruption* gathering around me," Jaq murmured sombrely. He added very softly: "As I suppose it must gather."

"Cults," continued Rakel. "I was to ask about cults. There is a private society of lust in the Mahabbat district of Shandabar. Aphrodisiacs, orgies. Mardal Shuturban attends its debauches. And his brother has heard rumours of a cult of 'transcendental alteration'. Evidently some people aspire to evolve beyond our human condition."

Grimm asked: "Do these dental alterationists by any chance file their teeth to points so they look like Genestealers' fangs?"

"Mardal has only heard vague rumours. My startling change in appearance seemed to explain my interest."

"Could be a remnant of Genestealer hybrids, Boss."

"Or else unwitting disciples of a certain Power, who foolishly imagine that evolutionary change is virtuous! Oh the Courthouse is surely all too lax in its investigations," declared Jaq. "Praise be that there is an Inquisitor here, to test how lax."

The next night, two hours after midnight, Jaq and Lex were lurking amidst the piled-up wreckage of vendors' booths which had been demolished during the furore of the unveiling.

It was that hour when body and spirit are at their lowest ebb, the hour when people most frequently die in their sleep. This nocturnal ebb seemed especially melancholy in the great space fronting the temple. By now the flood of visiting pilgrims had quit the city. Where a throng of tents had been, only scattered beggars slumbered, their bodies fully covered against the cold, dead to the world. Maybe in the Mahabbat district vigorous beggars were still holding out hands to drunks departing from brothels, to lucky winners leaving gambling dens. But not here. Here, the inert shrouded beggars seemed to epitomize the exhausted *tristesse* of the city in the aftermath of the frantic climax to Holy Year. No one stirred. Not even a cough to be heard.

The sky-wide stipple of stars only feebly illuminated the temple square and the looming domes of Occidens. Deprived of his power armour and interface with its calculator, Lex could not see telescopically. No magnified image fed directly to his visual cortex now. He strained to perceive the obscure tiny figures of Grimm and Rakel upon the temple rooftops. Maybe he wasn't even seeing them at all, but only a trick of darkness and starlight. Maybe Grimm had already propped the ultralight telescopic ladder against the dome above the atrium so as to reach the lowest vent. Maybe Rakel was already descending into smoky darkness, relieved only by a myriad pin-pricks of burning incense. Lex kept his enhanced ears alert for any outburst of gunfire.

How his hands itched to caress the thigh-bone and to power up his graving tool. Such meditative peace of mind that would bring; such reverent serenity. Let the theft not fail. Theft, indeed! It was the restoration of a sacred bone into the rightful hands, so that Lex could honour whoever that Marine had been, dead for millennia perhaps. The exploit must succeed.

"With your permission," he whispered to Jaq, "I'm going up on to the roof in case there's trouble."

"I shall pray there isn't," was the reply.

A great shadow departed swiftly.

Grimm's eyes stung and watered as he peeped down into the atrium. The rope had gone slack in his hairy hands. He had pulled it up a good way, in case some insomniac priest went a-wandering and noticed. The end of the rope was highwayman-hitched to a spur of stone with a knot Grimm had learned on a

world of nomad herdsmen where highway trails were beaten out
by hooves across vast grassy steppes, and where steeds were
tethered thus for quick release. A steed could tug on its tether
until it was blue in the face. A rider need only jerk on the end of
the rope for the knot to collapse.

Even with keen Squattish eyesight Grimm could hardly make
out the grossest shapes below. He might have been peering
through a porthole upon a smoggy fuming dark nebula in which
tiny dimmed stars burned feebly at a vast depth. Mustn't silhouette himself too much, even so! Might seem like a voyeurish
gargoyle. Bit like keeping watch down a chimney. Grimm suppressed a ticklish urge to hawk and spit phlegm.

In the basilica a thousand candles burned. Light waged its perpetual doomed war with darkness. Light must eventually fail, for
darkness was a fundamental condition.

In such an array, inevitably many candles were guttering. Their
flames leapt and faded, leapt and faded. Shadows quivered like
insubstantial night-creatures infesting the side-chapels. Rakel, in
black, was merely one such shadow.

An eroded legend read: FEMUR SINISTR** BENEDIC**.

Silently Rakel lifted from the altar a crystal monstrance resembling a supernova outburst. Next, some altar bells. Finally, an
iron candelabrum in the shape of an upright battleship. She
pulled away the altar brocade.

This plasteel altar had only been locked for a few decades.
Tumblers yielded to her lock-picks. She raised the heavy lid.

What a burden the battered reliquary was! To shift it she had
needed to climb inside the altar, then heave with all her might,
using the lip of the altar as a fulcrum. But not before she had
dragged a malodorous body-bag into position to act as a cushion
to deaden the fall. Otherwise, the din of impact upon a flagstone
would have rung throughout the basilica.

Now that the reliquary lay upon the floor, she scrutinized the
dead woman's head. She memorized for the morrow the rictus of
teeth and shrunken sunken eyes. She unknotted the throat-
thong. She unpeeled the camelopard hide from the abused body.
Although ten days deceased, the corpse seemed unlikely to fall
apart yet.

With a monomolecular blade she severed the dead woman's head at the base of the neck. Grimm had contrived a hooking device. One hook would anchor inside a gap in the reliquary. The other would lodge within the decapitated head of the corpse. Thus to fasten the two together.

Rakel had scarcely begun to thrust a hook up through one of the artery apertures in the base of the skull when a voice called out, *"Who being there?"*

There in the chapel she crouched. She froze.

Sexton? Deacon? Priest? Footsteps were padding close.

"Being you, Jagan the Wakeful?"

Rakel had a laspistol. Firing the gun in itself would be silent. A hit would result in a bright explosion. If only the night had been thundery; but it wasn't.

What choice was there but to use the miniature needle-gun? This would fire a tiny sliver doped with powerful toxin. The target's body would convulse. He would choke and suffer stroke and heart-attack all at once. Hopefully he would fall with no more than a thump.

Why, now she *was* an Assassin! As the snooper entered the chapel, she crooked a finger at his silhouette.

Instead of a noiseless mini-needle, a jet of chemicals spurted from the baroque ring. Igniting in the air, the volatile liquid wrapped the intruder's chest in flames—and he screamed. How he screamed. She had mistaken which digital weapon the needler was. If she had fired higher, her victim might instantly have sucked flame into his lungs and been unable to shriek . . .

Head thrown back, he howled in agony as he tried with seared hands to tear a burning cassock loose. He was a shrieking torch—a screeching illuminated alarm, capering away from her.

Time almost stood still. Each moment seemed so prolonged. Adrenalin was racing in Rakel. Discard the body-bag plan! Separate the relic from the bulk of the reliquary! Three seconds were becoming four. Already she was clawing with Grimm's hook at the once-glorious gold, prising and ripping. No one was responding to the screeching yet. Four seconds becoming five. How much longer, how much longer?

"Oh me Ancestors, how could I be so stupid!"

At the first ascent of that scream Grimm had let the gathered rope drop. A moment later he was over the lip of the vent. He crammed himself through the aperture. He slid down the rope at high speed, braking perfunctorily with his boots. If his hands hadn't been so calloused, he would surely have suffered rope-burn. What if he'd met Rakel ascending from the incense-pricked gloom? Some collision! However, she wasn't in the way.

He had crashed to a standstill. He had dashed across the colonnaded atrium. Immediately he spotted the screaming torch. He pounded past it.

He knelt beside Rakel, helping rip the reliquary apart, bless his tough hairy hands.

"Oh me Grandsires, how could I be so dumb!"

Screeching only spasmodically now, the torch fell over. A lambent aura spread around him as though some psychic energy had come into play. Reflection of the flames from the flagstones?

"Ach—!" At last the great femur came free from its ruptured golden container. Bit bulky, that bone, but far easier to shift on its own.

Here came trouble, in the shape of numerous scurrying figures in various states of dress and undress—temple personnel brandishing stunners, autoguns, shotguns, laspistols. Beware of those stunners especially. Priests mightn't be prepared to blast off shells and fragmentation shot amidst holy chapels.

That aura around the burning sexton! Why, the floor itself was softly on fire! Grease and soot deposited by generations of candles had ignited. Higher up the walls of the basilica there must be an even thicker skin. Dumping the thigh-bone temporarily, Grimm fired his laspistol over the heads of the oncomers. Swivelling, he fired in other directions.

Energy packets bloomed dazzlingly upon the walls. With a soft *whoosh*, a lustrous and almost gentle flame rolled outward from the site of each explosion.

"Run for it, Rakel! Keep low!"

The temple-dwellers had halted to goggle up at this phenomenon which was spreading swiftly around the interior surface of their basilica. Those who held stunners were themselves stunned with awe. The whole edifice was becoming radiant as if itself it were a candle. Everywhere candle-flame glowed yet did not consume. Surely this was a miracle. Surely what had ignited it—its wick—was the dying sexton who still writhed. Him, and those

other outbursts of psychic fire! Was this some visitation from the
Emperor's spirit, some wondrous and unexpected epiphany for
Holy Year?

As the miraculous flame spread across the great ceiling, in
majestic yet seemingly undamaging fashion, beads of molten wax
began to drip. The faces of those below were stung. A deacon
wailed as hot wax hit his eye.

Realization dawned.

"Being fire—!"

"Being arson—!"

"Incendium—!"

Grimm and Rakel reached the archway to the atrium. They
were spotted. Heedless of damage to columns, someone opened
fire with high-velocity shells. Reason deserted many minds. Were
they all not now in a vast oven, beginning to be basted?

Grimm and Rakel reached the rope. No time to unfold a fish-net
for the relic.

"Climb, lady, climb!"

She began to ascend, hand over hand.

How could Grimm possibly shin up a rope with a great bone
under one arm? Impossible!

The bone was far too big to clamp his teeth on to.

He timber-hitched the end of the rope around the bone. This
was a scaffolder's knot for hoisting a spar. No sooner done than
he began climbing after Rakel.

Wondrously, the rope was rising as he climbed. It was being
hauled up powerfully, by a familiar superhuman winch which
loomed over the vent above.

Pursuit had arrived among the forests of smoking incense-sticks.
The disappearance of the fugitives bewildered the searchers
briefly. Some dashed towards the oratory.

Could the intruders have taken wing? At last someone stared
up into the smoke. *Something* was on the point of disappearing
through a vent.

Warmth wafted upon Lex's face as first he hauled Rakel clear. He
inhaled greasy combustion. Then Grimm came through the hole,
followed by a tail of rope on which a great bone wagged to and

fro. Shots followed soon after. Several shots winged through the vent, and skyward. Others exploded within, the lip of the vent serving as shield, and shrapnel sprayed downward. Reverently Lex unknotted the bone.

They left the rope, still hitched for quick-release. No point, now, in removing evidence of the means of access. Let furious deacons fix plasteel grilles across the dozen vents. Away across the rooftops they scrambled, to commence a circuitous descent.

Jaq had heard gunfire, muffled and faint. Armed men spilled from the portico. They were gesturing to one another to head around the side of the temple complex.

He aimed his laspistol from within the wreckage of the booths. Sub-vocalizing a prayer of forgiveness—since those people were the loyal disciples of Him-on-Earth—Jaq fired surgically. A modest energy blast toppled a target, though the man still squirmed and writhed.

Jaq fired again, and another man fell.

A high-velocity shot crashed into the timber near him, spraying splinters. Jaq withdrew. Ducking, he darted away through the darkness. Deacons and sextons would be busy for a while, shooting at wood.

A couple of hours later, they had rendezvoused back at the mansion . . .

Lex sat upon a black slate floor with the thigh-bone across his lap. That bone was pitted with antiquity. Lex's fingers roved over it as though it were some musical instrument which had lost its strings. Before he could begin engraving he would need to sand the bone finely then immerse it in hot paraffin wax to seal its pores and thus prevent the ink of the designs from bleeding. Meanwhile, he caressed this sacred femur with a sense of serene inner joy. Might it even once have belonged to an Imperial Fist, several aeons ago? Rather than to a Blood Angel or a Space Wolf or whomever else. Probably not. Yet no matter.

"I'm obliged to you," he told the false Meh'lindi.

"And I to you," she said, "for pulling up the rope so quickly."

"Huh," said Grimm. "Took three of us to steal a bone, and no gold at all. Besides setting fire to the temple." The little man shrugged. "Set fire to a chimney to clean it!" The flames had been superficial. That sooty grease must have consumed itself or been extinguished by foam. Otherwise, the night sky would have glowed with the bonfire of Occidens.

Deacons would have found the ripped reliquary, empty of its relic. This must seem to have been a religious, sectarian raid. Staged by whom? By Oriens loyalists? Hard to imagine who those might be! Not after Genestealer infestation, and thorough cleansing, and all the subsequent decades. So was the raid mounted by the Austral temple? That's where the finger of suspicion might point—provoking a bitter and futile religious feud . . .

Had Rakel been tested sufficiently? Had the robbery proved to be partly a fiasco? Brave endeavours were often derailed; yet all four participants were safe, and remained incognito.

"Tomorrow," Jaq said to Rakel, "you will go to those Shuturban brothers bearing a ruby more precious than gold, prised from our book. Tell those Shuturbans that you found the ruby along with the reliquary. Say that the gold was merely gilding over soft copper. Buy any details about the Courthouse, especially where data is stored. Local builders were employed."

Grimm grinned encouragingly. "Best plan once you're inside the Courthouse might be to knife an Arbitrator and steal his black gear and mirror-mask. You'd better practise your exercises, mock-Assassin."

Jaq was staring at the counterfeit woman with such bitter wistfulness. Of course she must assassinate some official while inside the Courthouse! What other course of action would a devout Inquisitor require to galvanize Judges in their duties? What else would sow confusion and paranoia amongst them?

During the night, yet again, Jaq dreamed of Askandargrad, ravaged and ravished . . .

Raven Guards, in their black power armour, were advancing through smouldering ruins, their bolt guns ready to fire at whatever moved. Many Brothers were also armed with chainswords.

Whatever moved could only be an enemy—whose joy was to kill, but especially, and lustfully so, by rushing in close with power sword or chainsword. Lethal close contact was the delight of these devil-Marines—an erotic, sadistic impulse which sometimes impelled them to berserk recklessness.

So long as a Raven kept calm, these assaults could be ideal opportunities to kill or cripple a renegade.

How could one keep calm? Chaos spawn scuttled, spiderlike, over the smoky terrain. How nauseating if these creatures leapt at a Raven, to cling to his armour. They could hardly harm a Marine in armour, but they could disorient. Worse, and far more sickening and dangerous, were the *daemonettes*.

Their exquisite single breasts. Their lush thighs and loins. Their green eyes—uncannily elongated—and their manes of blonde hair. The razor-sharp pincers of their hands! And the barbed tails which sought to impale!

To be assaulted by such a creature was sickening, dizzying, destabilizing to a devout Marine. Daemonettes materialized as accomplices of renegades. Daemonettes were manifestations of the vicious lusts of the Chaos warriors.

Along with a Captain of the Raven Guard, Jaq wearily surveyed the advance from the low roof of a warehouse. Hooded ventilators were like monkish sentries to Jaq's eyes. He hadn't slept for fifty hours or more. Neighbouring buildings had collapsed, forming ramps of rubble. The destruction was disproportionate. Numbers of the iniquitous Legionnaires were now hosting daemons, daemons with powers, whose joy was to destroy . . . people if possible, but people's property too, so it seemed, so that their victims should be as nakedly vulnerable as could be, utterly defenceless. To the Legionnaires of Slaanesh the battle was an orgy of foul delight.

The Captain had been scanning rune displays within his visor of the disposition of his own men.

''*The Emperor's Children*!'' he exclaimed bitterly to Jaq. Those renegades had been merely a dark item of history to him, until now. ''How dare these fiends still call themselves by such a title! Our Emperor protects the innocent.'' He whispered hauntedly, ''Daemons are in their ranks . . . Such hideous creatures!''

Was this superbly trained man approaching snapping point? Badges of honour upon his inky-black armour told of past heroism. A scorch mark blistered his shoulder pauldron. His back-banner had been shot to shreds.

''We will win,'' the Captain assured Jaq. ''We must win.''

For if not, then his badges and those of his men would be taken as trophies; and worse, far worse, organs and hormones would be extracted from the corpses of the Ravens to create drugs of delirium.

Shrieking, a daemonette pranced up the ramp of rubble ahead of . . .

. . . that must be a *Chaplain of Chaos*!

The armour was rampantly adorned with male-and-female runes of Slaanesh, and with obscene hermaphroditic insignia. That armour shimmered unnaturally, wreathed in baleful energies. This wasn't only a Chaplain of Chaos, but a Chaplain *possessed*. He had given himself as host to a daemon, or he had summoned one. The chainsword in his hand shrieked as if in sweet torment. His bolt gun jutted phallically and ejaculated a bolt. The bolt penetrated a ventilator column close by the Captain. It ripped right through the backside of the shaft, *swooshing* onward before exploding belatedly in mid-air.

Forcing himself to ignore the onrushing daemonette, who was now so close, the Captain fired back at the perverted Chaplain. Those energies which cloaked the Chaplain seemed to catch the bolt and sling it far away.

Praying and summoning his psychic power, Jaq aimed the sleek black force rod, in the use of which he had quite recently been trained. Embedded with a few arcane circuits, the force rod was a solid flute, virtually featureless.

"Begone into the warp!" Jaq yelled.

The flute discharged.

The daemonette pitched forward. She wrapped herself into a ball—of buttocks and barbed tail and clawing arms, hugging herself. The knotty ball of daemonic anatomy bounded up the rubble, bounce after bounce.

Of a sudden the ball was shrinking, ever so swiftly.

Only something the size of a pea bounced towards Jaq's boot—and he crushed it.

Another bolt from the Captain of Ravens failed to penetrate the Chaplain's defences. Waving that chainsword, the Chaplain came onward. He did not trouble to fire another bolt. His rabid desire was to carve through the Captain's armour intimately, not kill from a distance.

Jaq directed his force rod. Could he summon another discharge of sufficient power so soon after the first? He prayed to the Emperor. He exerted all his will.

The rod throbbed.

An orange glow, as of a ship entering atmosphere, engulfed the

Chaplain. Billows of orange hue swept away behind him, curling and coiling and evaporating. His armour was being stripped of its devilish occult shield.

The Captain fired, *RAAARK, RAAARK*.

CRUMP, CRUMP. The bolts impacted, detonated.

The Chaplain lurched. He reeled.

Dropping the rod, Jaq snatched up his own bolt gun and added his fire to the Captain's.

The Chaplain's breastplate had burst open. Scarlet blood welled. The blood did not harden to cinnabar, as was the way with a regular Marine's blood. It coagulated into bright wobbling jelly, as if polyps were emerging from that mutated man. The chainsword fell from one hand; the bolter from the other. The armoured monstrosity toppled, crashing upon rubble.

"We *will* win!" vowed the Captain.

Jaq awoke, disoriented. Night pressed upon him, dark as Raven armour.

Ah. Sabulorb . . . Shandabar . . .

So far in time and space from Askandar.

The Raven Guards had indeed ousted the Emperor's Children from that city, and from that world. At much cost.

There was always cost.

Casualties were often appalling in the brave struggle to hold dissolution at bay. The fight could only be waged savagely. Anyone who had witnessed the rape of Askandargrad could imagine the universal horrors—multiplied a million-fold—if Chaos were to ravish the whole galaxy with slaughter and plague and depravity, with anarchy and mutation.

Closing his eyes again, Jaq meditated wretchedly about the Emperor's Children, tools of Slaanesh. They were no children of Him-on-Earth now! Biologically they never had been, except in the sense that the Emperor's scientists had created their gene-seed. As for the Emperor's true children—his immortal Sons—*did they even truly exist?*

Chapter Seven

Orgy

The Shuturban brothers were duly impressed by the ruby. Word had already reached them of a fracas outside the Occidens Temple—and undoubtedly within as well, and perhaps involving a fire, so it seemed. Two residents of the temple had been shot outside its walls. Searchers had climbed up on to the rooftops. In the morning the sextons hadn't opened the temple doors as usual. Worshippers had queued in vain.

Evidently one of the beggars who lived in the vast courtyard had been alert enough to make his way across the city to the Shuturbans.

Rakel the Thief now wished for certain details about the imperial Courthouse? Was there no limit to her enterprises?

The Shuturbans' source had noticed a robed man fleeing from the vicinity of Occidens; while another beggar had told the same informant how he had spied a giant and a dwarf in the vicinity that night . . .

Details about the Courthouse were possible—such a fine ruby was persuasive. However, Chor Shuturban insisted on giving such information to Rakel in the presence of her mysterious *patron*—whose existence she could not reasonably deny. Chor wished to meet this new sponsor of crime. The new-style Rakel had left her former lodgings in a hurry. A wagging tongue said that a giant slave had escorted her away.

The meeting should be on neutral ground. Rakel had been curious about cults of lust, hadn't she? Therefore the neutral ground should be a certain building in the Mahabbat district a week hence. Rakel's sponsor, and herself, were invited to an *entertainment*.

Chor assured Rakel that there was no obligation to join in the frolics physically. Entirely up to herself and her patron! The giant and the dwarf could come too. Those two might be amusing performers.

"Chor Shuturban hopes to unsettle our minds," said Jaq, "so that one of us may be indiscreet."

Yet did he himself not wish his sanity to be unsettled and deranged?

"My mind is staunch against carnal temptations," declared Lex. Now he had the thigh-bone to caress if need be. Already Lex had begun to prepare the femur for scrimshaw, by sanding and waxing. While he worked he would pray to Rogal Dorn, silently in case Rakel overheard his prayers.

Grimm pouted. "Huh, that a Squat like me should join in some orgy with *regular* human beings! Slim chance. If there were some sturdy dwarfesses I might be tempted."

To wait a whole week was frustrating—though it would take the Shuturban brothers a week to marshall the information which Rakel had requested. In the meanwhile, though, there was much to be done.

Rakel filched a hypno-casque from the Mercantile College in the southerly Saudigar district. This posed no special challenge to her talents; but a casque was needed. The data-disc in this particular casque was programmed with standard Imperial Gothic, for the use of exporters who intended to travel off-world. Jaq discarded the disc.

Next, Rakel stole a laser-scalpel from the Hakim Hospital. Grimm bought certain equipment in the industrial district. Lex rigged up an imaging system so that he could observe Azul Petrov's warp-eye without looking at it directly.

Might the eye still be lethal to the beholder when viewed on a screen? Proof was provided by a leper whom Grimm led blindfolded by a roundabout route to the mansion on promise of fifty shekels which would buy the wretch consecrated ointments at the same Hakim Hospital.

This leper wasn't one of those whose disease had begun to

attack his nerves painfully. Hitherto, the leprosy had robbed him of almost all bodily sensation—which he prayed that the ointment might restore. Did the leper fear ill treatment at his unknown destination? His hosts, if ill-intentioned, could hardly make him suffer greatly, since much of his necrofying flesh was already so numb.

Within an unseen room a large hood was put over his head and the blindfold removed. Before the leper's eyes, sharing the vacancy within the hood, was a small display screen. He was simply told to stare at that screen, and to describe what he saw.

"Being a black ball," the leper had said. "Being held in a clamp. The front of the ball being carved with a shape, with a rune—"

"Continue staring into the ball."

After ten minutes of staring without apoplexy, the leper was blindfolded once again, and led back to the vicinity of the Hakim Hospital, and released—with fifty shekels in his mutilated paw indeed.

Evidently the dwarf who had accosted him had been a miraculous intercessor in his destiny.

Out of curiosity, Grimm had hung around the entrance to the hospital. Half an hour later a hideous leper, now naked but for a loin cloth, had lurched out, shrieking, screaming for water to be thrown over him, crying to anyone that his body was on fire. The consecrated ointment must certainly have stimulated his numb flesh and nerves. In default of water the leper writhed in the chilly dust of the street to cool himself in vain.

While the thigh-bone was soaking in paraffin wax, Lex set to work on Azul's eye with the laser-scalpel. Lex had no calculator to assist with gradients and curves—and he had to study the process on screen, not directly—yet his beefy hands were dextrous and fastidious. It would have been a wonder to stand by and to watch him—if an accidental glimpse of the actual eye might not have ravaged the observer's nervous system or killed him outright. Lex himself wore blinker-goggles so as to prevent any inadvertent glance aside.

For the sake of symmetry of the lens, the rune on the front of the eye must needs be pared away. What of it? That rune was a guide to the Black Library in the Webway—to which they did not wish to return.

Ah, how Jaq's Ordo would crave to possess such a guide.

The Inquisition and the Ordo Malleus must needs be disappointed — though before commencing Lex did take the precaution of copying the rune on to camelopard vellum. If in future some other Navigator was willing to sacrifice the broad spectrum of his warp vision, a replica might be made upon that volunteer's eye.

Surely no one in the cosmos had ever before made a monocle out of a Navigator's warp-eye!

The resulting lens should be slim enough for Jaq to see through, if need be. Finally enough material had been shaved away from the obsidian-hard eye for a murky lens to be slotted inside a fat monocle frame, with thickly enamelled covers hinged at front and back.

Would the killing gaze of the warp-eye be greatly diminished by the removal of so much substance? Or would the lens prove to be a quintessence, a lethal concentrate?

"Doubt if we can bring the same leper back here," Grimm remarked. "Probably drowned himself in the Bihisti by now. Still, I s'pose it has to be a person we expose, just to be sure, not another damn monkey . . ." The little man scratched his head and grinned. "No need to do it here at home, though. You and me, Jaq, we should go for a walk in a dodgy neighbourhood and await some trouble. Then it'll be the fool's own fault."

Not a walk in company with Lex. His physique would be a big deterrent. A walk with Rakel, on the other hand . . .?

Thus it was that the three had set out for the industrial area, the Bellygunge district. Jaq wore his mesh armour under his robe. Grimm trusted as ever in his quilted flak-jacket. Rakel wore a shimmery silken blue gown over a clinging thermal undergarment. *She* would not be an immediate target for knife or bullet. For attempted abduction! For outrage. But not instantly for murder.

Jaq strolled arm in arm with Rakel, flaunting her like some seigneur with his courtesan. Grimm trailed a little way behind, a dwarfish dogsbody.

The smoky factory slums of the Bellygunge district were home to hundreds of thousands of souls. Any little factory producing a component for vehicles would be habitation to the whole family who worked there. The street immediately outside would accommodate another family busily manufacturing nails by cutting and sharpening wire. Around the corner would be a dozen other

enterprises, busily soldering or laminating or dipping wing-nuts
into noxious fluids to galvanize them. Each sweatshop jealously
guarded its cluttered territory. Inside and outside the rickety
buildings, equipment rumbled and thumped and throbbed and
vented smoke and fumes. Conversation was conducted in shouts.
Coughing was endemic. Sellers of water and sherbet and fish pas-
ties contributed to the hubbub.

For someone perceivedly rich to saunter through this ants' nest
of industry was to invite attack sooner or later.

The giant sun hung above the fumes like a red-hot lid. Indeed,
because of all the spewing fumes and hectic machinery, Bellygunge was a few degrees warmer than the rest of chilly
Shandabar. Many labourers would habitually strip off their calico
dungris.

Presently, in an alley, four skinny fellows accosted Jaq and
Rakel and Grimm. Those waylayers had been trailing after the trio
for a while. Now they had taken a shortcut to bring them ahead.

Stub guns emerged from the rags of two of the opportunists.
The two others produced gaudy swords shaped like meat-cleav-
ers. Evidently the sword blades were of plastic—sharp flexible
plastic, its substance dyed a streaky blood-red in the manufacture
so as to convey a menacing impression, of butchery. One red
blade bore the motif of a green snake's head poised to strike. On
the other was a baleful green eye.

An eye. How auspicious. How appropriate.

Grimm laughed.

Did Jaq's hooded monocle lend him a foppish rather than a
sinister appearance? "If being wise," he drawled, "getting out of
my way."

"Your way ending here," was the reply, "unless that woman
accompanying us for sale in Mahabbat." The speaker had been
chewing blood-nuts. He spat a scarlet splash into the dust.

"If being wise," warned Jaq again.

Another man waggled his sword. "Being blind in *both* eyes?"
he enquired.

The first man had tired of dialogue. He fired his stub gun at
Jaq's chest, that being the broadest target.

Under Jaq's punctured robe his mesh armour had stiffened instantly, absorbing and spreading the impact. Compared with a hit
from an explosive bolt the blow had been almost trivial. The
squashed bullet fell at Jaq's feet.

Another slug hit Jaq as he drew his laspistol and fired. The erupting energy packet threw the gunman backwards. The other dumbfounded gunman fell to a shot from Grimm. Snakeblade turned tail, and was hit in the back. One remained: the man with the eyeblade.

"Not moving! Or lasering your legs!"

And thus becoming a cripple . . .

For a moment the man glared at Rakel as if he was tempted to hurl his sword at her to deny the silk-clad woman to the rich trespasser, or at least to deface her.

"Dropping your sword!" bellowed Jaq.

The man complied. Kneeling, he babbled for mercy.

Grimm moved behind the fellow. He knelt on his calves to pin him. He clamped the man's wrists behind his back. Then he shut his own eyes as if it were the Squat who awaited execution.

Jaq knelt in the rubbish-strewn dust in front of the captive. One-eyed, Jaq stared at the shivering subject of their experiment.

At this stage Jaq did not intend to look through the lens which had been Azul Petrov's warp-eye. Such an extremity must be reserved for a time when, possessed, he must gape at himself in a mirror and either purge a daemon from his mind, or else die in the effort. He simply flipped up the front cover. Of course the captive stared to see what such a cover had been hiding.

A gurgling arose from deep in the man. It was as if his very soul was being heaved loose from somewhere in his belly — along with all the breath from his lungs. The man's eyes bulged, haemorrhaging pinkly. A death-rattle choked into silence as he swallowed his tongue. His face became puce. His scrawny frame spasmed.

Jaq lowered the lid over the lens. He removed the monocle and slipped it inside his robe.

"You can look again, Grimm."

Grimm released the man's wrists, and the body fell forward. Then Grimm picked up the eye-blade and thumped it into the dying man's back, almost up to the hilt.

"Looks more natural this way." The little man nodded towards a small knot of spectators further along the alley.

They departed from Bellygunge without hindrance. Jaq no longer linked with Rakel. Yet she still walked alongside him. The blue gown she wore must be hateful to a thief. It was so revealing.

"Tod Zapasnik the magician," she muttered.

"You know very well," he said sharply, "that it was merely the nucleus of a Navigator's warp-eye which killed the man."

"Merely," she echoed. She shivered despite her tight thermals. "What sort of *merely* will there be when we go to Mahabbat where I would have been sold by those ruffians?"

"Listen, Meh'lindi," he told her, "*we* shan't be participating in the debauch."

He realized how he had addressed Rakel. His expression anguished, he strode on in silence.

To travel to the Mahabbat district, they had hired a limousine. Security men in cheap grey flak armour mingled with the crowds outside the pleasure houses, of gambling and gourmandizing and lust and drugs. Illuminated signs flashed.

> COMING TO MAHABBAT, COMING TO DELIGHT!
> HYGIENIC EUNUCHS HERE!
> JOY-JUICE JUST FIFTY SHEKELS A JAG!
> WINNING A MILLION!
> HAVING SPECIAL NEEDS?
> HEAVENLY HUSSIES!

Copper-skinned, with piercing blue eyes and hooked noses, those security men all seemed to hail from the same clan or tribe. None were particularly young. All wore their black hair gathered up in a topknot, like a big shiny button upon their crowns.

"Armour looks like a job-lot of cast-offs from the Imperial Guard," opined Grimm.

Sabulorb, of course, contributed its tithe of a regiment of its best fighters to the Imperium: specialists, in this case, in cold desert war. The Sabulorb Regiment would be elsewhere in the cosmos. These men must have served their term of duty and returned to their home world. The branch-office of the Departmento Munitorum which supervised recruiting wasn't here in the capital but on another, harsher continent to the north. There in the north was the main base for the planetary army, which Lord Badshah preferred to keep well away from the capital. In case of emergency, troops could be airlifted to reinforce the garrison in Shandabar. Meanwhile the bulk of the army suppressed various recalcitrant warring tribes, and press-ganged new soldiery, the best of whom would be sent off-world.

The private patrolmen toted autoguns but they smiled at passing patrons. They smiled at Jaq's party when the four alighted from that limousine with tinted windows. Evidently interstellar experiences had accustomed these former Imperial Guardsmen to the sophisticated pleasures of a city, although none of them could have been soft men to have survived their military years.

The domed edifice to which the Shuturban brothers had invited Rakel and her sponsor was known as The House of Ecstasy. A fat gold-braided flunkey escorted the visitors into the main chamber. Erotic holographs shimmered languidly amidst the clientele seated at drinks-dispensing tables. Upon a central dais male and female acrobats performed suggestively. The air was heady with musk and patchouli.

Through this main chamber they passed, onward to the Sensuality Suite, which was reserved for special guests and private parties.

The floor of this suite was of rosy velvet padding, cushioned and supple. Soft low couches bulged, as much a part of the floor as a bosom is of the anatomy. Upon these velvet bosoms there lolled some fifty expectant pleasure-seekers dressed in multicoloured silks. Most were men of middle years. A few were mature women. Lighting was dim and rosy. A nymphette whose limbs and torso were painted with black spirals circulated, carrying a luminous tray of inhalants. Each step she took across the flexible floor made her body seem to pulse, spring-like.

"Please be discarding shoes and boots, good Sirs—"

Lex had no boots to remove. How different this sybaritic den was from the plasteel decks of a fortress-monastery.

How different, save for the crepuscular lighting, from the funereal interior of Jaq's lost *Tormentum Malorum*.

"Didn't wash me feet," mumbled Grimm, embarrassed, as he hauled off his big combat boots.

"Ah," breathed Rakel, "there are the Shuturbans—"

Two men arose from a soft divan. Both had curly dark hair, broad brows, large liquid eyes, snub noses and gleaming grins. Several teeth were of gold. Extravagant moustaches separated grins from the bantam noses.

"Chor's the stouter one." The sly one. On Chor's right cheek was a tattoo of a camelopard which seemed to trot on the spot whenever he flexed his facial muscles.

His quick-tempered brother sported a scar on his right cheek. Sewn to the scar was a large deep-red fire-garnet. This carbuncle seemed like a permanent eruption of lava from within him.

"Be relaxing with us," invited Chor.

Jaq and the giant and the dwarf and the thief-lady in her blue silks were soon ensconced in a half-circle of supple divans, along with the two Shuturbans. On behalf of his party Jaq refused inhalants from the springy nymphette. Lex restricted any responses to gutter-grunts. Grimm eyed the nymphette derisively. No girth to her!

"Robbing the Occidens temple of a sacred bone belonging to Oriens," probed Chor.

Jaq nodded dismissively towards Lex. "A bone for my mastiff to be chewing on. We were testing Rakel's skills."

"She being quite altered from when we were first knowing her."

"Home world being planet of shape-shifters."

"So she was telling us." Chor leaned forward. "You being magician of change? Rakel asking us about transcendental alterationists."

"Those being whereabouts?"

"Identity still being whelmed in mystery, Sir Tod."

"A fine ruby buying much information." As Jaq glanced at the garnet on Mardal Shuturban's cheek, a surge of fury seemed to course through the brother. Did Mardal suppose that Jaq was comparing the garnet unfavourably with a ruby? The brother seized a bulb of inhalant from the passing nymphette and crushed it under his nostril, breathing deep.

"Coming here to be relaxing," Mardal remarked. "Discharging tensions."

Chor probed some more. Jaq riposted. Chor waggled a ringed finger. Upon the ring, like a signet stamp, was a half-shekel-size data disc. Evidently the plans of the Courthouse were recorded in that disc. Before surrendering the ring Chor wanted to know more. Yet he seemed in no great hurry.

A door irised open—and the waiting hedonists sighed as an attendant pushed a balloon-wheeled cage into the chamber.

Squatting in the cage was a blind mutant woman. As the contraption rolled forward on to the springy floor, she clutched the bars to steady herself. Her body was scaly. Its texture was that of the mesh-armour which Jaq had worn again tonight. Maybe that woman was actually dressed in a tight body-stocking of lizard-skin fabric rather than her skin itself being squamous—for her white face was smooth. Hard to tell in the dim light.

Then it became evident that the woman's legs were fused together below her hips. Snakelike they curled and tapered around her, seemingly made only of muscle without bone. Her eyes were balls of boiled albumen—very like an Astropath's who had undergone soul-binding! Glittering bangles adorned her arms.

"Lamia, Lamia!" the clientele greeted her.

Why was she caged? So that she should not squirm out amongst them? So that the clientele should not invade her personal space? So that she might keep a grip on herself, assisted by bars? What was her role?

She swayed to and fro hypnotically.

The mutant woman must project erotic illusions into people's minds! Was this how she had escaped being smothered at birth when her worm-body emerged? By seducing her parents she had survived . . . Was this also how she had escaped being killed by neighbours or priests or mutant-hunters? When she grew to adolescence, had she actually been acquired for astropathic training despite her deformity? Had she even been soul-bound, resulting in her loss of eyesight and enhancement of her telepathic talent?

Jaq strove to imagine her functioning as a regular Astropath, transmitting and receiving coded messages or streams of commercial data.

Compelled from her earliest moments to sway minds sensually in order to survive—yet with physical gratification forever denied her by the frustrating fusion of her legs—what a powerhouse of libido she must be!

"Lamia being here," the snake-woman called out in a sinuous and caressing voice. "Letting all your secret desires loose. Becoming tangible to your nerves."

Oh, she was no caged and exploited freak, this snake-woman! Not at all. She was a veritable madame, a queen bawd of the inner sanctum of The House of Ecstasy.

"That's Bhati Badshah over there," confided Chor with a nod at a lascivious-looking fellow sporting large hooped silver ear-rings. Dangling gymnastically from those hoops, one could just make out miniature nude manikins of a shining iridescent icy blue—

crafted of titanium, no doubt. "One of our Lord Governor's nephews . . ."

High society indeed!

This was not to be the debauch which Jaq had expected. It was to be a mind-debauch. To refrain from participating might not prove so easy at all. Jaq could resist the snake-woman's sendings psychically—if he chose to. What of Grimm, or Lex, or Rakel?

Already, the sexual séance was beginning. Under Jaq's clothing fingers seemed to rove over his flesh, caressing him. It mattered not that he wore a corset of mesh-armour. Those immaterial fingers were not deterred. How did they know so cleverly which nerves to tease and stimulate? Why, because he himself knew. He had been touched thus by Meh'lindi, trained courtesan that she was—as well as Assassin.

Was it Meh'lindi who was now communicating dumbly with him from beyond the grave—in a tactile wordless language, imperative and enchanting? Was her succubus hovering only a membrane away from him? Would total surrender to her embrace drag her closer to existence once more?

Or could this open the way to possession by a daemon of lust? Aye, right here and now. Jaq had seen Vitali Googol succumb to Slaaneshi possession. Jaq had been within the doomed Navigator's aura when a daemonette ravished Vitali. Oh to become possessed right here, raging with lust—and yet somehow to stagger to a mirror, to pull the eye-lens from within his robe, to uncap it, to stare his possessed self in the eye, *withering* the daemon, banishing it back into the warp! Thus to become illuminated! Might this be possible?

Phantom fingers roved all over Jaq so sweetly and tormentingly.

He began to pray in the hieratic language. *"Veni, Voluptas! Evoe, oh appetitus, concupisco lascive!"* Such a prayer he had never prayed before. It was the opposite of any devout prayer to Him-on-Earth in His everlasting suffering. A summoning of lust personified.

All around him, celebrants in this obscene rite were moaning. Most were oblivious to one another. Several had rolled over and were writhing upon velvet couch or soft velvet floor. Others lay back, panting as imaginary bodies of delight conjoined with them.

Dimly Jaq understood that the snake-woman in her self-appointed cage was soaking up the feedback of fevered fantastical sensations. The cage served to restrain her from squirming forth futilely amidst the wallowing bodies, losing control of her own psychoerotic energy. If this were to happen, daemons of lust might very well heed. They might speed here to this beacon. They could displace the succubi of one's own imagination with materializing daemonic forms, given substance by the conversion of that energy. *Jaq was on the very verge of invoking this, as he extended his psi sense in monstrous invitation.*

Rakel was squirming in her own delirium.

Grimm was gasping, "Grizzle, Grizzle!" That dead wife of Grimm's must have been genuine, after all . . .

Lex's left hand was slapping his face violently. His lips resolutely framed the name: *Rogal Dorn!*

Mardal Shuturban was grinning and drooling with joyous abandon. His brother Chor was still alert.

Of a sudden Lamia shrieked out:

"One is here who has known no woman ever since he was transformed into a superhuman! Another is here who lusts for a Lady of Death—"

How Chor Shuturban harked to Lamia.

Aspects of the Chaos God of Lust were gathering. They were on the verge of seizing a channel—and of manifesting in the flesh. In Jaq's flesh? Or in someone else's?

Wretched sanity clawed Jaq back from the brink. Resisting the immaterial fingers, he drew the force rod from within his robe. Too late.

Within her cage Lamia reared. She mewed loudly and lewdly. The snake-woman was being possessed! Because Jaq had resisted, the powers of Chaos were entering the vortex of Lamia's psychoerotic energy.

Sighs of ecstasy were changing pitch to cries of painful pleasure as if sharp fingernails were raking bodies now.

Lex was shaking Rakel like a rag doll to restore her senses. Then he belaboured Grimm, sufficient to bruise though not to break bones.

Lines of blood appeared upon the silks of the pleasure-seekers, as unseen razor-claws stimulated their bodies with a delicious perversity. Blood was beginning to soak silk and velvet.

The garnet of Mardal Shuturban's cheek was aglow. Passions

overwhelmed him. In a paroxysm he launched himself at his
other self—at Chor. Mardal's thumbs pressed Chor's eyeballs inwards penetratingly. Chor screamed in agony, too devastated by
pain to know how to resist. Mardal was frothing at the mouth. He
kissed his brother in a crescendo of vile rapture. His thumbs were
pressing harder, to break through into the brain, into the ultimate
communion with another.

Lamia was about to burst from her cage—to try to walk upright
upon her mutant tail.

Lex seized Chor's flailing hand. He failed to pull the ring loose.
Unwilling to snap off the data-disc in case he damaged it, Lex
bowed his head over Chor's hand. When Lex raised his head
moments later, Chor was lacking a finger. Lex had bitten off
finger and ring. They were inside his mouth, for safe keeping.
Chor's mutilated hand was limp. Chor was dead by now, or had
been reduced to imbecility by the squashing of brain tissue. Mardal roared, enraged. His thumbs were trapped in the bony bloody
orbits of his brother's skull.

Summoning heartfelt revulsion, Jaq discharged his force rod at
the cage. Energies coruscated. A wild flashing of lurid rays illuminated the velvet chamber and jerking bodies stroboscopically. A
caul of jagged lightning surrounded Lamia. Then it imploded inwards to swallow itself, and her soul.

Rushing shapes of light remained loose in the padded chamber.
Bright dancing silhouettes!

Jaq discharged his rod again, more weakly. Lex was hauling
Rakel and Grimm, one in each hand like marionettes. The motion
he imparted taught them to stagger, then to regain use of their
limbs.

The main door had opened. The same gold-braided flunkey
gaped disbelievingly into the Sensuality Suite. Sprawling moaning bloodstained bodies seemed to be proof of attempted
massacre rather than massage. A glowing silhouette rushed at
him. The flunkey shrieked alarm.

The silhouette popped out of existence.

As Jaq and Lex—still lugging wobbly Grimm and Rakel—burst
past the flunkey into the main chamber, silhouettes followed
them. As moths to candle-flames the silhouettes flew towards the
posturing erotic holograms. The holograms altered. Eyes were
slanted and swollen and green. From gorgeous rumps barbed
tails sprouted.

Panic erupted. Tables overturned. A klaxon began to shriek.

This alarm quickly brought a pair of the copper-skinned security men with those big black buttons of oiled hair on their craniums.

Such a mêlée there was in The House of Ecstasy! Such horror at the floor-show! Leaping on to tables, and bellowing, "Down, down!" the ex-Guardsmen aimed their autoguns at the hideously mutated holograms. Jaq and party ducked behind a larger-than-lifesize nude female figure of solid white marble. The high-velocity shells passed straight through the holograms, impacting in walls, and in the bodies of the clientele. Chips flew off of the marble giantess as a couple of shells caroomed off the statue.

The live acrobats had ceased their act. Were they not part of the floor-show, which had so terrified the clientele? Shells killed several of the acrobats—even as the fearful holograms were winking out of existence one by one.

On the way back to their mansion in the limousine Lex spat out the finger from his mouth. They were separated from the driver by a privacy screen, and insulated fragilely from Shandabar by smoked glass.

Rakel had recovered her voice.

"That could be a Finger of Glory," she declared, "if Tod's a true magician—"

"*I am not that*," snarled Jaq. He had rejected the opportunity which came so terribly close and so unexpectedly.

"Hey, what's a Finger of Glory?" asked Grimm.

"It's a finger from someone who died abominably," she said. "You pickle it during suitable invocations. You dry it. If later you light it, it'll show your way and at the same time hide your presence—until it burns out."

"Just the ticket," said Grimm, "for breaking into a Courthouse."

"Superstition," snarled Lex. He half-closed his left fist, and whispered into it, "Biff and Yeremi, you aided me back there. I bless your names; and Rogal Dorn's . . ."

"Not a superstition," murmured Jaq. "A morsel of effective daemonry. So I believe."

"There is only one Glory," Lex affirmed, "and that is the Column of Glory in His palace on Earth." There, where the skulls of long-dead Imperial Fists grinned from their shattered armour embedded nobly in a tower half a kilometre high.

"I'll need new boots specially made for me, damn it," said Grimm. For he and Jaq and Rakel were still as barefoot as Lex.

All four were shaken by what had happened in The House of Ecstasy. Morale required a feast from Grimm. Fine foods such as imported Grox tongues should be accompanied by the best local *djinn*, and strong ale.

Initially, it was Grimm who mainly indulged in the *djinn*. Rakel followed his lead. Would the real Meh'lindi ever have allowed herself to become intoxicated, as Rakel was becoming? Jaq sipped, since he had sanctioned this indulgence. Lex also drank the fiery spirit ceremonially, to be detoxed by his special organs.

Presently Grimm, well in his cups, began to hiccup.

"Oh Ancestors—*hic*—I think it's me name day today. Oh well—*haec*—if it ain't today it must be sometime—"

"Remember your *body*," Lex reproved him.

The little man bridled. "Is your body a temple of glory? Well—*hoc*—in that case mine's a hog-pen. Who cares? When there's havoc, a hog-pen can often outlast a temple." Grimm raised his glass. "Here's to you, Lex, in yer temple! Here's to the Sons of the Emperor, wherever they may be, assuming—*hic*—they're anywhere. Here's to them conniving Illuminati. Here's to you, Boss!"

Abruptly Jaq seized a flagon of ale—and drank, and drank, to disorder his senses. He swigged from the bottle of *djinn*.

Seated there in the black-curtained dining room, Jaq swayed. Was arcane energy still hovering nearby? Did his vision swim as he gazed at the false Meh'lindi? To Rakel he said bluntly: "Come to my room now." With him he took the amputated finger.

What rite did he perform with Rakel—known only to Secret Inquisitors who had plumbed depths of perversion by proxy during their investigations of evil?

When both returned later, Rakel was white-faced and trembling. Jaq was sweaty and feverish. Grimm snored by now, his head resting on the table. Lex sat with the waxed thigh-bone before him, as if that were indeed the remains of a mastiff's meal. He was polishing the bone meticulously.

"Lust—or Change?" Jaq asked aloud, of the very air. He brandished the finger, now bereft of ring and data-disc. The finger had become stiff and leathery.

"Behold a Finger of Glory! A lumen for my mock-Meh'lindi thief, whose body is willing—though her soul evades me! Perhaps I'm becoming a Magus without recourse to Slaanesh or to Tzeentch . . ."

Grimly Lex polished.

After a while the Marine said to Jaq, "If you become insane, My Lord Inquisitor, despite my vow I may need to kill you."

Jaq swept an empty bottle of *djinn* from the table. The bottle shattered upon the black slate floor. Even this crash did not wake Grimm.

"Killing me," said Jaq, "might be righteous, yet it would ruin all hope."

"Perhaps it would. Use that corpse's finger as you please. My own fingers revere this bone."

Rakel listened numbly.

Chapter Eight

Courthouse

Jaq felt tainted and psychotic as he waited with Lex and Grimm in that same warehouse of saddles and bridles near the Courthouse. The rear door had been reinforced with a wooden bar. Lex had easily broken the bar. Tumbled racks had been restored to an upright position. Purity tassels had been fastened to them, which the trio ignored. Now that all pilgrims had departed from Sabulorb, the rear alley was forsaken but for charred dog bones which rats had gnawed. Here in the warehouse was the rendezvous point for Rakel—who trod alone, right now, inside the Courthouse.

As lookout, Grimm had watched Rakel commence her entry by way of a locked manhole cover giving access to a dry sewer which had been wrongly positioned during the long process of construction. Now she was alone amidst hundreds of servants and clerks and detectives and Arbitrators and Marshalls and Judges.

Filth clung to Jaq's soul. The taint of betrayal—of himself, of the devout Marine Captain, of the memory of Meh'lindi, most of all, of Him-on-Earth. Nevertheless, under the film of gathering psychic scum was his soul not still pure and intent on the light? Was it not through transmutation of foulness that he must aspire to a potent alchemy? Such sensations—and worse—he must endure, without provoking Lex to execute him.

A line from an old song in the creole dialect of a world Jaq had once helped cleanse came back to him: *Two madonna taboo, eh, Johnny Fedelor!*

'Eh, faithful Johnny, Johnny Fidelis, to admire two Ladies is forbidden!' was the translation he had been told. There could not be a pretend Meh'lindi and a real Meh'lindi. Might embracing the pretend Meh'lindi ritually invoke the real Meh'lindi—or exclude her?

Surely such musings were the stuff of psychosis.

Psychosis might be the instrument of enlightenment.

"What you humming, Boss?" asked Grimm.

"Nothing, Abhuman!"

"Huh, my ears deceive me. Say, while we're waiting shall I recite one of the shorter Squattish ballads?"

"If Rakel takes as long as that," Jaq said dourly, "she has either been caught or else she's dead."

"Regard my ballad as a thief-timer. Like an egg-timer. When it runs out, we'd better bugger off. And don't tell me that we'll go into a Courthouse after Rakel! I shan't do it, boss. The temple was another matter . . .

"Actually there's a *Ballad of the Boot*, about a roguish Squat freebooter who tramped all over the galaxy in his pirate merchant ship." Grimm hoisted a bare dirty foot, and tore at it vigorously with a horny fingernail. He peeled off grime and hard skin. A new pair of custom-made boots had been ordered. They would take a week. Once sewn, they needed to be battered and distressed for comfort, otherwise they would give him corns.

"Two madonna taboo, eh, Johnny Fedelor?" whispered Jaq.

"*Eh?* Is that some kinda invocation, Magus?"

Jaq's skin crawled. "*Esto quietus, Loquax!*" he ordered. "I must meditate."

"Likewise," Lex told the little man sternly.

It was two hours before Rakel joined them. When she did so, Jaq's heart skipped a beat. His Meh'lindi was suddenly amidst them as if from out of nowhere—as though she had materialized at that moment from out of the sea of lost souls.

"I succeeded," she said.

Between two fingertips of her left hand Rakel was holding up what seemed to be a data-disc. No: it was a greasy wafer from which a last wisp of smoke arose. It was the final residue of Chor Shuturban's Finger of Glory, now consumed entirely. It was which had hidden her coming into the warehouse—even from Jaq's psychic sense, even from Lex's special ears.

In Rakel's other hand dangled a heavy satchel.

Black-clad and black-faced, with two lethal rings on her fingers, Rakel had entered the Courthouse dungeons. Infrequent electro-lumens glowed redly like hot pokers in the prevailing darkness. Softly she had padded, hearing distant groans—then laughter from a guardroom. Its plasteel door was ajar, outlined by light from within. She bypassed this place and mounted stone stairs to a higher subterranean level, a maze of storerooms; then she mounted again . . .

She had spent hours at the mansion studying on screen the layout of the Courthouse—multi-level, labyrinthine, a dense and complex fortress-municipality. Otherwise she would surely have become hopelessly lost—as lost as a legal case in a great archive.

Rakel avoided internal courtyards. She favoured dark corri-dors. She was darkness embodied, slinking from darkness to darkness. As she climbed higher, baroque glowglobes were alight, and there was more nocturnal activity. In vaulted scripto-ria, clerks were scrutinizing scrolling screens and scribing. Although this Courthouse was only decades old, great mounds of documents had already been generated—as if the place was a vast rich nutrient tank wherein data-bacteria multiplied exponentially without any necessary reference to what lay beyond its confines; where, perhaps, different strains of bacteria contended for supremacy, corresponding to the varying opinions of Judges in their high chambers.

Night-ushers prowled with sheafs of print-out. Cyborged servi-tors trundled. These sucked up dust and fallen documents. Slow ceiling-fans, resembling rotating brass pterosaurs, stirred papers into motion, to escape from desks. Were it not for the fans, stale air might accumulate in suffocating pockets. Grilles protected weaponry and ceremonial whips and maces.

Just as truth emerges from perplexing obscurity, increasingly there was illumination. Now Rakel's black garb would betray her. She resorted to the Finger of Glory. She lit its tip with an igniter. Soft shimmery flame fluttered. She allowed herself to be seen—but she was not seen.

As she traversed arcades and galleries, so the finger consumed itself, burning down to the middle phalanx.

A dark-clad Arbitrator emerged from a side corridor. Armed

with a lasgun, he blocked her way. In his mirrored visor she saw
the flame of the finger flickering. The Arbitrator was puzzled. He
couldn't make out Rakel as she stood silently, holding her breath.
Some polarization of light must be letting him see the finger-flame
which she held, as if a luminous moth were hovering in mid-air.

"What's there?" came his voice. He spoke in standard Imperial
Gothic, being within an imperial Courthouse, and being very
likely of off-world origin. The Arbitrator shook his head as if to
dislodge the intrusive image. "Where are you, Corvo?" he called
out. "There's a flaw in this visor. You usually use this helmet,
don't you?"

The colleague named Corvo did not seem to be nearby.

The Arbitrator removed a hand from the lasgun, so that its barrel dipped. He raised his hand to his visor and lifted upward. A
thin intense face appeared. Twin pendants dangled from the
man's nostrils, like hardened plugs of mucus. Probably those
were gas filters. Frowning, he stared directly at Rakel.

Rakel's lungs were bursting. She simply had to breathe out. At
the sigh of her breath the gun jerked upward, awkward in a
single hand.

Rakel crooked a finger. She had remembered aright this time.
The toxic needle hit the Arbitrator in the cheek.

He was convulsing. Darting forward, she caught the lasgun as
it fell. The Arbitrator toppled against her. Her sudden rush had
extinguished the finger. In his few last seconds of horrified lucidity, the Arbitrator may have glimpsed Rakel's eyes, in her
blackened face, emerging out of nothingness like some predator
from the sea of souls, to snatch him.

His body spasmed against her as if experiencing some perverse
counterpart of ecstasy. His helmet was slipping. She must drop
the finger to catch the helmet. Lasgun in one hand, helmet in the
other, Rakel let herself sink to the floor to break the Arbitrator's
dying fall. How he writhed upon her, until suddenly he became
limp.

She extricated herself. Found the candle-finger. Dragged the
corpse into an alcove. Stripped him of his black uniform. She
dressed herself in that, and donned the mirror-helmet. The remaining portion of finger and the igniter, she slipped into a
pocket . . .

The data-store she sought was near to a Judge's chambers.

Carved doors to the chambers stood open. Fruitily scented oil-lamps burned in a vestibule panelled in intricate mosaics of dark marble spelling out ancient legal judgements.

The thick plasteel door of the data-store was open too. Light spilled forth. She tiptoed.

The store wasn't large. No towering iron shelves of tomes, such as Rakel had already glimpsed elsewhere, nor ladders nor gantries. Instead, there was one enormous central book taller than herself and mounted on a turntable. Its sail-size pages of stiff plastic fanned open through three-quarters of a circle. Like so many words upon those pages hundreds of discs were mounted in lines and columns above reference codes.

A silk-clad clerk was turning a page, seeking for a disc. The clerk was singularly tall and thin, as though he'd been stretched on a rack to assist his clerical duties, or bred for height and reach. His long thin arms were those of some spider-crab.

The clerk searched on behalf of a burly figure in gorgeously trimmed ermine robes and a towering black turban. This dignitary's eyes bulged behind incongruously small silver spectacles, betokening minute attention. A collar of goitres, lapped by fine fur, swelled the Judge's neck. His head seemed but the summit of a veritable mountain, snow-clad below, capped with volcanic soot. He was fiddling with a metal rod around the end of which a blue energy field flickered. That was his power maul, with which he could clout a malefactor insensible, or on a higher setting smash through a wall.

As the supposed Arbitrator entered, the Judge smiled at the image of himself and his power mirrored in the visor.

"Ah, Kastor, you find me still here—" This Judge must have been expecting an Arbitrator of that name to visit him in his chambers.

Respectfully Rakel inclined her head and helmet.

"You're early, Kastor. So hurry up, Drork," the Judge said to the clerk. He flourished the maul. "Surely the disc cannot have been misfiled!"

"Surely not by me, my Lord," replied the skeletal Drork, "since to the best of my recollection it has never been called for during the whole of my indenture. Misfiled by my predecessor, perhaps." Apparently there was a certain informality and mutual understanding between this clerk and the Judge.

"Alien lingo disc for a hypno-casque," the Judge explained to the false Arbitrator. "I've finally been able to appoint you a Marshall of the Court, my trusty Kastor."

Rakel inclined her head even more lavishly. If only the Judge did not demand a verbal response. If only she were able to ask about this lingo disc!

The energy field of the maul faded into virtual invisibility. Thoughtfully the Judge rubbed a great goitre with the tip of the maul, massaging his deformity.

"I appreciate your reticence, Kastor! I want you to form a small discreet team. Three other Arbitrators and yourself should suffice. Yesterday our Astropath received a bulletin—which I alone am privy to as yet. Several bizarrely-clad aliens landed on planet Lekkerbek, purporting to be itinerant entertainers. Members of the Eldar race. Such clowns also appeared on Nero Nine. Likewise on Planet Karesh—without any obvious means of transport there. Doubtless they hid their ship somewhere in the wilds. On Karesh a fracas occurred, resulting in the death of two of the trio of aliens. The third alien vanished. In case a similar visitation occurs here on Sabulorb, I wish you and your team to be ready to arrest and interrogate these aliens in their own tongue—"

"Ah," said Drork, "here is the disc in question." The clerk plucked the coin-like data-disc from a towering plastic page.

"Take it and use it, Kastor."

Rakel inclined her head obediently. She accepted the disc from Drork and secreted it within her stolen uniform.

How soon would the real Kastor be arriving? Had not the Inquisitor said that she should conduct herself as an Assassin, as well as a thief, here in the heart of the Courthouse?

The Judge continued to rub at his great goitres with his inactive maul. "If fortune blesses us, I shall be in the ascendancy amongst my learned colleagues. Tell me, Marshall Kastor—"

Tell him? That was an impossible demand! Instantly Rakel raised the lasgun and fired at that fur-clad mountain of a man. Even as the blast erupted against the Judge, his hand was activating the maul. Blue energy raged—and promptly died away again. Sidelong he collapsed upon the floor.

Her second shot threw Drork backward against the book of discs. The turntable spun. Two tall plastic pages clapped together, trapping the dying clerk between them.

"Your Honour!" A call came from along the corridor. That must be Kastor now.

Try to shoot him too? Noises may have forewarned him. She laid down the lasgun. Pulled out the stump of finger. The igniter flared.

Kastor was still lingering near that fruity-scented vestibule, lasgun at the ready. When Rakel rushed past him unseen he must have felt the displacement of air. What could account for this sudden breeze?

"Your Honour!" she heard him call again.

She was running away as quietly as she could.

Soon Kastor would enter the data-room and discover his Judge dead—inexplicably dead—and the clerk too. Now no one remained to explain anything about Eldar aliens, unless the Courthouse Astropath was questioned. Fearing for his or her own skin, the Astropath might deny all knowledge. He or she had divulged that bulletin only to the Judge who had now been assassinated. The perpetrator of the murder might be some rival Judge . . .

Rakel paused to extinguish the Finger of Glory. Chor's finger had burned down as far as the proximal phalanx. She proceeded onward as a mirror-masked Arbitrator with an urgent errand to attend to—and a perfect right to be in any part of the Courthouse. She would need to light the finger again, closer to the dungeons where she would discard her stolen costume. She was determined to retain a little stub of the metacarpal part of the finger with which to surprise the Inquisitor and his giant and his dwarf.

Let them respect her. Thus might she continue living. Thus Jaq Draco might accept her as an adequate substitute for the dead woman who inflamed his soul as a venomous thorn inflames flesh.

"What's in the satchel?" asked Grimm. "The head of a Judge?"

"No," said Rakel. "But I did assassinate one, as instructed." She opened the satchel. "I came across *these* in an armoury while I was making my escape."

Clips of explosive bolts! Well over a dozen clips! Enough for Emperor's Peace *and* Emperor's Mercy *and Lex's bolt gun to utter their opinions many times over.*

Reverently Lex reached into the satchel, took out a clip, and kissed it—almost as if bestowing a kiss upon Rakel.

"I did right, didn't I? This theft should confuse the Courthouse doubly—these being relics here, and a relic being stolen from Occidens too." Her speech was fluctuating between standard Gothic and Sabulorb dialect. After her exploit she was tired.

Had the real Meh'lindi ever betrayed fatigue?

"Tell me everything quickly now," Jaq said, "in case some accident happens to you. Give me a fast summary."

Rakel hastily related about the Judge and the clerk and the disc and the astropathic bulletin.

"You performed well," Jaq praised her. "After we return home I must reinforce your image with that special Tarot card, and with psychic pressure. You shall not suffer flux."

"Pity," said Grimm, "about those Eldar snobs closing in, eh Boss? If Harlequins do come here, it might have been better if a Judge was planning to dungeon 'em."

"Not at all!" said Jaq. "If some Eldar arrive here mysteriously we'll know for sure there *is* a Webway portal hidden on Sabulorb. If they arrive by passenger merchantman, we'll know that there isn't one. If they arrive in a ship of their *own*, then the portal's on the outermost rocky planet or else on a moon of one of the local gas-giants."

Indeed. The Eldar race had never given rise to the Navigator mutation, whereby human beings were able to pilot warp-ships swiftly from star to star. The Eldar only had their Webway to rely on, and short-distance interplanetary vessels.

Perhaps Eldar seers could have engineered a Navigator gene into some of the children of their race—but the Eldar scarcely *dared* enter the warp. Their fall had given rise to Slaanesh. Slaanesh forever resonated with Eldar minds, a perpetual curse upon them, hungry to engulf the survivors. For the Eldar to journey into the warp would be to offer themselves as sacrifices. The web was their only safe channel for interstellar travel.

"Besides," added Jaq, "once I've learned the language I shall need a tutor to master the reading of the runes."

"A Harlequin chained in our cellar, persuaded to tutor you by torture?" The little man still remembered his treatment at the hands of Jaq and Meh'lindi in the engine room of *Tormentum Malorum*, before he confessed his dealings with Zephro Carnelian, who had duped him. Meh'lindi and Jaq had duped him too. Grimm's torment had been almost a hundred per cent suggestion, working upon an inflamed imagination.

Jaq said to Grimm: "I've told you that physical torture is in-efficient. There's a much better way to persuade an Eldar."

"What is it?"

"First we need to catch our Eldar—rather than them catching us. We must go now—get away from this neighbourhood!"

"Soon be red dawn," said Lex. "Soon be red day."

During the next week, Jaq's nights were spent wearing the hypno-casque. By day he practised phrases which none of the others could understand.

"*Níl ann ach cleasai, agus tá an iomad measa aige air féin,*" he would recite.

Only the real Meh'lindi would have been able to respond. Jaq's verbal exercises constituted a kind of one-sided dialogue with her departed spirit.

Only occasionally did he gloss a cryptic utterance. Rakel happened to be listening when he intoned, "*Níl ann ache cleasai . . .* ' Jaq stared at her achingly familiar yet uncomprehending face, and translated into Imperial Gothic: "The trickster thinks too much of himself. That," he commented, "will be our motto as regards Harlequins."

While Jaq studied the Eldar language, Lex began to scrimshander the thigh-bone with his silicon carbide engraving tool. In lieu of a report to his Chapter—which he must not attempt to make as yet—Lex began to engrave an image of that Chaos world where a daemon had sat fishing from a low sickle moon, and where brave Fists had died resisting the onslaught by Chaos Marines.

When Rakel happened to peruse his progress a few days later, she said accusingly, "But you're picturing nightmares!"

Was she herself suffering nightmares?

"Nay," he said, "I am picturing reality. Or rather, I picture a hideous *unreality* which nonetheless exists. You should not look upon such things. Those who behold such sights merit mind-wiping."

"Mind-wiping?" she echoed. "In that case I shall never look at your art again." She had fled from the room.

No, she should not look at his etchings. Next, he intended to picture Meh'lindi speared to death by the terrible Phoenix Lady in the Webway.

After much minute attention to the details of the Chaos world, Lex strolled into the garden to rest his eyes.

Grimm was staring at the huge red sun.

"It's warmer today," said the Squat. "Warmer than it's been since we arrived here on Sab. Can't you feel it on your bare skin?"

Lex wasn't one to pay much heed to heat or cold. Besides, he'd been focusing his attention upon the fine lines wrought by the graving tool and how well those lines corresponded with appalling memories. Surprised, he agreed.

"But at the same time," said Grimm, "that ruddy sun looks, I dunno, smaller?"

Lex mused a while: "As I recall," he said, "that vast red orb is actually the outer atmosphere of the sun expanded across hundreds of millions of kilometres. Deep within, hidden from our eyes, will be a white-hot core, a dwarf core. By the time the radiance of that core reaches the extremities, the temperature is only that of an iron poker in a fire." His brow furrowed. "I've heard that the radiation output of white dwarfs can fluctuate. This is to do with the alchemy of elements." He regarded Grimm sardonically. "A dwarf can be unstable."

The little man scratched his head under his forage cap. "Maybe we're in for a heatwave, eh?"

"We must hope not! Who knows what the upper limit of a heatwave might be?"

"Don't you try to scare me, you big lunk. This world has harboured life for aeons."

"Aeons are merely seconds on the clock of time."

"I'm aware of that!"

"Maybe a relatively minor shock might be enough to destabilize the white dwarf core. A warp-storm occurring locally. Even a warp-ship materializing accidentally within the star and disrupting the fabric of space before evaporating."

"Thanks for the reassurance."

"The cosmos does not exist for our benefit, little man, any more than a dog exists so as to harbour fleas. The fleas may think so, but they are wrong. Heroism is to accept this fact yet continue to strive in the Emperor's name."

"Do you *know* His name, by the way?"

Lex flexed a fist warningly.

"No one knows His name by now," came Jaq's voice in reply. Jaq too had stepped out into the garden. "Nor can He possibly know His own name after so many millennia of transcendent anguish and cosmic overwatch. *Bíonn an fear ciallmar ina thost nuair ná bíonn pioc le rá aige,"* he recited enigmatically in Eldar, and strode forth through the shrubbery.

Chapter Nine

Jester

A few weeks later, Rakel brought word about a trio of amazing new performers who were drawing audiences to a theatre in the Mahabbat district.

Two of these acrobatic artistes were clad in kaleidoscopic motley, the hues of which changed from moment to moment. These artistes also wore holo-masks which could display a whole gamut of personae. In repose, the faces which these masks displayed were affably human. No one ever saw their actual faces of flesh and blood behind the masks.

The third member of their tiny troupe wore a skull-mask. White bones decorated his black costume. What a grin that skull exhibited! How frolicsome its wearer could be. He was the one who spoke Imperial Gothic, though not the dialect of Sabulorb itself. Much could be accomplished by mime. What fine mimes his companions were.

"Everyone seems to assume they're human," recounted Rakel. "Bit tall, maybe. But with arms and legs and heads in the right places."

These exotic artistes had arrived in Shandabar by camelopard caravan from the city of Bara Bandobast across the Grey Desert. They must belong to some nomad tribe.

Rakel's informant about these performers was Mardal Shuturban. The man was still ravaged by the fratricide of his brother. His thumbs bore scars where he had finally torn them free from the

bones of Chor's skull. Mardal believed that by wizardry 'Tod
Zapasnik' had saved himself and Mardal too from death during
the delirium in the Sensuality Suite. Sly brother Chor had hoped
that the snake-woman would snoop upon Zapasnik's mind. The
plan had gone unimaginably wrong. What did it matter if Chor's
finger had been bitten off impatiently? Compared with what Mardal had done to his brother's eyes and frontal lobes, a finger was a
trivial matter.

Mardal had babbled impetuously to Rakel. He was deeply dis-
turbed by his experience. At the same time, a criminal could not
afford to convalesce. Mardal had seemed on the verge of propos-
ing some kind of alliance with Rakel's powerful and scary patron.

"Oh my brother, oh my brother!" he had wailed. "Oh my wise
thoughtful brother!"

Why was Rakel asking about exotic artistes on behalf of Sir
Tod? *Chor* might have had an inkling of why. Chor was dead.
Zapasnik was an enigma.

Had Rakel really entered the Courthouse? Members of the caste
of garbage collectors who were allowed limited access to bring
away toxic ashes from an incinerator had heard cooks talking
about a murdered Judge. No need for Rakel to say a word about it
unless she wished to! Ah, how hot it was right now. How one
sweated. Never before in living memory had anyone perspired so
much in Shandabar—outside of a chamber of sin in the Mahabbat
district! In the Grey Desert dust was dancing thermally.

"Oh brother mine, brother mine!"

Ah yes, those strange artistes . . . Mardal would keep watch on
them for Sir Tod; but he would do nothing impetuous.

"Obviously," Jaq said to his companions, "the Eldar Harlequins
are searching for the stolen book."

Rakel's eyes had widened at this new revelation.

"The book contains many dire secrets," he told her. "We removed it from the Black Library of the Eldar located in the
Webway which leads through the warp. Only an Inquisitor could
penetrate such a place. This is all forbidden knowledge—which
you now need to know."

"Knowledge is a curse," she said, "not a blessing."

The Harlequins must be spreading their scouting forces thin, so
as to touch as many likely worlds as possible.

Groups of Harlequins sometimes visited innocuous worlds of the Imperium to present their pageants of dance and mime. A feast for the eyes! An enigma to almost all human spectators! A troupe would generally consist of at least a hundred of the aliens—including costume-makers and operators of holo-projectors, and even the elderly and children, in addition to the core of costumed players who were also warriors. For as few as three players to visit Sabulorb implied that many similar visits were being made by other Harlequins to as many worlds as possible. Often at great risk, no doubt!

Here on Sabulorb, the Harlequins were passing themselves off as exotic masked tribesmen. The local Judges now knew nothing about the astropathic bulletin. On other worlds, too, the Eldar might pass as human beings of ethereal grace; as visitors from some luxurious imperial plant where the population knew nothing of rickets or goitres or skin diseases. The Eldar would sometimes even boldly reveal their identity as aliens, endowed with lavish funds—as they had reportedly done on Lekkerbek. On many other planets such as Karesh they must be risking their lives, and even losing them, victims of strict Judges or zealous Preachers or xenophobic mobs.

All to recover the book!

The alien trio had arrived from the direction of Bara Bandobast, not by way of Shandabar's spaceport.

Jaq gave blessings that there was indeed a Webway entry and exit somewhere at hand. He and Lex and Grimm began to form plans, which should involve Mardal Shuturban and his men.

Jaq's party now had three fully-loaded bolt guns, as well as las-pistols. Yet how rash to go unaided against three alien warrior-troubadours, particularly when one was a Death Jester. Those Death Jesters were heavy weapons specialists. Ah but this Jester could hardly have brought a shuriken shrieker cannon fitted with anti-grav suspensors into Shandabar in his gear! If the Harlequins had ridden armed jetbikes through the Webway to Sabulorb, they must have hidden those far out in the desert before joining the camelopard caravan.

A problem was that the Eldar were far more sensitively psychic than human beings. The population of Shandabar generated a mental babel, a seething slurry of emotions and half-formed images. Doubtless the Harlequins were attempting to sieve this foetid torrent for any relevant nugget (though without the least guarantee of finding any).

What might stand out from the babble, as unusual?

Turmoil at a temple, as priests and deacons of Occidens tried to discover whether the Austral temple had been responsible for the theft of the thigh-bone . . .

The mysterious assassination of a Judge . . .

A gruesome Slaaneshi manifestation at the House of Ecstasy, branded in survivors' minds: *that* should rivet the attention of any Harlequin . . . Assuming that the sensitive Eldars were able to extract such needles from the haystack of circumstances!

Mardal Shuturban might be radiating intense horror at what had happened in The House of Ecstasy. His horror might be associated with visual images of a certain wizard—a wizard who had access to priceless jewels . . .

Shuturban needed an aura of protection cast around him as soon as could be.

Either that, or kill him.

His help was needed.

The walled mansion was far enough from the Mahabbat quarter for mind-noise to drown out any direct trace of Jaq's presence. Jaq could shield his thoughts psychically. Lex had no helmet shielded with psycurium—but Lex could always intone a mantra of *Rogal Dorn, Rogal Dorn* . . . Could Jaq maintain protective auras for Grimm and Rakel, and for Shuturban too?

"Lex," said Jaq, "I want you to start up a prayer-mantra in your mind as a screen against psychic intrusion. Grimm: I want you to start reciting your longest Squattish ballad to yourself—*silently*— and don't stop. Rakel: I need to conjure protection around you. I need to embrace you with protection."

Did a moan escape her lips?

"Next," he told her, "I need you to hurry to Shuturban and tell him that his life is in danger from those performers unless I protect him psychically."

"He'll believe you're a wizard for sure, Boss," said Grimm.

"Maybe," Jaq said to the little man, "I am becoming one." Briefly a rictus twisted his face. "With your faithful help, my Squat factotum, and with yours especially, Captain d'Arquebus."

It was the first time that Rakel knew for sure that the giant was a Space Marine—an officer of the Marines.

She gasped—and Lex clenched his fist. In salute, or in reprimand? He loomed over the false Meh'lindi. His heels came together. Had he not been barefoot, those heels would have clicked.

"Lady," he said formally, "I present myself: Space Marine Captain Lexandro d'Arquebus of the Imperial Fist chapter, travelling incognito as escort for my Lord Inquisitor Jaq Draco. This fist will snap the neck of anyone who betrays my identity, or my Lord Inquisitor's."

"Yes," murmured Rakel. "I hear you." She mumbled some prayer to herself. How many terrible secrets could she tolerate?

Jaq told her: "We'll need to rendezvous with Shuturban somewhere private well away from the Mahabbat district."

"Somewhere in Bellygunge?" suggested Grimm. "Now that our bolt guns are full of ammo!"

"And empty them for no good reason?" Lex said acidly. "We can do without a commotion."

Where, then, could they rendezvous? The ruins of Oriens harboured too many beggars. That saddle warehouse might be booby-trapped by now, by its owners—and it was too close to the Courthouse.

The little man piped up: "How about the cobbler's where I got me new boots?" Grimm stamped appreciatively. The successors to his old boots indeed had a long-lived-in look to the leather. "Meeting there has no obvious rhyme or reason. So it's ideal. It's nowhere near Mahabbat. Mind you, we must turf the cobbler out first to save his skin—I'm grateful to him."

Jaq nodded. "Shuturban shall bring as many bodyguards as he pleases." He turned to Rakel, and took the Assassin card from inside his robe. "Come with me, my mock Meh'lindi, *in nomine Imperatoris*, to be clasped with protection."

Amidst iron lasts and pincers and buffing wheels, amidst stitchers and scourers and sole-cutting shears—so many bolt guns and laspistols and autoguns! The cobbler's workshop could never have seen such a gathering of hardware as was in the hands or belts or holsters of Jaq's party and of Mardal Shuturban's half dozen men.

The workshop was a long broad room, lit by electrolumens in sconces. A hundred pairs of boots and shoes hung on hooks from joists.

The fat bald proprietor, Mr Dukandar, had been evicted into the night along with his stout wife and two apprentice sons. This happened as soon as Jaq's party arrived, in advance of Shuturban and company. The Dukandars couldn't remain in their upstairs quarters in case they eavesdropped. Take a walk for a couple of hours if you know what's wise! Cool though the night air might be, for Sabulorb the temperature was almost balmy. The Dukandars wouldn't catch cold.

"We are meeting again," Mardal greeted Jaq, with sombre respect. "My life being in danger once again?"

"In dire danger from those exotic performers. Being alien psyker-warriors—"

Mardal smashed a fist into his palm.

"Yes, crushing them," agreed Jaq. "But I am absolutely requiring *one* of those aliens as my prisoner, to be questioning about how they were arriving here. Mardal Shuturban, you are reeking of recent sorcerous assault. Your intention soon becoming known to the aliens. The flavour of what was happening to you in The House of Ecstasy attracting those psykers as carrion-flies to gangrene. Needing me to be protecting you with a conjuration of concealment. And then we are striking, *swiftly*."

"A conjuration?" Sweat pimpled Shuturban's cheeks.

"So that you being immune from psychic surveillance. I shall be extending a mental shield, Mardal Shuturban. Requiring me to be reciting certain anathemas, and blessing you with this." Jaq exhibited his sleek black force rod, accumulator and booster of mind-energy.

As Jaq led a compliant Shuturban aside, amidst the pliers and rasps and sole-stitching machinery, Grimm smirked momentarily. Oh, the Boss could extend an aura of protection around a whole ship. He wouldn't use a force rod to do so. That rare ancient weapon was for blasting at daemonic manifestations. The Boss was vamping for Shuturban's benefit. Shuturban was duly impressed . . .

By now it was well over half an hour since Jaq's party had arrived at the cobbler's premises. They were about to leave together with Mardal Shuturban and company, bound for a certain theatre in Mahabbat.

From outside in the night an amplified voice reverberated:

"BEING COURTHOUSE PATROL! PREMISES BEING SUR-
ROUNDED. FOUR PERSONS WITHIN ABANDONING
WEAPONS THEN EXITING ON KNEES ONE BY ONE WITH
HANDS BEHIND HEAD! DWARF WEARER OF NEW BOOTS
BEING FIRST OF ALL!"

"Oh me Ancestors!"

Jaq rounded on Shuturban. The man mimed protestations of in-
nocence which seemed perfectly sincere.

"BE SURRENDERING PEACEFULLY FOR LAWFUL
QUESTIONING BY DETECTIVE ARBITRATOR STEIN-
MULLER!"

The boots, the boots . . . That was the fatal flaw. A unique pair
of boots had been abandoned in the ravaged Sensuality Suite of
The House of Ecstasy. Someone had reported this fact to the
Courthouse. Could have been one of the ex-Guardsmen, acting
secretly as an informer for the Courthouse. Could have been the
Lord Governor's lascivious nephew, or one of the other patrons,
infuriated at how the orgy had endangered or injured them . . .
Someone of status, who could appeal to the Courthouse to investigate.

Item: the dwarf who lost his boots had been with a giant slave
and with a robed bearded man.

Item: the bearded man had played a part in the trouble rather
than being just a victim.

Thus: find the dwarf, and discover the true facts of the case.
Proceed astutely, without letting it seem that any investigation
was under way. Therefore, amongst other procedures: visit all
cobblers throughout the city in the hope that the dwarf needed
new boots.

It must have taken Detective Arbitrator Steinmuller a while to
arrive at the plan of action. By the time a bailiff of the Courthouse
had actually visited Dukandar, Grimm had already collected his
new boots. When Grimm returned to evict Dukandar, the cobbler
had raced to the nearest unvandalized com-equipment.

Or did he even need to do so?

Dukandar would already have revealed the fact of Grimm's
earlier visit. On the off-chance that the distressed boots might
prove faulty and a grumpy customer might return, the bailiff

might have been keeping watch on the cobbler's from another building.

Now a squad was outside, and around.

"DWARF EMERGING WITHIN TEN SECONDS," came the voice. "NINE . . . EIGHT . . ."

Grimm readied *Emperor's Peace*. Jaq levelled *Emperor's Mercy*. Lex aimed his bolt gun at the door. Shuturban's men pointed autoguns and laspistols at the shuttered windows. Mardal had produced a laspistol.

When Shuturban and company arrived, the bailiff must have been occupied messaging the Courthouse. Those extra unexpected visitors had not been spotted. The Arbitrators believed there were only four miscreants inside Dukandar's place; not a dozen.

Nor could the Arbitrators know that three were armed with fully-loaded bolt guns . . .

On the count of zero, deafening explosions blasted the front facade of the cobbler's. Rubble vomited. Clouds of dust billowed. The whole of the wall and its door and shutters disintegrated. Beams and rafters sagged. Plaster from the ceiling cascaded upon tools and benches. Still sustained by side walls, the upper storey did not pancake down upon the ground floor, yet the building groaned almightily.

Those Arbitrators had fired a volley of krak grenades to open up Dukandar's premises. The explosive effect of these were entirely concentrated at the target, without collateral blast. Would the Arbitrators now be switching to choke grenades to disable those who lurked within? Or tanglefoot grenades?

"Out, out—or gettin' caught!" bellowed Lex at Shuturban's men, remembering to use scum patois. "Out, and killin'!"

With a roar he launched himself into the wall of dust and scrambled over rubble. As did Jaq, hauling Rakel with him. As did Grimm. As, with only the briefest of hesitation, did Mardal and his men.

Five mirror-visored Arbitrators were immediately evident, out in the dusty dark street. Two were indeed porting their weapons, busy attaching different grenade tubes to the long barrels.

RAAARKpopSWOOSHthudCRUMP
   RAAARKpopSWOOSHthudCRUMP

RAAARKpopSWOOSHthudCRUMP

The first *RAARK* of explosive bolts—like the rowdy growl of some carnivorous terror-lizards or of hell-dogs erupting from the dust—caused the Arbitrators fatal instants of hesitation. Bolts penetrated chest or belly. Bolts exploded, *CRUMP*. Blood sprayed. Autoguns were racketing too. Ducking, two surviving Arbitrators loosed laser pulses which hit one of Mardal's men simultaneously. Each had chosen the very same target. And a lesser target, too! Perhaps Lex seemed more like a force of nature than a mortal adversary. The dwarf mustn't be shot. As for the bearded man, was he using that woman as a shield? The woman might be important to the investigation. Wrong decisions, wrong.

Emperor's Peace and *Emperor's Mercy* roared adieu to those two Arbitrators.

Which one of the five corpses was Detective Arbitrator Steinmuller?

From an alleyway around the side of the cobbler's three more Arbitrators were coming to assist. From a passageway on the far side, two more emerged. Crossfire flew. An energy blast caught Grimm on the very edge of his flak-jacket, bowling him over, but the Squat was able to scramble to his knees. Another of Mardal's men screamed and fell.

RAARKpopSWOOSHthudCRUMP
RAARKpopSWOOSHthudCRUMP

The raving of the autoguns! The gaudy flowering of energy shells on impact!

Did the fight last for fifteen strobing seconds? Perhaps not as long. Yet it seemed to last for several minutes in slow motion.

Arbitrators were all dead, or at least severely injured. Lex roved quickly from one body to another. He checked by starlight for signs of life. Where he found life lingering he ended it, so that the Courthouse would be unenlightened.

Where was the cobbler?

"Mr Dukandar!" Grimm called into the night. "Your shop is damaged!" How sadly the building sagged. "It's time to salvage your tools, Mr Dukandar!"

Once the victors departed, shadowy beggars might flock to loot the premises of its boots and shoes—and of its pincers and shears and nails and leather. No cobbler showed himself. If Dukandar was wise he was already hastening with his wife and sons to lose himself somewhere in the smoky entrails of Bellygunge.

*Did a bailiff still keep watch through a cracked shutter in some neigh-
bouring building? Was he whispering urgently into a communicator?*

Lex raked the street with his gaze.

"Us gettin' outa here!" he shouted at Shuturban.

"To the theatre!" cried Jaq.

Grimm paused briefly to scoop up one of the dropped lasguns
to which an Arbitrator had been attaching a new tube of grenades. The little man jammed the barrel diagonally inside his belt.

To the theatre, indeed—to the Theatrum Miraculorum on Khelma
Street in Mahabbat—like some intoxicated nocturnal revellers
eager for even more exotic entertainment . . .

En route, Mardal Shuturban collected five more men armed
variously with shotgun or chainsword.

Mardal's group now totalled nine fighters, plus himself. Would
fourteen persons be sufficient to deal with three warrior-troubadours, sufficient to slaughter two and subdue a third? Mardal's
men believed so—especially those survivors of the encounter at
the cobbler's. They were flushed with having exterminated a
whole patrol of Arbitrators.

Elegantly clad in silks and furs, patrons of this night's performance were spilling out from the domed foyer of the theatre into
Khelma Street to meet bodyguards and chauffeurs. Balloon-
wheeled automobiles and gilded carriages pulled by snuffling
snake-necked camelopards crowded the thoroughfare. Feet and
hooves and wheels stirred dust. Rich perfumes competed with
the weed-smoke of cigars and with exhaust fumes and with the
odours of camelopard dung and urine.

The irruption of the fourteen through this secure normality
seemed almost like a continuation of dramatic spectacle—especially since no armed robbery or abduction or murder seemed
intended as regards any theatre-goers. A swift frontal approach
through an excited crowd which was venting psychic noise might
take the Harlequins unawares. Was this not a time and a place for
an Inquisitor to act flamboyantly? Let the Courthouse suspect the
secret presence of an Inquisitor—aye, and of an imperial Assassin
too! This would perplex and perturb.

Weapons weren't being brazenly flourished, though eye-wit-
nesses could hardly fail to notice the toothed blade of a

chainsword or the long barrels of shotguns or of lasguns filched from the dead. Well and good. Had not Shandabar seen a Gene-stealer uprising and a cleansing by Marines, and the pious and bloody riots of pilgrims? At times death was a currency as common as the shekel. Jaq and associates lagged a little, letting Mardal and his men take the lead.

The domed auditorium was almost deserted. Chandeliers of electrolumens glowed brightly. A spangled curtain hid the stage. As the intruders advanced down aisles, some ushers ducked behind plush seats.

"Master Jadu!" cried one of those attendants piercingly.

Glittering, the curtain swept up and sideways, bunching tableau-style—to reveal the impresario peering from the wings. What a peculiar fellow Jadu was. Exaggeratedly high heels and short skinny legs elevated a little barrel of a body clad in purple velvet appliquéd with crescent moons and comets. With a red coxcomb hat upon his head he resembled a plump fussy poultry-bird. One could imagine Master Jadu flapping his arms and clucking and crowing resoundingly.

Behind him—much taller than him—multicoloured spangles shimmered where no part of the curtain should be. A ghost of Jadu's own moon-face swayed in mid-air. It was a Harlequin in chameleon mode. Its holo-suit was copying the surroundings. Its psychoactive mask imitating the impresario's own face! A device seemed to float unsupported: a sleek gadget with a sheen to it. Something wrought of psycho-plastic.

A shuriken pistol!

A stream of what seemed like tiny spangles sprayed along one aisle. One of Mardal's men screamed. Blood laced his clothing. His chainsword fell from a crimson hand, from which two fingers also fell. No spangles, those—but tiny spinning razor-discs propelled at high speed by a compact gravitic accelerator. Those tiny discs would scalpel through flesh, severing arteries, piercing internal organs, cutting bone. The man behind spasmed in a delirium of pain and injury, and collapsed.

Autoguns opened up. The impresario-bird seemed to fluff out his feathers as shells tore into him.

RAARKpopSWOOSH, spake Lex's bolt gun, as he fired over seats.

RAARK-RAARK, declared *Emperor's Peace* and *Emperor's Mercy* in chorus.

Explosive bolts ripped through the spangled drape as if through tissue, and one surely detonated in alien flesh. Ethereally tall, kaleidoscopically fluxing, a figure seemed to drift forward. Its false face was now a private nightmare to whoever beheld it. Mardal shrieked, "*Chor, no don't*—!" Rakel squealed, seeing some nightmare of her own. Was that figure on stage the Assassin whom she imitated, coming for her?

Shuriken spangles sprayed, scattershot. Blood flew from a nick on Grimm's rubicund cheek. Blood welled from the upper slope of Lex's brow as a new companion to old duelling marks appeared. The blood immediately hardened to a knob of cinnabar.

RAARK
RAARK

The Harlequin danced his last dance.

The raiders hurried backstage past a lanky alien corpse masked in horror and past the dumpy, slaughtered-turkey corpse of unfortunate impresario Jadu.

They found the Death Jester lurking in a blue room walled with lapis lazuli.

Oh such a lanky mischievous figure of death he was. His costume decorated with real bones. His skull mask, framed by a great clownish yellow collar like the fully-open petals of some huge jungle flower. A wild spray of inky hair fountained from his crown . . .

The first man through the doorway was greeted by a Harlequin's Kiss.

Strapped to the back of the Jester's forearm was a tube bonded to an egg-shaped reservoir. The Jester clenched his fist and punched the air in front of him. Briefly the interloper wobbled as if he had become a jelly; and collapsed. What had been a man had become a bag of minced organs braced with bones.

Such was the consequence of the monofilament wire which had leapt from that tube to pierce its victim's body and uncoil within his entrails. Thrashing about like a whip, the wire had reduced guts and liver and lungs and heart to a slurry.

The wire had already leapt back into its container, curling tight.

Already it was jumping out again, kissing the next man with the same consequences.

How swiftly a third! The third was Mardal Shuturban himself. Mardal jerked. He was a bony jelly containing warm soup. He spilled upon the floor.

The Death Jester might kiss everyone who came for him before they had a chance to fire their weapons.

Dropping *Emperor's Peace*, Grimm hauled out the lasgun, cranked the grenade tube, and fired several times into the room of lapis lazuli.

Gas billowed within.

Until that moment Grimm hadn't known precisely what type of grenades would pop out of the launcher. It was a fair guess that those Arbitrators had intended to capture rather than kill or maim. Now Grimm caught a whiff, and his eyes watered—and he caught his breath.

Jaq had dragged Rakel backward. Mardal's other men were beginning to gasp and cough at the seepage from inside the blue room.

"Ceasing fire!" bellowed Lex. "Killing anyone who is firing again!"

Unlike the helmets worn by Eldar Aspect Warriors, that Death Jester's mask wasn't sealed against the atmosphere. Inside the cloudy room the tall figure was staggering, bending over, racked.

Lex was gathering himself. He would rush into the room with his eyes shut tight and seize the Jester and haul him out. Just then, the Jester lurched for the doorway, fending wildly at whoever might be in his way. No longer was he able to use his kiss. He himself might blunder into the wire when it retracted.

Lex seized the emerging alien. He snapped the Jester's wrist. The Harlequin wouldn't be able to clench his fist and punch again. Lex threw the Jester, skidding, along the passageway, away from the gas. Launching himself upon the choking Eldar, he dragged the long arms behind the bone-cloaked back. Discarding the lasgun, Grimm was beside Lex a moment later. He pulled from a pouche a plastight manacle-loop to cuff sound wrist to broken wrist. Struggles would only tighten the tether. A second loop fettered the Jester's ankles. Quickly Grimm retrieved *Emperor's Peace* before the precious weapon might be stolen.

"This one being *ours*," Lex roared at the coughing bystanders. "Yourselves finding the third Harlequin and killing him!"

Jaq knelt by the disabled choking Jester, and stated in Eldar: *"I have your book of fate. We will take you to it, Jester."*

This should ensure that the Harlequin of Death wouldn't try to kill himself by swallowing his tongue or by some other guile.

Mardal was dead. Only Mardal had imposed any discipline upon his gunmen. Whatever discipline there had been now quite disintegrated. Orders to search the rest of the theatre for the other Harlequin were heeded only insofar as the gunmen would keep an eye open while they were escaping to safety.

The third Harlequin must also have escaped rather than blending with his surroundings in ambush.

They had left by a door at the rear of the Theatre Miraculorum. Lex carried the Jester slung over his shoulder at a fast trot by way of inky back alleys. Sirens wailed distantly, and there was an occasional crackle of gunfire.

No Harlequin, dappled in darkness, shadowed their route. Lex would surely have heard whenever he paused alertly. Jaq would have sensed. The third Harlequin must have judged it wiser to flee from Shandabar. To steal a camelopard. To ride it into the Grey Desert until the beast's heart gave out—on his way to wherever the hidden Webway entry was.

Would that Harlequin return a few days later accompanied by Aspect Warriors riding jetbikes? Or might the spy declare that the mission to Sabulorb had proved lethal yet inconclusive?

The Jester was chained in the cellar near to the lectern, unable to touch it physically. After removing the Harlequin's Kiss, which the Jester bore stoically, his wrist had been splinted and bound up.

Less stoical was his reaction to the removal of his skull-mask. He had bucked and writhed—but off had come the skull to reveal a lean, sinisterly handsome face with the highest of cheek bones and slanting turquoise eyes.

Next morning Jaq began learning the runes.

At first the Jester was uncooperative—until Jaq ripped out half a page from the *Book of Rhana Dandra* and lit the vellum with the same igniter as Rakel had used to light the Finger of Glory.

Flame climbed. Runes writhed as if alive. Runes crisped and

crumbled to ash. Smoke laced the air as if the consumed words were attempting to maintain a ghostly existence. Jaq swept the smoke aside as brutally as a power gauntlet breaking cobwebs.

This sight wrung such a groan of grief from the Jester, more agonized than any physical torture might have caused. The destiny of his race had been diminished.

"Page by page," vowed Jaq in Eldar, "I shall destroy the book before your eyes, Jester. I shall cram the final page into your own throat to choke you!"

"To destroy what you cannot understand—that is the human way!"

"Precisely. So therefore I wish to read these runes."

The Jester laughed wretchedly.

"Hieratic High Eldar runes! Do you have a spare month, and the mind of a calculator?"

"I have all the time in the cosmos, and a mind honed by my Ordo, and I shall conjure concentration."

Jaq made to wrench out the remaining half of the page. Runes squirmed beneath his fingers.

"No!" cried the Jester. "I shall teach!"

The Harlequin's name was Marb'ailtor, which signified something akin to *Corpse-Joker*.

Jaq waited until the next day to demand, "Marb'ailtor, where *exactly* is the Webway entrance which you used?"

The Jester demurred. Jaq tore out a whole page from the book and set it alight. Might that be the very page upon which his own involvement with Eldar affairs was inscribed?

"You are insane!" shrieked the Jester.

Jaq smothered the half-consumed page against his robe. He displayed the remains tauntingly. Thus he had been taught how to torment a person.

"A day's march east of the city called Bara Bandobast," confessed the Harlequin, "there is a labyrinth of rock. Humans regard the place as haunted because holes in the rocks give the wind a voice. Near the centre are six giant stone mushrooms. There is the gateway."

"I think you're lying," said Jaq. He relit the page.

The Jester howled impotently. Evidently he had told the truth.

"How," asked Jaq, "can there be *stone* mushrooms?"

"The wind whirls around stone pillars. Grit in the wind abrades the stone. Big grains of grit cannot rise as high as little grains. The lower part of a pillar wears away faster than the top."

Later, Jaq demanded, "Where do the Emperor's Sons have their stronghold?"

"I do not know, I do not know!" insisted Marb'ailtor.

In the matter of the runes the chained Jester was certainly co-operative—scrupulously so, sometimes *repetitiously* so. Did Marb'ailtor aim to prolong the period of instruction in the hope that he might be rescued before Jaq could read the prophecies fluently enough?

Yet at other times the Jester seemed almost impatient to accelerate the process. It was as if Marb'ailtor were torn between two conflicting outcomes—both of them undesirable.

One outcome must be that Jaq would soon achieve mastery of the book of fate—and therefore he would take the stolen book elsewhere with him, to act upon what he had learned. The other outcome was that he and the book would remain on Sabulorb for a while—with what consequences? The worst consequence must be the destruction of the book so that it was lost to the Eldar forever. How was the book likely to be destroyed, other than by the sort of vandalism with which Jaq had earlier threatened the Jester?

Even in that cellar beneath the mansion the air was perceptibly less chilly. Upstairs, despite the permanent black drapes which cloaked the windows, rooms were warm. Outside, the temperature was almost sultry. For what must have been the first time in millennia Shandabar sweated. Discernibly the great red sun had shrunk somewhat.

Lex was troubled. Rakel was bewildered.

"How can a sun shrink," she asked, "and yet be hotter?"

"Gas shrinks inwards and compresses," Lex said. "Thus more gas will burn in the interior. Thus more heat radiates."

"We've already been through this," said Grimm. The little man pulled off his forage cap. Derisively he mopped his brow. "Phew, we'll roast—and the *Book of Dandruff* will burst into flames. Look, Lex, you're talking about oscillations. This planet would already have been cooked to a crisp if oscillations were extreme."

"That is true," admitted Lex.

"Marb'ailtor," Jaq said severely, "do you believe this planet is about to burn?"

The Jester stared at Jaq with those eerie unmasked turquoise eyes.

"You," said the Eldar softly, "would play games with forces of Chaos. I have sensed the lure of corruption. According to the doctrine of *Tranglam*—which some call the Theory of Chaos—our Farseers declared that a small perturbation sometimes has huge consequences when circumstances are vulnerable to change. A night-moth flutters its wings and causes a subsequent storm half a world away. If this is true of a mere moth, how much more so of energies spilling from the psychopotent warp! The weather gives cause for concern."

"Continue decoding the runes," Jaq ordered.

Due to thermal gradients whipping up winds in the interior, in the desert which lay beyond the Grey Desert a sandstorm was arising. Ribbons of sand were snaking along, rising higher and weaving together into a speeding, undulating flying carpet.

In the Grey Desert itself, dust was storming aloft and becoming a dark wall rushing onward. Behind that wall, no sunlight could filter down into a suffocating realm black as night . . .

Chapter Ten

Renegades

Flame-haired Daemon Prince Magnus had looked out through the warp from his watchtower, seeking a trace of the Eldars' lost book of fate.

Oh to gain possession of that mysterious and mutable text! To be able to rove through its alien runes, looting its secret prophecies! By mind-force he might alter the words and twist the very future. How Tzeentch would rejoice. How Tzeentch would bless Magnus and his followers.

Above the jagged crags from which the watchtower soared, the energy of the warp crackled in a stygian sky. Atop the tower there bulged a naked eyeball of elephantine size. At once crystalline and protoplasmic, this cupola pulsed inwardly, scrying through the warp into the realm of ordinary reality far from the Eye of Terror, detecting ripples of psychic activity.

Magnus only had one eye. It was set centrally above his nose. He had been thus when he was the headstrong commander of one of the boldest Space Marine chapters crusading to conquer the galaxy for his Emperor. Even then, unbeknownst, he was marked by Chaos, and had hungered for arcane wisdom.

He had hungered so eagerly that when the possessed Battlemaster Horus rebelled, Magnus must needs be a rebel too, forced to ally with daemonry.

And be blessed by daemonic energies and potency!

With his own single eye Magnus spied through the telescope of that other baleful cyclops-eye surmounting the watchtower. In a rapture of *rapport he had detected the divinations of alien Farseers desperate to re-cover the book of fate thieved from their secret library. His spying was part teleperception, part symbolic vision, part interpretative intuition.*

Through the warp his followers had flown to attack the site of those alien divinations, to disrupt and disorient. Maybe even to deal a mortal blow to that vast half-crippled Craftworld, so stubborn in its refusal to submit to its final fate.

The shape-shifting ships from the Planet of the Sorcerers each carried a crystalline seer-scope similar to the eye on the watchtower. By seer-scope they could track the glow of psychic activity.

From his watchtower Magnus had glimpsed, far away from cursed Ulthwé, a halo of sorcerous summons—a prelude to wizardry—allied to that lost book. By now the book so obsessed him that he was as a male musk-moth scenting a single molecule of pheromone released from a mile away.

Far away, a Tarot card of Tzeentch was twitching, animated by the ever-scheming Architect of Fate, and by some powerful psyker's tor-mented passion to unstitch time. A psyker in whose possession was that stolen book of destiny! In whom conflicting urges were at war. Foolish fidelity, and tragic craving. A harsh idealism—to bring a new light into the universe. A lust that change might occur; and yet that the tyrannous cripple on Earth might be sustained or purified.

Change-lust was the signature of that psyker's soul in turmoil. He might succumb to either the Great Conspirator or to the Lord of Lust. The balance might tilt either way. That it had not already tilted was due to a precarious conjunction of forces, and perhaps because of spiritual agony.

The Lord of Lust knew how to transmute agony into delight; delight into agony.

The Lord of Lust was Tzeentch's rival in the fourfold corruption of the cosmos.

Magnus had sent other shape-shifting ships speeding through the warp.

Oh Mutator, oh Master of Fortune, may the Chaos Renegades of Prince Magnus come swiftly to their destination.

Normally it was gloomy inside the curtained mansion at noon. But on this particular noon the world outside was cloaked in deepest darkness. Dense dust stormed suffocatingly across the city. Visibility outside was virtually zero. In the streets, a hand held directly in front of one's face would be hard to see—assuming that one had not already choked to death even despite wet rags tied over nose and mouth.

Thousands of street-dwellers and beggars must have suffocated during the past half-hour since the storm arrived. Once the storm passed over, sanitation squads would be busy for days carting bodies to mass graves. In the unaccustomed warmth, uncollected bodies would soon begin to stink.

Such a dust-storm might reach as high as three thousand metres into the sky. Within the lowest reaches of the storm, near the ground, airborne sand also swirled. It was the friction of grains and grit which accounted for the sickening headaches which had suddenly afflicted Jaq and Rakel and Grimm and Lex, like an onset of unwelcome possession. The electrical potential in the air must have soared to eighty or ninety volts per cubic metre, grievously disturbing the electrical field of a person's body and brain.

Jaq exerted his psychic power to combat this. Yet it was not a psychic assault.

So hard to think straight any longer. Maybe he ought to relax and welcome nausea as the harbinger of a frame of mind in which he might indeed be vulnerable to derangement and possession.

With this in mind, Jaq had donned the hooded monocle which had been Azul's warp-eye.

Outside, black wind howled, laden with grit and dust. Curtains quivered. All four had gathered in the same room on the ground floor as if the mansion were under attack from more than merely the elements. Was there not a dark sense of something impending?

Something which Jaq might invite, and absorb—while it strove to absorb him—and might then repulse by gazing into a mirror at his own reflection seen through Azul's eye . . .!

Was there a minimum time during which he must remain possessed by whichever power came—so as to become illuminated when he freed himself? And while possessed, what rite ought he to enact with the false-Meh'lindi?

Did the Assassin card twitch inside his clothing? Was the Daemon card vibrating in anticipation of trumping the Assassin card?

How Jaq's head ached, and his soul as well.

Rakel moaned. "My head, my head, I could claw it open—" Would Meh'lindi have moaned thus?

"Don't waste your energy telling me you have a headache!" Jaq growled. He must not sympathize. Meh'lindi had always regarded herself as expendable in a higher cause. In that rejection of self had resided the real Assassin's perfection. If Rakel were to lose her own self — yielding way to Meh'lindi's soul — then in that moment Rakel would at least participate for a moment in perfection; and that would be Rakel's reward.

But of course they had not yet reached the place in the Webway where time might twist. Jaq did not yet know *how* to reach it. Nor was becoming possessed a necessary precondition for resurrecting Meh'lindi. Or was it, or was it? How Jaq's soul ached with confusion, and his head too. This electrical interference induced such disorder in the mind.

From Grimm: "Oh it's bloody misery, this. Wonder how our Jester's coping? Hypersensitive snobs, those Eldars. Oh so intense! Nervous systems strung like catgut on a harp. Every sensation, heightened. Boggar it — but he might be having a brainstorm downstairs! Seizures and paroxysms! I'm gonna check him out, Boss. Maybe there's less voltage down in the cellars. You come with me, Rakel. Might clear your head."

"Go, go," said Jaq dismissively.

Grimm clumped down the stone stairs. Rakel padded softly behind him. Along to the cell they went. As soon as the little man set hand on the iron key in the lock he squawked and shook his fingers and spat on them.

"Damn it, it stung me!"

To avoid any further electric shock, Grimm used a soiled handkerchief to turn the key.

The Jester sat in his garb of bones upon the pallet mattress which Jaq had allowed him. A chain rattled as he raised a long-fingered hand in sinister greeting.

Grimm slapped his own brow. "Oh of course! His chains are earthing the electricity . . .' '

"What is happening?" Marb'ailtor asked; for it was he who spoke ImpGoth.

"Just a storm. Particles rub together. Voltage potential soars."

"The storm is caused by rising temperature," announced the Jester. "The sun will burn this world and everyone on it. There will be white skeletons everywhere. Yours and mine and hers."

"No, there won't be! The sun won't do that—'cos it never did before."

"This time it will happen, Abhuman. For Death is here. Death will play a prank on Sabulorb."

"Huh!"

"Free me, Abhuman. Help me to reach the Webway. The Eldar will give you sanctuary."

"From whom? Oh I'm sure I'd enjoy being looked down on by your sort for the rest of me life."

The Jester nodded at the locked chest which was out of reach of him. "The Eldar will reward you with bright jewels. A fortune! Your master is insane. He will become possessed. This world will burn. I smell daemonry coming closer. Your master will sacrifice you as pawns."

Grimm puffed himself up. "*I'm* the major-domo hereabouts."

Rakel shuddered. "What *is* really to be my fate?" she asked Grimm.

Grimm eyed her. "Not to worry. That body of yours will see many years of service yet. Keep up with your exercises, hmm?"

Did a hint of a tear appear in Rakel's eye?

"Shut up, you!" Grimm barked at Marb'ailtor. "You're scaring the lady."

Distantly from upstairs came a muted crash as though the wind had racked itself up to a hurricane force and had now exploded through a window. No, that noise was due to something else. Some other violent intrusion.

"Crazy Aspect Warriors!" A Squat's detestation of Eldar affectations went hand in hand with a sensible degree of respect. "Suppose the storm isn't deep. They've come up behind the storm on jetbikes, using it as cover. Now that they've smelled Old Bones here psychically, they've plunged right on in." Grimm clutched *Emperor's Peace*. Crouching in the doorway, he trained the bolt gun along the passageway.

"Get your pistol out, girl!"

As Rakel readied the laspistol, with those eerie turquoise eyes of his and by mime Marb'ailtor implored her to shoot the Abhuman. She shook her head.

Risk her body succumbing to flux?

"I s'pose," mumbled Grimm, "dust would clog engine intakes, though . . ."

"A visit by masked Arbitrators?" she murmured. "Masks all coated in dust. Nothing visible . . ."

"We don't move from here," said Grimm, "until we know for sure what's going on. *You*," he called to the Jester, "no singing out, or else you'll be biting on a bolt!"

The Jester didn't sing. He shivered.

"Daemons," he hissed. "Daemons."

Had Jaq—his brain circuits disrupted by the high voltage— gone critical upstairs?

"Oughta tell the Boss to cling on to a chain or summat," muttered Grimm.

Neither he nor Rakel were intending to move.

The first two raiders to burst through a sheet-glass window and rip black drapes aside with their metal fists would have glimpsed in the room two men: one robed and bearded—the other huge and stark. A barbarian slave in his groin-cloth and webbing, bare-chested, restless. Such thighs, such biceps, such pectorals, such a solid slab of chest—and such *vulnerability*, to persons similar to himself, especially when those persons were enhanced by power armour! Surely the stark giant was a Space Marine, one of the paralytical Emperor's despicably devout knights such as these raiders themselves had once been long ago! Witness the bygone medical scars on his anatomy!

Such was the glimpse enjoyed by the raiders, before choking dust surged into the room along with them, abolishing ordinary visibility.

But of course these raiders had image enhancers in their helmets . . .

For Lex and Jaq the brief glimpse was of vanes like axe-blades jutting above angular helmets. It was of monstrous armour utterly harsh in its lines and edges, except for the rotund shoulder pauldrons.

Around the terrible figures electrical discharge flickered. Haloes crackled. Auras sparkled. The armour was damascened with arcane hexes. It was enamelled with badges of jeering bestial faces. One Knight of Evil toted a heavy bolter cloisonnéd with screaming, fang-bearing lips. That back-breaking bruiser of a gun could knock out a lightly-armoured vehicle, let alone a man.

Power armour easily sustained such a weight. The bolter clutched in the other intruder's metalled fist seemed like a toy by comparison.

"*For Tzeentch!*" shrieked an amplifier, over the howl of the wind . . . as incoming dust blinded and choked Jaq and Lex.

Had these hideous emissaries come in response to Jaq's tormented soul-searching?

He may have been on the verge of inviting a daemon to possess him. But not of inviting corrupted human minions! Even though those might be sorcerers in their own right! Pride raked Jaq's soul even as he clutched a palm over his nose and mouth—not to prevent vomit from spewing forth, though nausea twisted his guts, but to filter the dust.

Dust stung his eyes. He must shut them. He must rely on tumultuous psychic cues. Oh, to have the nearsense of a blind Astropath who could inwardly and exactly detect persons in her vicinity. Jaq himself was blind, and holding his breath.

What use was a warp-eye lens when its intended victims could not see it? Blindly Jaq snatched out his force rod. How sick and confused he felt. He summoned repulsion and disruption and anathema. He discharged these into the swirling gritty darkness, sweeping his rod from side to side rather than aiming it.

The impact of armour hurled him against a wall, concussing him. Dizzily he slid on to the hard slate floor.

Lex had loosed a bolt from his gun—with what consequence he did not know. Armour embraced him, crushing him in a cudbear hug. The gun was plucked from his grasp. To keep hold of the gun would simply have been to lose his fingers as easily as a spider loses its legs to a vicious child. Stray electricity stung him. His nostrils were silting up. He must close down his breathing. Both of his hearts were thumping—in horror at the memory of being captured once before.

Aye, captured in a tunnel inside the world of Antro, deep down away from the ruddy light of a star known as Karka Secundus. On that fearful occasion implacable spiked hoops powered by pistons had immobilized him in his armour. He had been stripped of his armour in preparation for sacrifice to Tzeentch.

Now the armoured strength of Tzeentch's Chaos Renegades

was dragging Lex out into the inky duststorm. He could not exert himself even in *futile* resistance. He could not even give vent to a howl. To do so, he must breathe. If he breathed he would choke.

Jaq roused. Dimly he could see the room. Ruddy light was filtering through the dust as though he was perceiving the scene in infra-red. The drapes were fluttering like great predatory wings. A great angular suit of armour lay motionless upon the slate floor.

The storm was on the verge of passing over.

And the force rod had killed one of the Chaos Marines.

A convulsion of coughing racked Jaq. He hawked up gritty froth. He dragged a handful of robe across his mouth and nose. He coughed again and again as though his lungs might turn inside-out. At last the bronchial spasm subsided. He gulped air through the thick sieve of his garment. Then he forced himself to breathe more shallowly.

Lex was nowhere to be seen. The wind wailed past the shattered windows. Elsewhere in the mansion there seemed to be no sound of turmoil.

Chaos Renegades from the Eye of Terror were so close at hand!

A bolt gun lay on the floor. Lex's gun . . . Jaq pulled out *Emperor's Mercy*, aiming towards the dust-veiled garden.

Those Chaos Marines had come into this room. He had seen two of them before dust blinded him. Probably there had been one or two more. They had proceeded no further. They hadn't attempted—*yet*—to ransack the mansion. They had left. They had even left Jaq alive.

They had taken Lex as their prize!

"Grimm!" roared Jaq. More coughing convulsed him.

The little man came soon enough, *Emperor's Peace* in one hand. On entering the ruptured room, Grimm clapped his forage cap over the lower part of his face. Rakel, who was with him, began to sneeze.

Outside the wind was dropping fast. The view was clearing somewhat. The lightest dust would still take hours to settle.

Beyond shrubberies and gravel the far boundary wall was flattened—under the bulk of a ship as large as the mansion itself. A rectangular ship with giant pincers at the bow, and razor fins. Jutting from the ship's snout was what appeared to be a plasma cannon. Other armaments were mounted atop, and to the rear.

"Huh," spluttered Grimm, "I see we got new neighbours. Guess there weren't ever too many planning laws in Shandabar." He eyed the fallen armour with fearful curiosity. His teeth chattered. "Su-somebody du-deliver a new su-suit of armour for our bu-big hunk?" He squashed his cap against his mouth to control himself.

"Chaos Marines." Jaq spoke tersely so as not to cough again. He glared at Rakel as if to erase the words from her consciousness.

The shock of proximity to these impious tools of Chaos was intense—visceral and soul-seering. That these agents of abomination should be here, in this heartland of the Imperium, was ghastly. Chaos seemed to be all-knowing, all-powerful. The Imperium seemed like a vast, star-spanning *cobweb* seeking to thwart the hornets—and locusts, and viler plagues—of Chaos. The web sought to be of adamantium. How frail and rusty much of it was! Space Marines and Imperial Guards were so many spiders scuttling to sting the toxic hornets which ripped the cobweb. No wonder their stings must be fierce and sometimes indiscriminate. And perhaps the effort was doomed.

A forlorn fierce pride coursed through Jaq; and he grinned crazily.

"Chaos has come calling on us—yet hardly the way I dreamed!"

Why had the Chaos Marines withdrawn? The logic of Chaos was not necessarily the logic of mortals. Those knights must have come here in response to the Daemon card, and perhaps to seize the book of fate, which might well resonate its presence to such as they.

Had Jaq's force rod disrupted their reasoning? Jaq had been enfeebled by the high voltage in the air—and yet one raider had actually died. The force rod had scrambled their thinking. Maybe the strong electric charge had contributed. Would the metal of their suits have insulated them, or caused an accumulation of voltage?

Sickeningly, Jaq recalled Lex's confession. Lex had once been touched by Chaos—by the near presence of Tzeentch. To the Chaos raiders, Lex must have smelled of that past encounter. To control and corrupt a pious Space Marine would give them such perverse joy! Then to use that wretch as a tool against his former associates! How much more perverse than simply to kill Lex.

Had not Jaq assured Lex that the force rod could save him or kill him, if need be?

Grimm interrupted Jaq's reverie. "Uh, Boss, do we just wait here for their next performance? Or do we get the hell out of here with the *Book of Dandruff* and leave the Jester to 'em?—"

Does one wait for the approach of a lumbering perverted homicidal giant attired in borrowed Chaos armour? Does one discharge a force rod at Lex—mercifully? Or in vain?

Lex had spoken of maybe needing to execute Jaq ... How tables were turned, how fate was foxing all hope!

After killing Lex, await the onrush of many more armoured renegades?

Try to decamp with the book? Surely they would be detected by some radar or motion sensor aboard the dire vessel. The plasma cannon would gush, consuming the mansion and anything in the vicinity.

"Uh, Boss, are you hoping the local vigilantes will take umbrage at the ship in someone's back garden—and fire off their pop guns? We gotta get outa here!"

"*No.*"

"Uh, you hoping Arbitrators will cotton on that there are hostile Marines roosting in this suburb, and send an execution team? Natch, they'll be delighted to save our bacon, if they ain't all fried by plasma, which is much more likely!"

"That's exactly why we can't leave," snapped Jaq. "The Chaos ship has this mansion covered."

If only Arbitrators—or soldiers of the garrison—might render assistance. If only those who should rightly be allies might indeed combine! Jaq's lonely renegade status denied him so much.

He gazed at the fallen armour. "I shall need to board that ship with my force rod. Somehow I shall wear that armour so that they imagine their vile comrade is returning—"

"That's figging ridiculous. It's power armour. You don't have spinal sockets to control it. You ain't enhanced all over, and inside. Lex could hardly move in armour when his power went off, remember?"

"Maybe that Chaos armour is lighter—"

"Made of titanium? Looks like tough steel to me."

"Maybe I can force it to move a step at a time, as if I'm badly in-jured. Rage may lend me strength. I will pray hard."

"Oh *fig*. If only you weren't right about the plasma cannon."

Grimm scurried to the suit and knelt. He wrenched the vaned helmet aside, unsealing it. The dead face he exposed was shar-klike, harsh and lean. That face sported dozens of tiny tattoos of vermilion mouths as though it had been kissed repeatedly by rouged or bloodstained miniature lips. Pink drool had dribbled down the chin.

"Give me a hand, Rakel!"

Painstakingly, off came those rounded pauldrons. Then the sharp angular vambraces. Then cuisses. Then greaves. Then poleyns and groin-guard and cleated boots. Time was passing. Dust was settling slowly.

"There *ain't* no spinal sockets, Boss! Just things like puckered ulcers or suckers down the backbone. Or like *lips*—"

Lips of Tzeentch, which would open all over that daemon's body, uttering contradictory statements . . .

"Daemonry!" cried Jaq with a terrible joy. His prayer was answered. "The suit's sorcerously synched to its wearer. It's psychically synched . . ." How the words slithered from his lips.

The dead renegade's body was mostly coated in iridescent scales as filmy as those of a fish. This renegade seemed to have been in a state of metamorphosis. One might imagine him—in whatever Chaos citadel he inhabited—lolling in a marble pool, before arising to don his armour. Now the eerily lovely glitter was fast fading from the scales.

With assistance Jaq began to don unfamiliar armour.

By the time Jaq stood armoured, with visor still open, visibility outside allowed an even clearer sight of the Chaos ship. Jaq still wore the hooded lens of Azul's eye.

As though to compensate for its progressive exposure to view, that ship wavered. It began to shift its shape, at least in the eye of the beholder. Miniature holo-projectors studding the hull must be generating a false semblance, a faceted camouflage; unless the daemonic power of change could manipulate the very material of that ship into new contours and configurations.

The ship no longer seemed to be a ship, of angular and box-like aspect—but instead a building. It imitated the mansion from which the trio witnessed it. A casual spectator might have been fooled—especially with all the haze of dust still adrift—except that the hoax mansion straddled a crushed wall.

Were the occupants of the genuine adjoining property gaping from their own windows across their own shrubby gardens at this phenomenon, this mirage looming amid the dust-mist? Might it seem to them that Tod Zapasnik was a wizard who had shifted his own abode closer to them under the cower of the storm, intruding right over the boundary line? Might it seem that the storm had been so fierce that it had uprooted and shifted Zapasnik's home? Those owners would be well advised to cower, and not approach that trespassing structure.

Due to the freak warmth, and to apprehension and expectation, Jaq was perspiring. He prayed for unity with this unnatural power armour; that it might heed his psyche and obey his will.

"Oh *Ancestors*—!"

The sight which wrung this yell from Grimm was of Jaq's harsh armour transformed. Like the ship, its appearance had shifted. It wreathed itself in holographic or daemonic illusion. Briefly its colours were fluctuating: brightly green, luridly yellow, achingly blue. Then, as if blessed by some kind of glory, the armour was red, embellished in gold; and remained so. The axe-like vanes rising behind the helmet seemed to have expanded into a blood-red bat-wing of metal. Gilded fylfot crosses adorned the shoulder pauldrons. The knee-protectors were embossed with skulls. On the groin-hauberk was a golden scarab. Surely this was pious imperial armour—bearing witness to a long-lost purity of purpose.

Within the open helmet Jaq's grizzle-bearded face was distorted by some vision—associated with Rakel? Grimly he squinted at her. He took a step.

"Turn back!" he commanded. "Do not go onward! You must not!"

Ahead of him, Jaq saw Meh'lindi lying asleep in that cul-de-sac in the Webway. Grimm lay nearby, and Marines, and his own sleeping self—and also the doomed deceitful Navigator.

If Meh'lindi went onward, it would be to her death, speared by a Phoenix Lady. Was this the moment when he could snatch her back from her fate? Was this when her soul could be plucked to

safety and enshrined in . . . in . . . in . . . He could not think
clearly. His thoughts were in turmoil, as though Chaos were
about to submerge him.

From the turmoil arose an image of a wench's oval face, vague
as a wraith. Her name came to him: *Olvia*. Jaq had been intimate
with Olvia aboard the terrible Black Ship carrying him and her
and hundreds of other young psykers to Earth to be consumed so
as to feed Him-on-Earth; and some few of them to be sanctified as
Astropaths or Inquisitors. Not Olvia, though. Not her. She was
already lost to her life. Just as Meh'lindi was lost!

Oh loss, oh loss! Oh agony of loss. Oh *damnum, detrimentum!*

Words tore from Jaq:

"Turn back! Do not go onward! You must not! I swear this by
Olvia! Go back!"

His other self, there in the Webway, roared in repugnance:
"Ego te exorcizo!" A fierce repulsive force rebuffed Jaq overpower-
ingly. That nook in the Webway was shrinking to a vanishing
point.

Yet he was still staring at Meh'lindi's face!

Ach no, at *Rakel's* face.

With his steel gauntlets he could have assaulted that tantalizing
face in frustration—except that it was sacred, in a private profane
corner of his soul.

"Boss? You back with us yet?"

"What do you mean?" demanded Jaq.

"You've just been standing there like some statue all stupefied
and bewitched."

Aye, caught up in that vision of the Webway where time
passed differently . . .

"How long was I thus?"

Grimm told him, and Jaq groaned. "So *long*!"

The little man added: "If I weren't a loyal sort of tike I'd have
taken off on me own in the meantime!"

"And if it weren't for the plasma cannon," Rakel reminded
Grimm.

"What *happened* to you, Boss?"

"That doesn't matter!"

Jaq could hardly have plucked Meh'lindi's soul from her
doomed body while she was still alive and brought it here. His
vision, induced by the Chaos armour, was futile.

"He looked so noble in his armour," Rakel murmured.

"Glorious and red and gold," agreed Grimm. "Skulls on the knees, scarab on the groin."

Now Jaq was harsh and angular once more; and the armour had become a dull blue . . .

They had seen him exactly as he had seen himself on that earlier occasion in the Webway.

"Couldn't help but admire you, Boss. 'Cept for your paralysis. Course, how you looked just now wouldn't have impressed any Chaos Marines into imagining you was one of them! Just as well you didn't budge from here."

Had this been the meaning of the illusion projected by the armour: that true honour and purity still resided within him despite a dalliance with daemonry, despite a pathological addiction to Meh'lindi? That these obsessions were indeed the route to virtue?

When he donned the Chaos armour just now, had the shining path touched him—after so long? Had the Numen transfigured him? Might the Numen now guide him into that Chaos ship, as once it had guided him through the Emperor's palace and into the throne room itself? Guide him unseen and safely?

Was he already illuminated, unbeknownst, without needing recourse to daemons? Without first needing to surrender his soul? Had he not already surrendered himself to this steel suit of Chaos—and exorcized himself?

"I'm going to the Chaos ship," he growled. "Give me my force rod, Grimm." He was on the point of closing the visor, to hide his face.

"Oh me Ancestors," cried Grimm. "You're too late."

From the direction of the Chaos ship, Lex came lurching. His face was contorted by a psychopathic snarl.

Chapter Eleven

Tzeentch

It was Lex's worst nightmare come true.

Oh, the threat of sacrifice to Tzeentch had been *actual* enough in that cave within Antro—but Terminator Librarians had saved Lex and Biff and Yeri. Nothing could save Lex now.

Worse still: his present tormentors were corrupted Marines who had rebelled against Him-on-Earth ten thousand years ago. If Lex had been elevated to a superhuman condition by surgery and by the gene-seed of Rogal Dorn, these former Marines had become radically inhuman. Daemonry had sustained their twisted lives, endowing them with hideous powers. Their existence was the vilest blasphemy in the cosmos.

Worst of all: it was not their intention simply to sacrifice him or to torture him to death. They intended to make him into one of them; into a daemon-ridden cadet of Chaos . . .

Contours inside the Chaos ship were wilfully deviant: askew and slanted and crooked. Ornamentations were tortuous and devilish. To gape at those was nauseous. They seemed to pluck at the mind. Sulphurous incense burned, perhaps to mask a lurking foetor.

With their power gauntlets two of Lex's captors easily held him, by wrists and ankles, upon a grooved iron table. They disdained the shackles which were welded to either end of the table. Thus they could turn him over, like a huge child, to examine his spinal sockets, and to let a comrade in corruption insert a chilly probe into those sockets. The mere touch of this probe made Lex writhe.

How many captives—how many vulnerable psykers—had been examined upon this table until they become insane or became serviceable slaves for these renegade sorcerers?

Now a captive Fist had fallen into their hands. He must strive to hide the actual identity of his chapter lest it be dishonoured. Would they recognize his cheek-tattoo, his personal heraldry as a Fist?

What a dry chuckling he heard from those who had raised their visors. Facial electro-tattoos, thus exposed, shifted slyly in shape and hue.

What was missing from a Marine's body was a suicide gland. What was missing was the ability to will oneself to die.

How could such a facility ever be contemplated? Even if hideously and fatally injured a Marine must strive to endure, at least until his progenoid glands could be harvested. Else how could a new Marine be kindled to replace him?

Sheer pain, Lex would welcome. Pain, he could convert into adoration of Dorn.

Not this impious *prying*, this intimate invasion . . .

A black-nailed finger traced the puckers on Lex's forehead from which he had torn out his service studs.

"You would seem to be a deserter," said his tormentor, his daemonic tattoos pulsing. "A runaway traitor. You have found your new family, deserter! Yet your hormones reek of loathing for us. They stink of loyalty to your wretched Primarch and to that thing on Earth. How can this be, how can this be? Let us see, let us see."

The voice became hypnotically sing-song. "All is change, all is mutation and alteration. We shall mutate you and initiate you, so that your soul shall conform to the semblance of renegade. You shall become one of us—a lesser one throughout the next few centuries, yet one nonetheless. Capable of serving our master Tzeentch, and of being rewarded with attributes, and of aspiring to potent sorcery. Oh yessss—"

During stages in Lex's novitiate as a future Marine he had been initiated dauntingly enough—by a feast of foul excremental unfood and by other formidable ceremonies.

The forced rite of initiation which took place like a ravishment within that Chaos vessel was execrable and almost unspeakable. How could Lex obliterate from memory the Kiss of Corruption, the Communion with Chaos, the Prayer of Perfidy, the spells and the invocations?—and all the while he was experiencing the slither of tendrils within his spinal sockets. These invaded his nervous system, generating nauseating visions of the fragility of the cosmos, of the feebleness of reality which daemonic fingers sought to unpluck and reknit—with such vile success.

Lex in torment saw the whole cosmos burst forth from a mere bubble in the energy-warp. A sparrow's fart the universe was! That fart inflated suddenly. It caught fire and exploded outward. Gas became matter. Space ballooned to accommodate the gush. Matter became the stars and worlds of a billion galaxies. All was mere froth upon the surging unseen ocean of the warp. Finally the pull of the warp would drag all galaxies and all space back together again, abolishing this temporary interruption which was the whole of space and time, and all of struggling suffering life.

The lusts and rages of life caused terrible entities to coalesce in the warp, and to give rise to sub-entities, to daemons and sub-daemons. Daemons clawed at reality to try to drag it and its denizens back into the warp prematurely. Tzeentch and his sub-daemons especially sought to twist the future of the cosmos askew. Tzeentch would triumph.

The Emperor on Earth was no more than a guttering candle in malevolent darkness. The radiance of Rogal Dorn and other Primarchs were pathetic glimmers.

What of the shining path which Jaq sought? What of the good light which might be awakened by benevolence and compassion and self-sacrifice arising universally? A sparrow might as well fart into a hurricane. The spirit of the Numen slumbered, unaware of itself except in dreamlike spasms.

Oh, do tell your tormenting initiators that the name of your chapter is the Imperial Fists! Oh, do hand over the book of fate to the worshippers of Tzeentch! Oh, do join them joyfully in the disruption of this futile cosmos, and be rewarded.

All along Lex's nerves, and in his mind, potent daemonry squirmed like an invasion by tiny ants which were really all one collective multifold beast.

"Which chapter did you desert?" Lex heard.

He gibbered. His mouth frothed. His very soul was being drowned in vileness, and revived, and drowned again. Soon it would no longer be his soul, but Tzeentch's property; and he would be a willing puppet.

"Which chapter?"

As he opened his lips to reply, his left hand tore free from the gauntlet which held it. His left hand rose as if to stifle him, to throttle him. That was the hand on the bones of which were inscribed the names of Biff Tundrish and Yeremi Valence of Necromunda, and of the Imperial Fists . . .

Lex seemed to hear from afar in the sea of souls the voices of Biff and Yeri crying out to him to resist—no, to let *them* resist on his behalf, to let them be his strength and his salvation. Yeri particularly had always yearned to protect Lex, hadn't he?

Let Biff and Yeri be his own protective daemons who would lurk within; who would snatch his soul back to safety even though it seemed to be lost to Tzeentch. The inscriptions hidden upon the bones of that left hand were the most potent sorcerous runes. By virtue of those runes, his left hand clasped Rogal Dorn's own hand through the intermediary of his dead comrades. Though he fell, they would raise him in the final moment.

Sweating and shuddering, Lex submitted to the Chaos Marines.

The name of his chapter? He could tell them that without blame, because it was the proudest of names.

The book of fate? He could betray that. They already knew it was nearby.

Who should they wickedly send to fetch it, and to kill or be killed, but this traitor, this new cadet kinsman in Chaos?

"*That's* his initiation test!"

"In that house they'll think he has escaped from us—"

"Instead he will kill or concuss—"

How Lex relished the prospect of incapacitating the Inquisitor with his bare hands. How he hoped to hand Jaq over to his new brothers in sorcery. How he relished the thought of swatting the impudent Squat to death or tearing him limb from limb. As for Rakel, that sham—what fate would be best for her, to torment Jaq the most? To inject her again with Polymorphine so that she would go into fatal agonizing flux—providing the visible dissolution of Jaq Draco's stupid ambitions!

There was also the Death Jester, to serve up to these new *elder brothers*.

Lex could relish these deeds and allow his hormones to riot—because his left hand enshrined his salvation. That hand was calm now. It feigned.

Chaos Marines were laughing. What if their new initiate were killed as soon as he returned to the mansion? Why, he would die utterly subverted—traitor to his chapter of naive musclemen and to the ramshackled Imperium. *Then* the Princes of Chaos would overwhelm the mansion and seize prizes. Lex himself was a prime prize—but a prize best enjoyed perhaps in the squandering of it.

"He's coming for us!" bawled Grimm. He levelled *Emperor's Peace*.

Jaq waved the force rod. "Don't shoot till I've used this! I may purge him and cleanse him."

"That's all very well for you to say. You're wearing armour."

At least Lex wasn't wearing any Chaos armour.

"I order you not to use the bolter. Otherwise I'll kill you."

"Oh Ancestors, maybe I'd rather be killed by you than by what'll follow—"

By what would inevitably follow . . .

Whatever Jaq achieved with Lex would surely be futile. Suppose Jaq could restore Lex to sanity, what price another pair of hands, however muscular, to fire another bolt gun—against armoured Chaos Marines? Ultimately, against a plasma cannon?

"Shall I free the Death Jester?" cried Rakel.

What, and arm the Harlequin? Gamble that the Jester might temporarily ally himself with his captors so as to save the book of fate from being seized by the forces of Chaos?

What a trusting—or desperate—assumption that would be.

Lex loomed in the vacant window frame. Promptly his left hand clutched that frame to slow him and hold him back.

His face was a mask of homicidal hatred. How he snarled at the hand. Relaxing its grip, the hand made a defiant fist—which then struck him brutally and dazzlingly on the chin.

"He's at war with himself—!"

Urgently the hand gestured at Jaq not to use the force rod. Jaq refrained, temporarily at least.

"He's possessed, and he ain't!"

The hand mimed opening a book. The hand pointed down in the direction of the basement. The hand urged going there. A nimbus of light glowed around the hand, leaving quasi-phosphorescent traces in the dusty air like blazons of a luminous route which should be followed.

How urgently Lex gestured.

This matter was urgent indeed if the renegades aboard the ship were observing—with mounting bewilderment—through oculi.

"Basement's the best place to be when a plasma cannon lets rip! That way we can be buried alive and roasted more slowly—"

The lambently glowing left hand—a *whole* hand rather than a mere finger of Glory—reached out toward Jaq, not so as to interfere with his force rod—but to invite Jaq to clasp the hand with his free gauntlet. That hand was becoming translucent, as though it were an alabaster X-ray. Bones showed within, scrimshaw bones with words inscribed upon them over and over elegantly and minutely in cursive script, words almost too small to read. There was no time for closer scrutiny.

As Jaq accepted the hand, light flickered around his borrowed armour, and once again it wore the guise of glorious red and gold. Would the renegades right now be watching something so inexplicable and occult that the mystery of it might deter them for a few more precious minutes? Might they imagine that Tzeentch was somehow manifesting himself within the mansion? That Tzeentch was causing such strange changes! Such a seemingly noble metamorphosis!

The hand assisted Jaq in his manoeuvring of the suit. The Hand of Glory led him.

"Stay, Grimm, stay!" ordered Jaq. "Rakel too. The renegades must see someone still up here or they might come to investigate."

"Oh Ancestors . . ."

Rakel was gaping numbly at a pair of sorcerers about to leave that violated room.

How those turquoise eyes widened. How crazily the Jester grimaced at the sight of Lex and Jaq. Jaq, in that spuriously splendid armour. Jaq, led by Lex whose illuminated hand leaked phosphor streaks which lingered briefly in the air. How Marb'ailtor wrenched at his chains.

"Deamhan diabhal!" he uttered in dismay. The giant stank of
daemonry—although his glowing hand seemed like a living torch
which was keeping dark evil at bay. That resplendent armour was
a phantasm. It was lustrous silk draped over razor blades. Something momentous had happened, and was still happening. What,
what? Surely Death was about to jape the Jester—who would die
in ignorance.

Lex and Jaq entirely ignored Marb'ailtor.

On the lectern the *Book of Rhana Dandra* lay open. With his
glowing hand, Lex assaulted the tome. His shining fingers
seemed to sink into the vellum as if it were dough. As he lifted his
hand clear, did runes drip phosphorescently from his fingers?
The runes on the page were writhing.

Marb'ailtor howled at the desecration.

With his Hand of Glory Lex gestured urgently at Jaq's force rod,
and then at himself. Lex's other hand, his possessed hand,
clamped itself upon Jaq's shoulder pauldron. This contact caused
the splendid semblance of red and gold to arc and flash and fade,
stripping away that heroic illusion, revealing the renegade
armour in its harsh angularity.

Jaq understood. Lex was trying to expel the daemonry into Jaq
himself, as lightning might arc through a conductor. Thus, to
empower Jaq!

Jaq pressed the force rod against Lex's chest.

"Yield up the evil in you! Let it pass into me! *Ego te exorcizo!*"
Jaq discharged his rod.

The flash threw Lex backwards ponderously, to crash into the
door jamb. Lex pivoted slowly. His fading fingers of Glory
dragged four phosphorescent claw marks down the stone as
slowly he slumped to the floor. He rolled over. His eyes were
alert with a light of salvation as he gazed, still alive, towards Jaq.

Jaq reeled and might have fallen but for the corset of his armour.
The rod fell from his gauntlet. He gripped the lectern to steady
himself. He was gazing down upon shifting shimmering runes,
flowing like spilled mercury.

What did he wish the book to tell him? What did he want it to
yield?

His fate, his future . . .

The location of the place where time could twist . . .

Or of a place where a soul could be redeemed from death . . .

A place of redemption, of deliverance.

A place in the warp from which the shining path originated. To arrive there might supercharge the dormant Numen. The Chaos Child might begin to awaken to divinity and to transfiguring power—and might even incarnate a fraction of itself in the illuminated mortal who visited its Chaos cradle.

Surely this was impossible, a megalomaniac fantasy!

And yet . . . at that pivotal place to resurrect someone worthy from death might surely send a shining ripple through the whole fabric of the warp and the cosmos too . . .

Someone as worthy as Meh'lindi . . .

Yes, oh yes.

Personal passion and cosmic salvation might both be served. The Imperium might be saved and transfigured, along with Him-on-Earth. Oh to bring healing balm to that wounded God, to reconcile Him restoringly with the Child of Light.

How Jaq ached for Meh'lindi to be resurrected, reincarnated. She was like an amputated limb. Her ghostly presence persisted and persisted.

A haunting cackle lurked in his mind. Yet how his perception was enlarging. How shiningly he saw: a sentence descending circuitously down into the page. The sentence curled around and within itself like some burrowing silver worm. The initial word of that sentence served as a compressed code which now gave rise to a whole stretch of instructions. Instructions which were simple directions. *Clé, Ceart, Lár*: left, right, middle. Directions through the Webway! Directions to Jaq's destiny.

When the rune had appeared to Azul Petrov in his agony-vision—the rune which revealed the route to the Black Library—the starting point had been precisely where Petrov had happened to be at that particular time.

So it must be with this snaking sentence.

With the tip of a steel-clad finger, Jaq flipped up the hoods from his lethal monocle.

Of a sudden the sentence was jagged and forked. No longer was it a sentence at all but an intricate network. What Jaq saw through the lens exemplified rather than described. A particular route through the network was luminously traced. Sometimes it returned upon itself. It crossed itself. Twice it cut over a major axis—those must be Wraithship passages.

Of course! That place of power in the Webway, that node which Great Harlequins were said to seek, was in no one particular place. It could become present anywhere at all—if and only if you followed a precise combination of routes from any starting point whatever.

No wonder Great Harlequins had never found the place. Potentially it could be anywhere. Yet it never was found, because no seeker had ever yet followed the exact combination. Who in their right mind would cross through the vast tunnel of a major Wraithship axis?

Jaq peered. A small gap existed in the route. Another gap, elsewhere.

What could those gaps signify but that the quester must quit the Webway somewhere and then re-enter it nearby? Within Craftworld there were too many Webway portals to make the right choice except by sheer chance. These gaps must relate to planets upon which there were not one, but two openings. You must travel across the surface of a world from one portal to the other . . .

The rune of the Black Library had been pared from the warp-eye. Jaq sensed now that the rune of the route to the place of power was inscribing itself psychically in thin black lines upon the warp-eye lens.

As it did so, the page ceased to have hidden depths.

Jaq hooded the lens, as a beetle collector might enclose a fine specimen. Whenever he chose to look through the lens, overlaid upon whatever scene he saw would be the *route*.

Was the route still implicit in the page? Might others discover it? Roughly he ripped the page out and rolled it up.

Lex was squatting now. His chest was blackened as if by soot, yet the injury seemed superficial and irrelevant to him, a negligible flash-burn.

Jaq tossed the scroll at Lex.

"Tuck that into your webbing. Don't lose it. Help me get out of this cumbersome armour! Hurry, we haven't long—"

How yearningly the Death Jester stared at the scroll. He must believe that his captor-wizard had found some prophecy of immeasurable value, outweighing the rest of the book of fate!

Marb'ailtor remained utterly ignorant of what had been dis-covered, or that the route was written upon the lens—or that a Chaos ship had landed above, so close to the mansion. The Jes-ter's nostrils still flared at the odour of daemonry, yet surely that daemonry was here beside him in the cell.

While Lex helped Jaq strip off vambraces and greaves and paul-drons, Jaq probed himself inwardly.

He seemed clean, yet he persevered . . .

. . . and he encountered a presence.

A sensation had taken up temporary residence in the big toe of his right foot. How insignificant it seemed, like a wart. It was hid-ing as far away from his brain as it could find.

No sooner detected, than the presence reached out like some sea anemone opening up its fronds. Those fronds extended numbingly out and out. Jaq's right foot became numb; wouldn't obey his will. The foot jerked sideways. The presence controlled it.

Jaq's leg was numb to the knee—to the thigh. The invasion was coursing up through him, rising like floodwater up a drain. Hasty incantations had little effect. This energy-thing from the warp was wild to seize a material body for its own use.

Jaq's hands were still his own. But to use the force rod upon himself might injure him severely. Lex had been protected by that luminous hand of his, and the daemon had anticipated trans-ferring into another body. Jaq must rip the daemon from his own marrow and banish it all the way into the warp.

While Jaq still controlled his own voice, he cried out to Lex, "Don't look at the lens! Hold armour in front of my face as a shield and a mirror!"

Lex understood. The giant snatched up the rounded pauldron. Even as Jaq beheld the reflection of his own rutted and bearded features with his ordinary vision he flipped up both lens-hoods again. He gazed through the eye of the warp at himself. The rune of the route interposed a filigree lattice. Energy seemed to leap through the lattice into his brain—raw warp-energy, akin to the daemon within him yet without any consciousness of its own nature.

Like a wave which had crashed ashore, this energy began to withdraw powerfully, sucking at his soul. This was when mortal

men might lose their lives or go mad. The energy was also sucking at the daemon which was rising up so swiftly within Jaq.

The daemon's momentum became part of that powerfully
ebbing force. It was being dragged with the wave, losing identity,
shrieking.

Out of Jaq the daemon was sucked.

Jaq had shuttered the lens and was breathing deeply.

Lex had discarded the pauldron and had slammed the *Book of
Rhana Dandra* shut. With his ceramically toughened fingernail he
ripped precious gems loose from the binding, and jammed these
into a pouch upon his webbing. He was planning ahead. If they
could conceivably escape from the mansion there was little that
they could carry with them other than weapons and the con-
densed wealth of jewels.

"Are you illuminated?" Jaq asked Lex—in wonderment at what
had happened.

Lex ignored the question. How could he possibly have become
illuminated when he had never been a psyker to begin with? A
miracle had happened. That miracle had been due to the names
upon his finger bones, to intervention by the souls of dead comrades, to the intercession of Rogal Dorn the shining light.

"Are *you*?" Lex barked at Jaq.

Jaq did not know. Analyse himself as he might, an awareness
of illumination eluded him. Oh, he had seen luminously into the
book of fate, assisted by that hand of glory which glowed no
more. Oh, he had been semi-possessed, but not profoundly in his
soul. When he reached the place of power and reincarnated Meh-
'lindi, *that* would be the supremely illuminating moment.

Upstairs, a bolt gun began to racket. There came the muffled
sound of heavier fire in reply.

The renegades must be returning to the mansion in force. Only
Grimm and Rakel were in their way.

As Jaq and Lex ascended from the cellars in haste, leaving book
and Jester abandoned, a pandemonium of explosions began
which could have no imaginable explanation . . .

The reason was both wonderful and terrible.

Chaos Marines had spilled from their ship to advance on the
mansion once again. Grimm had waited till they came half way

before opening fire. He was determined to die dearly and cause a little delay.

His shots provoked a thunderous response. And then—moments later—flying machines hove into view in the dusty air above the ship. Armed machines. Two-person machines. Half a dozen of them.

These were Eldar Vypers—somewhat larger than jet-bikes. Some sported twin shuriken catapults. Others, single shuriken cannons. Three of the Vypers carried heavy plasma guns in addition. The other three carried lascannons. The pilots and gunners were a squad of Craftworld Guardians wearing pale green wraith-armour and dark green helmets. Green banners rippled.

A seventh Vyper was keeping its distance. In the gunner's, the passenger's seat, was a shimmer of hues. The third Harlequin had indeed reached the Webway portal. He had brought vengeance back with him. Vengeance—or reinforcement? In spite of Jaq's psychic shielding had the Harlequin sensed something of the true motive of the attack at the theatre? Had he sensed—or guessed—the link with the lost book of fate?

That Harlequin could not have realized that the Death Jester had been captured instead of killed, otherwise there should have been another Vyper with an empty seat for rescue.

Those Vypers had flown to Sabulorb on the very coat-tails of the storm—such an ideal cloak. Had the Eldar spied the Chaos vessel descending upon the shrouded city? If not, its daemonic aura must have caught their attention and demanded investigation. Oh, let not the book fall into the clutch of Chaos.

A Vyper opened fire with plasma cannon and lascannon upon that ship which disguised itself as a mansion. Pilots and gunners had seen renegade Marines leaving that place. No mere mansion, that!

Incandescent shells of plasma burst against their target. Waves of heat radiated, accompanied by thunderous shock. Parts of the target were converted into superheated ionized gas. If confined, this would have been thermonuclear in intensity.

Energy shells from the lascannons delivered their massive punch.

Camouflage vanished, revealing the boxlike vessel. The giant pincer at the front was crippled. The plasma cannon at the snout had burst open. Part of the hull had stoved in. A razor fin had

sheared off. That fin was flying through the air like some flat predatory creature. It impacted in the roof of the adjoining mansion,
showering a scurf of tiles. Its blade must have shorted out some
power unit, because a moment later the whole roof of that large
house erupted, a small fireball rising, followed by gushing black
smoke.

The ship's upper plasma cannon discharged itself dazzlingly.
One of the Vypers became an expanding ball of scorching lurid
gas.

Plasma cannons took quite a while to recharge after the ex-
penditure of such energies. The pilots of the remaining Vypers
were turning their attention to the armoured renegades out in the
open—just as those renegades turned their attention upon the
Vypers. Shuriken discs streamed and cannoned from above.
Heavy bolts and energy packets flew upward. Blasted, a blue-clad
gunner fell. Punctured a score of times, a Chaos renegade staggered.

Grimm fired almost affably, out into the garden.

It was at this moment that the plasma cannon near the *stern* of
the Chaos vessel opened fire past the blazing mansion, at its vine-
clad perimeter railings.

Traffic was coming into view. Half-track armoured vehicles,
mounted with heavy stub guns or autocannons ... Trotting
alongside were ebony robots with mirror-faces. *Arbitrators*, armed
with lasguns.

Plasma disintegrated the railings and caused some casualties.
The half-tracks revved and headed directly through the dispers-
ing heat and gas. Before the rear plasma cannon could recharge,
the half-tracks were speeding past, on either side of the grounded
ship.

What did the Arbitrators make of those alien flying machines
swooping and banking, pitted against ferocious angular Marines?
The armoured vehicles and the Arbitrators on foot opened fire im-
partially   on   all   disturbers   of   the   Emperor's   peace.
TUB-TUB-TUB-TUB: heavy bullets belched from the big stubbers.
Laser-packets rocketed pyrotechnically. They were like fireworks
hurled against steel. Those renegades were armoured strongly
enough to cause heavy bullets merely to ricochet.

The fight was threefold and insensate. By now Jaq's mansion

was suffering enough collateral damage to bring masonry crashing down, interspersed by showers of glass from upper windows. Noises of detonations were deafening.

"Let's get outa here!" shouted Grimm.

Jaq seized his discarded robe to don over his mesh-armour.

"My bone!" exclaimed Lex. What about the thigh-bone on which he had scrimshandered for the sake of his chapter, should he ever rejoin them? And for the sake of his soul!

Stray las-fire ignited curtains. Flames climbed to lick the ceiling.

"Gotta leave your bone, you great mastiff," yelled Grimm.

Lex groaned with grief.

"What about the Jester?" shrieked Rakel.

"Leave him to roast, of course!" shouted Grimm. "And the *Book of Dandruff* too. Give his snooty pals something to occupy their minds. If those guys can deal with the Chaos boys as well as with the mirror-faces then they'd better take up fire-fighting pretty damn fast—"

Distracted by the nuisance of the Arbitrators, Chaos Marines were succumbing to the aerial onslaught. The damaged Chaos vessel began to throb and to vent wisps of plasma. Despite its damage it was preparing for take-off. The pilot was preparing to abandon all the surviving Chaos Marines.

Amidst such bedlam it *was* indeed possible to escape to the sidelines and away—blessing the dust which still hung in the air and the smoke drifting from explosions and fires.

As Jaq and companions were fleeing, a small sun seemed to rise against the hazed ruby immensity of Sabulorb's own sun which was now reasserting itself in the sky. A small and wobbling minor sun: that was the plasma torch of the Chaos ship.

With a vane missing, and with the other weakening it had suffered, that ship might well be unsteerable. If it achieved escape velocity the renegade ship might only plunge onward through space . . . until in a few days time—or much earlier, depending on velocity—it fell into the embrace of the vast red sun. How deeply would it penetrate the furnace-hot outer gases before exploding?

Or would the pilot suicidally activate the warp-drive to escape this fate, annihilating his vessel and disrupting space in its vicinity, sending a shock-wave inward through the contracting red giant?

On the vast scale of a sun, this would be a puny enough shock-wave—but perhaps significant . . . A dying butterfly begetting a tempest . . .

Chapter Twelve

Firestorm

It happened that an airborne troop carrier arrived at Shandabar's spaceport from the northerly continent just prior to the storm. On board were two hundred hardened soldiers. They were due to be sent off-world to join the Sabulorb Regiment. A transport ship of the Imperial Guard had landed at the spaceport to receive the new intake. Two squads of veteran Guards were escorts.

Half of the Shandabar garrison was routinely stationed near the perimeter of the spaceport, the remainder being near the Governor's palace. In the wake of the storm these received a static-crackly radio message from the senior Judge at the Courthouse in the city. Aliens coming from the direction of the Grey Desert on armed two-person flying vehicles had raided a suburb. That same suburb had already been invaded under cover of the storm by other formidable armoured warriors. Extraterrestrial raiders had chosen Shandabar as the venue for a private war. Many Arbitrators had died. Urgent assistance was requested.

Due to the assassination of a Judge and the massacre of a patrol in the city the Courthouse had adopted a policy of rapid response to sightings and reports . . .

Veterans and hardened recruits disembarked from the spacecraft to be met by all available surface troop carriers of the spaceport garrison, bulging armoured skirt-plates protecting their huge desert-tyres. Shortly after these vehicles had left the spaceport, an unidentified vessel descended from orbit without warning or permission. During the final stages of its descent, it fired a plasma cannon at that almost empty Imperial Guard ship upon the ground. The Guard ship exploded. Scattered wreckage crippled the nearby troop carrier.

No sooner was the intruder down than a burst of plasma demolished the control tower. Next, the terminal was torched.

Huge warriors in terrifying power armour emerged from the angular vessel . . .

Elsewhere in Shandabar many jet-bikes were sighted, steered by tall figures in green armour and helmets resembling great smooth hoods . . .

Citizens who had sheltered from the storm emerged to find dust-choked victims lying dead in drifts of grit in every street. A syncopation of distant explosions and gunfire from various quarters suggested that gangs must be taking advantage of the confusion.

Indeed deacons in camouflage clothing had set out from the Oriens Temple to launch an attack of retaliation upon the Austral Temple—though this was not the cause of *most* of the crackle and thump . . .

Viewscreens, set up throughout the city for the ceremony of the unveiling, still had not been dismantled. A Judge messaged the Oriens Temple, ordering its high priest to use the camera link to proclaim a state of emergency and immediate curfew via those public screens. City being under alien attack. Arbitrators restoring order mercilessly, being assisted by Imperial Guards.

In the meantime devotees of the imperial cult had begun flocking through grime-clogged streets to the courtyard of Oriens to pray. As prayers arose, like a portent there appeared above the vast courtyard a small armed flying vehicle—with *Death* as a passenger. Riding pillion was a bizarre lanky figure with a smoke-blackened skull of a face and a body of sooty bones stitched to a smouldering cloak. Death seemed to be in agony, and insane, and perhaps himself soon to die.

Through a loudhailer Death proclaimed to whoever could hear: *"YOUR SUN IS ABOUT TO MELT YOUR WORLD! YOUR SUN IS ABOUT TO BOIL YOUR SEAS! YOUR SUN IS ABOUT TO BAKE YOUR DESERTS! ALL FLESH WILL CHAR, ALL BLOOD WILL BOIL, ALL LIFE WILL END!"*

The shocked High Priest transmitted this scene to dust-coated screens throughout entire districts of Shandabar. Most viewers did not fully savvy the standard ImpGoth of this apparition. Yet the scorched Jester's gist was clear. The sun pulsed heat through the lingering dust. The whole sky seemed aflame.

And then Death the Jester fell from his perch—as if he had been shot in order to silence him. Down he tumbled to sprawl burned and broken.

Rescued from the blazing mansion by the wild bravery of two green-clad Guardians who had heeded his psychic cries—rescued together with the smouldering *Book of Rhana Dandra*—Marb'ailtor had suffered serious burns.

Even so, Marb'ailtor insisted to his rescuers that this city must be plunged into absolute anarchy so as to allow the Eldar to cope with the Chaos renegades and to safeguard the book of fate without interference by organised human authority—and so as to be able to track that mad magus-Inquisitor who had carried off a crucial page.

Let there be utter anarchy!

Marb'ailtor would endure long enough to bring this anarchy about.

Once the Death Jester had fallen from the Vyper, and once the Vyper had sped off, the High Priest finally uttered the curfew order. This command from the Courthouse was completely at odds with Death's warning about imminent calamity. Or was it at odds at all? Let the people passively await extinction—while, unimpeded by crowds, the authorities used some escape route!

Panic rippled through Shandabar. Panic, and outcry. The curfew was ignored. If two million people (minus a few thousand suffocated corpses) all disobeyed, what could mere hundreds of Arbitrators do?

Fires were soon burning here and there in the city. The Austral Temple was in flames.

Fire. Heat. The furnace of the sun, slowly sinking. Dust-haze, heat-haze, plumes of smoke, including one from the direction of the space-port . . .

Rumour of an escape route spread like a flash-fire. Not of escape by way of the spaceport! The spaceport was crippled. A hostile warship sat there. Whenever a freighter attempted to power up, a blast of plasma would strike it; a new explosion would rock the city.

Escape by way of the broad Behishti river? Flight upon its cool waters? Thousands of people mobbed boats. Boats capsized under the burden of bodies. Thousands of people drowned. That could not be the route. Boats were too slow. None of the authorities were fleeing by way of water.

A zealot preached about penitence in the desert, salvation in the wilderness. "Be confronting your souls in the desert as a test of faith! Be seeking the crucible of tomorrow's dawn!"

The vast majority of people had no clear idea of what was happening except that there was desperate urgency to distance themselves from Shandabar. Shandabar would burn. Soon a massive exodus was beginning. In its hysterical surge this resembled the ceremony of the unveiling, though on a greater scale.

By land-train and by trucks and by limousines—all bouncing along upon balloon-wheels—and by rickshaws and sand-sleighs and carts pulled by camelopards, and on the backs of camelopards, and on foot—on at least a million feet—the evacuation commenced in entire disorder. As the sun at last withdrew its ruddy light and intemperate heat, sinking below the camber of the world, a whole population was fanning out southward across the Grey Desert in the general direction of Bara Bandobast.

Minor battles accompanied the mass migration. Islands of violence eddied within the flood of folk. Highly mobile homicidal Marines fought running skirmishes with lightning-swift aliens. Imperial Guards were involved, and Arbitrators. These rolling skirmishes cut minor swashes through the exodus, serving as further goads to the mass of refugees. How much dust so many people were raising too. What with the dust and the setting of the sun, there was soon a blind lemming-surge, illuminated only by the discharge of weaponry.

About the time when Shandabar would have receded to a bumpy line along the horizon—had there been any visibility—a chain of distant explosions rocked the desert. Seconds later a scorching gust from the north carried much airborne dust away, revealing a wall of flame along that same horizon, a bright and rippling banner, and bringing uncanny illumination to the desert.

"What in the name of all me Ancestors—!"

Grimm and Lex and Jaq and Rakel were jammed inside the cabin of a single-carriage land-train. Until now the driver, obedient to the bolt gun held at the back of his neck, had been steering by the hazy beams from the transport vehicle's lamps. Suddenly: that great brightness from behind was reflected in the ornate mirrors jutting from either side of the cab.

If nomad bandits ever loomed in those mirrors, sprinting on foot or riding camelopards, hoping to board such a train from the rear, automated autoguns were mounted at the rear and half-way along the carriage roof to deter them. On the route to Bara Bando-bast bandits were rarely a problem. Yet right now the roof of the land-train was packed with refugees who had climbed and clung, dense as the fleas on the head of a swimming cudbear. Jaq hadn't wanted boarders shot off. Those people were a cloak, comparable to the human cloaks worn by many other vehicles. They were camouflage.

The goods carriage was full of thoroughbred camelopards from breeding stables on the southern outskirts of Shandabar. According-ing to the driver, the beasts were being sent to take part in annual desert races at Bara Bandobast; hence this journey of his, which Jaq and company had hijacked. The storm had died; he had been setting out when other events supervened.

Those animals were hobbled to prevent them from kicking each other. They were muzzled to stop them from biting their neigh-bours. Their weight and that of all the refugees up top caused the land-train's engine to labour somewhat. Jaq did not wish for high speed. If they outdistanced the mass stampede, they might become conspicuous. As things were, how might pursuers of whatever affiliation be able to single them out amid untold vehicles and a fleeing mass of a million people or more?

That light which pierced the dust, that blast which blew dust away temporarily, that wall of flame—!

"Has Shandabar been nuked?" exclaimed Grimm.

Lex shook his head.

"I don't think so," he said. "Even ordinary dust at a certain number of grains per cubic centimetre in an oxygenated atmos-phere can explode if there's a trigger. I think that the force of the storm may have exposed huge deposits of carbon and sulphur and nitre of potassium in the Grey Desert. It bore these aloft and mixed them. It spread them as an aerosol across the city. This thinned to a critical density. Plasma explosions ignited the mix. The city exploded in a fire-storm."

"Do you mean to say we're travelling across a desert of gun-powder? *This can explode too?*"

"I doubt it, Abhuman, otherwise flame would be reaching us by now. Other factors in the city could be lingering electrostatic charge due to friction, and the effect of Chaos. We ought to offer up a prayer of thanks that Shandabar exploded."

"Eh?"

"In the morning when the sun rises, the temperature will soar. The mob would be wise to return home. But now home has been annihilated. We will continue to be a needle in a very vast haystack. Eldar and Chaos renegades and local peace enforcers might kill each other. They will certainly become fatigued. *Not revving too fast, driver!*"

They must try to catch some sleep, or half-sleep, in the crowded vibrating cab while Lex or Jaq or Grimm in turn supervised the driver. Rakel could sleep as long as she pleased, or was able to.

How could Jaq's party know that a second Chaos vessel had landed at the spaceport?

Why should they need to know, when the fire-storm had already scorched that vessel?

Come the dawn, the smoke from Shandabar was a distant smudge upon the northern horizon. In all directions the desert was dotted with vehicles and with the fittest foot-sloggers who had kept up their best pace throughout the menacingly warm night. Amazing, really, that there were still pedestrians in the vicinity. Fear of death was such a fierce spur. But also, bargains must have been made.

Vehicles would have broken down fairly recently, or run out of fuel, shedding occupants and hangers-on. Nearly all functioning vehicles were slowed by the burden of hangers-on. Vehicles lumbered along surrounded by a gang of would-be boarders like sweat-flies accompanying a tormented and exhausted ox. Social organization had emerged amongst this vast rolling flood of fugitives so that people would take turns to ride and to jog.

The rumour endured that a route to safety existed. Who actually knew the route? Who would wish, in ignorance of that route, to outdistance whoever might possess this knowledge?

Did the route simply lead to Bara Bandobast? If the sun were about to destroy all life on Sabulorb, Bara Bandobast would burn too!

Might the secret of the route involve the fierce aliens? Or those terrible armoured marauders? Dispersed amidst the immense exodus, survivors of both factions continued to skirmish wearily with one another and with local forces. Come dawn, only one armed flying-bike seemed to be still aloft. None of the two-person fliers could be seen. Intakes choked by dust, had their pilots abandoned them? Had they been crippled by shots? Who could say? Skirmishes were akin to the dartings of frenzy-fish amidst a shoal of sprats. Where the sprats were so numerous, and the skirmishes comparatively few, the chance of being killed in crossfire was actually quite small—except for the persons actually killed. Sprats and vehicles and camelopards were being used as moving cover by the combatants.

Did one really wish to distance oneself from those fighters who might know the way to safety? Fighters came from off-world. If the world was to burn, safety must be off-world. Rumour spread, pantingly, of a huge fleet of starships waiting in the deep desert to evacuate people whose faith was strong, whose faith was now being tested.

Quivering, the sun shouldered up over the eastern horizon. Soon heat began to beat a gong upon the desert floor.

The sky glared.

Mirages burgeoned: of phantom vehicles floating along amidst the actual vehicles. Of floods of spectral people. Of distant shimmering towers. Surely those must be the starships of the rumour. Mirages appeared of a wide shallow river through which far-off refugees seemed to be wading.

How could one be certain which sights were real and which were imaginary? How excellent these many mirages. How confusing for anyone trying to find a needle in all the hay, now that the desert was bright.

Of a sudden the driver slumped over the controls. He was asleep. The land-train swerved and stopped abruptly. A couple of clingers were pitched from their perch. One scrambled to claw his way back up over the front of the cab. He stared in at the congestion within the cab, and at the driver seemingly dead—of a heart attack, of a stroke? The refugee gestured, offering himself as a substitute driver.

Pushing the driver aside, Grimm switched on the powerful dust-wiper to sweep the petitioner away. The man lost his hold. As he fell his hand closed on the wiper arm, dragging it down, bending it away from the windshield.

The driver woke groggily.

"Whaz happening—?" His hand flailed. He was in no state to drive any more. The throbbing engine had cut out. They could hear feet on the roof. They could hear drumming too. The hobbled camelopards were thumping their hooves in complaint.

That other man who fell off must have broken his leg. Grimacing, he stretched up an arm in appeal. And now two inverted heads peered down from above to snoop into the cab through the windshield.

With a grip upon the neck, Lex stilled the worn-out driver. He undogged the cab door briefly, threw the man out, and dragged the door shut. Grimm scrambled into the driving seat. He shouted at the peering faces, "One of you climbing down and straightening that wiper or else I'll be switching on the guns up top!"

As a man descended hastily, Grimm restarted the engine. While the fellow wrestled with the wiper arm, the land-train moved slowly forward. Maybe the balloon wheels missed the man with the broken leg. To run over him might be kinder than to leave him behind.

They were travelling south amidst the migration in the general direction of Bara Bandobast. That labyrinth of rocks and the stone mushrooms, of which the Jester had spoken, was supposedly to the east of Bara Bandobast. A day's march to the east, Marb'ailtor had said. Some fifty kilometres. Soon they would need to change direction towards the south-east.

If a single land-train were to deviate from the general direction of the trek, it would become conspicuous.

The air in the cab was so hot and vapid, so lifeless. It would only become hotter. Sweat trickled; lungs laboured. The cab possessed a ventilation system. A concealed fan whirred. But no vehicles on Sabulorb had hitherto needed a refrigeration unit, only a heater. Though the cab heater was switched off, it seemed to be operating at maximum output. Under Jaq's robe his mesh armour was becoming oppressive. Flexible, porous, and light-weight it might be—how could he think of forsaking its protection?—yet it taxed him.

Grimm rubbed salty sweat from his eyes. "We gotta open the windows."

Jaq agreed. "And it's about time we changed course."

A manual winding mechanism operated the window against which he was crushed. In miniature the mechanism reminded him of a torment machine he had once studied as a probationary Inquisitor. He wound down the armoured glass and shouted, "All you up there! Hearing me!"

Heads appeared.

"We are knowing the true way to safety! I am swearing this by Him-on-Earth! We must not be heading to safety in isolation—" He needed to stop and summon up saliva to lubricate his words. It was a while since they had drained the cab's water canteen dry. "Otherwise aliens and renegades will be stopping us. This whole trek must be veering south-eastwards. You must be running to other vehicles to be spreading the word. They must be spreading the word in turn. When enough vehicles are changing direction, only then are we doing likewise. Destination being stone laby-rinth in the desert fifty kilometres east of Bara Bandobast." He swallowed dryly. "Be going and saying this now! Only we here are knowing whereabouts in the labyrinth. I am guiding you to safety. Be going and returning. Otherwise I am shooting you off the roof on a count of ten . . . and nine—!"

Grimm halted the land-train. To any suspicious observer it would seem that the vehicle had simply broken down. Men and women were descending. Several gestured at their throats or croaked for water. How could they say anything without a few sips?

Oh but they could. Jaq mimed the absence of water in the cab. A man bit his wrist, and sucked on trickles of blood.

How could they *run*? Nevertheless, they managed to stagger, casting fearful glances backwards at the stationary carriage. It re-mained where it was—nor by now were there any other potential boarders in the vicinity.

"Nervous fools," growled Lex. "We need them back, as a crab needs its shell."

Not quite as many refugees returned. A few must have collapsed while away from the land-train. Nor could all manage the climb up to their former scorching perch. Nevertheless, once more the train had a coat of people.

Presently the tide of migration began to veer sufficiently, and over a wide enough expanse, for Grimm to begin heading east by south. A mass momentum accumulated. Word of mouth was no longer necessary. Vehicles far away were altering direction merely because so many others were doing so.

For some while they had been hearing a punctuation of modest explosions. The brisk bangs seemed unrelated to any skirmish. Abruptly an explosion rocked their land-train. The cab lurched to one side.

Another detonation. The train lurched again.

"Someone's shooting at our tyres—"

A third explosion. The vehicle was dragging. The floor was at an angle. How the engine toiled.

"No one's shooting," Rakel said huskily. She gestured as a nearby limousine subsided suddenly upon ruptured flattened rubber. "Heat's expanding the air in the tyres. The tyres are bursting—"

The land-train was disabled; and they had abandoned the control cab.

Far and near, balloons were banging. With bolt guns and las-pistols Jaq and Grimm and Rakel covered a small crowd of dizzy refugees who had quit the roof. Lex let down a ramp at the rear. He led out the camelopards one by one. Still hobbled, the animals shuffled with mincing steps. Long necks snaked from side to side, attempting head-butts. Lex had found no slosh of urine inside the hot carriage. Overheated, the animals were retaining their bodily fluid. Out in the open, each instinctively shifted to present the minimum profile to the great hot sun. How stupidly malevolent the beasts' whiskery faces looked. How scrawny their bodies. Ribs and other bones stood out prominently as if hairy rubber were wrapped around skeletons. The humps were like giant erupting boils.

These beasts weren't even sweating. Nor had the air inside the carriage reeked unduly. Camelopards must be able to tolerate higher temperatures than people. Probably the lack of fat on their bodies—apart from in the parasol humps—would allow heat to radiate away more rapidly.

Before the start of human colonization camelopards must have been introduced to Sabulorb with an eye to a possible future rise in temperature. Untold generations of beasts must have shivered for aeons, unable to evolve fat on their bodies because their gene-runes had been locked.

At last the beasts were coming into their own as regards climate.

Perhaps not for long. If radiation from the sun continued to intensify, the camelopards' summer of happiness might only last for a few days—until they all died of heatstroke, though rather later than their erstwhile owners.

A dozen animals stood shuffling, too hampered to attempt an escape or too stupid to think of it. Dazed passengers eyed the beasts covetously. Refugees might have surged feebly had it not been for the guns.

"There'll be *water* in those *humps*," Grimm enthused hoarsely. "A figging cistern of water. I'll stick a knife in as a spigot—"

"Sir, sir," croaked a dusty woman, whose obesity must be causing her great discomfort. "Sir, not being so! Humps storing fat, not liquid."

The little man motioned her to advance.

"Be explaining."

"Fat needing burning for releasing water."

"Damn it, there ain't no time for cooking humps."

"The blood, Sir, the blood—"

"Damnfool idea drinking salty blood!"

"Blood not being salty, Sir. Red bloodcells being filled with water when camelopards drinking. Bloodcells stretching, engorging. Bloodcells expanding to a quarter-thousand times their original volume—"

"Bloodcells swelling two hundred and fifty-fold? Tosh!"

"Being true! Beasts being watered before journey. Be observing how swollen the humps—"

This was indeed the truth.

The land-train's engine was sited mainly beneath the cab. Part jutted forward, protected by a hump-shaped hood. Lex soon unlatched this hood. Wrenching it loose, he hurried back to the camelopards.

A Fist thought. A Fist planned.

With a sand-shovel from the carriage Lex dug a shallow pit to accommodate the hood. The hood was now a big basin.

Litres of blood from two butchered camelopards filled the basin. In turn Rakel and Jaq and Grimm and Lex lapped their fill, under the hammer of the sun. Those not drinking pointed their guns at the increasingly desperate refugees. Lex filled the canteen from the cab with blood. Then they let the refugees loose upon the ample remaining blood.

The other camelopards had watched the fate of their stable-mates with what seemed a smug disinterest. From the carriage came reins and rope and four leather saddles.

Lex hauled the fat informant to her feet. Her face was blotched with blood. So was his own face. So were those of his companions. Dried blood and dust would provide protection against sunburn, which no one on Sabulorb could ever have experienced before.

Lex had seen camelopards ridden in the streets of Shandabar. Ordinarily a saddle was strapped behind the hump. These were racing saddles, though, and racing beasts. Maybe different circumstances applied.

"Saddle going behind the hump, eh woman?" he demanded. The pretence of only speaking scum slang was so irrelevant now.

"Otherwise their heads snaking back, Sir, to be biting."

"Not keeping mounts muzzled?"

"Needing to race with mouths open, for air!" She hesitated, gazing at his bare fused chest abulge with muscle. "Your *weight*, Sir. Your mount not racing, only cantering."

Thirst slaked, refugees turned their attention to the two corpses. Knives emerged. The immediate object wasn't meat but hairy hide with which to contrive oozing shawls to cover heads and shoulders.

"How ordering a beast to run?" Lex demanded. "What words being best?"

"Taking me with you?" wheedled the woman. "Clinging behind the dwarf?"

"Maybe," conceded Lex.

"Myself knowing much about 'pards, Sir."

"What about *your* weight, Momma?" interrupted Grimm.

The woman's gaze strayed to those ropes which Lex had brought from the carriage.

"You will be leading spare mounts behind you," she said in accusation. They would not be abandoning spare mounts for refugees.

"Hurry up!" called Jaq.

They were in no danger of being left behind by the migration. This was still scattered all over the hostile and increasingly hotter terrain, never mind how many hundreds of thousands had fallen behind, or fallen, never to rise. Yet sooner or later someone who hunted Jaq's party must surely find them.

Rakel aimed her laspistol at the woman. "Be telling the words. If wrong, we are not going far." True indeed. If the beasts failed to gallop—or at least to canter—then the woman could expect swift punishment.

Anxiously the woman said, "To be starting, be crying out *Hut-hut, shutur!* To be cantering, be crying *Tez-rau.* For galloping, *Yald!* For stopping, *Rokna!*"

Though perceptibly smaller than even on the previous day, the sun was still gigantic. How its heat beat down.

Lex told his companions, "Listen, we can make it. The heat isn't quite as bad as it seems. Not yet! It's bad by contrast with beforehand."

"Huh!" All very well for Lex to say so, when he was modified and trained to endure extreme temperatures. Still, Squats could tolerate enough heat in the deep galleries of mines. No doubt it was madness to continue this journey by day. Brain-boiling madness. What other choices did they have? Some of the refugees, having flayed shawls for themselves, cut hunks of raw dripping sinewy meat and retired inside the empty carriage for shade.

Jaq shed his robe, revealing the scaly mesh armour beneath. He unpeeled this from his body, resumed his robe, then he rolled the flexible armour up and tied the roll to a saddle like some shrivelled armadillo.

Rakel was swaying. Abruptly she vomited blood—as if some tiny missile had entered her unseen and unheard and ravaged her internally. Ach, that was only camelopard blood she was chucking up.

A shallow depth of liquid blood still remained in the basin, though around the edges a brownish purple rim was coagulating.

"Damn it, you'll drink again!" Grimm told Rakel. He grabbed her by the arm. She submitted. She knelt. She lapped.

Lex began roping camelopards behind one another. One spare mount to run behind, for Jaq. One spare for Grimm. One spare for Rakel. And two spares for his own hefty self.

What, canter? When he could try to gallop? At least until his first mount burst its heart . . .

Lex secured the saddles. He arranged the reins. He unmuzzled the beasts, avoiding a biting. Finally he unhobbled the creatures, avoiding being kicked. The four companions mounted.

One beast remained.

"Last one being for *you*, Momma," Lex told the fat woman, "in gratitude for your advice. *Hut-hut, shutur!*" he bellowed. His camelopard lurched into motion. The 'pards' eyes rolled. Strings of spittle flew from floppy lips, peeled back to expose large yellow teeth.

"*Hut-hut, shutur!*" from Jaq.

  "*Hut-hut, shutur!*" from Grimm.

    "*Hut-hut, shutur!*" from Rakel.

"*TEZ-RAU!*" bellowed Lex. "*And . . . YALD!*"

Behind, for a short while through dust one could see the fat woman wrestling strenuously with the final beast. Her fellow refugees were hurrying from the carriage to contest ownership.

How sad that so many striving people must be treated as expendable! But Lex and Grimm and Rakel were all too likely to be expended before the day was out.

Chapter Thirteen

Heatwave

The air seemed to be molten glass. The glass was imperfect, full of flaws and distortions. These flaws served as channels for mirages, as lenses for images of far-off vehicles and camelopard riders, and of shuffling refugees on foot—and of corpses, increasing numbers of corpses.

Was this lumbering figure in angular power armour—who shouldered a storm-bolter—near at hand? Should Jaq or Lex or Grimm loose off explosive bullets at that renegade? The image wavered and vanished before they could decide.

A natural phenomenon, this! It seemed that the heat might be boiling the blood in one's brain, breeding lunatic fancies.

The hood of Jaq's gown shaded, yet did not cool his head. Grimm had his forage cap to protect his cranium somewhat. Lex had been trained to tolerate the intolerable—but might his brain boil, even so? His exposed spinal sockets looked like holes drilled neatly in him by a marksman's bullets. Rakel wore an improvised hat of vellum folded in a yacht shape, and secured under her chin by the red Assassin's sash. The sash lent her the appearance of someone whose throat had been cut bloodily from ear to ear. That vellum hat was the great page which Jaq had torn from the *Book of Rhana Dandra*.

Was the rest of the book of fate being carried to safety by a Harlequin somewhere amidst the dwindling migration? Had the book already been rushed to the Webway portal by Vyper or by jet-bike? Such questions seemed remote and meaningless.

Glare reflected from the ground. They rode upon a glowing anvil, with a hot hammer poised overhead. What an inversion of blacksmithery this was. Those on the anvil would not soften like metal in a forge. They would dry up and harden utterly. No one would pluck them up with tongs to plunge them into cool water to quench them.

They passed bodies which were already almost mummies, their fluid content evaporated.

Yet something might well pluck them up. Great whirling cylinders of grit were wandering randomly amidst the mirages and the real refugees. Localized thermal hurricanes, these, the desert equivalent of waterspouts. One such cylinder picked up a refugee from beside an overturned bicycle-rickshaw—and dropped him a short while later as a skeleton, scoured to the bone by the swirling abrasion of sharp particles. At all costs avoid such roaming cylinders.

Constantly stones were bursting and rocks were cracking, uttering loud reports; such was the exceptional heat.

A vision came to Jaq—of the sky as a womb of light. Therein floated a great bloated pulsing blood-red child, the sun. Or was that red mass itself the womb, and did a white-dwarf foetus lurk deeper inside it?

Jaq found himself praying croakingly to the Chaos Child: "Come into being! Become conscious! Show me the shining path again, the quicksilver way."

How could a shining path appear when all the world and all the sky seemed ablaze? Was his prayer not heresy?

Lex snarled, "Let me see the light of *Dorn*!"

The light was a hot red, edging into white.

Rakel began to babble huskily. "I *am* an Assassin, aren't I? An invincible Assassin who can endure any torment!"

This was fitting. Rakel was conforming to her destiny. Maybe the heat would erase some of the higher functions of her brain, making the transition from herself to Meh'lindi easier . . .

"Look!" gasped Grimm.

Water was fountaining from the ground ahead, falling back in a rainbow.

"Another mirage—"

"No, no. *Yald! Yald!*"

Nostrils flaring, the camelopards were already galloping faster.

Thus far only one of the beasts had collapsed under Lex. Re-silient creatures, these. During the time it had taken for Lex to transfer the saddle to his second mount, his three companions had simply sat upon theirs inertly. They *could* have changed mounts but none could summon the energy to do so . . .

The camelopards needed no cry of *Rokna!* to halt at the pool which was forming in a depression, fed by that liquid plume. Before Jaq and party could dismount a dozen other dusty burned refugees had arrived from out of the mirages. Three rode on camelopards. Half a dozen more were packed inside a white limousine. Steam billowed from the hood.

The fountain was a shining path, was it not? A vertical path, ascending for half a dozen metres before cascading back, bringing salvation to thirst, at least. Animals and humans crowded to-gether, slaking their thirst and soaking themselves.

Jaq arose, dripping. "We should give thanks," he said, "to Him-on-Earth for this blessing."

"Might as well give thanks to the bloody heat," said Grimm. "Cracking fissures in the rocks. Opening up a water-bearing stra-tum under pressure."

Probably this was true. It did not seem to be true. Surely they were the recipients of a miracle.

Lex eyed the steaming vehicle. The turbanned driver, who wore soiled white silks, was carrying water in cupped hands to cool the hood before he would contemplate opening it. A thinker, that one.

"Hey," Lex called to him, "you deflated your tyres, eh?"

The driver recoiled at the sound of standard ImpGoth, a stranger's speech.

"You were deflating your tyres in anticipation?"

"Yes." The reply was terse and defensive. Might this armed giant covet the vehicle?

"Doing well, fellow!" How many other drivers would have thought of this? Ten per cent? Five? That would still amount to thousands.

"Place of safety being here," declared one of the driver's pas-sengers. He sounded simple-minded. "We will be hiding all but our noses under the water."

Perhaps he was ingenious, but insane.

"Place of safety being further on," said another passenger. He spoke patiently, as if it was necessary to reason with the canny madman or else they would break some social bond which had brought them this far. "Being the haunted stone labyrinth, remembering? First we must be passing the hermitage I was describing."

"Haunted?" cried a rawly sun-burnt young woman who had been riding upon a 'pard. "How being haunted?"

"What hermitage?" asked her companion, a stouter older woman whose long black hair was stringy with oily sweat.

"Ghosts howling in that labyrinth," declared the informant. "Being a former resident of Bara Bandobast, I am knowing this. Labyrinth being taboo, yet we must be braving it. On the way we must be passing the Hermitage of the Pillar Ascetics."

"Who?" asked the simple-minded soul.

The reply came: "The Secluded Solitary Stylites are praying for His face to appear in the Sun so that our Sabulorb will become the prime pilgrimage planet in the whole Cosm."

"Excusing me," interrupted Grimm, "but how many hermits praying?"

"Hundreds."

"Excusing me again, but how being hermits if such a crowd?"

"Each hermit sitting alone atop a different pillar of rock!" Was this dwarf stupid?

"Huh, so they'll be praying twice as hard today! Or falling off their pillars like flies."

From behind a low rise there lurched a tall figure in pale green armour, without any helmet. Although pinkly burned, his features were still graceful and achingly handsome. A plume of black hair spread out like a pathetic tattered toy parasol. One of the Eldar Guardians . . . He cradled a lasgun.

Inflamed skin pouched around his slanted eyes. He was squinting. He seemed half-blind.

He tripped. Using the long-barrelled gun as a crutch he rose again. Then he pointed the gun in the direction of the fountain, the little crowd, the steaming white limousine.

"Being alien—!"

Out came a stub gun. A bullet flew towards the Guardian, missing him entirely. To most ears what difference was there between the crack of that gun and the noise of another stone bursting? The keen-sensed Eldar must have perceived a distinction. Shouldering his lasgun, the Guardian fired towards the source of the sound.

He missed the gunman, but the energy packet erupted against the rear of the limousine. Bodywork tore open. Fumes gushed from a ruptured tank, igniting. Briefly a flamethrower was spouting into the air. And then flame flashed back. The whole rear of the vehicle exploded. Quickly the limousine was engulfed in an inferno.

How the driver howled. How he shredded his silks in despair at the sight.

RAAARKpopSWOOSHthudCRUMP spake Lex's bolt gun; and the half-blind Guardian died. Already Lex was remounting. Already he was gesturing urgently to Jaq and Grimm and Rakel to get into their saddles before the stranded passengers could recover from shock. The two women resumed their saddles even quicker than Grimm. They had arrived at the same conclusion. The passengers were stranded. Mounts were available.

Lex brandished the bolter and roared hoarsely, *"Hut-hut-shutur! Tez-rau! Yald!"* A chorus of *Hut-hut* and *Yald*, and the burning limousine and its former occupants were being left behind. At least they were left at an oasis—until such time as the sun might boil the water away. When that time approached would the ingenious madman lie underwater, scalding and boiling?

The two women were still tagging along with Jaq's party. Well and good. Thus the group might appear more normal—if anything was normal any more.

"Gaskets would have blown in any case sooner or later," remarked Grimm airily. "Cylinder block would have cracked. Best efforts don't always produce the best butter."

"Spare us your Squattish cookery mottoes," said Jaq. "I wish to meditate."

"You *could* have been leaving them your spare mounts," called out the younger woman.

"You two were hopping in your saddles fast enough!" retorted Grimm.

Rakel glared at the young woman. "Don't be messing with us," she warned. Perhaps this was indeed a helpful warning. "I," she continued, "being an imperial *Assassin*." Was she oscillating between sanity and insanity?

Pebbles continued to crack explosively. Fortunately these did not fling out shrapnel when splitting open.

Pillars of dark stone. Thousands of flat-topped rocky columns, ranging from three or four metres in height to upwards of fifty metres. These rose from the gritty desert over an area of many square kilometres.

This region seemed like the ruins of some prodigious temple. In the interior loomed a vaster hump of rock, honeycombed with cave-mouths. That might have been the inner shrine of the temple.

Atop a column knelt a white-robed hermit. What could be seen of his face beneath his cowl was brown leather. How the heat had baked him, exposed there up on that solitary height. Surely he had mummified.

Carved in the base of that natural column was the inscription: HIS GREAT RED EYE WATCHING US.

Further on, another hermit knelt high upon another pillar. This time the inscription read: PATRIARCH OF ALL.

Numerous other refugees were moving through the area. Some were on camelopards or balloon-wheeled trikes. Others were exhaustedly pedalling rickshaws. Many were reduced to pedestrianism. Every now and then, someone sprawled and did not rise. Tired tormented eyes barely glanced at the spectacle of the hermits on their pillars.

Many were the places in the Imperium where piety and insanity were indistinguishable. Insanity could often be contagious and persuasive. Pilgrims who had visited the holy city of Shandabar over the years, and been inspired with fervour, may well have been attracted subsequently to this desert hermitage. How many hermits there were, up on their pillars! The extent of the hermitage only became apparent as Jaq's group rode deeper.

All of the hermits were leathery corpses, desiccated by the heat or by the recent dust-storm—mummified into gargoyles in their positions of prayer.

Ordinarily these hermits would have sat high enough to escape storms of grit and sand. Yet during a dust-storm would they not be obliged to retreat inside that honeycombed central shrine to escape asphyxiation? From that place, indeed, their daily food and drink must emerge, transported by servants. Over the centuries or millennia that great rock had probably been extensively excavated, resulting in chambers and storerooms and maybe widespread catacombs beneath.

Obviously the hermits had sheltered from the dust-storm! When the storm passed, they had resumed their places. Then the rising heat had begun to kill them. The rules for these anchorites must include an exemption for dust-storms—yet not for a pernicious rise in temperature. Sabulorb was a cool world, was it not? Consequently the hermits had remained kneeling atop their pillars in ever more fevered prayer.

Within that central shrine-rock were servants grieving impotently? Maybe they were rejoicing to be free of duty. Maybe some mourned while others celebrated. Deprived of a rationale, the servants might even be at each other's throats—as the heat began to invade what may formerly have been a very cool abode.

Camelopards had slowed to a trot, partly because of the many pillars. Hereabouts a gallop might literally be breakneck. Yet this place also seemed to exert a certain charm over the snooty animals. How silent the area was. All pebbles with flaws must have cracked a while since. The 'pards padded circumspectly and refrained from snuffling, as if loathe to disturb the serenity.

Again, the inscription: PATRIARCH OF ALL.

Why not FATHER OF ALL? That was the more common usage.

Cold terror tiptoed down Jaq's spine. Upon a stubby spire a hermit opened his eyes, to glare down. Such mesmeric violet eyes those were. Cracked lips parted, revealing pointed teeth.

On other columns other hermits were stirring. Jaq kicked his camelopard in its ribs to urge it past that particular PATRIARCH pillar. He hissed to the others, "These are Genestealer hybrids!"

Growling oaths, both Grimm and Lex were readying their bolt guns.

The young woman called out, "What being happening?"

From Rakel: "What will they do?"

Something inside Jaq seemed to snap. Hoarsely he cried, "My true Assassin knew what Genestealers and their hybrids do. She took on their inhuman form. She tore hybrids apart with her claws."

Genestealers would kiss their seed into a human victim, male or female. Human parents would give birth to baleful offspring, upon which they could not stop themselves from doting, since

they had become slaves to their spawn. Some hybrids were monsters. Others almost seemed human, big-boned and bald, though
their teeth were usually sharp and their eyes hypnotic . . .

Such as these hermits upon the pillars.

Purestrain Genestealers were so strong and resilient. Their
claws could rip through steal. Hybrids shared enough of that
vigour and robustness to endure a rise in temperature. The leathery appearance of the hermits must be due to the emergence of
some mature 'Stealer characteristics—the horny purplish
hide—in response to environmental disaster.

If all the hermits out in the open were hybrids who could pass
as human, what monsters might lurk within the central shrine?
Hermits and monsters alike would all be brood-bonded in
empathy to a hideous armoured hog of a *Patriarch*! Sabulorb had
not been successfully cleansed after all. Survivors of a brood had
subverted this desert hermitage and multiplied . . .

If Meh'lindi were only here. If only she were still equipped with
Genestealer implants, whereby to confuse the hybrids on their
pillars. *No, that was a vile wish! Her implants had been an abomination.*

"She tore hybrids apart with her claws!" repeated Jaq.

Exhausted and almost demented, Rakel shuddered convulsively. "You have high expectations of your mistresses, my Lord
Inquisitor!"

Shame whelmed Jaq. His voice shook. "Your imitation of her is
sacred," he declared.

Yet no: it was profane.

Yet no again: Rakel's imitation of Meh'lindi would become
sacred when Meh'lindi was reincarnated within Rakel—and
when the Chaos Child stirred in the womb of the warp, sanctify-
ing Rakel's sacrifice of herself and Jaq's baptism of the new soul
within her!

"I apologize on behalf of the Ultramarines," declared Lex as he
surveyed pillar beyond pillar, upon which white-clad shapes
stirred slowly. "That the 'Stealers should have regained such
strength so soon! Truly it is better that this world be scorched."

A hermit had risen slowly to his full height the better to survey
the sluggish advent of the residue of the migration. His cowl fell
back, revealing a bald head glossy in the glare of light, and the
bony ridges of his brows. He stretched out muscle-corded arms.
He was inviting that advent onward, blessing it.

The scattered mass of refugees must have seemed like manna—or cause for imminent mania. Other hermits were rising. In time of crisis the absolute imperative was to pass on the genetic heritage of 'Stealers. Here came so many human cattle, to be inseminated.

Maybe this trek of human cattle was also welcome for the nourishment it could provide, if the heat died down rather than increasing. This desert was so barren. Did the hermits' servants grow food in the catacombs? Did hens cackle and lay underground? Were there tanks of algae? A feast of human flesh might be welcome; carcasses for pickling or smoke-curing.

Grimm sniggered hysterically. "Pad along softly, 'pard," he told his mount. "Keep up the pace, there's a good 'pard."

They passed another pillar, from the top of which a hybrid regarded them with magnetic eyes.

Thousands of flies were entering a web. The hybrids were like toads whose tongues are awakened by an appropriate flicker across the retina as prey moves within reach.

How soon would hybrids begin to descend? Maybe just as soon as mature 'Stealers erupted from the mouths of those tunnels in the shrine-rock.

This had been a hallucinatory, sun-struck journey—yet now the worst hallucination of all was real.

"Trotting a bit faster, there's a good 'pard—"

To break into a gallop or even a canter might precipitate the onslaught. Alas, their informant had not supplied the command for trotting. Grimm urged his mount with his knees.

"Hey," he called softly to the women who accompanied them, "what being the name for trotting?"

"Be saying *Asan*," was the reply from the younger woman. "*Easy riding* being the meaning."

"*Asan, shutur. Asan!*" This word was like a prayer. Grimm's mount picked up some speed. Others followed suit.

How Grimm yearned to be riding a power-trike rather than this lolloping quadruped. His rump was so stiff and sore.

In all directions hermits had arisen. All seemed to be straining to hear some sound. Were they awaiting an audible signal from the shrine-rock—or a psychic cue to attack? Yet their attention was focused northward from where the migration came . . .

"Aircraft!" said Lex.

Soon anyone could hear the drone of engines.

Into sight in the glowing sky came a large troop transporter, fly-ing slowly. Lex shaded his eyes and stared as the plane began to bank. It was intending to circle the hermitage.

"Imperial emblems, I think—"

How alert the hybrid hermits were now.

One of the aircraft's four engines spluttered and coughed and died.

"It's almost out of fuel—"

That aircraft couldn't have come from Shandabar. Shandabar was ashes and smouldering wreckage.

"Must be from the northern continent, from the planetary army base or the Departmento—"

After the dust-storm and before the city exploded, some Astro-path must have sent a message regarding intrusion by aliens and renegade Marines. Then Shandabar had fallen totally silent. A troop carrier had flown to investigate. To become so low on fuel, it must have met storms en route. The pilot would have counted on putting down at Shandabar. He would have beheld the utter and inexplicable destruction of the capital city. The plane had carried on. The pilot would have seen the signs of the migration: dozens of kilometres of corpses and abandoned vehicles; then refugees still struggling along, and camelopards—and that veer-ing in the direction of the trek, away from the obvious route to Bara Bandobast. The migration would have seemed to be heading for this place of pillars deep in the desert.

Airspeed would have ventilated the interior of the plane. Con-ditions on board might not have been too stifling. A hatch opened in one side of the plane. Bodies began to fall out. White chutes opened up. Bodies were drifting down—troops in mottled yellow and grey desert-camouflage, long-barrelled lasguns slung around their necks. Only one soldier's chute failed. He plummeted directly to the ground. Body after body plunged from the door. White blossoms opened. A hundred and fifty of the troops, at least!

One after another the plane's other engines coughed and cut out. Now it could only glide ponderously, its pilot hoping to reach open desert. An especially tall spire of rock clipped a wing. The plane promptly spun over and disappeared. The thump of impact threw up a cloud of dust but no fireball. No fuel was left for an explosion.

Troops were landing. Hermits were descending swiftly from their pillars, familiar with every finger grip. And the tunnel mouths of the shrine-rock vomited monsters!

Creatures with four arms, the upper set equipped with claws! Oh that characteristic loping gait. The speed, the sheer speed. Horns projecting from the spines. Bony sinuous tails. Long craniums jutting forward.

Behind those purestrain monsters, boiled forth a mob of hybrids who were far from human in appearance. They were such vile satires upon humanity with their swollen jutting heads and jagged teeth. Even from a distance their distortion was conspicuous. Some brandished a claw instead of a hand. Spurs of bone jutted from the backs of others.

Those hideous hybrids were armed with a motley of autoguns and shotguns and regular swords and chainswords. Of course the purestrain 'Stealers used no weapons nor tools other than their own fierce armoured bodies.

Having reached the ground, hermits were pulling stub guns and laspistols from under their white robes. A hermit cried out, "Silver-tongued Father, your saliva salving our souls!"

In the largest of the tunnel mouths, to survey the massacre which his brood intended, had appeared the Patriarch. Oh what a leering fang-toothed hog of a Four Arms! Armour-bones protruding from its curved spine were the size of loaves. Three-clawed hooves raked the rock on which it stood. Too far to make out its rheumy violet vein-webbed eyes.

Yet far too close as well!

Grimm shot the nearest of the hermits, wrecking his chest.

"*Tez-rau, yald!*" shouted Jaq.

They cantered, they galloped. Already one 'Stealer was racing to intercept them. The bouncing of Lex's 'pard spoiled his aim. A bolt was wasted on destroying the inscription upon a pillar. With a prayer and a bolt from *Emperor's Mercy*, Jaq halted the monster. It remained alive, writhing and ravaging the gravel.

Hermits were waylaying weary sun-struck refugees, often killing bare-handed. Hermits stooped to suck blood to slake a thirst. The toughest refugees defended themselves with stub guns. Scattered all over a great area, troops in yellow and grey were firing

energy packets wildly as 'Stealers or hybrids rushed towards
them. Most 'Stealers reached their chosen victims and tore them
apart. Attracted by the sight of the descending chutes—and now
by the detonations of this lethal affray—a half-track vehicle came
speeding. Upon it was a black-uniformed Arbitrator. He had lost
or discarded his mirrored helmet. Skin was peeling from his inflamed face. A 'Stealer raced from behind a pillar towards the
half-track. The Arbitrator swung the serpent-mouthed auto-
cannon mounted upon the vehicle. Shells blazed towards that
monster which should not have been present upon Sabulorb. A
high-velocity shell took off one of the lower arms of the 'Stealer.

On account of the extra revving perhaps the driver inside the
half-track succumbed to heat prostration. Or perhaps he tried to
swerve the vehicle away from the oncoming monster. One of the
vehicle's tracks locked, hit a rock. The vehicle skidded and began
to overturn. The autogunner was thrown clear. The 'Stealer
bounded faster. The Arbitrator rolled and tried to pull a side-arm
from a holster. Claws closed upon his burned bare head.

The 'Stealer turned its attention to the capsized half-truck.
Claws impacted in metal, seeking a hold by which to wrench a
panel loose.

A jet-bike was coming.

A streamlined aerial shark with a rune on its sloping nose, and
short stabiliser-wings each shaped like a double axehead, it
dodged its way between pillars, flying at only twice the height of
a man. It had made a close approach before being spotted. Such
low-level flying risked a 'Stealer leaping and clutching at a wing.

In the seat of that jet-bike: a confusing blur of hues—a Harlequin whose holo-suit was in kaleidoscopic flux. From either side
of the shark's snout jutted, like tusks, shuriken catapults. The
twin guns dipped momentarily, and spat discs of razor-metal
ahead almost too swiftly to be seen. A 'Stealer was crippled. Discs
had sliced through its rugged carapace into its softer core.

The jet-bike was angling towards the shrine-rock from which
the Patriarch surveyed the carnage. Blatantly, 'Stealers were
here—and *here* was comparatively close to an entry to the Webway. Guardians of a vile secret, the hybrid-hermits would not
have ranged far from their pillars in the past. Not as far as the
stone labyrinth. Survival of their brood demanded isolation, not
exploration. But now Sabulorb was about to burn. If the Patriarch

of the brood realized that there was a way to escape, hybrids and
purestrains would do their utmost to find that place. Purestrains
certainly could survive the mounting heat for long enough. 'Stealers could be loose in the Webway, able, if fate played a black
enough trick, to find a Craftworld.

This must not happen. The Harlequin angled the jet-bike
upward toward the shrine-rock, toward the terrible shape in that
tunnel mouth.

*A hail of shuriken discs bracketed that four-armed hog. A good many
discs hit it. The armoured hog staggered but did not collapse. One of its
two humanoid hands hung by a single remaining ligament. An eye had
burst, but the shuriken disc responsible must have lodged in especially
tough orbital bone, not piercing through to the brain. Injuries wept gluey
ichor. An armoured knee was shattered. Yet the creature's will was indomitable. Perhaps fatally injured but alive, the Patriarch still stood
defiantly.*

*All this the Harlequin would only have a couple of seconds to perceive.
Maybe it had been the Harlequin's original intention to destroy the
Patriarch—then at the last moment to swoop up vertically, avoiding col-
lision with the shrine-rock. Now he dared not do so.*

*Still hurling discs, that shark of a flying bike crashed into the
Patriarch's chest. The impact hurled the beast backwards into the tunnel,
along with jet-bike and suicide-rider. Then the jet-bike exploded, and
cleansing flame gushed from the tunnel mouth.*

"Yald! Yald!"

Jaq's group was almost clear of the last of the pillars when a
hybrid hurled himself at the younger of the two Shandabari
women.

The hybrid pulled her from her mount. He sprawled upon her
as she writhed and shrieked. The hybrid was screaming incohe-
rently. He made no effort to spring up and seize her 'pard, to leap
into the saddle and ride.

"Don't slow!" bellowed Lex, staring back; for Rakel had shown
signs of reining in—something that the refugee woman's older
friend was already doing. "Keep up the pace! Yald, yald!"

The stout woman was swinging her mount around, to return.
"Helping us!" came her cry.

No help was possible except at the cost of delay. Delay in putting the hermitage behind them might easily outweigh the use of

the two women as a show of normality. One must pray that
enough combatants amid the far-flung pillars killed or incapac-
itated each other, so that no effective pursuit would occur.

The hybrid was still shrieking incomprehensibly as if it was he
who was pinioned upon the ground. Because of the death of the
Patriarch, a psychotic tempest must be raging in the minds of the
brood, disrupting any lucid behaviour. Maybe the stout woman
would be able to knife the hybrid and rescue her friend.

Chapter Fourteen

Grief

Though the great sun was well past its zenith, heat and radiance were ramping up by a further increment—like yet another crank of a rack which would finally spring bones from their sockets and craze a body with insensate agony.

The dusty stone mosaic of this part of the desert was becoming a vast griddle, painful even to the splayed hairy pads of the 'pards. The beasts had no choice but to proceed onward. To relieve the pain briefly required the shifting of a foot forward, and then another foot, perpetually. A permanent smell of singeing hair accompanied the camelopards.

Their riders might well have been dead in the saddles, mummified in position.

Few indeed were the scattered fellow travellers, all likewise now borne by 'pards. Mirage-travellers might well outnumber real ones. If one squinted sidelong into the glare, no vehicles were in sight—not even as mirages. In the quivering lens of hot air you could even spy mirages of yourself. Reality itself might have melted.

How many refugees had succumbed by now? A million and a half? Jaq's party must be in the very vanguard. No one in the thinly-travelled vicinity paid them any heed as possessors of special knowledge.

Those untold hundreds of thousands of dead Shandabaris would soon be only a fraction of the global death count—although no one would ever number them.

*

Occupying the terrain from east to west was what appeared to be a desolate city. Nooks of shade were visible, in dark contrast to the glare of the roofs. The camelopards trotted eagerly.

The city proved to be a shallow plateau which had cracked into great blocks, divided by broad canyons and by long narrow clefts. For millions of years gritty wind had been at work, carving out chambers and corridors and lanes, and sculpting bridges of stone. Here was the labyrinth at last. It extended over dozens of square kilometres.

Bone-dry it was. Stone-dry. Dry as death.

They took temporary refuge from the sun's direct heat in a natural chamber as big as the whole of their former mansion. Within the chamber the temperature must have been ten degrees cooler. Or at least: ten degrees less roasting. In other circumstances the place would have seemed like an oven.

They must drink. They must eat. They had long since drained the canteen which Lex had filled at the oasis.

The stone floor was smooth, presenting no natural bowl to fill with blood.

By croaks and gestures Grimm indicated a means. The little man had remembered a method he once saw on a primitive agricultural world.

Off came Rakel's vellum hat. Grimm removed the hat's long ribbon, that Assassin's sash which had secured the hat under Rakel's chin—that sash with a garotte concealed inside the fabric.

Summoning a reserve of strength, Lex restrained the chosen 'pard. He dragged its snaky neck low. Grimm looped the sash around the beast's neck. He tied that red ribbon as a tourniquet. The 'pard tried to buck. The 'pard snarled and spat, but Lex held firm.

With the point of his knife Grimm dug into the beast's carotid artery. Blood spurted into the Squat's face as the living heart pumped lifeblood strongly through the little hole. Promptly Grimm suckered his lips to the wound. He swigged and swallowed for all he was worth like some sturdy vampire baby.

Briefly he stoppered the wound with his thumb. On that agric world the peasants had used a plug.

"Your turn, Jaq."

Hardly able to speak, Jaq motioned Rakel to drink next. She was on the verge of expiring. She was precious to him. She was essential to what must transpire at that place in the Webway.

Staggering, Rakel latched on to the 'pard's neck, and Grimm pulled out his thumb.

Already the 'pard was struggling less, seeming somewhat drowsy. Hopefully the tourniquet wasn't tight enough to kill it. Its brain was simply receiving less blood, and its lungs less air.

Jaq suckled next.

What of Lex, who must hold the beast? Grimm tried to position the empty canteen accurately. Spurts were so erratic. No time to delay. Urgently he gestured at Rakel's hat which lay upon the floor. Couldn't fetch it himself. Thumb in the dyke, holding back the blood-flood.

Jaq scooped up that cleverly folded page from the book of fate. As if bearing a receptacle in a sacred rite, he tilted the hat. Grimm removed his thumb. Camelopard blood pumped into the chalice of vellum.

Jaq held the blood-filled hat for Lex to plunge his face into.

The beast was dead now, fully garrotted. Its fellow 'pards rolled their eyes, but perhaps they were only cleaning away dust.

Flesh on the body would be stringy, sinewy. Therefore Grimm butchered the hump. He exposed thick raw fat which he cut into chunks.

The taste was fetid.

"It'll burn like high-octane fuel in our bodies," Lex assured the others.

All very well for him to say so. Equipped with an extra stomach, Lex could cope with unfood and even toxins.

Yet they forced themselves to feast.

In the heat, the hump-fat seemed already to be turning rancid. Nevertheless, Grimm packed fat into pouches; and the canteen had been refilled with blood from the hat, after Lex had done drinking.

The heat, the heat. Dearly though they may have wished to lie down and sleep, they might wake to incineration. Though the sun had all but set, furnace light remained and the sky was still bright. Press on, press on, before darkness suffocated this labyrinthine place.

Jaq had retrieved the sash. He eyed the hat, coated within by congealed blood, its Eldar runes besmirched.

"May as well abandon the page," he told Rakel wearily. "If we haven't found the mushrooms by morning we'll all soon die." He secured the sash around his own waist for safe-keeping.

Lex led Jaq aside.

"Surely we should keep that page," he murmured. "I know we couldn't possibly have brought the whole book with us. To toss the last scrap of the text away seems wrong. To use it as a hat . . . that was the only way to save Rakel from sunstroke. To use it as a vessel for beast's blood, even if I was eager to drink . . ." Lex shook his head.

"Are you reverencing *alien* texts, Captain?" Jaq asked harshly.

"Doesn't the text undergo changes? Mightn't some reference to the Emperor's Sons appear even in that scrap? Forced by circumstances, we seem to be straying from duty, from sacred vows."

"Not so! Oh no, Lex, not so at all." How Jaq strove to convince. "At the place in the Webway where history can change I shall deny death by resurrecting Meh'lindi. This deed will send a shockwave through the Sea of Souls such as may compress and coagulate the Chaos Child—by at least an iota. Maybe by a crucial iota! The Eldar Theory of Chaos states that the flutter of a moth's wing may trigger a hurricane half a world away. Marb'ailtor said so. How much more potently must this be true at that crucial node in the Webway, within the very warp itself!"

Lex looked sceptical.

"I swear this, Captain! Did not the Hand of Glory guide you? Did I not take your daemon upon myself and cast it out?"

Lex nodded. This was awesomely true.

"Am I not illuminated? If I am wrong," added Jaq, "I pray that you kill me. I would beg you to take me prisoner and deliver me to the Inquisition—except that the Inquisition is infiltrated by conspirators, and at war with itself."

To what reliable authority could Lex deliver Jaq? To the Terminator Librarians of the Imperial Fists, should Lex ever be able to rejoin his chapter? The alien book of fate, the Emperor's Sons: these matters were altogether too large for a chapter of Marines to handle. And as Jaq said, the Inquisition was at odds . . .

"Hear me, Lex: we are participating in a process of perfection of spirit, to be undertaken by a hallowing sacrifice—"

Of Rakel's soul . . .

Lex shuddered, since sacrifice as such seemed to stink of daemonry.

"*Self*-sacrifice is sublime," he murmured.

The fire in Jaq's eyes!

"Do you not think I would willingly sacrifice myself if such sacrifice was possible? Let us pray silently that the luminous path blesses our lady thief with understanding. I shall certainly honour her. She is a sacred vessel. An Inquisitor must make hard, devout choices. Painless choices are mere heresy."

"Aye, pain is pure," agreed Lex.

"Meh'lindi's reincarnation will be an act of *love*," insisted Jaq. "That will be a seed-crystal of love inserted into the psychic sea. It will be a triumph over death and chaos, which the psychic sea must heed."

The psychic sea—or the *psychotic* sea?

If there had been any flies in the depths of the desert, those pests would have clustered around the four travellers as they made their onward trek. Flies would have been clinging to skin and clothing crusted with dried 'pard blood.

For a while their gait—especially Grimm's—was more like a duck-waddle, after all those terrible hours in the saddle.

They had abandoned the 'pards by now. They had followed a winding, narrowing canyon until it became a cul-de-sac—except for a corridor boring through the canyon wall. That corridor had commenced spaciously but then tapered until they were compelled to proceed on hands and knees through into the adjoining canyon.

Towering stone walls ran parallel to one another. Those walls were only a metre thick, yet full fifty metres high. Wind had bored holes here and there which were barely big enough to squeeze through.

Thermal winds blew through the labyrinth. Holes in stone gave voice to those winds. *Thees-way, thees-way*, the voices seemed to say—voices of the ghosts of the labyrinth, voices of dead travellers who had become lost here long ago, and who now wished for company in their empty misery.

Despite high-octane hump-fat, Rakel had collapsed from fatigue. Lex carried her slung over his shoulder. Sometimes he needed to drag her through low passages behind him.

Hidden by lofty walls the setting sun had vanished, though the heat remained as extreme as ever. Unaccustomed auroras danced in the sky, perpetuating light.

They met half a dozen stumbling refugees who were also searching the labyrinth for the place of safety—without any idea of what the place might be. No harm in telling the secret to a few desperate wretches, survivors of the lottery of exodus. Indeed, on the contrary!

"Have you seen a circle of tall stone mushrooms?" Jaq demanded.

These refugees had not come across any such phenomenon. Now they staggered away to search for it. Some went one way, some another. If they did find the place, they vowed to shout out in the hope that their hoarse voices might echo far enough through canyons and passages.

Jaq consulted the eye-lens. The rune of the route was clear to see, yet where in the real world was the starting point?

Lex clenched his left fist. "Oh Dorn, oh light of my being," he prayed. "Help me now. Biff," he murmured. "Yeri . . ."

What could summon the light of Rogal Dorn? The heat was not yet great enough to match the torment of a pain-glove, the unconsuming inferno of punishment which had brought him visionary insight in the past. What agony could summon enlightenment?

"Your knife, Grimm," Lex said. "You must stick it slowly in my eye—until I see our way!"

With Rakel still slumped over his shoulder, Lex knelt.

"Come off it, Big Boy!"

Grimm glanced at Jaq—yet Jaq was nodding anguished agreement. *Self*-sacrifice was a tool. A tool of transcendence. Furthermore, there was a pattern here, a cryptic equation which the Captain must have perceived, an equation between Azul's eye—which Lex himself had once cut out—and his own eye.

"Do you not see the harmony of circumstances?" Jaq asked Grimm.

The little man shook his head.

"An eye for a warp-eye," Jaq said softly. "Illumination through torment. The alternative might be our deaths, and total failure. Yours is an inspired soul, Captain. Would you rather that I held the knife?"

"I believe that the Abhuman will carry out this technical task as efficiently as any Servitor." No, Lex did not wish Jaq to wield the

knife. Was Lex some heretic, that he should submit to excrucia-
tion by a member of the Inquisition?

"You won't lash out?" Grimm asked the kneeling Marine.

"I shall keep my eyelids fully open, Abhuman. I swear not to
flinch. When eventually I rejoin my chapter, our chirurgeons can
fit me with an artificial oculus."

Well they might. Yet for a fighting man to yield up the sight of
one eye when the future was still so fraught with uncertainty was
brave indeed. Or was it folly?

"You must press very slowly to stoke the pain," instructed Lex.

Grimm commenced his task.

Lex held his breath.

At the moment when the eyeball burst, and humour flowed,
Lex's clenched fist became phosphorescent with such a leprous
eerie glow.

His forefinger opened out, pointing. Pointing the way.

As Lex walked, still shouldering Rakel, he swung his head from
side to side. Thus he compensated for diminished vision. The
Assassin's sash was tied over his ruined eye now, like a bloody
bandage. Without this blindfold his vision would be hopelessly
fogged by light falling upon that naked lens which resembled a
pool of pus in a burst abscess. His glowing index finger pointed
ahead.

By aurora-light they entered a natural plaza.

Six stone mushrooms rose to Lex's height and half again. These
stood in a circle almost cap to cap. Within, was an upright disc of
light, of misty blue. It was the doorway to the Webway. There
began a tunnel which led into the depths of elsewhere, far from
this labyrinth, far from Sabulorb.

Lex set Rakel down, and shook her. "We're safe," he grunted.

Arousing feebly, she gaped at his bandaged face. Her voice
wavered. "What happened to you?"

"A sacrifice," Jaq said to Rakel. "There comes a day when we
must all make sacrifices, even of ourselves. What are we in the
perspective of the godly Child of Chaos? Or of Him-on-Earth? Or
of the Sea of Souls wherein all the anguish and rage and lust and
also all the virtues of a trillion trillion bygone souls are dissolved,
awaiting apotheosis!"

"What does apotheosis mean?" she asked dazedly.

"It means to become divine. Whether balefully or gloriously! Although we are only flotsam compared with that sea, yet our self-sacrificial actions stir a current which becomes a powerful wave."

"Fine preaching," Grimm said. "How far is it to the first gap in the route where we set foot on some world? We gotta rest. I need a figging lotus world with lotsa food and drink and ease. So does she."

Jaq uncapped his monocle. He squinted at the misty blue tunnel. "I count only ten forks until we arrive at a gap. We're blessed."

Maybe because they were so close to safety, the heat seemed suddenly to become abominable despite the setting of the sun. The night air was searing.

Surely soon, on the far side of Sabulorb, the shallow seas must begin to steam and simmer. Ultimately those seas would boil away. All combustible material upon the continents would ignite spontaneously. Vegetation and buildings and corpses would become smoke. The very rocks and deserts would incandesce.

From the roll-call of a million worlds, one name would be erased: that of Sabulorb. Who would pay much heed to this minute subtraction, except for interested citizens of star-systems in the neighbourhood, and Navigators, and of course distant clerks of the Adeptus Ministorum (since they would be losing a planetary parish), and clerks of the Departmento Munitorium (since they would be losing a recruiting base), and members of the Adeptus Arbites (since they would be losing a Courthouse— though Sabulorb would no longer need policing).

Five thousand light years away across the Imperium, who would even have heard of Sabulorb? The mass of people would continue not to have heard of the planet roasted by its sun. The vast mass of people would continue to be ignorant of almost everything.

Might it be that the Emperor, embalmed in his throne, would shed a precious tear from one of his leathery eye-sockets?

Entering the Webway was like walking into a tunnel of ice. So great was the contrast that three of the four baked and blistered fugitives were soon sneezing and shivering convulsively.

Even Lex was affected to a lesser extent. The transition from excessive heat to a normal temperature—which seemed glacial by comparison—stirred deep memories in Lex of the Tunnel of Terror in the fortress-monastery of the Fists. In that dire tunnel, zones of torrid heat had alternated with zones of absolute chill—and of airless vacuum, and of induced agony . . . and with teasing pockets of safety.

This whole tunnel through the warp was a place of comparative safety—provided that they met no Phoenix Warrior, such as had harpooned the real Meh'lindi . . .

Apart from such a ghastly possibility, they would certainly not meet any ordinary travellers. At most they might sense a fleeting ghost passing by, out of phase with themselves. Such was the nature of the Webway. Each traveller or group of travellers occupied a unique quantum of time. Two groups who set out at separate times from separate places could not coincide at the same time and the same place within this galaxy-spanning network.

Whilst in the Webway, one's sense of duration evaporated. Had one set out through the network just a few minutes previously? Or an hour earlier? Or a day earlier? Impossible to say! In the Webway even chronometers were completely unreliable, recording a lapse of several hours, and then only of a few minutes.

It was this timelessness which would sustain the four of them until they could reach a gap in the rune-route, and emerge upon a world. Tramping the Webway was akin to travelling in a dream.

Led by Jaq, with monocle uncapped, they reached one fork in the network, and then another, and another. Lex lent support to Rakel. She must not expire. Would the real Meh'lindi have needed assistance? Would Meh'lindi have needed a helping hand till they could reach a world and water and food and some shelter to sleep in undisturbed?

A comforting world? A lotus world, in Grimm's phrase? Why should that be where they emerged?

Rather than some bleak and terrible place! Or even some world which had been engulfed by Chaos!

They stepped out of the misty blue tunnel into a damp and airy cave green with ferns. Ferns growing around a pool into which a spring prattled over boulders.

A shaggy brindled beast reared and snarled, baring hooked yellow fangs. A tufted tail thrashed from side to side. The cave was a den. With laspistol Grimm shot the animal twice. Its charred body toppled into the pool.

Because its snout remained underwater, no doubt it was dead. After a prudent pause, all four joined the dead beast in the water, gulping and dunking.

A stream ran out of the mouth of the cave, into golden woodland under a blue sky. On this world it seemed to be late afternoon, and autumn.

"Just look at us," grumped Grimm.

Blistered, peeling skin. Grime. Crusts of camelopard blood. Lex with only one eye. Rakel vomiting water.

Some hump-fat remained. Grimm moulded this between his hands then smeared it on to his smarting face. Huffing to himself, he anointed Rakel and Jaq and Lex likewise.

What species of beast had they killed? An unknown carnivore. *Red meat.* Unlikely that the meat would contain natural toxins. The beast had been well protected by its fangs and claws, until they came along. Soon they were chewing raw steaks.

A bland yellow sun was sinking. Lazy cumulus clouds gathered, painted orange and crimson by the evening light.

Hardly wise to succumb to sleep close by a Webway portal. Reeling with fatigue, they quit the cave. Lex carried the butchered remains of the beast some distance, to hide behind a fallen tree. Mustn't leave such a marker to betray that armed persons had recently used the portal. While the others waited, Lex returned quickly to bathe once more in the pool and cleanse himself of yet more blood.

They found a dell. It seemed safe to bivouac under a screen of torn-down branches. Half of Lex's brain would remain on guard.

Jaq gave thanks for this world, but Grimm was already snoring.

Lex shook Grimm awake.

Misty morning of pearly light. Dew illuminated thousands of gossamer webs in the gilded crisping foliage. Trivial webs woven by tiny things, which but for the dew would have gone unnoticed. At the exit from the bivouac, strands floated loose and torn.

"Rakel woke and sneaked out a few minutes ago," Lex murmured.

"Huh, you can guess why! Me own bladder's bursting with all the water."

Yet one must assume that her departure wasn't innocent.

Jaq still slept. His head rested upon Lex's arm. Lex didn't wish to disturb the slumbering Inquisitor.

After attending hastily to the call of nature, Grimm padded after Rakel, trying to snap twigs only softly. Realizing the folly of stealth, he began to bound through the woods towards the cave.

She might have gone in any direction. Yet in all directions except one she would be trackable. If she re-entered the Webway . . .

As Grimm approached the cave there was no sight of her. When he reached the cave, it seemed deserted.

He almost turned back, to look elsewhere.

No. Readying *Emperor's Peace*, he charged into the misty blue tunnel. How his big boots pumped along.

Meh'lindi, in the mist . . .

No, Rakel. She was hesitating at the first fork.

"Stop right there, Lady, or it'll be a bolt in the back!"

Rakel froze.

"Turn round slowly, and let's not be seeing any laspistols."

Rakel turned. "Grimm—"

How appealing, her voice.

"You shouldn't have stopped to choose," the little man said almost apologetically. "Left nor right wouldn't matter, unless you're superstitious. You should have run and run. Come on back now."

"To choose," echoed Rakel. "What choice do I have in my fate? I'm scared . . .' '

Something about her hand, her fingers . . .

"Hey, don't you crook your fingers at me!"

The hooded rings on her fingers: those digital weapons. One still remained unused.

"I wasn't intending—" Defeat was in her stance. Yet there was also a residue of angry defiance. "Grimm, tell me truly—by all that we've gone through together!—will I really go into flux if Jaq doesn't reinforce me?"

Oh, so that's why she had paused. She had seized her chance to run—to run into an exotic maze which spanned the galaxy. Thus, to save herself *from she knew not what*. What if she escaped only to succumb to Polymorphine spasm?

"That's absolutely true," Grimm lied brazenly. "Now don't be a fool, and come on back with me—willingly, not for fear of a bolt. You're going to live. You aren't going to die."

Her body wasn't going to die. That much was true. However, her mind and soul would vacate that body—if Jaq's sorcery succeeded. Maybe the sorcery might fail. If so, Jaq must somehow wean himself away from an obsessive dream.

"Jaq intends to use me *somehow*. Using me will destroy me, won't it?"

"I swear that it won't, Rakel binth-Kazintzkis."

Credit the thief with her full name. Honour and compliment her. Had Lex been reluctant to chase after Rakel because he might be obliged to dishonour himself by lying to someone who was virtually a comrade?

Rakel asked: "Will you swear by your ancestors, Grimm?"

Grimm's heart thumped. A binding oath, indeed, for a Squat. This same Squat still winced at how he had been duped by the lies of Zephro Carnelian regarding the supposed Emperor's Sons and the benign Eldar custodianship of the Long Watch of the Sensei Knights. Lied to, and fooled! Lies were a poison. One poison could sometimes counteract another poison.

"You won't swear, will you?" said Rakel. "Honest Abhuman that you are, more human than most humans."

"Huh, of course I will." Grimm strove to improvise. "That's just the point. I was thinking to meself that an oath on the Sacred Ancestors is binding between us Squats—but you regular humans don't have any Ancestors." He contrived a chuckle. "I don't mean that regular humans are all bastards! Lots of high and mighty lords would take exception! You just don't worship your Ancestors like we do."

"On *my* home world," Rakel reminded him, "our shamans would drink the lichen-juice containing unrefined Polymorphine so as to adopt the appearance of dead ancestors and enshrine their spirits temporarily. Communion with our ancestors *is* sacred."

She had said so during their first interrogation of her. She had indeed.

Futile to prevaricate any longer. Think of the higher cause, Jaq would have advised.

"Rakel binth-Kazintzkis," said Grimm solemnly, "I do swear by me Noble and Virtuous Ancestors. May they disinherit me spiritually and genetically if I lie. May I sire only limbless freaks. May me gonads wither. May I never live to become a Living Ancestor meself."

Ashes were in Grimm's heart as he accompanied Rakel back towards the cave. He believed this curse indeed. Now he would never reach a truly mature age and attain powers and wisdom. A spiritual worm would consume him inwardly. Not this year, not next, but after a while.

If he were to tell Jaq about this oath and how much it cost him, would the Inquisitor even be able to understand? Would Jaq comprehend how vastly and disproportionately this lie compensated for Grimm's former well-meant duplicity in the matter of Carnelian? Maybe Lex, self-excommunicated from the sacred companionship of his Battle Brothers, might be able to sympathise?

As Grimm and Rakel emerged from the cave together, the morning sun was already beginning to burn benignly through the early mist. Rakel looked around. She inhaled deeply, as though this was the first moment of a new and sublime phase in life—or as if she was storing such a moment as she might never experience again, the memory of which must be her precious consolation.

For Grimm, no such consolation existed.

Ashes, and grief.

Huh, Grimm thought to himself as they walked back, *Probably get meself killed soon anyway. Probably better that way. Get me head blown off. No more thinking. No more feelings.*

He ached, inwardly. How he ached.

Chapter Fifteen

Harvesters

By the time Grimm and Rakel returned to the bivouac, Jaq had roused himself. Jaq paid scant heed to the little man other than a quick glance. He and Lex were discussing the other portal which must exist somewhere upon this planet. The map upon Jaq's lens simply showed that there must be another point of entry to the Webway—but not in which direction, nor how far away.

Slowly Lex unwound the red sash, to expose the remains of his eye. What he revealed made Rakel squirm. Grimm seemed curiously reluctant to witness the injury his knife had inflicted. The little man gazed anywhere else.

"Seems like a pleasant enough world, this," Grimm muttered disconsolately. "Give or take the odd carnivore. Huh: trees and streams and a tame sun. Bet it ain't nice at all here! Nothing ever is. Wish I'd died along with me Grizzle in that earthquake." He rallied himself. "It's the knife again, eh?"

"I see no other way," said Lex.

"No other way: that ought to be our motto. Good job I left some of that eye of yours for further surgery. You wouldn't be much use to us totally blind, having to be led around and relying on your amplified ears."

Rakel said hopefully, "Maybe we ought to get to know this world a bit better before we do anything drastic? It seems so hospitable. There are bound to be people. People might know where that other portal is. They might think it something else than what it is. They might shun it, or worship it."

Grimm glared. "Oh you'd love to dilly-dally, wouldn't you? Have a holiday."

"We have the jewels," she said eagerly. "We can buy information. We can buy people."

"There aren't *bound* to be people," Jaq contradicted her. "There may be no one at all."

Grimm licked his lips. "Or else there may be nutty green-skinned Orks who would love to enslave us. Fancy being a Painboyz' slave?"

"I'm waiting," said Lex impatiently.

Sighing, Grimm took out his knife. He spat on the blade derisively as though to confer antisepsis. "This is just the sort of skilful surgery that Painboyz love to indulge in!"

"I don't know anything about such creatures," protested Rakel.

"Well, we'd better get off this planet sharpish before you have a chance to find out!"

"You're saying these things to pressure me. There's no evidence."

"Huh. Trees are green. Why shouldn't the inhabitants be green too?" Grimm sniffed. "Doesn't smell polluted," he granted. "Proper Ork world ought to be heavily polluted."

"You seem in a foul mood," Jaq said to the little man. "I think I ought to hold the knife."

"Foul mood?" Grimm echoed. "You wouldn't know. Course I'm not!" He grinned, ruddy-cheeked. "I'm just psyching myself up to torture Lex, that's all." Having sworn a false oath, he mustn't undermine its effect on Rakel by indulging his inner misery, or else that deceitful oath would have served no purpose.

While Lex knelt as if before an altar, Grimm applied pressure to that giant man—knife-point against lens.

Wondrously, the finger-light reappeared. The light of Dorn, swore Lex. Or of the luminous path. Maybe both were aspects of the same guiding radiance.

When Lex pointed eastward, his finger brightened. To north or south or west, it dimmed.

They gathered ripe nuts from low branches, and big sweet blue berries from bushes, and meaty fungoids. Lex ate first, to test the fare.

Non-toxic. Nutritious. Hospitable.

*

All day they tramped through forest without incident other than the scuttling of occasional half-glimpsed little animals. Towards evening, the trees thinned out. Stumps bore axe marks, some quite recent. Wood had been felled for fuel or for building materials.

Orks would have demolished whole swathes of forest indiscriminately, leaving vast scars. Had human beings wielded the axes?

Maybe wild Eldar lived here—those puritanical fanatics who had fled to the fringes of the galaxy before the Slaaneshi spasm devastated their civilization; and who had survived because of their self-denial. Such a world should not be linked to the Webway. Of course it might have become linked long after settlement.

Yesterday, sheer exhaustion had put the travellers to sleep before daylight departed. So they had not seen the night sky. If this world was out on the fringes, stars might seem thin. Black intergalactic void would be close at hand. Alternatively, depending on hemisphere, the vast bulk of the home galaxy might be radiantly visible all at once.

If so, this might indeed be a wild Eldar world, of Exodites, so called. Except for the Webway entrances . . .

Most likely this was a primitive human planet which had long lost touch with the Imperium, and even with the memory of colonization.

Eventually they came to a great clearing. Grey ash covered hectares of land. Charred stumps of beams poked up here and there. A whole close-packed town must have occupied this space, quite recently. The town had been incinerated. Tramping through the ash, they came upon a few burned broken skeletons. But not many, not many at all.

Had enemies sacked and burned the town? The degree of destruction seemed beyond the technology level of axe-wielders. Why were there so few bones?

A stony rutted road led away through more trees. Warily they followed that route. After some twenty kilometres they came to what must recently have been an even more substantial town. It had also been reduced to ashes. The road continued, utterly deserted apart from themselves. At dusk they bivouacked in a small clearing at a sensible distance from the road.

The sky had been cloudy during much of their march. Now it cleared, as light was quitting it.

Soon they were staring up at a chain of tiny moons strung pearl-like across the zenith. A hundred little moons, perhaps. Each like a bleached snail shell, or like some curled-up fossilized foetus, chalky white. A snail, or a foetus, with a beak perhaps. Stars were scanty—but those moons, those many moons in an unnatural ring!

Even as they watched, one of these mini-moons detached itself from the procession and began to dip down towards the atmosphere.

Lex blasphemed softly.

"What are those?" Rakel asked softly, as if in fear that those eerie moons in orbit might hear her voice.

Lex's reply was as cold and hard as marble.

"You saw Genestealers in the hermitage on Sabulorb, Rakel. Now discover a terrible secret. The creatures in those ships up there are what created the 'Stealers. They are more dreadful than 'Stealers. They are known as *Tyranids*. Tyranids harvest whole worlds of their biological material to mould and mutate into abominations. They strip worlds bare. The process had begun here, with the harvesting of the highest life-form, Man—"

Tyranid hive-fleets came from way across the intergalactic gulf, two million light years or more. Presumably they had stripped a previous galaxy bare of all life. Life was their raw material. Out of this raw material they made such abominations as Screamer Killers and Fleshborer guns and scavengers.

Of course, *Screamer Killer* was merely a name which human survivors of early encounters with Tyranids had bestowed—upon heavy rotund battle-creatures which shrieked horrifyingly as they scuttled forward, virtually invincible, flailing their razor-edged arms and spitting toxic bio-plasma.

Merely a human label—for something vilely inhuman.

Fleshborers, likewise! Merely a name, screamed by psychotic survivors, in an attempt to describe a hand-weapon which was a brood-nest of vicious beetles, beetles which the weapon would goad to leap convulsively towards a target, to gnaw through flesh and bone like paper . . .

Their very ships were organic creations, compounded of thousands of modified creatures slavishly linked by an empathic central gland. Throughout the vast fleet of millions of vessels and sub-vessels a collective mind presided. Destroy ten thousand vessels (if only one could!) and still the mind presided. Destroy a hundred thousand (vain hope!) and still the mind would be relatively unimpaired. Its units would continue stripping worlds of life to assemble more parts of itself.

Neither the ravaging warriors—whom the Marines knew as Tyranids—nor the Zoat creatures who served as sly intermediaries, nor the Carnifex Screamer Killers, were individual entities. Each was only a specialized cell in the colossal multifarious organism of the hive-fleet. The infiltration of the home galaxy had been under way for a couple of centuries or so—a menace as deadly as the powers of Chaos which for aeons had been spreading their cancer within the galaxy.

The Tyranid swarm was yet another incontestable reason why the Imperium must conduct itself remorselessly and even mercilessly, lest humanity be devoured . . .

Might it be that deliverance from Chaos could only come about in the end by the absorption of all life into the Tyranid swarm? What a vile and terminal remedy this would be.

Lex pounded his fist into his palm, without extinguishing his finger of glory.

"I have fought them! I have been inside a Tyranid vessel on a raid. We were backed by a battle fleet. I was wearing full combat armour—"

Now he was one Marine alone, and almost naked. Dressed in mere clothes, his companions might as well be naked. As for their pathetic armoury . . . If a Tyranid even glimpsed them, they were doomed to become raw material.

How could they sleep that night, with those snail-like ivory vessels in the sky? With vessels descending periodically, and others rising into orbit, conveyers of captured flesh!

The first wave of the onslaught had already passed through this region, removing the highest life-forms for use. Lucky old carnivore in its cave, to have escaped harvest, and then to be blessed with swift oblivion!

The four travellers must move on as soon as could be, following the finger, praying that the other portal was not five thousand kilometres away, nor even a thousand, nor a hundred. How could they hope to cover even a hundred kilometres before a new wave of harvesting passed across the surface of this doomed world? First they must get some sleep.

Sleep; they must sleep. If, during sleep, a harvester might detect and seize them, how could they possibly doze off? Terror would keep them awake, and exhaust them. Unless—

"I'm no Assassin," Jaq said. Did his gaze reproach Rakel that she was no real Assassin either? "I've witnessed a certain Assassin kill with the touch of a finger upon the neck. A lesser pressure renders a person unconscious. I understand the principle. I know the vital nerve. The Inquisition teaches us the frailties of the human body. I propose—"

To render unconscious. Unconsciousness might segue into natural restorative sleep.

Lex was trained to be able to nap during any lull in combat. It must be Lex who would numb the others.

Jaq demonstrated. Then he, and Rakel, and Grimm lay down.

"Don't push too hard," said Grimm. "In fact I think I'd rather be bashed on the head with the butt of a bolt gun . . ."

A moment later he lay still. Was he unconscious, or dead? Attentively Lex bent low over the little man.

"Still alive. Squats are tough."

From Jaq: "I commend my spirit . . ."

Lex rendered Jaq unconscious, checked his vital signs, then turned to Rakel.

"Wait—"

"Yes, Lady?"

"These Tyranids . . . I never knew how hideous the universe can be. The 'Stealers, and those Chaos renegades . . . And Sabulorb, a whole world incinerated . . ."

"That was due to variability in its sun. Unless Chaos somehow acted as a catalyst."

"It's all so terrible . . .' '

"I've seen worse, Lady. I've seen a Chaos world itself. Compared with that madness, a Tyranid vessel is relatively comprehensible, however execrable."

"It's too much, too much. We *are* true companions, aren't we, after a fashion? Four companions in a hell . . ."

"After a fashion," he conceded. He would never have dreamed that an Imperial Fist might be asked to regard a thief as a companion. Yet a Marine was a protector of the vulnerable. Ach,

Rakel was an instrument for Jaq to play upon. She had been this
ever since she made the terrible mistake of trying to rob the mansion. Could it be that he felt pity at this moment? How futile, in a
pitiless cosmos.

"Put me to sleep now," she begged. Was she really asking for
him to kill her, in such a way that she would never know?

"No more talk," he said, "or we might wake the others up."
With his finger of glory he touched her neck powerfully yet
gently—more gently than he had touched Grimm or Jaq, though
with the same result.

Jaq had cast an aura of protection. Would this suffice against a
sweeping mass of scavenger creatures endowed with an instinct
to harvest life? Or against alert Tyranid warriors if any remained
in the vicinity?

The stripping and processing of the life of this world was only
commencing. The full task might take ten years or twenty. Time
was no object to an immortal hive-mind which had coasted
through the gulf between galaxies for hundreds of millennia.

Meanwhile the forest remained with its freight of lesser life.
Empty, now, of man's presence. Man's burned places were
empty alike of dog or horse or goats. All taken, selectively, as the
initial prizes of the harvest.

Eventually even worms and beetles would be gathered, sifted
out. Even microbes and bacteria would be gleaned by microscopic
nano-collectors—until there was utter sterility, and that sterility
was further sterilized by fire.

Lex's finger was glowing more brightly.

Let it be, let it be, that the two portals were close together.
Twins, in resonance with one another. Energy-tubes which had
divided only at the very last moment of formation.

The rough road had veered away from the direction which Lex's
finger indicated. They were hiking through golden and scarlet
woodland untouched anywhere by axe. These trees were both
strange yet familiar. A *tree* was not a species. It was a biological
structure, obeying similar constraints of gravity and photosynthe-
sis.

Undergrowth was sparse, probably stunted by chemicals
secreted by the roots of the trees in the eternal battle for space and
resources.

Steep crags were rising amidst the woodland. Here and there, deep rocky shafts plunged vertically down amidst the loam and humus: deep natural wells. Sometimes snapped branches had fallen across these wells and accumulated a mat of debris. These might have been the lids of traps. To tread this woodland unwarily by night could be fatal.

Deep down in the water at the bottom of one sheer wall, there floated a segmented horny hunchbacked body—a six-limbed gargoyle. Twice the size of a man, wrought of amber and russet coral, the hue of the autumnal trees—!

"That's one of them," whispered Lex.

Rakel did *try* to stifle her cry of panic and dismay.

Wasp-waist. Armoured haunches. That long lurid head.

Its claws had grooved the sides of the well in vain. Eventually it must have drowned.

Deep down, golden eyes opened. Those eyes glared upward. The body convulsed in the water. Claws raked at stone. If only the golden gargoyle could scale the slippery vertical sides.

Yet it couldn't, despite the lure of flesh peering from overhead.

"Kill it?" asked Grimm.

"No," said Lex. "Our guns are too noisy. Even the lasers. The echo in the well shaft would boost the din."

"Pity we don't have a needle gun." Grimm glanced at Rakel's expended digital weapon, and shrugged. "Would have done you good, Girl, shooting your fears."

Rakel swallowed several times, suppressing an impulse to vomit.

Down in the well that great tough coral body doubled up, as if to impale itself with its own barbed tail, thus to boost itself upward like some rococo missile from a silo.

Jaq twitched at the empath-call. The psychic howl impinged on him only slightly, rather as the ultrasonic cry of a bat might register upon a sensitive ear as the faintest twitter. Yet it was perceptible.

"It's signalling. We must run—"

How they ran.

Wary of hidden well shafts. Alert for distant sounds.

Lex's stabbing finger was radiant. *Ahead, ahead.*

From a good way behind—yet ever closer—came a whinnying inhuman shriek of pursuit. That warbling whistle might have been meant to panic or manipulate prey which had ears to hear. Maybe air was squeezing through certain ducts in the external skeletons of the loping pursuers, causing this moaning wail.

Glancing behind: a distant flash of amber and russet—which was certainly not foliage in motion.

Another glimpse.

Tyranids were a-hunting.

One of the monsters had sighted them. Impossibly, its pace seemed to increase. In its upper set of arms it was clutching what seemed to be a great golden drumstick which might have been torn from some ostrich-like bird.

Lex knew that instrument all too well.

A *Deathspitter*.

One of the vilest bio-weapons used by the Tyranids. The organic gun consisted of three types of creature bonded together. In a hot wet womb, hard-shelled toxic maggots were bred as ammunition. When firing occurred, a slimy spider-jawed creature would seize a maggot and strip it of its shell, laying bare the corrosive flesh. To rid itself of contact with the caustic body-fluids, the jutting bowel of the gun would spasm, ejecting the poisonous maggot-flesh through the air at high speed. The slimy flesh, itself burning in agony at contact with oxygen, was like phosphorus to any victim which it spattered against.

Such nauseating devices did the Tyranids turn other creatures into, in their biological conquests.

During the time which the raiding party of Fists had spent aboard a Tyranid vessel, Lex had seen armless humanoids whose heads were clamped by organic lamps . . .

To imagine oneself—or Rakel—similarly transformed! Shorn of arms, and of will-power! Converted into a mobile lantern.

Perhaps only the prisoners' protoplasm and their gene-runes would be exploited to manufacture such servitor creatures.

Either way, the prospect was unbearable. This ghastly fate was befalling the former inhabitants of this planet right now; and might in a few more minutes befall Lex and companions. *That*, or caustic high-velocity maggots from the Deathspitter . . .

"What," panted Grimm, "what's that thing it's carrying?"

"You don't want to know!"

At that moment Rakel tripped and sprawled.

Lex skidded. He doubled back. He hauled her, hand under armpit, even as she was trying to scramble up. How he lugged her along. He might have plunged into another of the well-shafts but for Grimm's shout of warning. "Watch out!"

Pain lanced urgently through his finger of glory. Pain, the signal; pain, the revealer. His finger glowed so brightly that in another moment it might well ignite.

"It's here, right here!" he bellowed.

Grimm paused. Jaq swung around. Lex craned to stare down the shaft, half-blindly, holding Rakel over the edge so that she gasped and writhed.

Lex prayed to see—and prayed not to see—an opening to the Webway somewhere down below in the precipitous wall of the well. To see, because then they would have found it. Not to see, because without ropes the entrance would be unreachable. Ropes, and many spare minutes! The tall Tyranid was loping nearer by the second, thrusting its Deathspitter forward like some anti-grav device which was towing it headlong, aimed at the humans. More Tyranids were in view. That wailing warble might have been a war-cry if these creatures had been human or Abhuman or Eldar or Ork, anything individual and of this galaxy.

Lex only saw sheer sides of stone and blank blue water shining at the bottom of the shaft.

Water, so blue.

The entrance was horizontal, not vertical. It was underwater.

"Leap, leap!"

Lex tossed Rakel, shrieking, down the shaft. He seized Grimm and hurled him likewise.

To the robed Inquisitor on the far side of the well: "Jump, Jaq, jump!"

Two disappearances of prey-samples. Capture, no longer a concept.

The Deathspitter farted its first shrieking maggot-slug from that bowel of a barrel—as Lex dived.

What if he was wrong? When he hit the water, what if Rakel simply surfaced nearby, and Grimm alongside her—and there they would all float impotently, staring up for a few last moments until fierce inhuman heads loomed above?

Lex clove the water.

Blueness blinded him. Down he travelled, down. The water twisted him around. The water was thrusting him upward:

And, *oh Dorn*, he did break surface—to squint at Rakel bobbing close by, spluttering, and Grimm bereft of his forage cap, wallowing, and only moments later Jaq's grizzled water-slicked head was breaking surface too; and all four were treading blue water confined by stone.

Above, bending down, were long drooling jagged heads.

Chapter Sixteen

Warworld

Disorientation departed. Above was the roof of a cave. Dripping stalactites grew downward. Those were the heads Lex had thought he saw. To one side the rim of the pool was high. Then it slanted down steeply to water-level. The high side was a smooth weir down which a film of water flowed. The low side was a natural sluice, draining excess water away along a subterranean channel. The spillage of blue light from below the surface of the pool illuminated the smooth mouth of a dry passage. Underground flood-torrents must have smoothed the mouth whenever it rained heavily on whatever world was above.

Soaked, they were recovering breath upon a slanting mass of rock beside that tunnel mouth. Lex's finger no longer glowed. The only light came from the Webway portal underwater, till Grimm produced an electrolumen from a pouch.

Items: bolt guns and a couple of laspistols and a force rod, wet yet seemingly sound. Jaq's monocle. His rolled mesh armour which had been secured under his robe. *Jewels*, and the paraphernalia of Grimm's pouches. Some spare nuts, soon eaten . . .

"Why ain't we back in the Webway?" Grimm was the first to demand of Jaq. "Flushed round a U-bend, we were, from one pan of piss into another." Grimm directed the light beam into the stone passageway. The passageway angled slowly upward before rounding a bend of its own, where it seemed to narrow considerably. "Let's get going! Those things can follow us."

"I think not," said Lex. "They have other business—harvesting."

Jaq prayed softly, but to what power?

Soon he said, "If a luminous finger no longer points elsewhere, that is because the proper place is right here. Do we understand all the intricacies of the Webway? Do even Great Harlequins understand? The entry to the Webway must be right here, in the pool."

"Boss, this entry leads to a well with monsters up top!"

"This was unlike any other Webway link. Hardly a link at all!"

"You mean more like a topological twist? A geometrical anomaly? Sort of like causes the zero-energy containment field controlling the warp-core in a neoplasma reactor?"

Jaq glared at Grimm, who added hastily, "You'd need to ask one of our Engineer Guildmasters about that. Me, I'm just an ordinary engineer."

"An engineer who probably thinks himself superior to the Technomagi of Mars."

"Those Technomagi," Grimm muttered under his breath, "whose devout experiments with Squattish warp-core tech resulted in the buggering up of Ganymede."

"What did you say? Never mind! Here is some such twist, I do believe. Diving back into the portal from this side ought to take us into the true Webway."

Rakel's voice quavered. "Dive . . . back in again?" She turned to Lex in appeal.

He rose, still wet. He gripped her by the arm, to lead her.

"Rakel, we'd better dive from the highest bit of rock before we lose our taste for water."

She fought in vain. "Those monsters . . . I never knew the horror!"

"I told you there are worse than those."

"Our lives are spent in a torture chamber—"

"Nevertheless," said Lex, "it happens to be a vastly large torture chamber. Billions of naive people do actually survive relatively unscathed until a natural death."

"Not I. Not I."

Rakel screamed as he leapt with her.

They had emerged, sprawling, into misty blue Webway. The end of the tunnel was liquid, held back by some membrane which permitted the passage of living beings but not of inanimate matter. Was this membrane a creation of the Eldar during an earlier era? Or was it a phenomenon of the Webway itself? In this universe, as Jaq knew all too well, the unknown and unknowable vastly overshadowed the entire vault of knowledge.

Quickly they travelled away from this place, with the rune-lens as their guide.

Jaq was first to step from the Webway—into what seemed at first glance to be an authentic, although deserted, torture chamber.

Lit only by the soft blue radiance from the Webway, a sombre crypt housed a succession of fearsome toothed iron machines. Blades jutted from these. Such was the muffled rumbling and thumping percussion which assaulted the ears that one might imagine that these machines were in operation. Yet the equipment was eerily motionless. The muted din came from elsewhere. It came from above. It reverberated through the walls. Such was the vibration that dust descended slowly through otherwise stale and motionless air.

Was a vast factory of the Cult Mechanicus in operation above, and outside of this crypt?

A series of sharp *crumps* suggested that on the contrary a major battle was in full swing.

Grimm swept the crypt with the beam from the electrolumen. Due to the rays of light shining through dust the air was full of geometrical patterns. It seemed as if subtle force-fields radiated from around those cruel machines. The purpose of all the apparatus must surely be to—

"Don't move!" yelped Grimm—too late.

Jaq had taken a pace forward on to a floor of black tiles each marked with a dark red arcane symbol. A tile creaked underfoot. With a grinding whirr one of the machines came into operation—to hurl its dozen blades at Jaq.

With a raucous shriek, the device succumbed to age and rust. Its spars and springs and ratchets fell apart. Rust cascaded. The whole machine crumbled and collapsed. Blades clanged down upon the tiles, fracturing apart—so fragile had the metal become over the course of untold centuries.

"They're all booby traps," cried Grimm.

Aye, they were all devices for flinging blades at whatever might emerge from the Webway . . .

And all of them were utterly antiquated. Nothing could have emerged from this Webway exit for thousands of years. Pressure of a foot upon a tile would still cause a machine to come into operation—and then it would merely disintegrate.

With a howl of glee the dwarfish engineer capered across the crypt. He danced upon those hex-patterned tiles. A dozen machines wheezed and grated and gave way into piles of rusty scrap.

The dull external clangour and vibration continued.

A sweep of the electrolumen beam revealed no obvious outlet from the crypt. No flight of stairs. No iron door. No visible hatch. Walls were great blank slabs. Supporting the huge slabs of the ceiling, semicircular diaphragm arches sprang from low engaged columns along the walls, unreinforced by any buttress. The effect was of an artificial cave, secure and massive, fortress-like. It might have been a fine shelter against crude missiles hurled by catapults or gunpowder, built by primitive though clever masons—had there been any way in or out. The absence of any exit indicated that the massive masonry existed to confine the Webway opening, to incarcerate it forever along with those primitive killing machines.

Presumably no one knew any longer that this sealed crypt existed. A building would have been piled on top to cap the seal. That building might have collapsed millennia ago, providing foundations for a subsequent building, which in its eventual collapse would have formed a further layer of footings for some other edifice. Such was often the way. Cities rose high upon the rubble of their own former selves.

Judging by the audible tumult they could not be too far underground. Might as well be under hundreds of metres of stone, even so!

Thump-thump-thump-thump. Sounded as if a massive thudd gun was firing off a quadruple salvo from overhead.

"Me stomach's grumbling," complained Grimm. "Lex might be able to eat rocks and rust. Damned if I can."

"I might very well be able to *chew* such things," snapped the giant. "But they would not nourish me. Switch your light off. Save power."

If they went back through the Webway to a different world in search of food and drink, they would break the pattern which led to that special place. Here was the second gap in the pattern. They must cross that gap. Not to do so would compel them to commence the sequence all over again. How would they fare, if so? Lex had already lost the humour and the lens from his eye. Only the retina and the optic nerve remained to torment, if need be.

"A thudd gun's a significant target," said Lex. "We must hope that a battle cannon or a big beam projector is used to take it out . . . soon, and devastatingly." He scanned the unreinforced arches ingeniously holding up the roof of slabs. "We should shelter just inside the Webway portal, and pray for a direct hit."

Before intoning such a prayer, Jaq thoughtfully unrolled his mesh armour. He cast off his robe, drew on the flexible armour, and resumed the robe again. All four sat within the Webway and bowed their heads, in the posture of people awaiting a missile attack. Rakel's teeth chattered. Grimm's utter silence went unremarked, since imperial prayers were never of any account to a Squat.

The thunderous detonation of a prayer being answered rocked the whole crypt as if it were a crib in the claws of a carnosaur.

The roar continued, increasing in volume. Some edifice was collapsing overhead, ramming tons of rubble downwards. The arches of the crypt groaned mightily—then snapped inwards. Choking dust billowed into the Webway.

When the dust had cleared enough to see through, a slab was half-blocking the portal. Enough gap remained for a Marine to squeeze through.

From somewhere up above, hazy natural light filtered down. Fortunate, indeed, that the masons of this world built massively. Great slabs and blocks were canted upon one another in vast vertical confusion—up which, through fissures and chimneys, it would be possible to clamber . . . towards the pandemonium of conflict.

Such a sight greeted their eyes.

The demolished stronghold, which had been a firing platform

for the now-disintegrated thudd gun, was atop a precipitous hill
overlooking a sweeping valley. The hill might be the core of an
ancient extinct volcano, with the remnant of a mini-crater. The
crypt had been built in the mini-crater. Above had been piled the
stronghold, now reduced to a jumble of jagged stone teeth like
some Orkish idea of battlements. Ideal location for a thudd gun,
which lobbed shells high in the air. From here they would travel
further than usual and descend with a more devastating armour-
splitting impact . . .

Some corpses had been hurled against tilted slabs. Others must
have hurtled down the precipice. No signs of life in the immediate vicinity. Yet the immediate vicinity was of no account
whatever compared with the vista!

A rolling sea of men and machines were at war. A multitude of
mites were in muddled combat. Such vehicles were in their midst!
Battle tanks and superheavy tanks, mobile battle cannons,
specialist artillery carriages, four-barrelled lasers on motorized
track-units. Dwarfing all these were numerous Titans, gargan-
tuan marching machines with auto-cannon and plasma cannon
and chainsword arms, their energy shields flushing as they
soaked up a surfeit of incoming fire.

The thinnest of drizzle drifted down from a uniformly grey sky.
Together with the drifting smoke and fumes this mizzle bestowed
a pastel impressionism upon the prodigious spectacle.

Those Titans were like erect tortoises, striding ponderously,
their cleated feet crushing whatever infantry were in the way,
whether friend or foe. The auto-cannon arm of one hung crippled. Another's leg was rigid, so that it must swing its way slowly
forward. A great glowing crater in the distance marked where the
reactor of another Titan must have overloaded.

Mites fought mites. Tanks fought tanks. Titans fought Titans.
Rapier lasers targeted Titans, trying to bring their four thrusts of
energy to converge exactly upon the void-shield of a lurching target. Titans blasted at the track-units carrying the massive rapiers.
All was in convulsive conflict. Wreckage and corpses littered the
battlefield like so many crushed ants. A thousand minor fires
burned. If there had ever been villages or fields or orchards in this
valley, no trace of those remained.

The ruined stronghold vibrated with shock waves. The air
drummed. How the hordes of humanity struggled. How potent

and ingenious the weaponry. Some of the Titans were Carnivore class, armed with multiple rocket launchers and turbo-laser destructors. Some were Warhounds with plasma blastguns and mega-bolters. Oh the cannons and battle claws, oh the gatling blasters and power fists. After an encounter with Tyranids, this sight of regular human conflict filled the soul, almost, with the boon of blessed familiarity—rather than with horror. The sight almost restored faith in human endurance.

Rakel whimpered.

Considerably overtopping any other Titan was a red castle mounted upon two flaring rounded bastions. Smoke had veiled it. Now it became more clearly visible. From its topmost spires, plasma cannons and lascannons jutted. Two of the four spires were ablaze. Human mites had taken refuge on the ornate battlements below. Those battlements were borne upon vast metal shoulders. A glaring skull could swivel upon a neck-dome. On either side were two massive pivoting weapons arms—a multi-melta and a plasma cannon, from which flapped the smouldering remnants of battle banners. That dome was set directly upon a horizontal and cylindrical pelvis. Great pistons—surely of adamantium—plunged into the great boot-like bastions. One of the bastions was wreathed in flames.

An entire castle, humanoid in general appearance, and wondrously ornamented all over with golden skulls and imperial eagles, with fleurs-de-lis and fylfots!

One vast red boot of the castle moved. It grooved a wide pathway. The whole edifice lurched forward a step. No mere castle that, but a Titan amongst Titans! At the base of the moving boot were wide stairs resembling claws. From an arched doorway troops streamed down the claws.

"Bloody hell," swore Grimm, "the Adeptus Mechanicus have been busy."

Even so, that Titan of Titans was in trouble. Its spires and one huge foot were ablaze. Its plasma cannon was seemingly disabled. The multi-melta arm still beamed infernal heat, reducing tanks to puddles of glowing slag. Even as they watched, one of the lesser yet redoubtable Titans scored a plasma hit in the castle's groin. Although the scene almost eluded analysis, it seemed that imperial forces were suffering a set-back.

A groan drew attention to what they had assumed was a corpse nearby. The golden epaulettes of the man's high-collared great-coat were like fronds of a sea anemone. Sleeves and breast were adorned with pious icons and honour braids. Miniature steel skulls studded wide gauntlets. The man's face was flash-burned. His legs had been shattered. Very likely his pelvis too. Blood seeped.

His groan—of recovered consciousness and of revival to pain—became a defiant growl of fury at his inability to move. Was his spine broken too? He shifted his head and inhaled.

"In the Emperor's name, assist your Commissar!" he ordered.

Was the man hallucinating that the giant and the Abhuman and the robed man and the woman could possibly be members of the Imperial Guard? Regiments of the Guard were a motley recruited from many worlds, preferably from the cream of planetary defence forces, though often from violent gangs and barbarians. A Commissar's duty was to impose obedience and unity and purity of purpose.

How could these four well-armed persons be here upon the obliterated stronghold unless somehow they were participants? If they were rebels—as must seem probable—the injured Commissar appeared determined to browbeat them into obedience through awe at his sheer strength of purpose. A plea, or surrender, was inconceivable.

And then Jaq realized.

The explosion which destroyed the thudd gun emplacement had blinded the Commissar as well as crippling him. The man was guessing that if he had survived then there might be other survivors too. Any such must help him at whatever cost.

Jaq made his way to the ruin of a man and knelt.

"I am an imperial Inquisitor, Commissar," he declared.

"At last," snarled the man. "At last!"

"I would show you my palm tattoo, except that you are blind—"

"At last!"

Wondrously it seemed the Commissar had been praying for an Inquisitor to arrive. Thus what was happening here was no simple rebellion—but some pernicious heresy. That heresy appeared to be triumphing on the field of battle.

This Commissar must be disoriented by pain and blindness. Yet one could not take such a dedicated man for granted.

"We were captured soon after we landed," lied Jaq. "We succeeded in escaping only recently. We have been searching for you. Those officers of the Guards whom we have encountered hitherto are not exactly subtle men. In your own words, Commissar, how do *you* define the nature of the heresy?"

"Why, the rebel Lucifer Princip claims to be the Emperor's son—and heir to the Imperium. His followers believe that this world of Genost will become the new Earth. This is simple enough, and foul enough—" Pain wracked the Commissar, and he bit into his lip deliberately.

The news staggered Jaq.

An *Emperor's Son* . . .! One, moreover, who seemed fully aware of his origin—unless this Lucifer Princip was merely an opportunistic and persuasive liar who had concocted a bogus story . . .

If Princip was not a liar, had roving Harlequins identified him at some time in the past? Had Harlequins enlightened him? If so, the man had evidently avoided further involvement with the Eldar . . . Had Sensei Knights found him and informed him of his true nature? Princip was hardly engaged in any secret Long Watch . . . What might Princip know about those Knights or about Emperor's Sons? If those did truly exist, and were not a fabrication!

"Is this not simple enough?" repeated the Commissar. Was there a growing suspicion in his tone? Commissars were trained to detect deviancy and to root it out.

Simple? How very far from simple!

Said Jaq: "It is the experience of the Inquisition, Commissar, that simplicity may often mask deep deceit and corruption. Tell me, does Lucifer Princip claim to be immortal?"

"Of course he does! Yet no one is immortal, except for Him-on-Earth." A cough wracked the Commissar, tormenting his broken bones. He bit his lip again.

Jaq's next question was: "Is Princip originally from this world of—" For a moment the name eluded him. "—this world of Genost?"

"That's unknown. How did you escape, Inquisitor? Who else is with you? My name is Boglar Zylov. What is yours?"

Jaq simply asked, "Do you know of a mysterious misty blue tunnel, Zylov, within say thirty kilometres of here?"

That other portal, which Jaq must find, may have been used by

the Eldar to visit Genost, and to discover Princip—*if* Princip was a
native of this world, and *if* the Eldar were at all involved.

Supposing that Princip was indeed immortal, and genuine,
how very unlikely it was that he would still be on the planet of his
birth over ten millennia after the Emperor had scattered his seed!
These enigmas vexed Jaq almost as much as Zylov's broken bones
and blindness must vex him.

"No blue tunnel," growled the Commissar. "What is it? Why?"

The portal beneath this stronghold had been painstakingly
sealed in the distant past. The other portal must likewise have
been hidden and fastened away in a similar fashion.

"Do you know of any ancient structure resembling this one
within say thirty kilometres?"

Zylov's head inclined towards the valley where the war continued to thunder.

"Your questions mystify me, Inquisitor!"

Jaq replied, "I sincerely hope that the intention of our imperial
forces is to capture the rebel alive."

"The intention right now is simply *to survive*."

"Tell me: how many other Commissars apart from yourself are
with our forces?"

"Three. No, Gryphius was killed. Two—and myself."

Gently Jaq said, "You are no longer fit for duty, Commissar
Zylov. Would that you could see my palm tattoo. I need to adopt
the mantle of Commissar to aid my inquisitorial inquiry. I shall try
not to hurt you unduly while removing your greatcoat."

That ornamented coat, although soiled, would immediately
identify Jaq to the imperial forces as someone requiring absolute
obedience.

"Certain Inquisitors prefer to work in secret," Jaq confided to
Zylov. "Thus we learn more; and Princip's heresy requires—"

"—*eradication!*"

"That is a Commissar's commendable view. I must take a wider
view, *in nomine Imperatoris*."

Zylov was confused, and agonized. He submitted.

"Grub!" cried Grimm.

While Jaq had been interrogating the Commissar, and while
Lex had been watching the progress of the battle from behind a
slab, the little man had discovered some scattered ration packs
and canteens of water amongst the ruins.

Hands full, Grimm eyed Jaq attired in decorated greatcoat with epaulettes.

"How posh. How ruthless-looking. What's the idea, Boss?"

To mention Emperor's Sons right now might confuse Grimm, as well as wasting time. It was a supreme priority to discover the true nature of Lucifer Princip. Princip would be utterly protected. It would take a true Assassin—not a bogus one—to reach Princip. It would take an Assassin of the Callidus Shrine whose hallmark was cunning! How utterly Jaq needed Meh'lindi for this mission. She was not really too far away by now. Merely dead, temporarily. Her resurrection—which would cause such a psychic quake, devoutly to be desired as another supreme priority—was merely a dozen or so more avenues distant through the Webway.

Jaq said, "We must find some place resembling this one here. The place may already have been wrecked by battle, and the portal exposed. If not, we shall need to wreck the place ourselves. We require transport and protection and perspective and heavy weaponry. Therefore are going to commandeer an imperial Titan."

Lex cleared his throat. "Along with my comrades," he said darkly, "I once hijacked a rebel Titan."

Dropping the ration packs, Grimm clapped in morose applause.

"How fortunate for us. Now we can really jump into the frying pan."

"To know how to operate the Titan," continued Lex, "it was necessary for my comrades and me to eat the fresh brains of the crewmen we killed."

Rakel swayed, aghast.

"It is pointless," said Lex, "for any of you to eat brains in the hope of acquiring new skills. You lack a Marine's Omophagea organ. That is essential for digesting the facts of a person's life from their flesh."

"Huh," said Grimm. "I was once advisory engineer with a consignment of Titans shipped out of Mars. So, Big Boy, I'm already well aware how complicated they are."

"I said," roared Jaq, "that we shall commandeer a Titan, not try to climb up one and force entry and kill the crew. The crew will obey us. In my righteous office as Inquisitor I am assuming the duties of Imperial Commissar, and appropriating that rank. How can the Emperor's forces be losing here unless there is lack of faith?''

Unarguable logic.

"So you see," said Grimm to Rakel, "there's nothing to worry about. By my Ancestors there ain't! We simply sneak into the valley of death. He flashes his epaulettes. If we haven't already been evaporated or boiled or roasted or blown to pieces we can all take a ride in a colossal target.''

Chapter Seventeen

Me, Lindi!

How long had the battle already been raging in the valley? Since dawn? By now sheer exhaustion must have been taking a toll as well as casualties—exhaustion of men and of weaponry too.

Cacophony resounded. Titans still plodded. Outpourings of energies cut swathes through men and machines. Tanks rolled. In many respects the mingled armies were more like a pair of punch-drunk pugilists locked in a clinch, each equipped with several hundred thousand arms. As Lex analysed the situation, some form of disengagement must occur. The imperial forces had lost the day, yet the rebels could not hope to annihilate such a multitude—unless all discipline and all faith collapsed.

Disentanglement would hardly be easy or quick; any more than if those pugilists, or wrestlers, were smeared in strong glue.

A combination of battle fatigue and luck—and Jaq's aura of protection—finally allowed the four to approach an imperial Titan. On the way they had been obliged to kill rebels. Jaq's borrowed greatcoat was a provocation. He himself took several hits, which his mesh armour withstood. Lex caught a flesh wound in the upper arm. His welling blood hardened immediately to cinnabar, as if Lex had received a humble chevron of rank.

Ahead towered a largely intact Titan. Skulls and double-headed eagles adorned the splayed fairings of its legs. Its remaining tattered banner displayed a militant white angel slicing off the head of a green serpent. This Titan was partly equipped for close support. One weapons arm consisted of a power fist—and the other was a laser blaster. On the carapace above its turtle-head a defence laser pivoted proudly, though a companion weapon was unidentifiable slag.

Jaq clambered upon the burned-out wreck of a superheavy tank. He spread his arms wide in the Commissar's greatcoat. He semaphored.

The turtle-head took note. The Titan's lurid green eye-shields seemed to glare directly at Jaq, though of course these eyes were of almost impenetrable adamantium. Behind those eyes, in the armoured control bubble, the Princeps of the Titan would be staring at two slanted oval screens which faithfully reproduced the outside view.

Crushing corpses with its huge cleated feet, the Titan paced towards the tank, then halted. Its defence laser covered the forward terrain, and the frontal right energy shield ceased to glimmer. Large as a land-raider, the unprotected power fist began swiftly to descend.

Usually a crew would board from a gantry. Jaq had expected a flexible metal ladder to snake down from the rear. Clearly the Princeps of this Titan was an officer who could improvise. Urgently Jaq motioned the others to join him. Lex carried Rakel bodily up on to the tank.

The metal fist opened its fingers invitingly. The four climbed upon the palm. Already the hand was rising, carrying them up into the smoky air. The weapons arm locked horizontally. Along that titanic arm they scrambled. Ducking under the shield of the carapace, they negotiated a narrow maintenance catwalk round to the entrance hatch.

Inside the head of the Titan, the temperature was almost worthy of Sabulorb en route to incineration. Hot fumes mingled with the reek of pious incense. Sweat broke out at once all over one's body. This despite the laborious inhaling and exhaling of ventilation gargoyles.

Grimm stayed with Rakel in the red-lit escape chamber at the rear, while Jaq and Lex made their way into the forward cabin to confront the Princeps. For four people to cram up front right away would be confusing.

Graffiti decorated any spare surface of the escape chamber. *Death's the Destination! Enema to Enemies!* To right and to left, short fat passages led to those pods in the shoulders where four Moderati controlled the power fist, the lascannon, the defence laser up on the carapace, and . . . The fourth weapon was slag. Synched to it by servo-motorized fibre-bundles, its Moderatus might have been fatally injured by feedback.

If the Titan's reactor overloaded, the pods of the Moderati would cannon pneumatically into this escape chamber just prior to the whole head blasting free. Should this happen, Grimm and Rakel would be pulverized—unless, at the moment that a klaxon shrieked its warning, they instantly scrambled forward.

Servos whirred. Stabilizing jets hissed. Gargoyles gulped and whistled.

Strapped in the gimballed control seat, protected by padding and armour, the Princeps faced those great slanting eye-screens. Bronze bones framed the screens. Across an array of lesser data screens diagnostic icons scuttled like phosphorescent beetles. A spaghetti of cables led from his reinforced mind-impulse suit into ducts. Cables coiled from his shoulder pauldrons, and wires from his impulse-helmet—which now swung round to scrutinize the newcomers.

Behind a goggle-visor: weary blue eyes.

Below the visor: a hooked nose with sapphire rings through each nostril, thin lips, and a depilated chin tattooed with tiny silver pentacles.

Jaq brandished his palm tattoo of the regular Inquisition. "I am Imperial Inquisitor Tod Zapsnik," he declared. "Do you know what an Inquisitor is?"

Blessedly the Princeps nodded.

"Commissar Zylov is dead," lied Jaq. Perhaps, by now, he spoke the truth. "I have assumed his authority, and his uniform. My companion is a Captain of Space Marines, undertaking covert reconnaissance—"

"*Ah*," breathed the Princeps. He admired that bare giant with the red sash over one eye, and with the bolt gun.

"I must not distract you long from controlling this Titan, Princeps. I hereby commandeer your splendid machine, *in nomine Imperatoris*, as is an Inquisitor's right and privilege. It is vital that we locate a building resembling that former thudd gun emplacement up on the crag to the west. Have you detected any such place within thirty kilometres?"

The outlook from the Titan was high. Although drifting smoke veiled much from ordinary observation, the eye-screens could operate in infra-red. There was also radar.

The Princeps summoned an electro-map upon a gridded screen. He willed a cursor to flash.

"Maybe you mean the so-called Tower of Atrocity twenty-five kays east of here. There is little else."

Lex released a breath. His eye may not need to be ravaged again. Destroying the optic chord would require the implanting of nerve-wires into his brain as well as the fitting of an artificial oculus. He did not wish to burden the chirurgeons of his fortress-monastery unnecessarily.

"Take us there as swiftly as possible," ordered Jaq.

"With respect," said the Princeps, "it is well away from the battle zone. Well away from our main force. We may seem to be deserting. A reversal may become a rout. I ought to radio—"

"*No*. The rebels may intercept your message—and then intercept us."

"Two hundred thousand men may die. We may even lose our base on this world."

"Nevertheless!" It anguished Jaq to deliver such a pronouncement. More gently he added, "There are higher considerations, Princeps. The apparent defection of one combat unit cannot possible be a pivot upon which so much hinges."

Did he himself not behave as though major aspects of the future pivoted upon his own actions?

"*In nomine Imperatoris!*" he repeated. He swirled his filched greatcoat. He rested his tattoo lightly upon the butt of *Emperor's Mercy*. Surely only a person of sublime authority might carry such a precious ancient gun plated with iridescent titanium inlaid with silver runes. Or an associate of that sublime person.

"Princip's heresy must be crushed!" said Jaq. "The key may well be in that Tower of Atrocity!"

"I will brief my Moderati," agreed the commander of the Titan.

Disengaging from the struggle required some use of the defence laser and lascannon, as well as the hurling aside of battle tanks by the power fist. At one time the Titan's rear void-shields seemed likely to overload and fail. The temperature soared higher as energies radiated. Eventually the Titan was striding at its briskest

pace towards the east. It stomped through a carbonized forlorn
waste of former vineyards, deserted but for furtive grimy plun-
derers of corpses.

A sinking sun had at last pierced through the mizzly overcast to
paint orange blood across the sky. The cabin was cooling somewhat—as was the escape chamber, where Grimm snored
obliviously and where Rakel sat hunched, hands clasping her
knees.

Long evening shadows made the tower of slabs, upon an isolated
knoll, seem even more sinister. Embedded in that windowless
tower were hundreds of rusted up-curving iron spikes. From
some of these, bleached skeletons dangled. A scree of white
bones lay around the base of the tower. Its sides were streaked
with brown trails. This tower was a place of execution for those
who had committed atrocious crimes. It could not have been used
as such recently, otherwise some body would surely still be
decaying. Some dying malefactor might still be impaled high up,
squinting afar in slow agony.

Was this disuse a symptom of Lucifer Princip's heresy?

The tower had survived the ravages of war. No one must have
wanted to climb the rungs of those spikes to mount a gun on top.
The tower would not survive the attentions of a Titan—which
now mounted the knoll.

The Moderatus of the lascannon fired energy packets which
blasted and shook the structure. He performed a kind of dentistry
upon the tower, as if the erection were a vast barbed tooth which
required drilling prior to capping with a ceramite crown. Masonry
tumbled, blocks with long wicked hooks jutting from them.

The tower appeared to be solid throughout.

On instructions from Jaq—relayed by the Princeps—the Moderatus blasted repeatedly at the base. A cloud of bone-dust filled the
air, swirling snow-like.

The Titan advanced closer. Its power fist punched the weakened remains of the tower repeatedly in the style of a wrecking
ball. During this pummelling the Princeps edged the carapace
against the fabric as a massive lever. With a great groan, the
ancient edifice finally uprooted itself and collapsed.

Stooping, the Titan clawed into the foundations. The power fist
dragged out chunks of masonry and threw these aside. It excavated soil and stones. Bending almost double, hydraulics

shrieking, lamps blazing, it smashed through the roof of a subterranean chamber.

As rubble tumbled into the chamber, murky antique iron
machines jerked forth blades—and fell apart in rust.

"You have served the Imperium nobly," Jaq congratulated the
weary Princeps.

The Titan's lamps no longer glared. Upon the open palm of the
power fist the four companions rode down into the breached containment chamber, and into a soft blue glow.

Above, dusk was gathering. Nobody staring down from above
would be able to see the portal itself. During daylight hours the
glow might not even be visible. By night a spectator would certainly notice. That spill of light would seem to be some baleful
form of radiation.

A few thousand years ago, this portal might have been hidden
deep in dense wild woodland—which was subsequently cleared.
Jaq was sure that the knoll was artificial. Tonnes of stones and soil
had been heaped up around the containment chamber to form a
base for the Tower of Atrocity.

He would need to come back to this world once he had resurrected his sublime Assassin. When he returned, the war of
righteousness against the heretic Lucifer Princip would still be
continuing. Unless the imperial forces now present on Genost
had been annihilated! Yet if so, others would come. Space
Marines might arrive through the void, to cleanse such blasphemy. Eldar forces might sneak through the Webway, hoping to
seize a self-proclaimed Emperor's Son; or to bargain with him.

Jaq needed the route to remain open, yet protected. Therefore
he had told the Princeps that with a finger of the power fist the
Titan should gouge radiation hexes on the sides of the knoll,
amidst the rubble; and never reveal what he had done. Knowledgeable people would believe that a burrowing missile or mole
torpedo had destroyed the tower, leaving a stew of lethal long-life
radioactivity buried in the site. The ignorant would be too superstitious to investigate.

Thus, once more, they entered the Webway, Jaq leading with
his monocle.

The misty blue tunnel branched several times. And then it
opened out, upon immensity.

To right, to left, and above was boundless blue mist. No, not exactly *boundless*. To left and to right the walls of the Webway could be seen, now vastly enlarged.

The capillary-tunnel had pierced one of the major arteries of the Webway. Here was a channel spacious enough for sizeable ships to fly through from one Craftworld to another, or from star to star.

This was as the rune-lens had indicated. The reality was daunting. To hike across the bottom of that gulf without losing one's bearings! To find the blue of the corresponding capillary against the greater blue!

"We shall set out one by one," stated Lex. "We shall keep at a right angle to this wall. When the first of us is about to disappear, the second will set out. We shall shout out our names regularly in turn to identify where we are. We'll stay in a straight line, linked by a rope of voices."

With his enhanced hearing, Lex should be able to detect deviations, and to call out corrections to left or right.

Jaq would go first into the mist. Grimm, second. Rakel would follow. Lex, as anchor-voice, would bring up the rear.

Presently a call came: "Jaq here! I've found it."

By heading for the beacon of Jaq's voice presently they were re-united.

More branches ensued. Presently the capillary-passage entered another major artery. How close they were now to the place they sought! Cross this second gulf—and only three more forks remained.

Jaq was across. Grimm was across. Rakel was approaching. Soon Lex would loom.

An eerie throb was discernible at the very edge of audibility. Maybe it was not a sound so much as a vibration of the mist. The throb intensified quickly.

"It's some Eldar ship in transit," yelped Grimm. "Wraithship rushing this way. Run, Rakel, run," he yelled. "Run, Lex! Wraithship coming!"

The mist began to billow and stream. The approaching ship would be out of phase. The sheer size and momentum of even the ghost of a Wraithship was bound to have some impact.

What if two out-of-phase Wraithships were to fly towards one
another through the same artery? They might pass one another
by. The artery was ample enough. Or might they pass right
through one another? Detection equipment, or some exclusion
principle, must prevent disaster. The crews of such sizeable vessels must experience drag and disorientation. How much more must
travellers on foot experience, so tiny in proportion?

Rakel was arriving apace, her eyes wide with fright at the
motion of the mist and the throb and the urgency of Grimm's cry.

Lex came pounding after her.

"Run, run—!"

Ever so briefly, a vast white butterfly, wings erect, seemed to
rush past. This filled the view momentarily—almost too fast for
its faint huge image to be glimpsed. Parting, the blue mists
surged in a tsunami of vapours. Suction tugged at the three
where they sheltered inside the tunnel.

Lex was bowled away, mist-borne. He was pulled in the wake
of a ghost-ship. Turning over and over, he had vanished from
view in a trice.

Grimm yelled Lex's name periodically for many minutes.

No answer came.

Yet they waited. Undoubtedly more than one pair of capillaries
joined this artery. How to tell one from another except by the presence of comrades who were in phase? What if another
Wraithship came rushing by? Lex might be carried away across
half the galaxy. Yet they waited. Every now and then Grimm gave
a call.

Time was elusive in the Webway. Was it an hour or half a
standard day before they heard a reply? Before Lex came loping
out of the mist!

"Huh," said Grimm, "the big brute's back." He wiped a cuff
across his eye.

Rejoining his comrades joyfully, Lex breathed deeply to replenish his lungs.

"You took your time," piped the little man. "Pass many side
entrances, eh?"

"Six," said Lex. "Widely spaced. I reasoned that either you had
waited, or you had not. The greater gamble was whether I was

heading in the right direction. I had spun around so much that even I could not be sure which way I was facing finally. I prayed to Rogal Dorn to guide my choice."

"You could have tried sticking your finger in your eye."

"I should stick mine in yours, Abhuman." Lex clasped Grimm. He squeezed the Squat's shoulders, roared a brief laugh, shook the little man rag-like, and released him.

They had come to a place where four tunnels converged.

This crossroad could be no other than the *place*.

"We're here," said Jaq, harsh triumph and tragic hope in his voice.

Jaq had shut the monocle and stowed it in a pocket. Two sets of eyes—and one lone eye—regarded Rakel binth-Kazintzkis. She fiddled with the only one of the three miniature weapons on her finger which was still loaded, twisting it this way and that. She trembled.

"I feel wobbly," she said, as if it was high time for Jaq to re-inforce the integrity of her altered body by scrutiny of the Assassin card. "It is a fearful thing to fall into the hands of an Inquisitor . . ."

"Rakel," said Jaq, "in the warp, just beyond the walls of this Webway, there is a force of goodness and nobility and truth divine. There is a dynamic towards transfiguration. There is an embryo of a new God who may renew the old God-on-Earth or who may even supersede Him—may He forgive my heresy!—and, in superseding, release Him from His eternal agony into blissful triumph." Jaq spoke awkwardly. Could he fully believe in the possibility of such a victory?

Oh, he had experienced the luminous path. He had witnessed Lex's Finger of Glory glowing. Doubt must always remain.

Lex appeared to be racked by mixed emotions. Might Rogal Dorn lend scaffolding to his soul! Let not that scaffold be a gibbet of dishonour, a gallows for an unwitting traitor.

Grimm seemed deeply dour, as if somewhere along the route his soul had deserted him.

Had they not arrived where no one else had ever arrived? Let not doubt subvert this sacred moment.

Jaq and Lex and Rakel knelt in the centre of this four-fold junction bathed in the blue light of the alien Webway. Only Grimm stayed standing, defiant of piety, lacking grace.

Jaq prayed aloud to Him-on-Earth, and to the Numen, to the Luminous Path.

He turned to Rakel. Appropriate words would not come.

"You are asking me to accept my own death," Rakel murmured. Fleetingly she glanced at Grimm.

Frustration coursed through Jaq. "What have you told her?" he cried at the dwarf.

"Nothing!" howled Grimm. "I swear by my absent Ancestors, *nothing*!"

"I did strive," said Rakel in a shaking voice. "I strove so hard. Please give me oblivion before such nightmares as Tyranids seize me. Or Chaos, or other horrors."

"Indeed," Jaq said softly. All was well, after all. "The real Meh'lindi wished for oblivion too," he told her. "She denied oblivion to herself."

Rakel was weeping. "Now you wish to drag her back into horror and suffering! I understand your desire, you see."

"You great soul," exclaimed Jaq, in wonder. He experienced a surge of exalted rapture. This must augur well for what was surely so soon to happen.

"You great soul . . ."

Yet not a soul as great as that of Meh'lindi, who must soon supplant this woman from her altered body.

"I *need* Meh'lindi, do you see, Rakel? *I need her!* I need her by my side—to cope with Lucifer Princip."

"Oh you *needed* her," was Rakel's reply, "before we ever heard of Lucifer Princip. I do accept my destiny. I accept! Send me into darkness to save my eyes from seeing any more abominations such as I already saw. I cannot face any future. All futures are fearful and foul."

"All, apart from the Shining Path, which your sacrifice will help kindle. Oh, Emperor of All," cried Jaq, "forgive me. Perceive that this is . . . *the way*."

Rakel wept. Yet she also nodded in affirmation. And her affirmation was at the same time the negation of her self—in favour of another, whom she so exactly resembled, even to the very tattoos, courtesy of Polymorphine.

Lex was deeply moved. "Companion," he said to her. He scratched at his itching left hand as if to scour away the line of life from his palm.

Jaq began to remove the Assassin card.

As before, unbidden, that other card sprang free. The card of Tzeentch shed its wrapping. It fell face up upon the Webway floor.

The daemonic countenance leered up at Jaq. He almost panicked. Hastily he slapped the Assassin card down upon the Daemon. The card depicting Meh'lindi but also mirroring Rakel trumped the Daemon card.

Had he not triumphed over Tzeentch in the mansion? Had he not ousted a minion of the Great Conspirator? Had he not overcome Slaaneshi temptations? Jaq felt not lust but pure adoration for this idol of flesh close by him, soon to be reanimated.

"Let us rejoice," he declared.

Rakel sobbed. "I rejoice in oblivion."

Those could have been Meh'lindi's very own words. Already Rakel was not merely Meh'lindi in body but partly so, it seemed, in speech.

Jaq gestured to Lex for the Assassin's sash. Lex unwound the red fabric, exposing his ravaged eye-socket. Dangling stole-like, Jaq draped the sash around Rakel's neck as if preparatory to a garotting.

"Stare at the Assassin card," Jaq instructed Rakel. "Stare deep into the eyes. Lose yourself in the eyes. Sink into those. You are going into the Sea of Souls to help stir a mighty spirit to consciousness by becoming part of that spirit through your willing self-sacrifice. *Spiritum tuum*," he continued solemnly in the hieratic tongue, "*in pacem dimitto. Meh'lindi meum, a morte ad vitam novam revocatio.*"

Grimm was shivering. Lex covered the ruin of his eye with his left palm, the better to keep vigil throughout a rite as macabre as any he had endured in the fortress-monastery of the Fists.

The semblance of Meh'lindi in the Assassin card was squirming.

"At this place," Jaq intoned, "where time twists, by the power and the grace—"

Shuddering, Rakel slumped forward.

She squirmed. She twisted and flexed. She writhed as if in agony.

And from the writhing woman's lips a cry of defiance and assertion tore:

"Me, Lindi—!"

That was the shriek of identity of a savage feral girl taken from her jungle world to be trained by the Officio Assassinorum. That was the cry which had given rise to her imperial name, of Meh-'lindi.

Jaq gloried immeasurably.

Meh'lindi uncurled. Briefly her hands explored her midriff, where the harpoon of the Phoenix Lady had transfixed her, twisting her guts as on a winch.

"Me, Lindeeee—!" she screeched.

She rolled. She sprang to her feet. Her eyes were glazed with frenzy. One hand was a fist. The other was slanted, a chopper.

Those eyes! She didn't seem to recognize Jaq at all. Was she even *seeing* him?

Nor, as she flicked her glance, was she truly seeing Lex, or Grimm.

"Die, Phoenix Lords!" Meh'lindi screamed—and launched herself ferociously at Jaq.

Chapter Eighteen

Illumination

Could she be mistaking Jaq because he wore a Commissar's scorched and bloodstained greatcoat with high collar and golden epaulettes, and icons and honour braids upon the sleeves and breast?

No! The name she had called him was *Phoenix Lord*. Jaq and Lex and Grimm as well. *Phoenix Lords*.

Those were the Eldar hero-warriors who had no Craftworld to call their own. They roamed the Webway from world to world. Sometimes they disappeared for hundreds of years. They would heed a call of ultimate danger, and suddenly, devastatingly, they would reappear.

Lords? Immortal divinities, almost! Not *persons* in any ordinary sense!

In the distant past, each Phoenix Lord had been a warrior who had followed the path of war so utterly and absolutely that there was no turning back, ever, to the persons they had been before. If one of them died, his or her soul passed into the spirit stone within their armour. The armour itself would call another candidate to rekindle the same identity, phoenix-like—just as the ancient legendary bird arose anew from the flames of its nest.

It had been a Phoenix Lady, a Storm of Silence, who had speared Meh'lindi to death at the very entrance to the hidden Black Library of Eldar secrets . . .

*

The resurrected Meh'lindi was mentally locked in those last lethal moments of ultimate combat. She was reliving those moments. They had occurred elsewhere in the Webway, close to the Black Library. Here at this crossroads of time-twist, that previous climactic event dominated her consciousness. The manner of her death monopolized her reincarnated psyche. *And she fought*.

Meh'lindi fought her final fight all over again, like a soul condemned to a hell of agonizing repetition. Of *intensifying* repetition.

All three figures were Phoenix Lords. The terrible triple-vision possessed her as surely as a daemon might possess a victim. Such were the energies of the Webway, concentrated here, weaving tyrannical illusion.

She would not be a victim! She would not!

Her fist smashed into Jaq's chest under his heart.

The impact should have killed any unprotected enemy. But the mesh armour under Jaq's greatcoat had absorbed the bullet-like force of her blow. Aghast, he staggered back, shock scouring his soul.

She seemed to realize instantly about the armour. She was upon him, her hands seizing grips. She paused briefly so that the mesh armour might relax its stiffness. He stared appalled into her spellbound unseeing eyes.

"Meh'lindi," he gasped. Still she did not know him.

With implacable force, applied smoothly, she hoisted and levered.

Jaq's elbow snapped. Pain lanced through him as if the very marrow of his bones was lava, boiling, spurting. Momentarily he shrieked.

In his agony, she pivoted him across her hips. Jaq crashed to the floor of the Webway. The collision stiffened his armour for several tormenting seconds.

He had fallen heavily. A pang in his own hip must be from the monocle lens, crushed by his fall.

Meh'lindi swung, she leapt. The heel of her foot connected with Lex's wrist—just as he was bringing the bolt gun to bear from behind his back. The gun sprang loose from his hand.

This Jaq saw through a mist of pain. The mist blurred Meh'lindi's motions. Lex was fending her off with a mighty arm. Her clawing fingers tore at his ruined eye. She feinted. She was going to try to blind Lex entirely. Instead, she somersaulted—and she stumbled, although she recovered swiftly. Grimm sprawled upon his back. He was swearing. He was still alive.

It could only be Meh'lindi's unfamiliarity with her new body—its lack of perfect training—which had saved the little man. She wasn't quite as co-ordinated as she expected to be. This perplexed and incensed her.

Lex flexed potent muscles. He half-turned his head as if to avert his good eye. He hesitated. Meh'lindi's hostility was inexplicable—unless she was mad. Unless she had returned from the Sea of Souls deranged and demented! Unless a daemon was in her body. Yet she cried out again:

"Me, Lindi—!"

She adopted a feral crouch, her hands splaying out.

And now the three hooded rings on her fingers caught her attention. The miniature weapons. The toxic needle gun. The flamer. The laser. In exasperation, she howled. Not to have noticed straight away! Not to have realized! To have been so bound up in sheer *body*. In limbs and spine and nerves!

Meh'lindi stabbed a finger towards Lex. Whirling, she stabbed another in Grimm's direction. Swinging, she jerked a final finger at Jaq.

Instinctively Jaq interposed his uninjured arm. Energy exploded upon his hand, which no armour nor even a gauntlet sheathed.

The shock-wave stiffened the mesh upon his arm, all the way to his shoulder. Briefly his arm remained raised, like some crooked staff which might display regalia. The regalia consisted of scorched stubs of carpal bone to which blackened ribbons of flesh and gristle clung. The energy packet hadn't amputated his palm and his fingers. It had vaporized his hand.

Pain hesitated . . . before surging into tyrannical existence. Even though Jaq's hand no longer existed it seemed that it was being roasted.

Tears started from his eyes. A greater grief moaned within him, all-gnawing. Despair consumed him. All hope was crushed. Not only his own proud tragic hopes! Hope for humanity too. Hope that the Imperium might endure. Hope that salvation might emerge.

*

Meh'lindi glanced at the giant Phoenix Lord who still stood up-right and alive. At the dwarf Phoenix Lord who was recovering himself. She spared not a flicker of attention for the enemy whom her digital laser had disabled. Meh'lindi glared at her own betray-ing hand.

The miniature needle-gun had failed. The tiny flamer had failed. Neither had been loaded.

How could this be, how could this be? Why was her body im-perfect, inaccurate? Around her neck—not around her waist!—was her Assassin's sash. She plucked it into her fist.

These Phoenix Lords were playing a terrible game with her. It was as if she must fight with a hand tied behind her back. Oh, this she could have done! Or else died, attempting to! Something more fundamental was at fault.

What could it be? How could she have no knowledge that two of the digital weapons were useless? How could it be that her body did not perfectly obey her will? Oh, she was trapped in a night-mare! She must fight or flee. She was Callidus. She was cunning.

How short a time had passed. Before the giant or the dwarf could react, Meh'lindi fled at random along a blue misty tunnel of the Webway.

She raced, her long legs pumping. An intimation of fatigue registered. She forced herself to maintain her pace. Were Phoenix Lords rushing after her, armed with weapons of wizardry? Her gulping breaths were not as rich as they ought to be. Fireflies seemed to flicker in her vision. The blue tunnel forked. At ran-dom she ran to the right.

Jaq was ruined, in body and in soul.

An arm, shattered. A hand, seared away.

Agony flayed him. Tragedy scarified him. He might almost be partaking of the Emperor's own illuminated anguish.

The Emperor would fail. The Imperium would fail. Its death throes would be so appalling that honour and nobility and faith and proud perseverance would be mere drops of water in a caul-dron of boiling blood. No God-child could possibly awaken then. Humanity would succumb. Out of its screaming downfall there would vomit forth a great new power of evil unimaginable. Chaos would surge to engulf reality.

Despair gnawed Jaq like some ichneumon parasite devouring

his innards. He had committed heresy and betrayal. Meh'lindi's resurrection had been an abomination. If only she had destroyed him completely!

Lex had vowed to do so, if necessity demanded. The Captain had recovered his bolt gun. With the stump of his wrist, Jaq thrust himself up, snarling as he did so. He must not cause any more ghastly heretical harm.

He sagged upon his knees. He forced himself to withstand. He knelt, self-condemned. He riveted Lex with a glare of homicidal, psychotic hatred.

And he blasphemed. How he blasphemed.

"May the puny human Emperor shrivel! May the light of your Primarch wink out like a candle! Glory to Tzeentch! *Chi'khami't-zann Tsunoi!*"

Jaq was evoking the Greater Daemons of Tzeentch, in their own language. He must have become possessed anew.

Jaq bared his teeth in a bestial snarl. This time daemonry owned him utterly—so it seemed.

Lex steadied the bolt gun. With Rogal Dorn's name upon his lips, he fired at Jaq's head.

RAAARK—

A violent blow *upon* the vault of a skull might leave it intact. If the bolt had only struck a glancing blow a compression-wave would have been transmitted around the skull to the rigid base, which might fracture.

An explosion *within the skull* was another matter. It tore the great jigsaw pieces of the skull apart. And even though Jaq's head had not entirely disintegrated, what had been knitted together since childhood was separated now. The frontal plate was divorced from the sundered parietal plates of the cranium, and those in turn from the occipital plate at the rear. Liquified pulp of brain had gushed out of its broken container.

Grimm did try to wrench enough of the Commissar's greatcoat loose so as to hide the sight. He quit.

Lex had arisen from prayer.

Bitterly Grimm exclaimed, "I didn't think that a daemon could thrust its way through the walls of the Webway!"

With his one intact eye, Lex scrutinized the corpse. Slowly he asked the little man, "What are you implying?"

Grimm babbled, "As I savvy it, the Eldar don't dare travel through the warp in ships the way we do—because they would attract daemons all too easily. That's why they use the Webway for travel. The Webway acts as a barrier to daemons. How did a daemon get into Jaq?"

"Because of the unique nature of this crossroads!"

Grimm shook his head disbelievingly.

"Because the daemon was still hiding inside him!" declared Lex. "Ever since he exorcised me!"

"Where would the daemon go to from here?"

"I'm not responsible for the problems of daemons, Abhuman!"

"*If* there ever was a daemon—"

Lex clutched his bolt gun as if it were the hand of a battle brother offering support.

"Explain yourself!"

"I think that Jaq despaired!" cried Grimm. "He despaired utterly. Because of *her*." He jerked his head in the direction which Meh'lindi had taken. "It was insane to resurrect her. And *she* was insane."

"He despaired? Despite all vows?"

"*I* know what despair is! I can recognize despair."

Menacingly, Lex demanded: *"How is that?"*

Grimm sighed in grief.

"I don't want to say."

"You will say—or I will squeeze it out of you!"

Wretchedly Grimm confessed: "I swore to Rakel that she would live. That she wouldn't be destroyed. "I swore *by my ancestors*. I knew I was lying!"

"What does that false oath signify to you?"

Dully, Grimm told him, "It's as if you betray your Primarch. A Squat who perjures himself in this way will never sire any offspring. He'll never become a Living Ancestor."

Dread seemed to harrow the giant. "I have not . . . betrayed . . . my Primarch," he insisted softly. "I have not . . . betrayed . . . my chapter. Yet I have been led far astray. I must make amends. I must . . . redeem myself."

The little man wrung his sturdy hairy hands. "Don't do it by blinding your other eye! Don't disable yourself!"

"That would be blasphemy, you fool! We must return to Genost where those rebels rampage. We must find out all we can about their leader, Lucifer Princip. Surely battle brothers will come to Genost on a crusade to purge the rebellion. In another year. Two years. Three . . . Space Wolves or Blood Angels or Ultramarines. It does not matter which."

"When I was trying to adjust Jaq's coat . . . I felt in his pocket. The rune-lens is ruined."

"I can remember the route, little man! By Dorn, but it's time to take that route—away from this place of failure!"

Grimm blew his nose in his hands. He wiped himself. He grimaced. Bleakly he said, "Back to Genost, eh? A pretty rainbow beckons fools onward constantly in hope of hidden gold. Just so does a black rainbow beckon *us* onward—towards death or madness!"

"*Nay*," said Lex, "that is sacrilege. To succumb to despair is blasphemy."

Firmly Lex clenched his free hand into a fist—and Grimm may have thought that the Marine was going to strike him. But instead Lex smiled, contortedly.

However far away Lex was from his fortress-monastery and from his battle brothers—and although he was half-blind and near-naked—he remained an Imperial Fist.

"Come, little comrade," he barked. "And redeem yourself by serving Him-on-Earth."

RAAARK—
For the merest moment—
—pop—
Jaq knew—
—SWOOSH—
Then the universe exploded.

Bodiless, he was afloat within blue light. He was no longer a body, but only a point of view. From that point of view he looked down upon his corpse, lying ruined and defunct.

He looked down upon Lex, who was kneeling in prayer. He looked down upon Grimm who was trying in vain to cover the corpse's shattered face.

An astonishing serenity filled Jaq's soul, almost to overflowing.

Tunnels of blue light led in four directions. He knew that by a mere act of will he might rush afar along any of these tunnels. Or he might simply accelerate his vision along one tunnel or another, as though he were going through an expanding telescope.

He did exactly this—and his vision overtook Meh'lindi. She was loping headlong like a hunted animal.

Stop, stop! He wished her to hear his voice. But she could not hear.

As his vision accompanied her, he perceived a scintillating aura about her—in a way that he had never perceived before. He realized that she had behaved as she behaved because she was in a trance of combat, mesmerized by her dying moment. She had been akin to a Phoenix Lord, possessed by the path of combat to the exclusion of personality. Her lethal rapture would surely abate as her intelligence asserted itself.

That aura of hers was so complex. Could it be that Rakel was not entirely evicted from her former body? Could it be that deep down Rakel still lingered? That, in a sense, Rakel possessed Meh'lindi. Not directly, as a daemon might possess a person. But present, nonetheless, Or that Meh'lindi's spirit possessed Rakel's body, daemon-like?

Yes, yes . . . Rakel was not entirely dead.

Meh'lindi would be volatile. She would be unstable. Pray that her fierce will would prevail!

He could not communicate with her. He could not contact her, however much he might wish to do so.

Therefore Jaq let his vision range far beyond Meh'lindi—until a blue tunnel reached its terminus, inside a cave a-sparkle with crystals. His vision could travel no further. It could not leave the Webway.

Once more, he was gazing calmly down upon his own corpse.

Grimm was grieving. He was mourning for himself as well as for Jaq. Such despairing hues polluted the little man's aura, unseen by Jaq until now. Oh Grimm, Grimm! Grimm believed himself damned, because he had sworn a false sacred oath to Rakel. Yet he was wrong. For Rakel was not extinguished utterly.

If only Grimm knew. But there was no way that Jaq could inform the little man.

Four blue tunnels led away, branching and dividing into routes leading to anywhere in the Webway—to everywhere in this vast network spanning the galaxy. The immensity of this vision exalted Jaq. And in his exaltation, he sensed presences. It seemed that the four tunnels corresponded, in some manner, to the Eldar Phoenix Lords. Their transcendent identities intruded upon him. He understood their titles.

Maugan Ra, the Harvester of Souls.

Baharroth, the Cry of the Wind.

Jain Zar, the Storm of Silence.

Karandras, the Shadow Hunter.

They were such potent foes of Chaos . . .!

And he realized that because he had died at this special crossroads, his spirit had not entered the Sea of Souls but had become attached to the Webway instead. His vision could ride the Webway—although his spirit could not leave it. By riding the Webway, knowledge would suffuse him. He sensed, afar, the spirits of dead Eldar seers. He might commune with those seers in a way impossible to any other member of the human race.

He would be more illuminated than any living human Illuminatus could ever be!

Lex and Grimm were trudging away from the place where Jaq's corpse lay. Why hadn't they taken the force rod with them? The precious force rod! Neither Lex nor Grimm were psykers. Neither could use the rod. In vain Jaq strove to call out to them. To reassure them that his spirit had survived. To explain about Meh'lindi. To encourage them.

In vain.

Rapture filled him, at the promise of impending revelations. It was as if he was uniting with the Numen. He was becoming a tiny part of something wondrously noble, yet as diffuse as hydrogen atoms in the void, which would one day condense into a resplendent star.

If only he could commune with tormented humanity! The Eldar could commune with the souls of the dead through spirit stones, through wraithbone, through the infinity circuit. Jaq's personal Tarot card might have been a means of contact with the living. His Tarot card was long since destroyed, consigned to ashes scattered in space.

For a long while, riding the Webway, Jaq's vision followed Lex and Grimm as they retraced the route to Genost. In his sublime transcendence Jaq was impotent to intervene.